ESCAPE FROM PURGATORY

SCARLET DARKWOOD

By: Scarlet Darkwood

Copyright 2017

All Rights Reserved. This story is a work of fiction. Any likeness to persons living or deceased is coincidence. Sharing this work, physically or electronically, is prohibited unless there is written permission from the publisher.

Publisher: Dark BooksPress

Cover Design: Dark BooksPress

Images: Depositphotos

ACKNOWLEDGEMENTS:

I would like to thank my beta readers, Ellen and Chelsea for their honest feedback for this story. I appreciate Rebecca Poole for her formatting and tightening up of the cover and her cheerleading when I need it. I would like to extend my gratitude to Angela Rackard Campbell for her editing expertise and giving her blunt, honest feedback where it was needed. That's always tricky for an editor who takes on a new author. She helped make the book even better. As always, I want to thank my spouse, Phillip, for being the biggest, tireless cheerleader of all.

"Oh, breaker of spirits,
Destroyer of dreams,
Who covers the ears
To silence the screams,
Turn a blind eye
So you'll never see
The horrors of Hell
You've inflicted on me.
Wrench out my heart,
And lock it away.
Shroud it in darkness,
Death and decay"

CHAPTER ONE

Claire Wright gazed around the office, confused. Uneasiness crawled all over her as she sat on a hard, wooden chair. Where was her husband Adrian, and why was she waiting in a room inside the local asylum? The door squeaked open. A young gentleman dressed in a starched white lab coat entered. He greeted her with a polite nod and sat down at the desk. She watched intently as he removed a clipboard and pen from the top drawer.

"Mrs. Wright, I'm Dr. Dandridge. This is an intake interview, and I'll be asking you some questions."

"Excuse me?" Claire leaned forward in her seat. "What do you mean by an intake interview?"

Dr. Dandridge smiled. "No need for alarm. This is something we do every day. It won't take long."

Claire frowned. "I don't understand why I'm being interviewed. I came with my husband to deliver a hat. You interview people for that?"

"Mrs. Wright, I assure you everything is fine. It's just a few questions, that's all. You can talk later about anything that concerns you."

Claire stood up, indignant. "Now I really don't understand. Why on earth will I be able to talk later?" She stepped toward the door. "Excuse me, but I need to find my husband."

Dr. Dandridge bolted out of his seat, positioning himself between her and the door. "Please don't make this difficult." He guided Claire back to her seat. "Your husband left."

"Without me? That's crazy. He'd never forget and leave me somewhere." Claire struggled with the rising anxiety inside her. This situation didn't seem right at all.

The doctor scrutinized Claire a few moments in silence. He cleared his throat and spoke again. "I hate to be the bearer of bad news, but his intent was to have you admitted here."

Claire grew pale at the words. She stared at the doctor, stunned.

"Can you think of any reason at all that your husband felt you needed psychiatric care?"

Panic hit her full force. "I can assure you I have no idea why." Claire tried making sense of the events that had transpired up to now.

The doctor said nothing, sitting motionless as he fixed his gaze on Claire.

"Dr. Dandridge, Adrian and I have always gotten along. We've had some issues lately surrounding the death of our son, but that wouldn't be an excuse to have me put away. It makes no sense at all."

"I see." The doctor scribbled a few lines on his paper. "Any moments of uncontrollable sadness or mood changes? Unable to do your housework?"

Scowling, Claire answered, "What ridiculous questions. Who wouldn't be upset that their child died?" She clenched her fists. "I want out of here now. You can't keep me here. I haven't done anything."

***

Claire found herself running in slow motion through dark, winding hallways and passages leading nowhere. Terrified, she turned a corner, tripped over something unseen, and tumbled to the floor.

With a jolt, she sat upright in her bed, in a real world of darkness, not a dream. Sweat dripped down her body, leaving her faded slip of a nightgown damp and smelling mustier than ever. Such was life here at Hatchie River Asylum For The Insane. She'd been here a week, and all she heard were screams, bitter crying, and laughter that came at the oddest times from the lips of those whose brains had been affected by an insult from nature. Claire wondered if these people weren't, in fact, blessed in some small way. They weren't aware enough of their surroundings to be driven any madder by this forsaken place.

Women sat for hours, their leg curled up beneath them. They stared out the windows for hours, oblivious. If they balked at all, horrid attendants retaliated. The asylum was a perfect place for letting sadistic natures run amok. Sleep had been difficult since the first night of arrival. Two hours of tossing and turning finally turned into catching sight of the first morning rays flashing through the flimsy curtains covering the window.

"You all right?" The lady in the other bed sat up, bedsprings squeaking in protest as she moved.

"Yes, I'm okay, Ruth. Sorry I woke you up." Claire rolled over and faced her roommate.

"You sure been tossin' around a lot. You sick?"

"I'm fine." Claire adjusted the sheet. "I had a bad dream, that's all."

Ruth shook her head. "Wouldn't doubt that for one minute. It's hard to not have them, being here and all."

Claire realized, for the first time, that she and Ruth hadn't said much to each other, except for simple pleasantries. Glancing at her roommate, Claire asked, "Did you have trouble when you first came here?"

"Couldn't imagine a soul not having trouble when they come in here. I'd be more worried if they didn't, if you ask me."

"You know something, I haven't been very friendly at all, a real big sour puss. I'm sorry for that." When Claire smiled, the other lady smiled back.

Ruth waved her away. "Aw, don't think nothing of it. It's partly my fault too. I'm not much into sayin' a whole lot around here. Sometimes it's better to keep quiet so you don't get yelled at or hit on the head by some crazy person. And I don't mean just the ones in here like us, neither."

Both women chuckled and settled back down in their beds. Claire closed her eyes and tried dozing a little longer before breakfast hours. Only a week in her life, and it seemed like she'd been here forever. Why hadn't Adrian come by for a visit? Why did he dump her off here? Had things been so bad that he felt he had no other choice?

"Time to get up! Get up, get up! Breakfast time, let's go." One of the asylum attendants banged on the door frames, yelling at the top of her lungs as she alternated between the right and left sides of the hall. The coarseness of her voice mixed with the horrid pounding of her fists against the wood sounded like the world coming to an end.

Grimacing in disgust, Claire braced herself for another day with "Nurse Grace." That's what Grace often made patients call her when the real nurses weren't around. Never would Claire forget the first time she saw the lowly attendant, with her sullen blue eyes, and how they lit up the moment she entered the receiving room and viewed Adrian. Grace appeared amiable enough as she and Adrian chatted briefly in one corner. In her mind's eye, she still saw Adrian grasping the hatbox, a mere prop in the ruse to lure her here. Grace had glanced down at the box and back up to Adrian's face, her head bobbing up and down with a knowing grin. When they finished, she gently led him by the elbow out of the room.

When Grace returned alone, she led her to Dr. Dandridge's office for the ill-fated interview. When the interview ended, Grace returned, leading her to the ward. She told Claire to "get settled in because this is your home now." It was the last admonition that chilled Claire the most: "You also better listen to me and do what I say, or I'll make your life a living hell." Claire never dreamt Adrian had signed her life away, making haste out another exit before the ink dried on the paper and she'd have a chance to protest.

Grace yelled out again, "Time to get out of those nightgowns and into your day clothes. Move, you worthless things." Grace made a special point of stopping in the entrance to Claire and Ruth's room, yelling louder. "That means you, too, Miss Uppity. You don't get no special treatment around here!" She strode in and jerked the sheet off Claire before grabbing her up by the arm and hauling her to her feet.

Claire struggled to keep her balance. When their eyes met, Grace's lips turned up in a sneer as she slowly shook her head. "You don't get no special treatment. I don't care how fine your husband's hats are. You won't be wearin' 'em here. Bet you thought you were high and mighty, didn't you, struttin' around town, all gussied up." The words spilled out of her lips smooth and easy, deliberate enough, but the bitterness in the tone bit down on Claire's soul as hard as the fingers digging into her arm. "I bet you miss that man of yours. Quite a looker. Real nice too." Grace clicked her tongue and the glint in her eyes sent a chill down Claire's spine as the nasty gaze looked her up and down. The sneer left her face. "Still can't figure out why he left you here. Maybe it's because you don't know how to please a man." Her face brightened up. "That's it, maybe he wasn't gettin' any from you." She wagged a thin finger in front of Claire's face. "You know it's not nice holdin' back like that, especially when he kept you up all nice and fancy." Grace moved her face within an inch of Claire's. "That's what you get when you snap those legs shut. At least that's what he told me." With another sneer, she released her grip and left the room. The booming sound of her voice faded as she walked down the hall.

Both Ruth and Claire stared at each other. After several moments of silence, Ruth took Claire's hand in hers. "You okay? Don't let her get to you."

"I-I haven't done anything to her. Ever since I've been here she's been nothing but mean."

Ruth shook her head, scowling. "I try to be nice and not say things about people, but I've lost everything since I've come here, including my religion. So I'll just say it. Grace is a bitch, plain and simple. I think she's really the Devil's bride in disguise." She wrapped an arm around Claire, giving her a quick hug. "C'mon, we better get washed up and dressed and on down to breakfast, or we'll have more than Grace breathing down our backs."

The ladies walked to the washroom located midway down the hall, where they waited in line for the next available sink. Inside a large, tiled room, only five sinks and three toilets served fifty patients. Nothing but a tiled divider wall separated the area for washing and the other for elimination. Performing activities of self-care in plain view of others had been a shock to Claire's senses the first morning she woke up to this ignominious routine.

Naked women at the sinks rinsed off with hurried swipes over their bodies. Some used bits of soap on the counter while most splashed themselves off with thin streams of water coming from the tap. Claire decided early on that no amount of washing at Hatchie River would ever relieve the foul odor lingering in her nose. Claire removed her assigned toothbrush from a designated rack, feeling lucky to have that luxury. Large rolling racks along a side wall held dresses and shoes. Patients selected their clothing based on assigned numbers given them on admission.

Twenty minutes passed before Claire and Ruth stood at the sinks. Ruth cleaned under her arms and breasts followed by her private parts. Claire swished her toothbrush over her teeth, splashed off her face, and finished rinsing off. She cringed at the reflection in the dull, spotted mirror, running her fingers through oily strands of limp hair. The long, silky mane of dark hair she used to style and pin up with fashionable clips and combs had been chopped off by the surly nurse who finalized the admission process. Grace had looked on with her usual evil-eye gleam and smirked as Claire fought back tears.

"We don't allow long hair or nails here. It's for patient cleanliness and safety." The nurse must have received a quick jolt of compassion, because she had glanced up at Claire, shaking her head. "The last thing you need is someone grabbing a handful of hair and leaving you bald."

Her pristine street clothes had been exchanged for the hideous dress she'd soon remove from the rack. Exhaling in despair, Claire turned away from the mirror. Nothing in the asylum would ever restore the looks she pulled off with style when she lived at home, in the community, in the real world where a woman's beauty meant something. When her beauty meant something to Adrian.

In the hallway, the two ladies joined the other residents. Each face reflected unadulterated depression. In their sockets, eyes brimmed with lackluster stares where brilliance of spirit had once shone. She often studied these faces. These ladies, like her, had been plucked from their life in society and carelessly dropped off at the doorstep. Each lady surely had stories, lives with loved ones, pets, walks on country roads and getting caught in the rain. Surely they'd received garden flowers gifted lovingly by children and grandchildren. Hatchie River had destroyed those lives, leaving nothing but memories and a bitter aftertaste.

The dining room hosted yet another dull breakfast, which took place like clock-work at seven-thirty each morning. Having received their trays of food, Ruth and Claire grimaced at each other and began eating.

"Bon appetit," said Ruth, faking a cheerful smile while lifting a chipped glass of milk. "Isn't that what you're supposed to say before a scrumptious meal?"

Claire chuckled and turned her attention to the stale toast, eying one corner. She pinched off a tiny bit of mold, wagering if she'd survive another meal without food poisoning.

The remainder of the day consisted of work. Never had she imagined the world of the asylum and how it truly functioned like a tiny universe. Each participant, including the patients, all worked together to ensure Hatchie River remained sustainable, growing food and creating clothing and other necessities. Claire admitted that work assignments instilled a sense of purpose, even for a fleeting moment.

CHAPTER TWO

After breakfast, Claire and Ruth made their way to the common room, joining eight women. Anne, another attendant, met the ladies and led the way to the sewing room where everyone would stay until lunch time.

The sewing room was located farther back from the wards and down a different hallway altogether. Claire memorized the direction, took note of unique architecture, such as ornate banisters and archways along the way, and burned into her memory every twist and turn. After her admission, Claire had taken a special interest in learning the design of the asylum, inside and out. In her opinion, knowledge meant survival.

The sewing room windows faced the back side of the building. The outside scenery held a peaceful allure. To her amazement, the sewing room had become an internal counterpart to the woods and fields.

She often sat quietly, stitching dresses, mending linens, and listening to the others chat endlessly about the asylum and the injustices

On top of a long table sat baskets of linen, clothing, and material, along with sewing supplies. Claire learned that only the safest patients selected by the head nurse were allowed sewing duties. Anne still performed the customary item counts at the end of the session.

"Okay, ladies," Anne began, her face filled with a warm smile, "I think we can start." She pulled some material from one of the baskets. "Who wants something different to work on today?"

She glanced around the room at each of the women. "You don't get a lot of choices here. I don't believe any of you are bad people or criminals. I don't make the rules, but I like to treat people like I want to be treated."

"You're one of our favorites, Miss Anne," Ruth spoke up. "Nobody cares about us. We're lost and long forgotten." The woman's face showed dejection.

Anne rushed over and put an arm around Ruth's slumped shoulders. "Aw, no need for a long face. We make the best of it, won't we?" "Sorry. Didn't mean to be so down." Ruth looked straight ahead as she quickly wiped her eyes.

"Now then, let's get to work." Anne returned to the baskets and handed Ella some sheets. "Ella, you can mend these." To Claire and Ruth, she handed out yards of fabric and some patterns, as well as some scissors. "You two do such a nice job at sewing these dresses."

Ruth wrinkled her nose. "Can't they give us nicer material? This is just plain ugly. Don't matter what you do to it."

"Sorry, it's all we can get." Anne pulled out some more from the basket and handed it to Bonnie. "We can't forget you. You're also a good one with needle and thread."

"You flatter me, Miss Anne." Bonnie pursed her lips and spread out a pale-yellow print. "Can't we make fun pockets or fancy bows? You know, spruce these things up a bit?"

Anne shook her head. "Rules are rules. I'd be in big trouble if I let you do that."

Ruth glanced up from cutting. "We don't want anything happening to you. You're our only saving grace."

"Considering the Grace we do have is pure hell," Bonnie blurted out, never taking her eyes off the pattern on her piece of material.

The other ladies murmured in agreement.

"We need someone who'll listen to us, instead of treating us like we're animals." Ella nodded at the slender lady with a pleasant face and brown hair standing in front of the baskets.

"I keep everything that's said to myself." Anne went over and delivered a soft pat on Bonnie's shoulder.

"If you ask me," Ella said, "some of you get too free with the tongue. People don't care what we have to say. Something gets back to the wrong person, and we'll be done in." The older lady stopped a moment and looked at each of her peers. "I don't want to be done in, even if I'm here in this trap for a while longer."

"For a while?" Bonnie squared up her shoulders. "You'll be in here until the day you die. That's the truth, whether you want to believe it or not."

"Ladies, please!" Anne clapped her hands. "No fighting. "And Ella, you're free to believe anything you wish. Bonnie, you are too. The only thing I have control over is making your time with me pleasant Just so you know, there are people who leave and go back to their families." Anne paused, forcing a light smile. "Maybe there's not many who leave, but there's always hope that you'll be one of them soon."

All the women had stopped and listened. Some shook their heads in disbelief, some politely agreed, others said nothing. Claire glanced around the room. The clenching sensation in her stomach confirmed growing doubt about being one of the lucky ones. Adrian hadn't called or visited. Each time she thought about calling him at work, she talked herself out of it. Fear of rejection had a strangle-hold on her.

Memories of home and the hat factory hit her harder than ever. Claire thought again about the earlier encounter with Grace. Even a mean, common woman knew about Adrian's hat's, which were prized by merchants and customers all over the Southeast. Time To Wear The Wright Hat. That was the slogan the two brothers concocted when they spruced up their marketing plan. Adrian had been so excited when he came home after work and shared it with her. When Claire suggested that all hats bear the label, The Wright Hat, Adrian made it happen.

He always shared the happy moments, like when he came up with new designs. Sometimes he took her to the small manufacturing building on Market Street and showed her new hat blocks he'd ordered from England. They shared warm twilight evenings with walks in the park, romantic nights dining at Jameson's on McNally Street, and sometimes catching a movie at the Lutesse Theater.

Sharing a bed with Adrian had been a taste of heaven. They both approached their private moments with anticipation, and carried on with equal excitement. The touch of his skin against hers as they engaged in lovemaking under luxurious linen sheets sent her into heady bliss. He knew all the different ways to make her body come alive, and she had learned how to pleasure him. Viewing his face in the height of passion left her brimming with satisfaction. She knew only too well how to please her man. That's why Grace's words still stung, down to the last ugly insinuation. Had he truly made such false statements, or had their declining intimacy as of late clouded his memory?

Twelve years of marriage disappeared in the blink of an eye. Could she have stopped the downward spiral? Did she even see it coming? Questions like these rolled endlessly around in her head when she sat in a rocker in the common room, or walked alone outside in the small amount of time allotted. Sad and frustrated, she realized the whys of her marriage crumbling may never be answered, but there was one certainty: She would find a way out of this godforsaken place, one way or another!

"Mrs. Wright, are you here with us?" Anne's voice called out.

"Sorry, I didn't hear you." Claire averted her eyes from her work.

"I asked you if you could tell us a little about yourself and why you're here. You don't have to tell anything you don't want to."

"Yes, do tell us. It helps boost the esprit de corps." Ruth reached over and patted Claire on the back. Her face bore a sober expression. "Really, Claire, it helps to talk a little. We may not have answers to everything, but we try to give all we got. Don't we, ladies?"

"We do," Ella said, plunging the needle into the sheet. "And don't mind our carrying on like wet hens. There's nothing else to do but try and console each other." She made a knot and cut the thread.

Claire took a deep breath. Never one to share too much, Anne's request put her on the spot. How embarrassing to admit how she'd been duped and tossed away like a used toy.

"I don't know where to start. Haven't been here too long, but let's just say, I'd rather be home."

"Amen to that, sister," Bonnie said.

Claire continued, "My husband brought me here, saying he had to deliver a hat to one of the doctors, and asked me to come with him."

"Deliver a hat?" Ella shot a look of surprise in Claire's direction, wincing when she stuck herself with a needle. "Damn it!" She focused briefly on her wounded finger. "Why would your husband be delivering a hat, of all things?"

"Because he's the one who makes those hoity-toity hats everyone dreams of wearing. Isn't that right, Claire?" Ruth beamed at the others. "Don't you wish we could wear them?" She let out a small cackle.

Ella pulled a new sheet off the pile and began stitching again. "Did he ever make special ones for you?"

"Let's just say I got to wear the first ones before they made it into the shops." Claire smiled as she sewed the garment in her hands.

A round of "Oh-h-hs" from the ladies filled the room.

"But what happened? He delivered a hat, but what did that have to do with you?" Anne spoke up.

"He went off with Grace, and you can guess the rest. I never saw him again. Never said so much as a good-bye or nothing." Claire found herself choking up as she relived the scene again in her mind.

"Any idea why he'd do that?" Ruth asked.

Ella offered her idea. "I know a lot of us have said something was usually going on when we were brought here, like being irritable all the time or mentioning that we were tired of taking care of a household. Some of us were sick and couldn't work like we used to."

"And I'll tell you something else," Bonnie stated, "you'll get sent here if your old man is simply tired of you. I've heard of it happening too many times. As for me, I found myself being on top of the world one minute, only to become ornery and cantankerous the next. I guess my old man Fred got over that real quick. Finally, I gave up on everything. And so did he. Next thing I knew, I found myself here. We talk occasionally, but he never promises to come get me."

Claire listened. She thought more about her life before Hatchie River. Perhaps losing two babies, one after the other, put a damper on the relationship between her and Adrian. She stopped working on the dress and thought some more, digging deeper for answers. As she pulled events together on her mental timeline, everything slipped into place, forming the grim picture she'd refused to see. Her mood plummeted to the lowest level, with every day turning into a struggle. Getting out of bed proved challenging. Carrying out her daily chores had become nearly impossible.

The loss was made worse because she'd carried this last baby full-term, and it died two months after it was born. Adrian didn't understand why she had withdrawn, crying all the time, becoming angry when she wanted to visit the grave as often as she did. Work became more important to him, so he stayed at the factory later. After that, everything went downhill in their relationship. It seemed like all the love had suddenly evaporated. No matter what she did, the old togetherness didn't come back.

"Yes," Claire said, answering the question Ruth asked her, "I think my husband simply got tired of me too."

The room grew silent. All the ladies focused on the work in front of them.

Anne spoke softly, "We're sorry to hear about that. I'm not married, but it has to be hard thinking someone loves you deeply, only to betray that love and trust by sending you to a place like this."

Claire wiped a stray tear trickling down her cheek. "I think of what might have been, dream of what could have been a happy future, and then I wake up here in this place. I still can't quite understand why he'd do that. Whatever was bothering him, we could have worked it out. I mean, why not? People do it all the time, don't they?"

Ruth stopped and wagged a finger at Claire. "Men are heartless cads. For the life of me, I can't understand what we want with 'em, anyway."

"Oh my, just listen to the song of the forlorn and downtrodden. You poor dears." A familiar voice came from the doorway of the room, and all the ladies turned their heads. Grace leaned against the doorframe, her lips turned up into a smirk. She pushed herself off the door-jamb and sauntered further into the room.

"What do you want, Grace?" Anne's voice rang out in a steely note.

"Just came by to check on you and your darlings." The exaggerated smile on Grace's face blended well with the higher vocal pitch at the end of her words, and the ladies wrinkled their noses, sniffing with disgust as she walked by. Grace ignored the rebuffs while she meandered through the room toward Anne, showing feigned interest in the work, leaning over some of the women and inspecting their progress. She paused by Claire, who stiffened at her approach. "My, my, you are handy at something after all. Not bad, not bad." Claire jumped at the series of firm pats from Grace's hand, each one landing between her shoulder blades with a dull thump. "I approve, I really do."

"Grace, state your business and let us get back to work." Anne made no pretense at her irritation.

"Hold your horses!" Grace lost the smile long enough to scowl quickly at Anne before resuming a new smile with full force. "I just wanted to see everybody and all the wonderful work they do around here." She viewed a little more of the handiwork. When she approached Anne, her face lost all expression. "Just wanted to remind you to get your supply list turned into Greta before the shift ends. She told me to tell you."

Anne returned the cold stare. "Fine, I'll get everything turned in."

"Fine, you do that." Grace turned on her heel, walked to the door, and disappeared from the room.

Bonnie jerked around in her chair, thrusting an up-turned middle finger toward the door. "Take that, you cow!"

All the women snickered. Anne put a hand to her mouth, hiding the beginnings of a laugh. When the group had settled back down to a nice pace of activity, Anne chatted with everyone again.

"Mrs. Wright, before you came here, did you used to sew and make new clothes? You surely had some nice clothes to go along with the hats you wore, didn't you?"

Claire kept working as she spoke. "I had nice dresses to go with the hats. I also wasn't shy with needle and thread at all." She paused and sat up straight, eyes sparkling. "I remember when Adrian surprised me with a Singer Featherweight. I squealed and jumped up and down like a silly five-year-old! He'd ordered it from England just for me. I made several nice pieces with it."

The women murmured their approval as they glanced in Claire's direction.

Anne asked, "Did you do other things besides sew?"

"I had a loom. I made some of the prettiest blankets and tablecloths. I even got smart and created some patterns that are mine. I've never seen them anywhere else."

"Hey, Miss Anne, maybe we can get a loom and she can give us a class." Bonnie stopped working. "Those tables in the dining room could use something to brighten them up. It's dreary in there."

Ella chimed in. "I'd like a new blanket and a scarf to keep my head warm."

All the ladies smiled and looked up at Anne.

"We don't have looms. I doubt we could get a fancy one like Mrs. Wright had."

When the morning ended, Anne called out the time. The group wound their way back to the dining hall for lunch.

With sadness, Claire remembered the lively lunches she had with close friends. She imagined how each of her current peers might look, dressed up in fine clothes, wearing one of Adrian's hats, and sitting in some high-style restaurant. What would they talk about, then? Would Ella's silvery hair be a different color? Would Bonnie have some manners? How would Ruth look with her hair styled, wearing cosmetics and a pretty dress? Claire missed being what Grace called "gussied up." Most of all, she missed being the apple of Adrian's eye. Now, the only lunches she had was stale food amid the company of scantily-washed bodies and vulgar mouths. Maybe she'd muster up enough courage to call Adrian the next time the day for phone calls came around.

CHAPTER THREE

The common room hummed with endless chatter, accented with staff yelling in frustration at other patients. The women had come in from working outside and now rested before dinner. Claire gazed across the room at the sea of unkempt women and a showy display of the oddest behaviors she'd ever seen. She'd also peeked inside other rooms, viewing patients who lay on the floor covered in their own filth, nearly starving. Other patients shared horror stories of women in isolation rooms, where they were often chained to the wall for days and weeks at a time, if not longer.

Claire gazed at Millie sitting in the far corner of the room, where she sat cradling an old baby doll. The woman's short gray hair stood on end, and her toothless mouth sank back in her face. When she looked at you with her wild-eyed stare and pursed lips, you prayed she wouldn't take a notion and hit you. Ruth had told Claire the lady was really "cracked in the head," and that she'd been at the asylum for several years. "These are the people that need to be here," Ruth said. Claire wondered what Millie would be like if she were sane. Did she have a family? Had she ever known romantic love? Claire had tried speaking to her, but got little in the way of lucid conversation. Sometime the male orderlies took Millie away from the room for a long time before they'd bring her back, where she'd find her old seat and go back to rocking her baby.

"Mrs. Wright, it's your turn to use the phone, if you'd like." Greta, the charge nurse, came over and stood by Claire. "You think you're up for it today?" A German accent coated the words as she spoke in a clipped, but soft, tone.

Claire followed Greta to the nurse's station. She held the receiver and dialed the number, trembling as she plunged her finger into the slots on the rotary dial. This process, so simple under normal circumstances, seemed like an eternity now. She considered giving up and finding another solution. However, Ruth had encouraged her to make the call. "Either way, good or bad, you'll know where you stand." Those had been her words. She made Claire promise she wouldn't back out. Three weeks had passed and still no call from Adrian. Had he truly forgotten that he had a wife who missed him, despite all their differences? Her heart had ached long enough. Now she needed to know her fate.

A woman's voice sounded through the other end of the line. "Wright Manufacturing. How may I direct your call?"

"I'm needing to speak to Adrian Wright, please."

"May I tell him who's calling?"

Claire blanched at the question. She should have prepared for this a little better. "I'm calling to discuss the Callahan account." Luckily for her, she'd remembered this customer he'd mentioned on several occasions.

"One moment, please."

Inhaling a deep breath, Claire waited.

"This is Adrian Wright speaking."

Her heart nearly stopped at the sound of the smooth, pleasant voice on the other end, the voice of the man she thought would love and protect her forever. For a moment, she froze in panic, scrambling for the right words.

"Adrian? It's me, Claire." Nervous, she cringed thinking what might happen. Would he hang up on her, or would he give her a good reason why he'd disappeared from her life with no reason or warning?

"Claire?" His vocal inflection rose to a higher pitch. "Why are you calling here?"

The nerve of asking such a question first set off a spike of indignation, followed by a round of tears pooling in her eyes. Ruth, who'd been standing nearby for moral support, gave her an expression of dismay. She'd most likely read the hurt feelings on Claire's face the moment she spoke into the receiver.

"I-I'm calling to see how you are. I hadn't heard from you." Claire took a gulp of air.

Adrian cleared his throat. "I'm fine. You?"

"Everything going well with the hats? Are you coming up with any new styles?" While she tried to sound casual, a large part of her died inside. His response what not what she wanted.

"The hats are fine. Everything's fine. Why wouldn't it be?" Now his voice contained a twinge of irritation.

Claire sniffed as tears trickled down her cheek. "I just thought I'd ask." Ruth gave her a sign to keep on talking, forcing a light smile and nodding for encouragement.

"Is that all?" Adrian's voice came over the line firm and strong.

"The real reason I called is because I'm wanting to know why you left me here and when I'd be leaving?

"I really don't have time to discuss this, Claire. I'm busy."

Now she panicked. "I'll do whatever you want. We can get through all this. Just please let me come home." She lowered her voice. "They're not very nice here, and I don't feel safe."

Just as those last words left her mouth, she tensed as a body brushed past. Grace looked back, her lips turned up into the same nasty smile she'd worn that morning. She turned around and kept walking. Claire closed her eyes, swearing under her breath. Of all the people she'd never want nearby to hear this conversation, Grace topped the list. No sooner than she focused her attention back on Adrian, she bristled at the series of taps on her back. Turning around, she saw Millie.

"Kiss it!" The older woman stood, holding out her doll.

"What?"

"Kiss it!" Millie thrust out the doll with more determination.

Claire placed her hand over the bottom of the receiver. "Go away. I don't want to kiss that."

Millie stood there, insistent.

"I'll do it later. Go on. I'm talking to someone." Claire gently pushed Millie away, at which point Ruth came promptly and guided Millie back to the common room.

"Sorry." Ruth mouthed the words, flashing her friend an apologetic look.

Claire turned back to the phone.

"Claire . . . Claire! Are you there?" Adrian's voice snapped like a nasty whip, his words stinging with equal intensity.

"Yes, I'm listening." The brief disruptions had distracted her, and she quickly rustled her thoughts together.

"Like I was saying. You'll be staying right where you are until you're better. You hear me?"

"Better? Why did you even put me here in the first place? I don't have to get better because I was never sick."

"Listen to me. You need to be there. That's why. When I talk with the doctor and he tells me you're better, then we'll see about you coming home."

She grimaced at his response. Nothing she said computed in his brain. Frustration mounted. "When will you be talking to a doctor, then? It's been three weeks. You haven't come. I don't care what these doctors say. I'll do much better at home."

"They know a lot more than you do, and this is the very thing I got tired of dealing with, you're sniveling moods, always dwelling on the baby. He's not coming back, Claire, no matter how hard you pray, no matter how much you visit a grave." His voice glanced off her ears, delivering a steely blow with every word.

"Please don't talk like that, Adrian! We haven't always been like this. Remember how we used to laugh and talk? We loved each other once. Lately, you've been so cold, mean and unfeeling. What's happened to you? What's happened to us?" Tears trailed down her cheeks.

Adrian continued, oblivious to her pleading. "Life's not fair; things happen. You never seemed to toughen up and deal with it, and I couldn't do anything with you, either. So now you're in a place where you'll learn to deal with it, whether you want to or not."

Claire grew numb. His words held a finality that frightened her. She tried to stifle the fear and temper the grips of desperation choking every muscle in her body right now. "Adrian, honey, I'm sorry. If you let me come home, I'll do much better. I promise. I won't mention the baby or even think about going to the grave." She closed her eyes and took in a deep breath. What else could she say?

"And just how do you promise that when you can't even hold it together during a simple phone call? Just listen to yourself, carrying on like that."

Claire cringed. "Don't you think I deserve an answer to all this?"

"The answer is you'll stay a while longer. Then we'll see when you can come home."

She tried one last desperate attempt to win him over, convince him to see the situation her way. "Don't you love me anymore, Adrian? I love you. I'm your wife. I miss you. Aren't you even coming for a visit? You're allowed to. Other people get visits from their family."

The other end of the line grew quiet, and Claire thought he'd put the phone in a drawer and went back to his work.

"I'll have to see. Can't guarantee when I'll can get away. We are busier than we've ever been."

Claire swore she heard his voice waver. He sounded strained, like having this conversation had truly fatigued him physically.

"Promise me you'll drop by. Adrian, this has broken me. I didn't mean for us to ever be like this. We had some good times together, you and me. Don't you even remember any of that?" The tears returned in full force, and she wiped her nose with a finger, cleaning it off on her dress.

His voice softened a little. "Let me see what I can do, Claire. I'll look at my schedule, I promise."

"I love you, Adrian." Claire choked out the words. Click, and the line went dead. She stood there, stunned.

"Mrs. Wright, are you finished? You're time's almost up."

Greta smiled in sympathy.

"I guess so." Claire hung her head in disappointment and handed the receiver back to Greta.

"The conversation with your husband didn't go as well as you'd hoped?"

"No. I knew I shouldn't have made that call. I just knew it. I had a feeling it would go bad."

Greta listened, nodding a little. "Maybe your husband just had a bad day. You can try again another time, and maybe things will be better. There's always hope. Never give up."

Claire turned her eyes up at Greta and tried smiling back. "Maybe you're right, but I'm just not feeling hopeful right now."

Greta turned her lips down in a show of sympathy as she placed the receiver back in the cradle. Claire walked to Ruth, who waited in the door of the common room.

"Sorry about that. I'd hoped your old man would have been in his right senses after not hearing from his wife for a while."

"Don't worry about it, Ruth. Something told me that calling would be a bad idea, and I don't know why I didn't listen to myself." Claire pushed her fingers through some oily stray locks of hair hanging over her eye.

Ruth found two empty rocking chairs by a corner window, and the ladies sat down. "You can't keep on beatin' yourself up like that. Like I said, you need to know where you stand in all this mess he left you in. Did he even hint at coming to see you, even just a little?"

"I had to beg him to say yes. But I don't think he will. Didn't sound all that happy to hear from me. Pretty much blamed me for everything."

The older lady beside Claire sat and rocked, shaking her head at times in disbelief. The evening sun pierced the sky, its hot glow shining an ugly light on every truth Claire didn't want to acknowledge, the truth that Adrian no longer loved her. The truth that she may die here.

Adrian had sounded like a foreigner, with the uncharacteristic coldness in attitude and speech cutting at her heart. He didn't sound like the man she'd married years ago, one who'd captured her soul with twinkling eyes and sure words, a torchbearer for undying love and devotion. Now all he left her were broken promises and ill words falling on her like cold spears—and the enemy was Adrian. At this moment, Claire turned her face down and let the tears flow in silence.

She cried about her current imprisonment, cried for an old life that had truly died an undeserving death, cried for her dead baby boy sleeping forever in Green Oaks Cemetery, not more than a mile from her former home. She cried for all the other women sitting around her, with their broken hearts and dreams. She cried for Millie, at all the injustice inflicted on her through Grace's daily brutality. Ruth didn't take her eyes from the window nor did she speak a word. No angel of consolation would come to heal the raw unseen wounds of two helpless women as they sat together, staring out the window at a bleak future. They, along with others, found themselves unlikely companions in a stormy sea of confusion, with little hope of a savior coming to their rescue.

An attendant cried out the announcement for dinner. Dinner time only ushered in the nighttime, which meant poor sleep on uncomfortable beds and bad dreams. She and Ruth followed the other ladies to the dining room.

"So, what will you be having tonight, my dear? The Filet Mignon or Duck a l'Orange?" Ruth cocked her head a little and cut an exaggerated grin at Claire, batting her eyelashes for more emphasis.

Claire couldn't help but smile. "Perhaps a taste of both. Money's no object. And I do want the best wine in the house."

Both ladies burst out laughing, but toned down the levity as they passed Greta, who nodded politely.

"I like her," said Ruth. "She's the best nurse here. When she's on duty, I feel a little safer. Can't say that with the others."

"Me too. You can't beat her and Anne."

In the dining hall, Ruth and Claire selected two empty adjacent chairs, and surveyed their trays.

"Where did you learn some of your fancy words, Ruth?"

Her friend spiked a dull slice of roast beef with a tarnished fork and paused it in front of her lips. "Spent several weeks in Cincinnati with an uppity cousin of mine. She always had an eye and taste for the finer things in life. Don't get me wrong, I enjoy all that, too, but at heart, I'm just a simple, country woman. No need for all that complicated nonsense." She leaned closer to Claire and said softly, "Meanin' no offense, but something tells me you're not much different from my cousin Fran, with your old man makin' hats that lots of people know about. Only people with good money could buy the kinds you sell. You just seem to act more prim and proper than most of us do around here, the way you walk, the way you sit. More just the way you come across, an air about you."

"That's okay. I'm not offended. But you're mostly right. I was used to getting pretty much what I wanted all my life. And my husband wasn't always like he sounded today."

"They never are. Charm the shoes off a snake, they do. But once they have you, they're the very devil. You can't trust 'em one lick."

"I'm beginning to see that." Claire swallowed a spoonful of tasteless mashed potatoes and looked out over the dining hall, taking in the details of patients, staff, and general surroundings. How easy it seemed to simply get up when staff had their heads turned and slip down the hallway and out the front door, especially if someone had forgotten to lock the door to a stairwell. She could sneak down to the end of the hall and make it out another way.

She whispered over to Ruth. "Do people ever just leave here, walk out, or run away?"

Ruth squinted her eyes as she turned the question over in her mind. "Some people have run away."

Claire sat up straighter. "Really? How do they get out of here and not get caught? And what happens when they are caught?"

Ruth put down her fork and gazed intently into Claire's face. "There's tunnels under this building that lead to the outside. Several people have sneaked out. I've seen a few come back with the police, and others I've never seen since."

"Where do you think the ones who never come back go?"

"Don't know." The lady shook her head.

Pressing on, Claire asked, "Why haven't you tried to leave here, since you seem to know a way out?"

"I never said I knew an exact way out, but I've heard talk here and there." Ruth slipped a fork of green beans into her mouth and wiped away the dribbles of juice with her hand.

"If you know people who've done it, why haven't you?"

Turning her eyes away, Ruth gazed across the room for several seconds before she answered.

"The thought of going out there in the world and making it on my own, trying to get along with everybody, scares the hell out of me, that's what."

"But why?" Claire stared at her companion. "How can being here be better?"

The older lady leaned in close. "Let me tell you something. This place is the devil's hole. I'll be the first to say it. But mark my words, and many here will agree, there's a certain security in being here. It sounds strange, but it's true. Even though it gets rough and the food'll nearly kill you if the staff don't do it first, there's still that sense of knowing what to expect. You know if you don't do what you're told, or get too yappy, you could get yelled at or slapped. If you hit a staff member or someone else, it might get you thrown in isolation where you might be left to die and rot, or killed just from being manhandled. Other than that, it's the same old routine, day in, day out. No surprises, no needing to think on anything." She paused and sipped some water while Claire stared at her in disbelief.

"And I'll tell you something else." Ruth moved her face so close to Claire's, their noses nearly touched. "Do you know what those orderlies do with Millie when they take her out?"

"No, but I've often wondered. I see them take her out of the common room sometimes."

"They take her to the old shed out back, the one near the field that lines up with our property. It's quiet out there, and you'll see that it's a good enough distance away and just enough out of sight, being hidden by the trees and all. You see, the orderlies, they sneak men out from the men's side, one by one, sometimes two or three at a time if they want to act like they're using them for some kind of work. But what they're really doing is using Millie as a free shot . . . you know . . ." Ruth pursed her lips and darted her eyes upwards and back to Claire."

Claire sat back in her chair, stunned beyond belief. "You mean they have . . . ?"

"Those bastards make money off her, getting what they can, or maybe the men have something for trade. Families sometime send money or bring little gifts. I think some of them get a kick out of watching crazies go at it. Don't think anyone is left totally alone. There's someone watching somewhere."

"Why would anyone want to do something like that with poor old Millie?"

"Men are cads and horny bastards, like I said before. They don't care how cracked in the head someone is. If they can blow their wads in a hole, they don't give one rat's ass who's or what it is. And staff usually turn a blind eye, anyway. Nobody reports it or says anything, because if you do, you'll be the one who ends up in the shed."

Thoughts of men invading a poor helpless woman, blowing their foul breath as they put their lips on her, taking advantage and pouring out their nasty filth, filled Claire with a deep disgust and loathing. What would it take before anyone decided to come after Ruth or her? She knew the male orderlies often slipped into certain rooms at night. In the hall, their footsteps echoed as they passed by her door. At times, when she couldn't sleep, she'd get out of bed and peep out of the room. Many a night she caught a glimpse of them entering a room where she knew a woman of lower mentality slept, all in the name of "checking in on them." Were they doing obscene things with women such as these, helpless victims with no clear voice to scream, perhaps lacking the clarity to know they were being violated? The men stayed in the rooms far too long for making simple shift rounds.

Ruth tapped her roommate on the wrist. "Mind what I say. I've been here for three years, and I've seen a lot. I've seen young girls come in here all feisty on their first day, and within weeks beaten down so hard and broken there was nothing left but a walking corpse. And I curse the ones who sent them here, hoping they'll rot in Hell. Keep quiet, keep out of trouble, try to blend in. Most of all, pray hard. Pray real hard. Even that won't guarantee you'll be safe. Things happen in the blink of an eye."

Claire nodded and turned back to her food, assimilating everything Ruth had told her. If cries for help fell on deaf ears or guaranteed retaliation, how could save themselves from the jaws of the great monster known as the asylum? One question intrigued her: If she ever reached the outside world; who would help if Adrian wouldn't?

When dinner was over, the ladies returned to the common room. Nothing in the physical environment had changed. Millie sat in her usual rocker, holding her doll. The same women paced nervously or sat in corners with their hands over their ears, while others rocked quietly. That evening Claire looked at asylum life and its inmates through different eyes, ones taking in a world where the brutal clarity of it all slammed against her with unforgiving force. She knew each day would confirm what she already knew, and there was nothing she could do but drink from the bitter cup. To do otherwise would be a futile dream.

Later that night, Claire opened her eyes when the sounds of feet passed by the door. Ruth snored softly, unaware. Claire strained her ears. The trail of footsteps ended up in a room across the hall. A female let out a groan, followed by a few quick sobs. The menacing, low-pitched voice of an orderly sent a chill through Claire's heart. She pulled the sheet tighter under her chin, closed her eyes, and said a prayer.

CHAPTER FOUR

Today was Tuesday, the day for "Hydro." Claire and Ruth had talked about treatment days, and both admitted being undecided on which one they detested most, hydrotherapy or the electric shock treatments on Mondays and Fridays. Thursday was the other day for hydro, leaving them with Wednesday, Saturday, and Sunday to recuperate. According to some, being "electrocuted," the term used for describing the shock treatments, didn't fare any better in the popularity department than being forced to endure time in an ice-cold tub.

Claire thought back to the first day she'd been "electrocuted." An attendant always gave the announcement with a loud "T-i-i-ime for therapy-y-y! Line up everyone! Let's go, over here!" And the women ambled over, following the attendant down the hallway to the treatment room. Heaven help those who lagged behind in the common room, because another attendant came around, jerked you out of the chair, and dragged you to the group. Ruth had already explained to Claire what to expect.

"No use showin' out. They'll whip your ass all the way to that shock room, come hell or high water, if you try to stall any. Just go in, do what you're told, and it'll be over soon. And don't mind all the carrying on you'll hear."

"What do they do to you?" Claire asked.

"They'll ask you to lie down on a bed. Once they've put those pads on either side of your head, you just go blank. It don't hurt or nothing, but it takes a bit to come to. You know, to clear your head again. But you always do. I don't like it much, but you can't fight 'em."

And the scene proceeded the way Ruth had described it. The room held an electrical smell, and a mix of other odors not easily identifiable. Women waited until their turn, several crying to get out of the procedure while their cohorts tried to say words of comfort. Claire remembered her body shaking with fear. Of course, Ruth never mentioned anyone actually dying from this. Or had she been too scared to tell Claire if it had happened? She took a deep breath and tried to concentrate on getting through this ordeal. Getting into the bed when it was her turn sent her into another round of shivers, especially when she sensed a cold paste being applied to her temples just before they placed the electrodes on her head. That was the other smell, the one mingling with discharged electricity against unwashed skin. Was that the only protection between her head and a surging electrical blast? That god-awful smelly paste?

Her hands had been strapped down, and a nurse stood at her feet to hold them when the shock was delivered. A piece of rubber had been placed in her mouth as soon as she got on the bed. An approving nod from the doctor, and all went blank. After that, she couldn't remember what happened next. She recovered with her lucidity mostly intact about a couple of hours later, but soon discovered that she couldn't remember what happened before treatments or immediately after. Like Ruth, she'd decided the procedure held something sinister, an indescribable essence she disliked. As much as she refused to admit it, once she got past the nausea and occasional headache, she discovered her mood had perked up a bit.

Hydrotherapy, on the other hand, posed another issue, most likely because time in an ice bath didn't go quickly, and Claire learned if you didn't pass out from the shock or hypothermia, you had too much time to think. At least rocking away in the common room or doing work in another activity burned off pent up energy. Being trapped in a tub, sealed in with a heavy canvas cover didn't afford such a luxury.

Today, Grace ran the tub room with the usual tenacity of the fiercest drill sergeant. When Greta stepped out for a moment, she took the opportunity to thrash Millie, who fought back as the cold water hit her skin.

"You just shut up and sit down!" Grace pushed the poor woman hard, sending her flailing into the tub.

Millie stuck out her tongue. "Bitch!" She shot out a hand toward Grace's face.

The attendant delivered a resounding smack on Millie's cheek, the sound of it filling the room with a sharp snap. Claire winced and turned away.

"Mind your mouth, you worthless fool. I'll drown you as sure as I'm standing here."

"Grace, enough!" Greta had entered the room again, clapping her hands as she moved in between Grace and Millie, who'd began fighting to pull herself out of the tub. Claire breathed a sigh of relief.

"Here, help me get this canvas over her. Now, dear, just be still. The water will make you feel better." Greta patted Millie's face and helped settle her into the tub. "There's a good dear. Yes, you'll feel so much better."

"How you coddle these idiots." Grace glared at Greta as the nurse positioned Millie's head. Grace yanked the canvas cover around Millie's neck, fastening it in place. She stood up and faced off with Greta. "What are you so riled up about, anyway? She got mouthy and tried to hit me. So, I let her know who's boss."

"You provoked that woman." Greta moved her face within inches of Grace's. "I'm aware of the way you and other staff treat these poor people. If anyone outside ever knew what really happens here, we'd be in big trouble. We'd find ourselves without jobs and homeless if this place ever closed down. All because of people like you." She poked a finger into Grace's chest.

Grace stepped back. Her eyes lit up with an evil gleam. "You know what, Greta, you really sound as paranoid as some of these patients at times. Know what I think? It really wouldn't take too much to convince these quacks we have for doctors that you're starting to lose your mind. Now, wouldn't that be something, you being a patient here? Of course, spending time around the loonies can make you loony, so we'd all understand. It's all right. It can happen." She postured and waited for a response.

"You better wipe that smirk off your face before I slap it off myself, Grace—just like Millie!" Greta's eyes widened in anger. She continued, "How dare you speak to me and threaten me in that manner. I'm in a higher position than you, so smarten up and know your place." She shook her fist and moved toward the door, ignoring Claire as she passed. Before exiting, she turned back to Grace one last time. "And I'll tell you something else, you shameless girl, you keep provoking these patients, and one day you'll find yourself on the wrong end of the bargain."

When Greta had disappeared, Grace put her right hand under her left elbow and raised her left arm in a movement depicted by society as an obscene gesture. Claire closed her eyes and prayed she'd get through this treatment today.

"You're next, Miss Uppity." Grace moved over to a spare tub, tapping her foot with impatience. Claire approached, pulled off her dress, and dropped it on the floor. She stared at the tub. The cold porcelain interior looked like a monster with a gaping mouth, ready to gobble her up. She hesitated before lowering into the hammock. Could she stand another day of being doused with cold water? She'd been at Hatchie River over a month, and surely these treatments had to end someday.

"Don't act like you've never done this before. Sit down and be quick about it." Grace's eyes seemed to launch a barrage of angry bullets as she shoved Claire inside.

Claire held out an arm, risking backlash from the young woman standing next to her. "I'm going. Don't push."

"Move it, then!"

The hammock in the tub kept the brutal, cold surface from sending shockwaves through her system as she lowered herself down. It took every ounce of resolve to keep from screaming when Grace turned the tap on. Ice-cold water lashed at her ankles and legs like a million angry whips.

"Warm enough for you?" Another smirk from Grace, and Claire debated whether or not to throw good sense to the wind and just sock Grace in the eye and be done with it all. Surely death couldn't be as bad as enduring the woman in control of the taps. She closed her eyes and gritted her teeth.

The water soon covered her thighs and crept up to her waist. No matter the number of baths, one simply could never get used to this torture. She decided then and there, electrocution was much better. Once the water had covered her chest, Grace shut everything off, fastened the canvas on top and walked away. Claire hoped she'd only spend no more than a couple of hours in the tub. She knew some of the other patients often spent hours and even days in this room, with attendants feeding them their meals.

Trapped under the canvas, unable to do anything but shiver and think, she spent the next thirty minutes imagining her body at a warmer temperature. She'd read magazine articles of certain spiritual men in other countries doing this same thing when they slept outside in the snow. The weather beat all around them, snowy and cold, and their bodies survived without any of them dying of frostbite or exposure, all because they willed themselves to stay warm. Needless to say, her intent failed miserably as it had in previous attempts. Perhaps these men possessed a special power she didn't have.

In her estimation, Hatchie River seemed bent on breaking down the resolve of every patient who walked through those front doors rather than heal them. The worse you behaved, the worse staff had it in for you. She witnessed one unfortunate patient having their own feces from the toilet shoved in their mouth after smarting off at an attendant. Greta had not been on duty that day, and the nurse in charge ignored the commotion. And yet, staff were never held accountable for their actions. "Keep quiet, keep out of trouble, try to blend in. Most of all, pray hard. Pray real hard." Ruth's words haunted her.

Claire's mind wandered back to life before entering the asylum. She'd learned this trick of forcing herself to think, to remember people, places, and events so her sanity remained intact during hydro sessions. Each time she tried extracting every detail from anything she could think of so her brain "wouldn't go soft." That's the term she'd heard when patients had finally been broken by the system. They'd lost their ability to think and reason. If she lapsed into unconsciousness, she feared her brain may never be sane again. She counted all the friends she'd made in her lifetime, attaching to each name their face and a trait she liked best about them.

Her mind wandered back to carefree days when she was eight years old, and ran through fields of flowers, with long braids trailing behind her as the sun smiled down from a brilliant blue sky. All through high school she'd been popular and treated well by friends and teachers, asked to parties, courted by young men. She counted all the parties she'd attended in her life and the number of boys who'd tried to steal a kiss. Her parents spoiled her with trips to the ocean, pretty dresses, anything her heart desired. She tried counting these, too, the number of trips, the number of skirts and dresses she'd owned. Her parents would be so shocked, maybe embarrassed, if they saw her now. She kept her mind pressing onward. At eighteen, her life changed when she married Adrian, strong, handsome, adoring, and fit with a solid mind to rule the household, business—and her. Had anything caused him to falter the way her mind faltered right now, this moment, trapped in a tomb of ice? Why else would he do such a thing as this to her?

Then there was Mitchell, Adrian's younger brother. She couldn't recall enough specifics to count anything regarding him. One thing she knew, he'd always struck her as something of an enigma, mostly because he wasn't around much until recently. When she and Adrian first married, Mitchell had refused to take part in the hatting business, choosing his own path and wanting a life away from family. This created great frustration in Adrian. Claire hadn't formed much of an opinion, writing him off as a rather distant sort. The only question in her mind was how Mitchell could have succeeded in his marketing career if he didn't have the personality for it? Maybe Adrian's younger brother came off as suave and debonair to others. Just because he didn't show that side of himself to her or his brother didn't mean he hid it from those who mattered—people with money to buy products he pushed. She tried counting all the salesmen she'd ever encountered.

 Claire thrashed her legs, hoping she'd warm up just a little. Fighting to stay awake, she closed her eyes and hummed as she shook her head several times. Where was she in her tracking of things? Mitchell being an odd sort, yes. She continued mentally recounting her knowledge of Mitchell. Two years ago, Adrian finally succeeded in getting his brother to see how they could influence hat fashion for the better, he creating the new styles, while the other marketed the business and collected orders. Mitchell relented, finally teaming up with his older brother if he agreed to split profits fifty-fifty. That was the only deal he'd accept.

 When he set up his office next to Adrian's, Claire saw more of this man, one who wore fashionable suits with shirt cuffs bound with gleaming gold cufflinks. He penned notes in a leather-bound journal using a sterling silver fountain pen. She bet he and Ruth's uppity cousin Fran might hit it off if they ever met. Fran was uppity, Mitchell seemed uppity. And apparently, she must have seemed uppity, too, because Ruth and ugly old Grace had both referenced her as such. Otherwise, she couldn't count any other faults in Mitchell.

 Her teeth chattered as her body temperature dropped. When Greta returned, she'd ask for warmer water. Treatment procedures had rules, and Greta meant to follow them mostly to the letter, but she had a heart. Claire's eyes closed. How long had she been in this forsaken tub? Maybe she'd be out of here soon and back in the common room. In the other tub, Millie had already fallen asleep, eyes closed, mouth open. If Grace didn't slap her any more today, at least this poor woman could rest a little.

The sound of splashing water and voices interrupted Claire's thought processes. Or had those thoughts been merely dreams? Her eyes fluttered open. Grace and Millie struggled against each other as Grace tried pulling her from the tub.

"Come on, you old hag. Time's up."

"Ow!" Millie cried out, slapping at Grace's arm. "That hurts." Her voice came out raspy.

"Quit fighting me or I'll knock the fire out of you." Grace pulled one last time before hauling the poor haggard woman out of the tub and onto the cold tile floor. Millie stood dripping wet, shivering. Claire saw too clearly the gaunt body, delicate skin, and sagging deflated breasts as the woman waited for Grace to dry her off and replace her clothes. However, the scene with Grace and Millie quickly took a back seat to the burning sensation in her bladder and the fullness in her rectum. The passage of time and cold water had wreaked havoc with her system, and now she panicked.

After helping Millie dry off and dress, Grace pulled her out of the room. Claire gritted her teeth and clenched her muscles, trying hard to hold everything in. A gripping cramp passed through her abdomen, so hard she cried out. It passed, but she knew her body wouldn't hold out much longer. Fumbling underneath the canvas, she worked two fingers through an area encircling her neck and pulled. The canvas had been tied down, leaving her a helpless victim. For once in her life she prayed for Grace's return. What would she do if Grace didn't return?

A rumble in her stomach left her with a sense of hopelessness. If she couldn't get out . . . Claire tugged once more at the covering, hoping by some chance of a small miracle it might slip loose, but no such luck occurred. Her ears perked up at the sound of footsteps. In seconds, Grace stood beside the tub.

"So how are you doing? Having the time of your life in there, not a care in the world?" Grace delivered a few hard pats on the back of Claire's head, rattling her nerves so bad she almost lost control of everything right then and there.

"Am I done? I need to use the toilet." Claire's words came out in a raspy whisper.

"You need to use the toilet?" Grace grinned down at her. "Sorry. I'd let you out, but your time's not up yet. Can't go against doctor's orders. When they order a certain amount of time, we have to follow it."

"I'm not in here as long as the others."

"And how would you know that? You don't see a clock in here, do you?" Grace tapped her foot.

Stunned, Claire looked up at her with pleading eyes. "I-I just know they let me out in about a couple of hours." She swallowed hard, holding back the tears. "You can put me back in here when I'm done. I won't give you any problem, I promise. Please just let me use the toilet."

"But why take you out, then put you back in? That's so much trouble when you're already here." Grace glanced at her wrist. "By my watch, you still have more time left." She turned her eyes up to the ceiling, pretending to think the matter over in greater detail, still engaging in that annoying foot-tapping.

A flash of anger passed through Claire. If she hadn't been trapped under that damn canvas, she would have jumped out of that tub and choke the life out of Grace.

Grace shook her head in mock sympathy. "Well, I really don't have any choice but to let you at least finish out your treatment just the way the doctor ordered it. To end it sooner or stop at all would make me look bad." She paused her tapping and leered down at Claire.

Claire blinked a couple of time, trying to steady her voice before she spoke again. "So, what am I supposed to do?"

"Don't know darlin'. You can hold it in or let it go. You make a mess, you clean it up when you're done. Hold it in 'til I let you out, and you can go then. Makes no difference to me." Without another word, she turned around and disappeared from the room, leaving Claire alone again.

"I hope you rot in Hell, you witch! One of these days, you'll pay for all you've done." Claire turned her eyes to the ceiling and spoke freely, her words an incantation filled with unadulterated hate. Wincing as another sharp pain lashed out in her stomach, she took several deep breaths, fighting one last time for a bit of dignity. She'd never make it to the toilet. Not now. With one last involuntary contraction, her bladder and bowels released a hot stream of urine and waste into the tub. Warmed briefly by the heat of her own fluid, she thought of the irony, a fleeting comfortable sensation of warmth mingling in the ice water. But the light touch of her own solid waste tapping against her skin if she moved the slightest bit filled her with an immediate sickness. This incident gashed her spirit. She remained perfectly still.

Other women had gone through this, she knew. She'd somehow had avoided such ignominy until Grace stepped in and made sure she suffered every horror imaginable. Claire envisioned herself killing Grace a thousand times, enjoying the dullness seeping into her eyes as she died a slow death. She sat brooding, counting the number of ways this woman could be knocked off. Yes, like The Maltese Falcon, Suspicion, or even Rebecca, those marvelous crime and mystery movies she and Adrian often saw at the Lutesse. The ones that kept you guessing or sitting on the edge of your seat. A blow to the head with a lead pipe, poison, drowning.

"Ach, you're still in here?"

The clipped German accent mingled with the swishing of a nurse's uniform skirt hit Claire's ears like the trumpet of salvation. She craned her neck, watching Greta come up beside the tub.

Claire turned her eyes up to a concerned face. "She wouldn't let me out. I asked her to."

Greta frowned. "That girl can't be trusted to do a simple job. I told her to let you out once she'd finished with Millie." She unfastened the canvas.

With a blush, Claire reached out for one of Greta's hands. "I've made a mess."

The nurse stood there for a moment, processing what her patient had just confessed. Her face colored in irritation. "Good grief! She didn't let you use the toilet?"

Claire hung her head in embarrassment. "I'll clean it up. She said I had to."

"You'll do no such thing. We'll get you cleaned up." She rolled back the canvas, grimacing when she saw the water. "Go ahead and stand up. Be careful."

Grabbing either side of the tub, Claire pulled herself out of the water, turning her head away from the foulness left behind.

"I was just coming in to get her out. Sorry, I got busy for a minute."

Both women glanced up at the sound of Grace entering the room, and Claire noted Greta's face turning redder than before.

In a cold tone, eyes smoldering with anger, Greta addressed the attendant. "Bring some extra towels. You'll need to clean out this tub."

Grace stood rooted to the ground, eyes fixed on Greta's. "You want me to what?"

"You know what I mean, you lazy girl. You never do what you're told." Greta angled her head toward the cabinet holding the towels. Grace still didn't move. In a final display of authority, Greta walked over and stood within inches of her face. "You'll move now, or I'll throw you in one of these tubs. I'll fill it to the brim with the coldest water, and you'll stay until you're shriveled up so bad your own mother won't know you."

In an instant, Grace's face paled, her eyes widening larger than Claire had ever seen.

"Move now!"

Those two words came from Greta's mouth in such a menacing growl, a hoard of goosebumps popped up on top of Claire's arms. She'd never seen the nurse stand up to a staff member this way.

Defeated at her own game, Grace whirled around with a huff and stomped over to the cabinet, jerking out several towels from a shelf.

"Bring me a few wash cloths."

Sullen, Grace reached up on another shelf and wrenched out a few cloths, sending several others tumbling to the floor.

"Wipe her off. All of her. Make sure her bottom is clean and dry." Greta's face had softened somewhat, and in her eyes a glimmer of amusement edged out the former angry glow.

"What if I just wet these and give them to her? She can do it better than I can."

The nurse replied with a sly grin, "You're the one who's supposed to care for these patients. You'll do your job, and for once do it right." Smooth and calm, the words came out in such an eerie tone. Claire shuddered. "And hurry up. She's freezing cold."

Grace grimaced and held a few washcloths under the water.

"I want them good and warm."

The attendant moved stiffly, adjusting one of the taps up a few notches. While the water streamed, the scowl gradually faded. With the most casual demeanor she said, "Why don't you go on, Greta. I can finish up."

Claire gazed in awe and fear at the attendant's hands, watching each muscle and tendon strain as Grace squeezed out every drop of water.

Greta crossed her arms. Her eyes lit up, flashing and dancing as she watched the attendant. "I'm staying right here."

"You sure?" Grace's hopeful expression faded.

"I'm sure."

For the next several minutes, under Greta's instruction, Claire stood while Grace wiped away the filth. In one final blow, the nurse insisted the tub be cleaned and disinfected while she supervised. Claire put on her dress and waited. When Grace finished, Greta escorted Claire back to the common room.

She should have felt like she'd just won a battle, but somehow Claire knew the war wasn't over. The pleasure of seeing Grace humiliated by her superior rang hollow. The attendant was surely planning her next revenge. For now, Claire had survived one more day at Hatchie River.

CHAPTER FIVE

Claire stopped and rested, leaning against her hoe as she stared out in all directions across the field. For the past few hours, the ladies had worked hard, pulling weeds and hoeing. Others gathered up baskets of vegetables and passed them off to staff who made sure everything ended up in the kitchens.

Today, the air covered everyone and everything in a muggy blanket of humidity so thick one wondered if they couldn't part it with their hands like Moses had done the Red Sea. Claire wished now she'd taken Ruth's advice and salvaged some of Anne's scrap material for making a handy headband.

She'd already begun a collection of "lady rags," the common term for monthly sanitary pads. "You won't get no Kotex here, so you better keep a bag full for when you need 'em." Such had been Ruth's explanation when Claire's menses had started. Bonnie taught her how to make a belt so the rags stayed in place.

Claire smiled. She found it interesting how one thought led to another while she toiled for hours. "Free Association." That's the term she'd learned from her weekly therapy sessions with Dr. Dandridge. While she didn't try to make sense of these ramblings outside of sessions, he afforded her no such luxury during times they met.

Dr. Dandridge had decided on using the "talking cure," a new popular form of treatment. He and Greta thought this approach would improve Claire's mood. She went along with it, much preferring to talk about how to get out of a hell hole such as Hatchie River, but doubted Dr. Dandridge considered such a goal appropriate for therapy.

The positive thing about these sessions was the lack of ice baths and electric shocks. They talked together like two adults. She remembered a recent session. After reclining back on a divan, as was the usual custom, He started off the session by stating, "We've spent some time talking about your home life before you came here. Today, I want you to talk more about feelings of abandonment."

"My feelings of abandonment?"

"Yes." He waited for a moment. "What do you want to say about that subject?"

Claire turned her eyes from the ceiling and glanced over at him. "I'll tell you what I want to say. Men have the power to do things to women, and no one ever questions them. We get labeled with words like "insane" or "crazy" so men can justify their reasons for what they do. They think that makes everything okay, but it doesn't."

He watched her, eyes scanning every movement, face void of expression. "Do you think you're insane?"

"Of course not. Grieving over my baby's death insane? That didn't mean I'd lost my mind. I wanted to go to the grave an awful lot, though. I couldn't help myself."

He cleared his throat and shifted a little in his seat. "And what did you hope to accomplish by visiting the grave as often as you did?"

Claire fought back the tears. "I'd hoped that God would give me an answer. An answer as to why he'd denied me something so simple as the happiness of having children, of having a family I could care for and love."

Nodding, he jotted down something in a notebook. For the first half hour, he spent their session asking her basic questions like these. During the last half hour, he asked her to do something a little different.

"Mrs. Wright, I want you to think about the word love and tell me what comes to your mind. Don't analyze what you say. Just talk, and we'll see what comes out of it before the end of our time."

"Talk about my thoughts on love and saying what comes to mind? Is that what you're asking?"

"Yes. It sounds like an odd request, but there is a point to it."

She'd turned her eyes back to the ceiling, wracking her brain. What did she feel? Did she even feel anything anymore?

"Mrs. Wright, I can see you're thinking. I need to you speak those thoughts, not keep them to yourself."

His tone hadn't been unkind, just insistent.

"Love. That's a bitter word for me . . ."

"Go on, please. Just let your mind flow."

"Well, I married for love. I married my husband assuming we'd be together until we died. He must have decided he didn't love me anymore because he brought me here. God doesn't love me, either, because he made my babies die. I think men and women are equal. We each offer different things in a marriage. That's what makes it work." She'd paused and looked at the doctor. "Is that what you want?"

"Yes, please keep talking. Don't stop until I tell you to."

She'd closed her eyes and continued. "Nobody should have the kind of power men have over women. I think the world's unfair. I had dreams, now I don't know what the future holds. I hate it here. I hate the way we're treated, beaten, starved, treated like animals. I hate the way the men take advantage of helpless women. I hate Grace Neil. She's the Devil's spawn. I think the Devil sometimes makes me think bad thoughts. I didn't used to be so ornery. Adrian said I couldn't deal with things, that I sniveled all the time. He said being here would cure me. I miss my baby boy. I imagined him as the most perfect creature on earth. I still think about him and what he'd be like if he'd lived. If he had been older, maybe he could have seen to it that Adrian wouldn't have left me here. He would have protected me, been someone I could have run to.

"I'm all alone. I'm scared. I usually know what to expect around here, but then again, I don't. Miss Greta and Miss Anne are the nicest staff members. They listen. They care. There should always be trust in a marriage between two people. Nothing should happen without the other person knowing about it. Differences aren't solved with indifference. I don't know what to do next. I want out of here. I'm not sure what it takes to get out of here. I don't belong in this place. I had a life, pretty things, friends. I don't have any family nearby. I'm alone. I saw Grace slap Millie across the face. She shouldn't have hit that poor woman. Millie can't help it. They say orderlies make money handing Millie off to the men around here. It's never quiet. People talk all the time. Bad things happen in patients' rooms. I hear it. My brain gets in a whirl. I don't know what day of the week it is. I want to go home."

"Time. You can stop now." Dr. Dandridge had scribbled furiously in his notebook for the next few minutes. Not once did his face show any emotion about the session.

Claire let out her breath in a loud huff. Maybe this talking cure worked after all. Part of her sensed a bit of relief, like she'd at least lightened the anchor weighing her down into all the muck and dark secrets of the asylum. It had a liberating effect, talking and unleashing her most painful thoughts the way she had just done to Dr. Dandridge. "So, let me ask you, Doctor, do you think I'm insane?"

He'd smiled an easy smile, the one reminding her of Mitchell. "What I heard was a lot of despair, fear, and disappointment. No, that doesn't make you insane. But we'll talk about all this some more the next time we meet. We're out of time now." The session ended with Anne coming and escorting her back to the common room.

Claire jumped at the jolt of pain slicing through her arm.

"Get moving! We haven't got all day."

An attendant had delivered a sharp slap, scowling back at her as they passed. Claire repositioned her hoe and viewed the remainder of the row. Ruth moved several yards down, attacking the ground with sharp stabs at the weeds. Off in the distance, Claire glimpsed the side of the old shed she'd heard Ruth talk about, the one sheltered by the trees. One of the orderlies led a ragged female behind him. The woman followed with a blind trust, no resistance. It was Millie. Claire screamed in silence for the poor woman and the horrors waiting for her inside. Tearing her vision away from the horrid shed, she stared down at the weeds. Like the weeds, she needed extraction from Hatchie River, uprooted with no chance of ever returning.

The hoe fell in a new rhythm as she moved on down the row, meeting Ruth in the middle. After the conversation with Adrian, she'd toyed with the idea of contacting her parents for help. How did one call their family and casually mention they'd been admitted to the local asylum, banished from society? Due to the distance between them, they couldn't travel to Ashe Grove and save her. Getting Adrian's permission to take her home would be an even bigger battle. She knew they could easily blame her for everything. No, she couldn't contact them.

If only she could write Adrian off, dismiss him from her life, but her feelings waxed and waned between love and hate. Someone told her once that love and hate belonged on the same spectrum, just at opposite ends of a feeling. Watching some of her peers break down in front of their families when they came for visits jump-started a deep pride in herself she'd never noticed until now. She'd be damned before stooping so low, groveling, begging her husband to come get her.

Like her grandmother said one time when philosophizing on the finer points of love, "Why in the world would you ever want a man who didn't love you?" Adrian had loved her well for many years. Surely one hateful conversation didn't mean Grandmother's words applied to her marriage? Like it or not, the awful truth pointed to the fact that a part of her may always love him on some level. But even if she forgave him, she could never return to him. If not him, who could help her? Who would help her? There remained only one hope. Her next plan of action: Talk to Mitchell.

Three days later, she found herself standing at the nurse's station, her stomach in knots.

"Okay, Mrs. Wright, are you ready?" Anne placed the phone on the edge of the counter. "Just remember what Bonnie, Ella, and Ruth suggested to you."

With a deep breath of apprehension, Claire picked up the receiver. "I know, I know. Stay calm, be nice, and ask my brother-in-law if he'd be kind enough to help."

Anne smiled. "That's right. Don't be scared." The smile of encouragement turned into a scowl.

Claire faced the person who sidled up next to her.

"So, you're up for a second round. Not giving up without a fight. That's real good." Grace drummed her fingers on the counter, her eyes narrowed. A mocking grin spread across her lips. "Are you calling your husband again? Got any sweet words or special favors you can offer to change his mind? If I were you, I'd just forget the words and go straight for the favors. That's all they want. If he's missing the warmth of a good woman, you might have a shot at getting him back . . . unless he's found . . . well, you know."

Claire stared at her in disbelief.

"You shut your foul mouth, Grace. It's no business of yours who she's calling." Anne came charging out from behind the counter, teeth clenched, eyes smoldering with irritation. "Get the hell out of here . . . now!"

Grace stepped back, waving her colleague away. "What are you so worried about? I'm just trying to help. These women need to know how to get their men back. You can't cry and carry on. They don't want to hear that. You gotta sweet talk 'em. Tell 'em it'll be more than worth their while to come take you home."

Her patronizing inflections as she spoke reeked with her trademark sarcasm. Visual exchanges between Anne and Claire reflected a restrained urge to trounce Grace, once and for all.

"Grace, don't you have some work to do?"

All three women turned and saw Greta, hands on her hips The grim look on her face showed that she was in no mood for squabbles or trifling conversation.

"I was just offering her advice. She's about to make an important phone call and needs to know what to say to the poor soul on the other end who has to listen to her." Grace rambled in her usual way. "Make it count was what I was telling her."

Greta steered Grace away from the counter and pushed her toward the common room. "You couldn't come up with decent advice if your life depended on it. Get back to those patients."

Grace threw back her head and laughed. "You tickle me, Greta. Always playing the savior." The smile on her face disappeared. She glared hard at the three ladies in front of her. "You can say whatever you want, but nothing will save these women. No matter how much they whine to their families, nobody's picking them up." She whirled around and disappeared into the sea of madness in the adjoining room.

"Never mind her, Mrs. Wright. Are you ready to make this call?" Behind Anne's eyes, hostility still burned.

"I think so. Wish me luck." Claire picked up the receiver and dialed.

The secretary answered. "Wright Hat Manufacturing. How may I direct this call?"

"Mitchell Wright, please. This is personal. Please tell him it's important."

There was a brief pause. Claire clenched a fist, in no mood for questions.

"Is there a name I can give Mr. Wright?"

Impatient, Claire answered in a curt tone. "No, there isn't. Please tell him what I suggested before. Thank you."

The sound of the call ringing through to Mitchell's office roused relief and fear. This would be her last chance for help from family.

"Wright Manufacturing. Mitchell speaking."

Smooth came the voice over the line, one sounding so similar to Adrian's it almost scared her. The hello froze in her throat.

"Hello? This is Mitchell Wright. Can I help you?"

Her finger hovered over the tiny white button to end the call. Willing every ounce of resolve, she moved her finger away. "Mitchell? It's me, Claire." She forced out the words, praying he'd be receptive.

"Claire? Oh my gosh! Where are you?" Mitchell's voice adopted a higher pitch of excitement. "Are you . . . having a good time, relaxing a little?"

His concern sounded genuine, at least a little. She cleared her throat and spoke again. "Not sure what Adrian has told you, but I'm not on vacation."

"Where are you, then?"

"You won't believe this, but I'm at Hatchie River."

Silence.

"Mitchell? Are you still there? Please don't hang up on me." A round of tears stung her eyes, and she blinked them back.

"Hatchie River? The crazy house? What are you doing there? Hold on, Claire. Let me shut the door."

In the background came the pounding of the phone as he placed it on the desk, followed by some shuffling and the sound of a door closing. Her heart beat faster. He didn't hang up on her. At least he wanted to talk to her in private. This was a good sign. She glanced at Anne, who'd been watching, and nodded. Anne smiled back and whispered in Greta's ear.

Mitchell's voice came over the line. "I'm back. So talk to me. Why in the hell are you calling me from the looney bin? What's going on between you and Adrian? One day we're talking. The next day, you've disappeared."

"Hasn't he said anything to you about bringing me here? I tried talking to him a few weeks ago, and he just blew me off. I haven't heard from him or seen him."

"Honestly, he's said very little. When I've asked about you, he's only mumbled something about you going away for a while, needing some rest. Didn't say much more. I just assumed maybe you'd gone to visit your family."

"I can't believe he wouldn't have said something to you about this, Mitchell." She shook her head in disbelief. So Adrian had lied about sending her here. This more than confirmed the strange behavior he'd been displaying lately.

"He and I aren't the biggest talkers in the world. When it comes to business, we do okay. But personal matters, it's a horse of a different color."

Claire grinned. "Mitchell, it wonderful to hear your voice. But I need help. I've been here for several weeks now, and I'm wondering how I'm going to get out of here." Her eyes panned the area, landing on Grace watching her intently from the doorway of the common room. She turned her back to the nurse's station and lowered her voice. "I can't go into a lot of detail. Too many people around. But is there any way you can get me out of here? Could I stay with you until I think of something else? I can't go home anymore."

She heard nothing but Mitchell's breathing. Her hopes sank. Claire closed her eyes and waited for an answer. If he refused to help, all hope was lost.

"I'm not sure how much help I can be, Claire. Let me see what I can come up with. First, I have to figure out how to bring this up to Adrian. Are they treating you okay there?"

Claire answered in a low voice, "This place is hell on earth. I can't hold out much longer. I need your help." Desperation welled up in her voice. "Mitchell, if you can't do anything, it'll be the death of me. You're my only hope. No one else can help."

"Mmm, I see." He paused a minute. "I'll check and see if I can get you back home or somewhere else. I still can't understand why he would do something like this. Honestly, getting him to make much sense these days is hard."

"I believe you. I don't know why he put me here, either. What's he doing with you?"

"I can't go into detail right now, for the same reason you can't talk because of where you are. Hold on a bit. I'll get to the bottom of this."

Claire breathed easier now. "You don't know what this means to me, Mitchell."

"Think nothing of it. You're a nice lady, and you've been kind to me."

A loud knock sounded in the background. Claire tensed. Was Adrian knocking?

"I've gotta hang up. Talk to you soon," Mitchell whispered. Click, the line went dead.

Claire placed the receiver back in the cradle, basking in a small sense of relief. She pushed the phone back to Anne. "It was a good talk. Glad I called."

Anne placed phone behind the counter. "I'm so glad to hear that. You know, Mrs. Wright, sometimes help comes from people you'd expect the least."

With a smile, Claire turned away and headed into the common room. She sat down in the rocker Ruth had reserved for her, and told her friend about the conversation.

"You're lucky there. Not many of us feel happy after a phone call. I've given up." Ruth stared out the window a good long while before she spoke again. "Claire, if you can ever find a way out of here, do it."

CHAPTER SIX

The kitchen pulsed with a life of its own, filled with whirring sounds from electric mixers, pots and pans clanging against metal wracks, and the hum of idle chatter interrupted by occasional shouts for assistance, and sharp commands from Liza, who supervised everything with the eyes of a hawk. Sitting at a metal table in the back corner of the room, Claire absorbed the scene around her as she peeled a large bowl of potatoes Her hands moved like an automaton, a rote task filling the time while she listened to the dialogue speeding from one person to the next.

Situated off the back side of the asylum, the cooking area reflected a less obtrusive atmosphere, and an abnormal lingering calm. The near congenial nature of it hit the senses hard when removed from the chaotic life on the wards. In the kitchen, frenetic movements of staff and culinary tools fell into a certain order and rhythm, a unified effort to get a job done.

In this tucked-away, shadowy world of the unseen, Claire re-acquainted herself with sanity again, coming alive as revitalization washed over her. She needed a safe harbor, a place for healing and licking her wounds. As luck would have it, she'd reached some semblance of a promised land at last.

"You okay back here?"

"Huh?" Claire stopped peeling for a moment, startled by the booming voice. Liza stood in front, scouting out the table, head thrown forward, eyes darting from knife to bowl. Her large frame and direct manner scared most people, but she and Claire took an immediate liking to each other, with Liza being anything but gruff when they spoke.

"Yep, you seem like you're on it today, just like last week when you first came down here. Doin' real good."

Claire smiled. "Thank you. I always do my best."

Liza turned and glared at two staff members squabbling across the room. "Knock it off over there, or I'll bust some heads if I have to." She shook her head and stared back at Claire with a much kinder face. "Lord, I wish I had twenty more of you. I'd be set, then. No problems, work would get done, and no one giving me fits."

"Like I said, I always work hard. Besides, I like it down here."

"Bet you do, honey. It's crazy up there. Hope I don't end up in one of those wards, but with these shenanigans down here, I'm liable to." Liza smiled at Claire. "Miss Greta did a real fine job picking you to come work in here. I told her, 'I want the best pick of the litter.' And she up and brought you."

"Do you need me to do anything else? I'll be finished with these potatoes in a few minutes. I can peel faster, if you like."

"I'll need you to come with me so we can get some meat from the slaughter house. They're runnin' a little slow today, so we'll get the cart and load up. Then we'll go to the dairy barn and bring back some cans of milk. I don't know which are bigger slowpokes, the killers or the milkers. Either way, we'll starve if we don't get on 'em."

Excited, Claire concentrated on peeling faster. This news rang sweet in her ears. She'd never followed anyone outside from the kitchen. Did she dare ask if they'd be using the tunnels? Her thoughts turned back to Mitchell. Three weeks had passed, and still no return phone call. Had he dropped the whole matter of helping her?

She'd appreciated the few blessings that slipped her way. All she knew was an opportunity for fresh information loomed ahead, one she planned on adding to her arsenal of knowledge. Knowledge, like how the privately owned back field she saw from the sewing room window lined up squarely against the asylum's property, and how the woods on the asylum grounds ran parallel to that field. If one continued a path in the woods and kept the field to their right, the main road lay to the left. Continuing on the main road would lead one back to town. If she could reach the field or woods, she knew the two-mile walk to town, where real civilization lived, was a possible task.

If it took miles of walking, camping out in the rain or heat, she'd do it. Other than a catastrophe of nature, she'd stop at nothing to leave Hatchie River and forget it entirely. But some images she'd never forget, no matter how much time had passed. They'd branded themselves inside her head and her heart. Unlike Ruth, she didn't fear the outside world, the people in it, or making decisions. In the outside world, one could run far away—and hide.

Trapped inside brick walls, bullied by real breathing demons scared her. Foul men with lewd minds and hot, eager loins scared her. Never knowing when someone was coming after you, ready to strike, scared her. Predictable unpredictability, knowing nothing would ever change, thus turning your brain into a useless grey mass scared her. Becoming so numb to life that you were certain you'd never feel anything ever again scared her most of all. No, the world outside didn't frighten her. Even its unpredictable nature could be borne with the help of good family and friends, people who talked to you and really listened, ones who believed in the virtues of helping another.

Had Mitchell, like Adrian, lost his sense of morality, all sense of charity, turning a blind eye to the virtues of helping or caring about someone? Did Mitchell ever have a shred of this emotion every Christian church called compassion? She thought Adrian had all of this, but it seemed that the business and the drive to produce great merchandise had killed something in him. She'd started to see it a little before she'd become pregnant with the first baby. Maybe the same drive and trappings of being number one had ensnared Mitchell.

"You ready, gal?" Liza had slipped up to the table, pounding the top lightly with her hands. "You look mighty thoughtful there, peeling those things like your life depended on it. What do you think about when you work like that?"

Claire shrugged. "Nothing much. I just sort of let my mind wander."

"Finish those last two in the bowl, and we'll go. I'll be back in a bit."

Several minutes later, she called out from across the room. "Come on, Mrs. Wright. I'm ready."

Liza and Claire exited the kitchen and headed down the hall to a side door. "We'll be using the tunnels. It's quick and easy. The best part, no one gets in your way." Claire's heart pounded with excitement. These were the words she wanted to hear.

The ladies made their way down the steps. When they reached the bottom, Claire immediately knew there was no other way out, other than to turn and follow the hallway all the way down to the end. At least this exit seemed easy enough if she ever needed it.

"Liza, tell me about the tunnels. I've heard of servant passageways from books I've read."

The older lady kept her pace. "These tunnels are the same way. They just let us come and go easier without dodging people."

"I guess they get used a lot, then?" Claire picked up her speed to keep up.

"We use 'em every day, all the time. We'll put our supplies into the elevator so we can send everything up to the kitchen. That way, we don't have to haul anything upstairs."

Claire almost decided against asking more about the tunnels, but curiosity and desperation overshadowed prudence. "Is this the only tunnel, or are there more?"

"Yep. They all run the length of the building, from front to back." Liza glanced at Claire, a quizzical look on her face.

Viewing her supervisor out of the corner of her eye, Claire picked up the pace even more. She kept her eyes focused forward. If she looked Liza square in the face, she risked giving herself away.

Liza continued. "As you know we keep doors locked around here for safety. Don't need anyone wandering around anywhere. This building's nearly a hundred years old. Parts of it aren't even used much anymore. You get a crazy person traipsing through these old halls and rooms, nobody'd ever find 'em."

"That would make sense. I couldn't imagine being alone in parts of this place. Too spooky, if you ask me. The wards aren't always the most pleasant place, but at least you're accounted for." The heat of anxiety painted a pink flush on Claire's face, and she prayed they'd reached the end of the tunnel soon.

Liza slowed her pace just a little and lowered her voice. "You know what else has happened?"

At this point, Claire turned her eyes toward the older lady. "No, what?"

"People have died in the field out back, the one that joins the back part of our land."

"I think I've seen it before." Ahead in the distance, Claire saw a metal door and breathed a sigh of relief. They'd soon be outside picking up food, and hopefully the discourse over tunnels would bear itself out. In silence, she cursed herself for bringing up the subject in the first place.

The ladies had reached the door. Instead of opening it, Liza faced Claire. "Like I was saying, people die in that field. The crazies who manage to get back there get all confused, don't have enough sense to find their way back, and they starve to death. I know this because I've heard it told that the owner comes and reports it when he's found them."

Dumbfounded, Claire stood blinking at Liza. The thought had never occurred to her of someone losing their way and dying in a field, especially so close to the asylum. "How big is that field, anyway?"

"Bigger than we probably care to know. Like I said, it don't pay to go running off around here when you don't know your head from a hole in the ground." Liza pulled out some keys, unlocked the door, and both ladies filed out into the sunshine.

The bright light blinded Claire, and she shielded her eyes. Though the air had diminished in temperature, the humidity insisted on lingering with the persistence it always did this time of year.

"Let's go over here and we'll get a couple of carts." Liza led the way to a small storage area, opened the door and pulled out two medium-sized wooden carts. "You take one, and I'll take the other. We'll head over to the dairy barn first. You'll carry the milk in your cart, and I'll carry the meat in mine."

"That sounds like a good idea to me." Claire grinned. For the moment, she'd forgotten her status as a patient. The idea of being a team with someone brought out the old sense of pride she used to have when she and Adrian talked about the hatting business, when he'd ask her what she thought of his latest style, and how she liked the hat once he'd made the prototype. A fresh sadness loomed over her, threatening to overshadow the sun itself. Would she ever be a team with someone anymore, someone who valued what she thought, how she felt? She tugged the cart, and away she went, following a few paces behind Liza.

The exit from the door led the women several yards past the garden where Claire and Ruth worked with the other women. Claire saw the last rows when she viewed her surroundings from the right. The old shed where Millie spent some of her ill-fated time had remained hidden from the present angle. Though Claire couldn't readily see it, she knew it was there, ready and waiting for the next vulgar scene. To her left, she spotted the edge of the woods, thick with trees and underbrush. Those woods called out to her, with promises to help if she ran away. Yes, someone could hide without much difficulty within the dense leaves and behind large tree trunks.

Her eyes followed an imaginary path leading down to the main road. If she could make a beeline for the woods and follow the road as a guide, the walk into town might be achieved with no one seeing her. Better yet, she'd be able to walk the length of those woods until she reached the first house marking the entrance to the residential section. In her mind, she saw the green lawns with homes standing tall and proud, some fronted with large white columns, while others flirted with steep rooflines, arched windows, and gingerbread porches. One of those homes belonged to her, a charming gothic-style cottage on the corner of Fifth and Abercrombie Street. Mitchell lived in a neat bungalow house on Watkins Avenue, five streets opposite Claire's house. If she marched into town at dusk, she'd reach his home first.

Cradled in the midst of the residential section, three streets held the heart of Ash Grove, where the lifeblood of the town flowed with the activities highlighting a steady, vibrant commerce filled with merchants and services.

If she continued through town, her steps would lead to Market Street, where small factories and manufacturing buildings, including Adrian's, lined the back part of town, close enough for convenience yet far enough out of view. Market street led the way out of Ash Grove and on to the big city of Memphis. And everyone knew if you wanted to leave West Tennessee, Memphis Union Station held the torch to the promise land of other towns and cities far away from Ash Grove. How long would it take to reach Memphis?

Claire eyes misted over. She wanted to go back to town, to the homes—to her home—and to the shops where people talked, laughed, and shared secrets. She wanted to eat at the diners again, and listen to the young girls, on the precipice of their lives, as they lamented over broken hearts while sharing a milkshake with their best girlfriend. She wanted to wander into the shops, smell the scent of new merchandise and polished floors, while selecting new shoes or pondering the benefits of the latest kitchen mixer and whether or not she really needed a new one.

She yearned for that life, to dip her foot back into the stream of the living before letting herself sink easily into the routine and happiness she once knew. Yes, returning home lay within her grasp. Just head for the woods, reach the main street, and walk straight on until she found her way to . . .

"Mrs. Wright, you need to pick it up a bit. You're laggin' behind, gal!" Liza had stopped, placing a hand on her hip while she waited.

"Sorry, I'm coming, right behind you." Claire picked up her feet and pulled the cart at a jaunty speed until she reached her supervisor.

Liza clicked her tongue. "Goodness, I hope you're not picking up some of those bad habits like the other ones have. I had faith in you. Don't disappoint me, now." The lady grinned and started walking again. Claire turned her face toward the woods one last time before concentrating fully on the task at hand.

The dairy barn held the smell of cow pies and dirt. Liza and Claire had stepped with caution through muddy spots, sometimes making a small jump over a puddle, to reach the entrance. Inside, several men tended the cows. Fascinated, Claire watched as men sat patiently on stools, working the udders with nimble fingers. Milk landed into tin pails with a rhythmic tinkle. Sometimes a cow let out a low moo. A light breeze blew through the windows, stirring up a fresh round of animal and waste odors. If she thought the sewing room and kitchen were interesting places to work, what about the barn? Claire imagined sitting on a stool, squeezing udders all day. But she'd never have the strength for lifting heavy containers of milk.

"Would you like to give it a try?"

"Huh?" Claire blinked and stared down at a pleasant-looking young man dressed in overalls.

The man smiled and offered again. "You seem a mite bit interested in cow milking, so I just asked if you wanted to give old Betsy here a squeeze. Ever do this before?"

"Oh, go on Mrs. Wright. We have a little time." Liza strolled up behind

Claire, gently pushing her toward the stool. The man stopped milking and stood up. Claire took his spot next to the cow that craned its neck in the direction of the voices.

"I've never done this before." Nervous, Claire sat on the stool and turned her eyes up to the man. "I'm afraid I'll hurt her."

"No, go ahead, like this." The gentleman took her hands, placed them in the appropriate place, and said, "Now squeeze, like you mean it. I won't hurt her." He smiled with encouragement, with Liza looking on.

Claire turned back to the cow, giggling to herself. What would Adrian say if he saw her milking a cow? She'd never been around animals much; she wasn't sure how much she liked them. With the right pressure and finger position, she had a new rhythm going, and a new stream of milk found its way into the pail.

The man patted her on the back. "You're a natural. Real good there, ma'am. Maybe Miss Liza will spare you a little so we can have an extra worker."

"Never! I'll let her come help get the milk, and she can do a little when she comes with me. Other than that, she's mine." Liza let out a loud laugh. "Come on, gal, we'll do this another time." She turned to the man. "Roy, help me get some cans into her cart."

He headed to the rear of the barn. "How many you need?"

Liza motioned for Claire as she called back. "About six should do it."

"Six, it is."

Roy returned with six containers, straining at the weight of each can. "There, I think that'll get it."

"Much obliged to you." Giving a light bow, Liza turned around, and both women headed outside.

"Now, to the slaughter house. And let me tell you, if you've never seen an animal being killed and gutted, you're in for a treat."

From the wide-eyed expression on Liza's face, Claire didn't know if she was merely joking or not.

As they walked, Liza chatted. "It's not a pretty sight in there. You'll need a strong stomach. Are you squeamish?"

"I've never seen an animal being killed before, so I don't really know for sure how I'll be."

"Just let me know if you start to feel sick, or if you just want to wait outside and let me get everything. It don't make no difference to me."

"I'll let you know. Don't worry."

The winding path led several yards up a small hill to a large wooden structure with a large iron gate. Seconds after their arrival, shrill squeals cut the air. Inside a large stall, two brutish men held a poor hog in place as a third man sliced into the jugular with a large glinting knife.

Claire winced, watching bright red blood pour from the animal. As its attempts at kicking free weakened, so did the life in its eyes, growing dimmer until nothing remained but the glassy look of death. "Didn't they bother to kill it first?"

"They usually try to shoot 'em and then drain the blood. But when you run out of bullets, there's nothing else to do."

"You know what, I think I'll wait out here. I'm more squeamish than I thought."

Liza opened the gate. "I'll be right back."

Spared from witnessing further brutality and gore, Claire spent her time surveying the landscape, taking in every detail, layout of building placement, tree line, and field. Off in the distance, movement behind a grove of trees caught her attention. Her position by the slaughter house gave her a view of the shed, the one where orderlies often secreted Millie away. She shielded her eyes from the glare for a better look.

She only saw the backs of the people as they reached the door. The scene looked the same, with an orderly present, but the woman with him wasn't Millie. This woman was larger in frame, and a little older. Because all the asylum dresses were the same, except for color or print design, she always had difficulty distinguishing an individual person on first glance. And though the view was a little clearer than ones she'd had previously, the distance still hindered the ability for a clear view of faces. The woman struggled with the orderly, trying to pull away. He grabbed her hair and yanked it hard. The door opened and the two disappeared inside.

The scene Claire had just witnessed filled her with a sense of uneasiness, one so strong that it left her blood running cold with fear. At the sound of the gate rattling and squeaky wheels from the cart, she whirled around. Her supervisor had left the building.

"I think we have everything now." The older lady straightened up her hair before grabbing the handle of her cart, which had been filled with fresh pork. "How 'bout we head over to the garden and steal us some fresh tomatoes or Tommy Toes? I'm thirsty."

"Sounds good to me." Claire turned an anxious eye back toward the shed.

"What's wrong? You look like you've seen a ghost."

"Nothing, I saw a man pushing a woman inside that shed way back there." She faced Liza. "Didn't look like she was all that keen on going in, but he made her."

Liza paled at this observation, and leaned in close. "Let me tell you something else. We don't talk about that shed over there. You ever heard anything about it?"

Fearful, Claire played dumb. "No, I don't think so. What about it?"

"We just don't talk about it. You didn't see anything. And my advice to you is never talk to anyone about it. You do, and you'll land in mighty big trouble."

The ache in her gut sent Clair into a tailspin of nervousness. "I-I hear you. Won't say a thing. I promise."

"See to it that you don't." A sharp warning glare from Liza, and the two walked down the path, picking up an adjoining trail to the garden. The supervisor picked some tomatoes and placed them in the cart with milk, while Claire pulled off some tiny tomatoes, Tommy Toes as she liked to call them, and ate a few. She pulled a few extra from the vine and followed Liza back to the main building.

Inside, they followed the hallway back the same way they'd come. Near the end, Liza led the way down a small hallway to the elevator. She and Claire loaded the milk and meat inside.

"There, we got it. We'll leave these carts here. I'll get someone else to come back and wash them off."

In the kitchen, Claire sat once again, chopping vegetables until her work time ended. She gathered up the Tommy Toes and followed an attendant back up to the ward. She took a deep breath, bracing herself for the usual chaos.

Millie sat next to a vacant chair, and Claire made her way to it. Millie didn't look at anyone, but held her doll in a limp fashion on her lap. The lady rocked aimlessly, her face highlighted with vacant eyes and grim lips. Claire stared down at the Tommy Toes and back at the withered face in front of her.

Taking a deep breath, Claire got up from the chair and stood in front of Millie, holding a tiny tomato to her lips. "Here, I brought something for you."

Millie stopped rocking for an instant.

"Do you want it? I brought some more, just for you." This lady brought out compassion, but at the same time, something about her created a sense of fear. This was the predictable unpredictable, not knowing if Millie would accept the gift, ignore it, or slap it away with some unexplained irritation.

The older lady opened her mouth, and Claire fed each piece to this poor woman, starved not only for food, but just as much for the kindness of another, an act of pure giving with nothing expected in return. Before Claire sat down again, Millie grabbed her wrist, holding it tight. Somewhere in the woman's eyes, Claire detected a knowing glint, a spark of life catching fire in the kindling of life known as the present moment. Claire's heart nearly caught in her throat with fear. What if this woman bit her?

In flash of lucidness, Millie brought Claire's hand to her mouth, and delivered a tiny kiss on the forefinger. Claire marveled at the uncharacteristic display of emotion. She marveled even more at the softness of the woman's lips and the warm heat of her breath as she exhaled. At once, the enigma surrounding Millie dissipated. In that moment, the tender gesture confirmed that she and Millie were companions of a sort, elected by an ill hand of fate to endure an arduous journey they'd never understand.

Millie released Claire's hand. The vital spark vanished. Her vacant gaze traveled back to the window. On an inner level, Claire sensed gratitude radiating from this woman's heart. In all her madness and bleak isolation, Millie had understood a benign gesture and appreciated it. Settling in her chair, Claire also stared out the window, waiting for Ruth.

Where had her friend gone? It wasn't like Ruth to be missing this long. Claire instantly perked up at the low rumble of male voices trickling into the room. She craned her neck around. Two orderlies walking in hushed, quick steps with Ruth in tow.

Each footstep echoed with a soft thud. The men held their heads down as they moved. Claire at once new their dirty secret. They maintained a grasp on Ruth's arms as if she might faint and fall to the floor, and swiftly guided her to an empty rocker in a shadowy corner across the room. Ruth dropped into the chair with a bump, while the orderlies disappeared from the room almost as fast as they'd entered, their gazes tethered to the floor.

Inside their sockets, Ruth's eyes emitted a glassy, listless stare. Her face held an expression of one who'd experienced a horror that would never be resolved. Her hair stood out in disarray all over her head like someone had grabbed fistfuls of strands and ground them against her scalp without a thought or care.

A succession of chills stung Claire's spine as her mind shot back in time when she'd seen a new woman with the men, someone who had fought against them and lost the battle. She shuddered at the remembrance of seeing Ruth forced into the shed and the door closed, shutting out the chance for help. And to think she and Liza hadn't been so far away that they couldn't have intervened.

At once she wanted to run away deep into the woods outside the asylum, and when she came to a private place where she was sure no one would hear, scream at the top of her lungs. She wanted to ease the soul of her injured roommate back to wholeness again, but the pale skin and empty eyes showed one who'd been changed forever, one who'd never return to her fiery knowing ways. Hatchie River had broken Ruth.

At dinnertime, Claire sat next to Millie, and the two ate in silence. Ruth didn't come to dinner. Anne and Greta had escorted her to bed, while Grace watched in mild amusement, lips twisted into her usual infernal smirk. Claire caught Grace turning her eyes from Ruth to her. Grace smiled wider, and a new fire in her eyes blazed hotter. Inside Claire's chest, her heart ached with the fear of impending doom. She picked at the rest of her meal with shaking hands.

When she crawled in bed at the stroke of nine o'clock, Ruth remained still with her face to the wall. Claire didn't speak. As she lay in bed, Grace's demon eyes came back full force with a hellish glow. For the remainder of the night, Claire caught snatches of sleep. The night had never seemed so long, and she prayed hard for morning.

CHAPTER SEVEN

Inside the tub, Claire took a deep breath and clenched her teeth. If the canvas covering hadn't already been secured around her neck, she would have scrambled out and run for safety. But finding an unlocked stairwell had always left her dreams of running away filled with apprehension. Staff were obsessed with locking doors behind them. At the uncovered end of the tub, Grace stood at the taps, preoccupied longer than usual in regulating the water flow and temperature. The water first came out scalding hot. Claire jerked her legs away, screaming in pain as piping hot water singed her skin. More than anything, she had a mortal fear of being roasted to death.

Grace turned off the hot water and twisted another handle, at which point the needle-like sting of cold water rushed against Claire's ankles, assuring a gruesome death by roasting may occur another day.

"Don't know what's going on with these taps. I can't seem to get the temperature I want." Grace flashed Claire a quick sinister smile. "But I think we have it right for today at least." When the tub was full, she anchored the canvas in place, trapping Claire underneath. "Have a nice bath. I'll come back when I think your time's up." With a series of hard pats on Claire's head, she bounded out of the room.

Claire winced and shook her head, thankful her brain hadn't been truly scrambled by Grace's tender affections. Tender affections. Somehow, she thought these words were funny. The water had already chilled her to the point where her mind was starting to slip, and finding a bit of twisted humor in what others would have seen as ugliness scared her a little. What if she truly started seeing events and people around her as genuinely funny? How could she explain this? She fought to keep a straight face. Giving into laughing meant one had reached a point of no return, the point where insanity truly began, leaving the sane world behind forever. This could happen. She'd seen patients who laughed at nothing, crouched in dim corners of a room.

She rested her head back against the tub. For some reason the surface seemed harder today, not that it wasn't harder any other day. And of course, dear Grace hadn't bothered to put a towel under her head to ease the discomfort. Anne and Greta always put something soft behind her head. But not Grace, the one with tender affections. Claire let out a startlingly loud laugh. She opened her eyes wide and glanced around the room to see if anyone had heard. Then she giggled. Of course, no one else was here but her. No one else had entered the room since her arrival.

Another round of giggles ensued. She paused a moment, listening to the silence, an eerie quiet she didn't hear often. For a change of pace, she opened her mouth and let out a small yell. She stopped again and listened. No answer, no rush of feet down the hall, and no other person yelling for her to knock it off. For the next few minutes, Claire belted out a series of wails, with different durations and unique pitches. When this activity bored her, she made silly sounds with her lips and tongue, taking an opportunity to stick her tongue out until she glimpsed the tip. Still, no one had come into the hydrotherapy room.

Undulating her thighs in the water, the shocking cold which had stunned her in the beginning had worked its wicked magic, sending her body plummeting to what might as well have been an icy grave. No matter how long one spent in these tubs, one never warmed up or got used to it. Had anyone ever died in these? Were the dead bodies in the field behind the asylum as cold as she felt right now? Her bladder burned, and her bottom throbbed as if might explode. The urge to urinate and defecate had been a continuing battle during hydrotherapy. If she got lucky enough to have Greta or Anne present, bodily functions weren't an issue.

But Grace and her tender affections managed to bring out all the discomfort she'd suffered in her lifetime, mentally and physically. Claire thrashed her legs again, cursing Adrian for destroying her life and Mitchell for not calling back. All at once hate set in, so strong the anger roiling inside scared her. She hated the world and everyone in it. Nothing or no one could make it better. Hatchie River and the staff had successfully declared war, disemboweling dreams and crushing the existence of all the women inside its walls, leaving mental carnage in its wake.

The last vestige of spirit had been plucked from her friend Ruth, leaving an innocent woman shattered and ruined forever, her eyes dry because all the tears had been cried out. Any shred of self-esteem or hope had been totally amputated, with only a dead stump in the psyche left behind. There was only grim remembrance of the past and no hope for the future.

Claire dug her head against the hard surface of the tub until the pain kick started a headache. She clenched her fists until her hands throbbed. Seething in anger, tears flowed. She wanted all of this craziness gone, to purge herself and be done, start anew. Relaxing her pelvic region, she released a hot stream of urine, enjoying a new emptiness inside. In one last act of defiance, she clenched the muscles in her bottom and heaved, the contractions inside her colon eliciting a final sordid burst of satisfaction. Once the drain opened, all the ugliness of the world would go down nice and easy. It had to. There was nowhere else it could go.

Time passed, and with it Claire's tolerance as she rested her head to one side, using the taut canvas as a makeshift support. For the first time, ice water didn't leave her whimpering and wishing for something better, nor did she spend time counting clothes, life events, or people to make a therapy session bearable. For the first time, she truly embraced anger, welcoming the emotion in all its fiery strength and glory. For the first time, she didn't try to understand why life had brought her to this point, this inexplicable place where she found herself. She rested against the canvas and opened herself to the flow of anger, marveling at the way each part of her body and each nerve tingled with a new energy, filling her with a resolve she'd never experienced before.

A rustle of feet infiltrated the silence. Learning the feet belonged to Grace fanned the flames of anger. Claire didn't acknowledge the attendant when she unfastened the cover and pulled it back.

"You look all crabby for someone who's just had a nice bath." Grace glanced down at the tub and grimaced as she pulled Claire out of the water and helped her out. "But I guess it's hard to enjoy a good soak when you shit and pee in it."

Numb to consequences at this point, Claire blurted out, "Maybe if you did your job right, like Greta says, you wouldn't have to clean up shit and pee." Her eyes locked onto Grace's, while her lips pursed together in a new rage.

Grace stepped back, her face blanching with surprise. "Oh, aren't you hoity-toity today. You got a lot of nerve saying that to me."

Claire stood her ground in cold silence, never removing her eyes from Grace.

"No wonder that man of yours dumped your nasty ass here. You're a sassy bitch . . . and a shitty lover to boot. I'd get rid of you myself if I was him . . ." With a fresh gleam in her eye, Grace reached out and pinched one of Claire's nipples. "Can't figure out what he'd want with those old saggy tits when he could get some young cute thing."

In a reflex action, Claire's hand shot out, and her palm landed squarely on Grace's cheek. For the next several minutes, time moved in slow motion. At once Claire noted a strange disconnect, a separation from her body, like her eyes had somehow floated out of her head and now hovered above.

Those eyes viewed a naked woman running out of a room and down the hall, trying desperately to make her way to the stairwell door. Behind her ran another woman, yelling and cursing in anger. The door didn't budge, no matter how hard Claire rattled the knob, praying hard for deliverance, a stroke of luck, perhaps.

Grace grabbed a handful of hair and yanked hard, holding Claire hard and fast. "Where in the hell do you think you're going?" The heat of her breath filled Claire's ear. "I hear you beggin' for the Lord to save you. You better pray hard because He won't help you now, and Greta isn't here today." She jerked the fistful of hair harder while Claire cried out. "You wanna run away, do you?" With a few quick maneuvers, Grace unlocked the door and pushed Claire into the stairwell, quickly pinning her against the wall. The attendant's eyes burned with fury, as her lips pursed themselves into a cold, grim line, an expression displaying an intent to kill.

Within seconds, Grace worked her hands securely around Claire's neck, locking her into a deathly chokehold. "I could just drag your sorry no account ass to the basement and lock you up where you'll never be found again." Grace shook Claire's head so hard, she feared her eyes might pop out of her head. "Or I could let you feel the warmth of a man again, and maybe that'll knock some sense in you. That old shed out back would do the trick, don't you think?"

Claire thought she might faint, but she'd remained conscious enough to hear Grace's words, especially the last ones. Fear kicked in an adrenalin rush. Aware of her hands again, Claire used the burst of power, pounding on Grace's shoulders, wriggling and struggling against the force that held her. Grace maintained her grip, stepping backwards down the stairs, pulling Claire with her. In a flash, Claire remembered one of the fight scenes in an action movie she and Adrian had seen at the Lutesse. Desperate, she rammed her knee between Grace's legs. The grip around her neck loosened. Claire struck out and wrenched free from the chokehold squeezing the life out of her.

Grimacing in pain, Grace wavered. Claire watched in horror as the attendant tried steadying herself, only to overstep the edge of the stairs. The woman who'd been standing in front, choking her to death, now tumbled down a flight of concrete steps, rolling and rolling until she landed at the bottom with a sickening thud. Claire remained rooted to the step for several seconds, not sure if what she'd just witnessed was a dream or a grim reality.

She turned her eyes toward the door, which had swung back nearly to a closed position. Not a sound echoed from the hallway. The motionless body at the foot of the stairs verified her fear. Claire knew one thing. Any association with a dead body held consequences, none of them good. Relief was now bittersweet. No would believe her story if she told it.

Claire swallowed hard and tried to think. Raspy breaths pushed against her constricted throat. Going back upstairs and screaming for help would be her undoing. Grace hadn't moved since the fall. Claire shuddered. The cool air against her naked skin reminded her that she didn't have any clothes, or even one of the towels from the hydrotherapy room.

From the silence in the stairwell, no one was coming around anytime soon. Claire took one last breath, warding off the dizziness setting in. She gripped the iron railing and crept to the bottom of the stairs. When she looked down at Grace, she detected the ring of keys resting beside her.

She studied Grace's eyes, their glassy surface reminding her of the pig she'd seen in the slaughter house. The face already held an ashen gray color. As Claire turned for a closer look, she saw blood in the strands of Grace's hair. The attendant's chest didn't move. A chill coursed down her spine, leaving her a little lightheaded. The seriousness of the situation hit her full force: a dead woman lay at her feet.

Leaning against the wall, Claire arranged in some semblance of order the typhoon of thoughts deluging her mind. If ever an opportunity presented itself, this one did. She took a mental inventory of what she knew, like her current position in the building, and how this position lined up with the layout of the rest of the building.

From her work in the kitchens and following Liza to different places, the tunnels had lost their mystery. Finding her way through Hatchie River and out a door wouldn't be a problem, especially if she looked like one of the staff and not like a patient. Her eyes panned back to Grace and the ring of keys.

The keys to freedom and salvation lay within her reach. With those keys, she'd could leave the asylum, through any wing, room, corridor, and door leading to the outside world. Claire viewed the woman lying in a rumpled heap. The clothing size came close to hers, and if she wore them, she'd be incognito. With keys in her possession, Claire had only to make her way to the tunnels, out a door, and head for the woods. She lifted her eyes and mouthed a quick, silent prayer of gratitude.

For the next several minutes, time sped by, leaving nothing but a blur in her mind. Fear and disgust at touching something so foul as Grace's dead body left her long enough to do what was needed. She stooped down and grasped at buttons. Every second counted, and she moved quickly. She strained, rolling the body first one way, then another, pulling off articles of clothing. Claire soon left Grace as naked as herself, except for the panties.

Armed with sure-handed speed, Claire put on a blouse, bra, skirt, stockings, and shoes. She even pulled the ribbon from Grace's hair, first checking for drops of blood, and secured it around her own head. After fastening the last button, she reached down, scooped up the keys, and glanced at the door above. Still no one had come. This opportunity would never come again, and in the wake of this nightmare, she tapped into her own bravery. She turned away from Grace and continued down hallways and stairs, never looking back until she reached the tunnels.

Inside the tunnels, Claire followed hallways, noting turns she and Liza had made until she reached the door to the outside world. Her hands shook as she breathed out a sigh of relief and lifted up the keys. Thankfully, only one person passed by, a youthful lady who seemed in a hurry and averted her eyes. But now another problem arose. Which key fit the door? Her heart pounded. Sweat dripped down her back. Had she ever seen the key Liza used when they visited the slaughter house and dairy barn? One option remained: try each key until she found the right one. Luck kicked in when she tried the fourth key. The lock turned with a click.

Sunshine filled the dim hall and the rush of a lukewarm breeze drifted through the open door. It was now or never. From a quick view of the sun, there was still a few hours before dusk.

A glint from one of the keys caught her attention. On impulse, she tossed them back inside, listening to the sound of metal gliding across the floor. Somewhere deep inside, she hoped more than anything that leaving them behind might somehow lessen her association with a certain attendant who'd not be needing keys anymore.

On the left, stood a grove of trees. She headed off, knowing this area would initially hide her from view. Once in the heart of the woods, she'd find a hiding place until dusk ensured a safe passage to town. Simple, really. So simple she almost laughed out loud. But where would she go? Right now, it didn't matter. She'd think of something. Satisfied no one else was around, she scurried over the grass, making a beeline for the trees.

From her quick estimation, the door from which she exited placed her facing the side property aligning the asylum, with the neighboring field perpendicular. The main road was several yards to the left. If her orientation didn't falter, she'd surely make it to safety. With each step, she carefully picked her way, stepping over large twigs and around knotty tree trunks, leaving Hatchie River farther behind. The smell of old leaves, acorns, and dirt filled her nostrils. Never had anything smelled as pure and fresh as freedom did right now. With the wind and the sound of nature in her ears, she walked what she thought was about a mile and a half before stopping to rest. Under one large tree, a bed of green moss filled the ground. Claire headed over and sat down, winded from running.

In the distance, she heard the rustling of leaves. Panic-stricken, the breath caught in her throat. Had someone followed her from the asylum, discovered what had happened? When she looked closer, the sound turned out to be nothing more than a squirrel scavenging for food. Claire breathed a long sigh of relief. Right now, she was still as good as invisible to the rest of the world. But what about Grace? Only a matter of time before someone would discover her absence . . . and then her own. She needed a plan of action.

It could be hours, or maybe a couple of days, before someone happened upon Grace. Just enough time to flee . . . to Mitchell's house!

Where else could she go? He wouldn't be home until the end of a work day. If he'd taken a trip out of town for business, she'd find herself in bigger trouble.

Claire pulled herself up from the mossy bed and walked until she detected a white wooden house in the distance. This house marked the beginning of the residential section, and on ahead, the streets led to the heart of town. The hum of traffic grew louder as drivers crowded into the streets.

She decided this was close enough. As an added precaution, she retraced her steps several feet back to avoid detection. Claire seated herself against an oak tree trunk and waited. She'd make it to Mitchell's before dark.

New-found freedom. What did it feel like right now? In her opinion, she'd not be able to internalize this freedom until miles stretched between her and the asylum. Miles and time. Folding her arms, she rested her head against her hands, falling in and out of a light sleep. Her ears remained in a heightened state of acuity.

Time passed, with golden shades of late afternoon sliding into the purples and grays of evening. Still, no one had found her. With a hopeful heart,

Claire got up and walked until the white house came into view. Glancing around, she didn't see anyone right now, but the trek into town would be a different matter. She started off, head down, eyes averted, and walked quickly.

Inhaling a deep breath, she moved toward the house, taking a left to the beginning of the sidewalk along the main road. She continued until the town came clearer into sight. How inviting the lawns and homes had looked, a veritable picture of quiet family life in a small town. In the distance, she caught sight of taller buildings peeking up behind the homes, those beloved department stores and other merchants she knew so well.

Cars had driven by, but she didn't glance in their direction. Claire ran a hand through her hair, fluffing out the locks. With short hair and wearing Grace's clothes, no one recognized her. She reached Watkins Avenue, crossed the street, and hurried to Mitchell's house, praying he'd be home.

Her heart quickened as his driveway came into view, next to which sat the neat bungalow with its whitewashed boards and inviting porch. Claire followed the driveway to the back where he kept his car parked in a separate outbuilding. No sign of a car anywhere. Had he parked it inside the garage for the night? She slowed down and glanced around again before scurrying to the building. The sky had darkened to a dull gray, but she still detected the car tucked safely away. He was home, after all!

CHAPTER EIGHT

Claire stepped lightly up the steps of the back porch to the door. Pausing a moment, she rehearsed some words she'd say to Mitchell. What would she do if he slammed the door in her face and left her on with no safe place to go? Trembling, she wrapped at the door. A minute passed, increasing Claire's fear even more. People knocking at the back door wasn't the norm. She peeped through the opening in the curtains. From what she gathered, her brother-in-law was in another part of the house. She landed another round of knocks, and to her relief, glimpsed a shadow of a person through the glass. In seconds, she heard the muffled sound of footsteps.

The door opened, and there stood Mitchell, with a dazed expression on his face. Claire stepped back, hoping she hadn't unsettled him too much. He poked his head out the door, checking all directions before turning his eyes back on her and staring several seconds longer.

"Mitchell, it's me, Claire." She forced a light smile on her face, nervously running a hand across her. "I know you may not recognize me like this. They cut my hair and . . ."

Mitchell opened the door without a word and stepped aside. Relieved, Claire stepped into the kitchen. Mitchell shut the door, turned the locks, and pulled the curtains until they hid the window completely. He checked the larger picture window by the breakfast table, adjusting the blinds until they, too, shut out any possibility of prying eyes. He turned and faced Claire.

"What are you doing here? How did you get out?" His eyes focused on her for the first time, and his lips pressed together in worry.

"I know this all seems crazy—"

"You could say that. Crazy, yes." His eyes widened in agreement.

"After we talked, and I didn't hear from you again, I got scared."

Mitchell shifted from one foot to the other. "So you just took it upon yourself to high-tail it out of there, huh?"

A cold chill radiated down Claire's spine. Numbness crept over her. Maybe he wasn't as accepting as she'd hoped. "I had an opportunity, so I just took it. I can explain, really I can." She glanced down at her hands, which throbbed with pain because she'd been wringing them hard in fear and desperation.

His face softened somewhat. In his eyes, a light of compassion flickered. "Here, sit down. I was making some tea. I'll make some for both of us, and then we can talk this whole thing out." The kettle whistled just as he reached the stove. For the next few minutes, Mitchell busied himself preparing the tea, while Claire seated herself in a vacant chair at the table.

How peaceful everything seemed here in this house, almost too quiet. In her mind, she continually reminded herself that there were no hateful staff members milling around ready to strike. No noise and wails from hallways and other rooms. No sickly stench of unwashed bodies and excrement from patients who couldn't contain themselves. She watched the man at the stove, pouring water into delicate china cups. He dipped a teabag into each one before placing them on a matching saucer. He'd removed his work clothes, changing into a rich embroidered dressing gown, no doubt a purchase from an English supplier. For a moment, she marveled at how handsome he looked, with a solid frame, smooth skin, dark brown eyes, and cocoa-brown hair neatly cut and shaped about his face. Aristocratic he seemed, moving easily and with a purpose.

"I'm all ears. So, tell me how on earth you got out of that crazy place down the road and ended up here." Mitchell eased himself into a chair across from Claire. From the cut glass sugar bowl, he removed two cubes and dropped them into his cup.

Claire added some sugar and stirred until they dissolved. After taking a sip, she sat back and related to her brother-in-law all the events leading up to her admission to Hatchie River, and launched into a more detailed monologue about the staff, events, and patients warehoused there. She told him about what happened with Ruth, and about Millie, and all about the treatments that were hailed as state of the art in treating crazy people.

She ended with more stories about abuse, hard work, and other horrors she witnessed. In silence Mitchell sat, wide eyed, occasionally lifting his cup to his lips before focusing his eyes hard onto hers. Much of the time he squinted at her, shaking his head in disbelief.

"Simply unbelievable. They treated you like that?" He sat up straighter and frowned. "I never would have believed that anybody could go through such an ordeal." The gentleman stared into his cup, thinking for a moment. "But you still haven't told me how you got out, and how you got here unseen."

Should she tell him what really happened? Would he believe her, or accuse her of murder and turn her into the police? Claire struggled in silence, detecting Mitchell's eyes filling with intensity and worry.

"Well," Claire began, choosing her words with care, "I managed to slip away when staff were too busy with everyone else, I found an abandoned stairwell and made my way out a door that had been left open." She studied Mitchell's face. His expression showed no signs of disbelief. "Staff sometimes got careless, you know, and would forget to lock the doors. On my way out, I found some old clothes in a room, so I thought it would be a good idea to change so I'd look more like a regular person. I just took advantage of whatever I could to get out."

"I can understand that." The brother-in-law nodded, lifting his cup to drink the last of the tea.

"Once I got outside, I ran for the woods and hid until it got darker. And here I am." Claire's eyes wandered from her cup to Mitchell's face and back again. Did he sense something else, a hesitation in her voice?

"And nobody saw you on your way out? No one at all?" His voice rose a little as he shifted in his chair.

"I only saw one girl, and we didn't pay much attention to each other. She was in a hurry like everyone else there." Claire let out a light, nervous laugh.

"I've heard some stories of people making it out of that place. Even heard they've found a dead body or two at times." Mitchell shook his head. "Poor souls didn't' quite make it after all, I guess." His expression sobered. "Did you ever hear stories of patients getting out of control and killing staff members? I have. You don't hear it often, but it happens."

Claire stared back in silence. Desperate to change the subject, she asked, "Mitchell, did Adrian ever tell you why he put me there? I called and tried to talk about that with him, and he more or less blamed it all on me."

Mitchell tapped his fingers lightly against his up as he thought. "I'm sure you've seen a change in him over the past two or three years. Subtle, but definitely there."

"Yeah, seems that way, now that I start to think about it."

"He's become a little odd, if you ask me." Mitchell paused, getting up and retrieving the kettle from the stove. After he'd refreshed the cups with water and the tea bags had been re-steeped, he continued. "Like I said, he's been acting strange. At times, he goes at hat-making with a crazed gusto, while other days he'll slow down, spending a week obsessing over one design. He's forgetting little things he used to know off the top of his head, certain formulas, or how he created a design in the past. Sometimes he has to stop and think about what he's just completed, like adding a floral decoration or finishing a fold right. And his temper has gotten out of hand. I hate asking him things because I don't know if he'll simply answer the question or bite my head off." Mitchell leaned forward in his seat. "And here's the really strange thing. There are days he's clearer in thought, not as cloudy or muddled. He seems to still remember things if he's been at them a while."

"Yes, yes!" Claire perked up, nodding in agreement. "He didn't always used to be that way, always pretty easy-going and a sharp wit. We basically got along, had a great time together. But once we started having the babies, it seemed to fall apart then. I thought he was mad at me because of what happened, losing them."

"No, Claire, I don't think it was you at all." Mitchell gave her a pointed look. "You know the hazards of the hatting business, don't you?"

"I've always heard of it. I hadn't given it much thought. Living for the moment, I guess."

Mitchell shook his head. "I don't know how much longer he'll be able to do this kind of work. He's been in the environment long enough. It's finally taking its toll. It's toxic, being around all the chemicals and working on creating those hats the way he loves to do."

"You think he knew what he was doing to me?" Claire took a quick sip from her cup, never taking her eyes off her brother-in-law.

"I don't know, but I think in his mind, twisted as it may be, he believed he was doing the right thing." Mitchell furrowed his brows.

She sat up straight and leaned forward in her chair. "He hurt me, Mitchell, more than anyone will ever know. I'll never forgive him for what he did. I don't care what the reason is." She gazed in earnest into her brother-in-law's face. "Honestly, a big part of me hates him now. And of course, I'm scared of him."

Mitchell pursed his lips together, nodding in agreement. "I don't ever believe in putting a woman away like that, not someone who's perfectly sane. Not sure I'd do it to someone even if they were a raving lunatic. I don't share a lot of the views most men have about women, you know." He glanced over at Claire and grinned. "Maybe that's why I stay single. Easy to keep your nose clean and your life simple."

"Aw, Mitchell. You'd make a great husband for some nice girl out there." Claire smiled back, kicking him lightly under the table. "You sure you haven't given it enough thought?"

"Don't know. I think I'm just a confirmed old bachelor. Like it that way. I can come and go as I please, and no one to give me any lip over it. There's something to that, I'll say."

Claire lost the smile and gazed at Mitchell. "What's going to happen to me? What do I do now? I don't have anywhere to go. And I haven't even told my family about all this."

He arched an eyebrow. "You may not believe me, but after our talk, I did do some thinking. I'll be honest. I have talked to a friend of mine, who's also one of our valued clients."

"Who's that? Have I heard of him?"

"George Parker. He owns a nice department store in Knoxville. G. P. and Sons. Been in his family for forty years and still going strong."

Filled with alarm, Claire shifted in her chair, her brow wrinkling into a frown. "What did you tell him? I hope you didn't say too much."

"Easy, Claire." Mitchell held out a hand. "George is one of my best and closest friends. I knew if anyone would understand and could help with a solution, he could."

"And?"

"Here's the deal." He cleared his throat and took a sip of tea. "I don't advise you to stay here. This town's too small for hiding. Let's face it. Like it or not, you're going to turn up missing at Hatchie River. They'll call Adrian. You can depend on that happening."

Claire blanched at the thought. Of course, they would. "That's true." The knot in her stomach tightened.

"He'll most likely tell me about it, and after that, I'm not sure. They could also notify the authorities, too. I don't know how much effort they put into searching for patients who escape. From the sound of things, it doesn't seem like much, which makes it easier for you."

"I don't know how that makes it easier for me." She sank back in the chair, staring down at the empty teacup.

"Listen, I have it all figured out."

"Great, and when had you planned on filling me in about it? I didn't hear back from you." She scowled.

He sighed, grimacing. "I know you thought I'd abandoned you, but I didn't. I had to work out the details on dealing with this situation. The big part, too, was how to deal with my brother.

"Mitchell, I was desperate. You don't know how desperate."

"I know. I know. You told me. I believe you. The good thing is, I've found a solution. Parker says he has a vacant house he can let you use for a while, until we think of something more permanent."

"Really? He has spare houses sitting around?" Claire shrugged a little. "Well, he must make some mighty good money in that department store of his."

Mitchell shot her an exasperated look. "The house actually belonged to his wife. She passed away three years ago. It's just sitting there vacant. He was only too glad to put it to use." He studied Claire as she sat in thought. "What do you think about us taking the next train out of Memphis and getting you out of here as fast as we can?"

Claire still didn't say anything. Her brother-in-law began drumming his fingers on the table.

"Well? Do we do this or not?"

"No, no! I'm not saying I don't like the idea. I'm just trying to make sense of it all. I'm leaving my whole life behind. I don't have any clothes, or my things. I'm not prepared for this."

"Were you prepared when you left Hatchie River?"

Silence.

"See? You saw an opportunity and, like you said, jumped for it. Did you take time to plot and plan, think about what you were going to take?"

Claire shook her head, blinking. "Not like I had anything to take."

Mitchell pounded the table with this fist. "There you have it! You made a run for it. That's what you're doing again here. Why? Because there's really no other way out of this, and the more distance you can put between you and this town, the better." He dipped his head down a little, following Claire as she lowered her face and stared into her cup again. "Look, you stay here tonight. I'll go first thing in the morning and buy some clothes, and we'll leave for Memphis just in time to take The Tennessean all the way to Knoxville."

"The Tennessean?"

"You heard me. We'll be taking the newest train on The Southern. She's a beauty. Caught a look at her in the paper."

"Didn't have access to a paper, so I didn't hear about that." Claire squared up her shoulders, lifting her head. She grinned at Mitchell. "So why are you so willing to help me?"

His face softened, and he reached over and placed his hand over hers. "I like you, Claire. Always have. You're a good lady, and I hate seeing a nice person unjustly punished for something they can't control. Like you, I don't condone Adrian for what he did, regardless of his state of mind. And if that place was a bad as you told me, it's a wonder you didn't wind up dead."

She flinched at his last word. "What Adrian did to me was like a knife through my heart. But you've saved my life. I owe you a lot."

He waved her away. "Just glad we've got something figured out so we can get you on your way."

The two sat together for a few minutes, lost in thought, neither saying a word. Her stomach rumbled, and now she thought about food. As if reading her mind, he spoke up. "Tell you what. Let's eat a little, and then you can take a nice hot bath. I'll find something for you to wear for the night. How about that?"

"I'd love nothing better." Claire flashed him an easy smile. The anticipation of eating normal food and taking a 'nice hot bath,' struck her as foreign. Would she ever be able to look at a tub the same way again, after her horrid memories of the asylum? What would a clean, comfortable bed feel like again, with a man nearby who vowed to help rather than harm or take advantage?

After gathering up the cups, Mitchell spent the next thirty minutes putting together a light dinner. As they conversed about the latest news in the community, about friends, and the business, the kitchen had taken on a warmer atmosphere. Smells from hot food stirred up her hunger. As enticing as a hearty meal seemed, she wanted a bath and a change of clothes.

She got up from her chair and help set the table. He placed a small piece of steak on each plate, followed by a modest portion of green beans and boiled potatoes. When the glasses had been filled, each took their place and began eating. Claire closed her eyes, savoring each fresh bite. The taste of spices hit her palate in the most delightful way, flirting with her tongue as she chewed.

"Is everything all right?" The brother-in-law put his fork down for a moment and waited for a response.

"I don't know what to say. This so delicious, the best I've eaten since the last day Adrian and I ate together."

Mitchell lowered his eyes in silence.

"At Hatchie River, we grew fresh vegetables and killed our own cows and pigs for meat, but we never saw any of the goods on our plates. All we got were the leftovers, and the worst of it."

During the meal, Claire reflected on how Mitchel had now become a generous kindred spirit. Kindness seemed at the heart of this man who'd once struck her as distant, one she didn't understand. After dinner, she washed dishes and cleaned up the kitchen. Mitchell spent time preparing the bathroom and finding something suitable for her to wear. He led her down the hallway and pointed to a doorway. Once the door closed, she found herself in a tiny room with the toilet, sink, and tub all within touching distance.

She stared at the neatness, clean bright porcelain, sparkling mirror, and a fresh fluffy towel and washcloth on top of a dark cotton robe. A fresh white bar of soap rested in the soap dish. The steel knobs and faucet in the tub winked at her in the light, and she eyed them with wonder, as if seeing these for the first time. Even now they elicited a certain fear.

Had she been away so long that she'd forgotten the simple luxuries of everyday living? The thought of undressing unleashed a confounding renewed sense of modesty she didn't understand. She surveyed the room again, making sure the blinds covered the windows. Slowly she removed all her clothing, stepped toward the tub, and twisted the knobs. The sound of water ran loud in her ears like it did in the tub rooms. She forced herself to remain calm and focused.

While water splashed into the tub, she relieved herself in the toilet, happy for cleanliness and plenty of toilet paper. Within minutes, she stepped gingerly into the tub, acclimated to the warmth, and sat down. She waited for an attendant to lock her under the horrid canvas, but no one came. For the first time, her eyes scanned over her body, on down to her feet. Nothing had wrapped her skin in such comfort as the clear warm water, and all she wanted to do was concentrate on how she felt right now.

A good meal, the first in months, and a clean bath free from her own waste had already begun a positive influence on her psyche. Her thoughts turned back to Mitchell's earlier suggestions of not remaining in Ash Grove. The suggestion had not totally surprised her. Under different circumstances the mere notion of it all would have struck her as romantic, the stuff of movies.

She reached for the wash cloth and soap. For the next several minutes she ran the cloth over every part of her body, including her hair, digging her fingers into her scalp like her life depended on it. Soon her hair would grow back, and she'd use pretty hair pins and scarves like she'd done before. Maybe she'd grow her hair longer this time, so long until it nearly reached her ankles, with nothing more to do than simply plait the strands in one thick, long braid. Ducking down under the water, she rinsed all the soap from her hair and off her skin. For good measure, she emptied the tub and stood under the shower until her skin glistened and strands of hair squeaked when she ran her fingers through them. Claire smiled. That's what a bath should be like for everyone! After drying off, she slipped on the robe and stepped out into the hallway.

"You done? Do you need anything else?" Mitchell walked around the corner.

"That was the best bath I've had in a long time." Claire grinned and shook her head a little to fluff out her hair. "Not having fifty other people around was the nicest of all."

The gentleman smiled, nodding in affirmation. "Did you want to stay up a bit and talk some more, read a book, or do you just want to head off to bed?"

"I think I'll go to bed, try to get some sleep. I'm exhausted. Haven't had a peaceful sleep in forever."

Mitchell led her back down the hallway to a room on the left. The light from a small lamp resting on the nightstand cast the room in a soft lazy glow. "This is my guest room. I'll be right across the hall if you need me for anything."

"Thanks so much." Claire turned and placed a hand on his shoulder. "You don't know how much I appreciate all this. I don't have anyone else in the world on my side right now, someone I can rely on anymore."

"I'm only too happy to do this for you. Get some sleep, and we'll take care of the rest of this in the morning. I'll think of something to tell Adrian."

Claire shut the door of the guest room behind her. She took a deep breath, inhaling nothing but clean air. Her eyes surveyed the room. At last, a real bed, with fluffy pillows, pristine linens, and a fresh-laundered smell she'd learn to appreciate from this point forward. Sleek maple furnishings lined the white walls. Next to the bed lay a woven tapestry-style rug depicting a renaissance couple kissing under a pear tree. Everything neat and in order. Even the hardwood floor struck the bottoms of her feet with a surface so clean she swore she could almost eat off them.

She slid between the sheets and turned off the light. As she lay there, the darkness swallowed her up, overwhelming and suffocating, leaving her almost gasping for breath. Other than the occasional settling of the house or stray cricket chirping outside the window, the house held the quietness found in a mausoleum. How delicious the quietness played against her ears, the noise of no noise, so quiet she almost heard her own heart beating in her chest.

With each passing minute, she grew more comfortable. So many thoughts and a brain too weary to process it all. She closed her eyes while her mind drifted between consciousness and dreaming. Just when she'd nearly dropped off to sleep, the image of Grace's death-filled eyes and lifeless face jarred her awake. She sat upright, clutching the covers around her like she had done many a night at Hatchie River.

Claire took a few deep breaths, adjusted the sheets, and dropped back down. Would she ever be rid of this hateful vision? A stab of uneasiness washed over her. Someone would find Grace and discover, too, that an inmate was missing. Adrian would know. Even through his own cloudiness, he'd understand well enough that his wife now roamed free somewhere, free against his will. What more could she say about what happened on those stairs, hidden away from patients and staff? In her situation, wouldn't anyone else had done the same? Of course! She wasn't the first to escape the asylum, nor was Grace the first staff to have suffered an ill stroke of luck there. Mitchell spoke the truth: she seized an opportunity and took it.

CHAPTER NINE

It was the voices. Always the never-ending sound of voices, angry, pleading, insistent, consoling. The voices never stopped. Claire opened her eyes, dazed. She glanced over, expecting Ruth, only to see a wall with a fine chest of drawers in front. The voices persisted, trailing down from the farthest distance, penetrating through the door into this room.

The voices weren't staff fighting with pleading female inmates. These voices were male, and one of them belonged to Adrian. Her eyes widened with fear, and she sprang out of bed for a peek through the window. Outside sat a parked car sparkling in the morning sun. Time hadn't dimmed her memory of Adrian's 1941 Chevrolet Business Coup. She'd helped him pick it out brand new from the car dealer earlier this year.

Clapping her hand over her mouth, Claire frantically reviewed the room for a hiding place. She spied the bed. Perhaps she could squeeze under it? The closet door caught her attention for the first time. She refused to go over and open the door, fearful something may fall out. With quiet, deliberate steps, she made her way to the door of the room and pressed her ear against the wall. The voices had died down, ending with the sound of the front door closing.

Claire ran back to the window and peeked through a small opening behind the curtain panel closest to the nightstand. Keeping herself hidden, she viewed Adrian making his way down the walk. When he stopped and turned as an afterthought, and stared toward the window, her heart nearly stopped. She backed away, closing her eyes a second, and peered out again. He had reached in his pocket for a handkerchief, and now swabbed it over his mouth. Eyeing him harder, she detected a shakiness in his hand, which disturbed her. He bobbled as he turned back around, and held out his hands, steadying himself. Had he been this wobbly when she'd last seen him?

Nevertheless, he was still attractive, with neatly combed hair parted on the side, trousers and shirt hugging a well-built frame, and a face, though somewhat tired in appearance, outlining the same aristocratic features as Mitchell. Under normal circumstances, the sight of him would have sent her dashing from the room. She would have thrown her arms around him, kissed his lips, stroked his hair, promised to make all the bad things disappear so he'd be the same strong, adoring husband she had fallen in love with. Maybe once he laid eyes on her he'd have a change of heart. But all she felt now was pure fear, mingled with strong loathing.

The car door slammed shut. The engine sounded, and Adrian sped away, the tires squealing as he headed down the street. Somewhere in her heart, she knew this may be the last time she'd ever see her husband again. Fighting off a surge of weakness, she collapsed back down on the bed, the first waves of real fear inciting a horrid clenching sensation in her stomach. The asylum staff had found Grace; Adrian had been notified. Footsteps echoed down the hall, and the door flew open.

Mitchell stood in the doorway, an angry scowl fixed on his face, eyes snapping with fury. On his face, the trace of fear showed loud and clear. He marched into the room and sat beside Claire. His eyes burned straight through her.

"I need you to tell me the truth. Did you kill someone? Yes or no?"

Claire, paralyzed with fear, stared at him, mouth slightly open in an effort to speak. But the words lodged in her throat and wouldn't come out. Her eyes focused on the corner of the sheet she held in her hand.

In frustration, Mitchell grabbed Claire's shoulders, shaking them so hard her teeth rattled. "Tell me now," he shouted, "yes or no? Did you kill someone, and why did you lie to me last night?"

Silence. She bowed her head, shrinking back in fear.

He moved his lips close to her ears and, in a low controlled voice, made the awful statement, "You'll either tell me the truth, or I'll drag you back to Hatchie River right now, and I'll see to it you never get out of there again."

Trembling, Claire spoke, "No, Mitchell, I didn't kill anyone. Grace stepped back and . . . it was an accident. It was just a bad accident, that's all." One by one, tears tumbled out of her eyes as loud ugly sobs crept out of her throat. This time she didn't think she could stop crying. Mitchell sat and watched, holding Claire's hand between his in a small act of consolation.

In a quiet voice, he spoke again. "Then I need you to tell me the truth, because that's the only way I'll be able to help you. It's the only way I will help you." His eyes found hers, and the two stared at each other for a few seconds. "Adrian said he got the call that you were missing. On top of that, they told him a staff member was dead. They suspect you had something to do with it. So, I need every detail of what happened. I understand why you've shown up at my door, but why didn't you tell me someone died?"

For the next several minutes, Claire related everything that had happened the day before, while Mitchell listened, nodding or frowning at intervals.

"And you didn't think to call for help or tell someone what happened?" His face had hardened again. "This whole thing may have been truly an accident, but didn't you think taking that woman's clothes might be stretching your luck just a little bit too far?" He sat up straight, running his fingers through his hair. "It all makes you look guilty, that's what."

"I was naked, for godsakes, Mitchell. What else could I do if I wanted to get out? I wasn't about to go running around naked through Hatchie River, trying to find clothes or call for help. And let's face it, this whole thing would be my word only, which nobody would believe, because I'm supposed to be crazy, you know." Claire's voice had risen several decibels.

Mitchell sat thinking, his eyes fixed on Claire's face. He let out a long sigh. "That's a good point. It's really your word against hers. And she's dead." He shook his head and looked back up into her face. "And you're right. The most they would do is lock you back up again, declaring you now criminally insane."

"Mitchell, they would have thrown me in solitary, locked in chains, little food or water, and left me for the rats to gnaw on. I heard those horror stories from people who'd experienced it and managed to make it out. I saw those cells a few times when I helped Liza take food to those women. It was horrible. The smell, feces everywhere, puddles of urine on the floors, blood on the walls, the hollow look in their eyes." She started crying again. "And that witch of a woman threatened to take me to the shed and let those nasty men do god only knows what . . . put their hands all over me—"

"Stop it, Claire. I've heard enough." He held out his hand, silencing her. "Enough. I know you'd never deliberately kill anybody, and though that woman's death was a misfortune for her, it turned out to be your gain." He scowled. "I still don't like the fact that you took her clothes, but if she hauled you out of that tub room, dragging you naked down the hall, I guess you really had no other choice."

"What do we do now?" She gazed at him through the remnant of tears, wiping a stray drop here and there from her cheek.

Glancing at his watch, he got up from the bed. "I played dumb with Adrian. Told him I hadn't seen or heard from you. All I can say is time is of the essence. He's at the factory now. It's nearly ten o'clock. You need clothes, but I've got to come up with some story, in case someone tells Adrian they saw me making such an odd purchase."

Claire looked up. "Or you could sneak into our house and simply grab some clothes from my closet, maybe my travel bag too? I can tell you where a spare key is."

"Wonderful," he answered back. "Let's see, risk being seen at a shop, or some nosy neighbor catching me at your house." He shrugged. "Either way, I'll be in trouble. You'll be in bigger trouble."

"There's no way I can wear Grace's clothes again." She shuddered.

"No! Those clothes didn't smell good, either. Pack them with you, and when we get to Knoxville, we'll have a bonfire out back of the house." Mitchell's face relaxed a little. "I think I'll take you up on getting your own clothes. If anyone asks, I'll simply say I needed to borrow a suitcase or something."

She smiled at him. "With Adrian's sketchy memory, he probably won't remember what you've told him, or if he gave you a spare key to get in."

"And that's if anyone even sees me." Mitchell smiled back. "Just sit tight here. And for heaven's sake, don't answer the door or the phone. I'll be back in a few minutes."

"You'll find a key under the flower pot next to the last post on the right as you face the back door."

Mitchell nodded, got up and turned out of the room. Claire sat still, her mind in a whirl. Everything still held a dream-like quality, Grace's death, Mitchell willing to help her. Even seeing Adrian for a brief few seconds reminded her this last vision could easily have been one of her dreams during a hateful night at Hatchie River. Her thoughts abruptly turned to the graveyard where her baby son slept, one who'd never hear his mother's voice singing or see his father's smile when he rode a bike by himself the first time or graduate from school.

By this time, she'd shed every tear her body possibly held. If she continued obsessing about this, she'd surely scream. Going back to the grave for one visit would be foolhardy, and after all Mitchell had done, she wouldn't dream of asking him for such a favor. Like it or not, Adrian had warned her about not moving on, that life wasn't fair. This time, her circumstances commanded she get on with life. Start over, completely over.

Do it now, or die a slow, agonizing death at Hatchie River. The asylum had graves, deep, dark, and waiting for people like her. When the end came, only death granted a person true asylum. She headed to the bathroom and straighten up her hair and face. Today was a new birthday, one just as real as the day she'd been born, the birth of her new-found freedom, a new life.

Within thirty minutes, Mitchell returned carrying a woman's tapestry print travel bag in his hand. He dropped the bag beside the bed and grinned. "I did it, and I don't think anyone saw me."

Claire opened it and rummaged inside to find clothes, nightgown, undergarments, stockings, and shoes. He'd even secured her cosmetic bag in a drawer of her dressing table. "Nice job. And thanks for finding my makeup." She smiled up at him."

"Personally, I think you'd be fine without it. I've never cared much for all that goop you women wear." Chuckling, Mitchell waved her off. "Once you're settled in George's place, you can get some more new clothes or whatever you need."

A flash of realization crossed her mind, and she sat on the bed, thinking a few seconds.

"What's wrong? You look worried." He sat down beside her. "Look, I know all of this is so fast, something you'd never planned on happening. I mean, who would, for crying out loud?"

"I don't have any money, no job. How am I supposed to even live?" New fear crept all over her, and she searched her brother-in-law's face for guidance.

He took her hand between his. "Don't worry about all that. I have money. I'll simply help you get on your feet, and we'll figure out what to do once we're in Knoxville. Right now, my biggest worry is getting you out of Ash Grove before Adrian gets a wild hair and starts looking for you."

"I'll repay you, Mitchell, really I will. That's an awful lot to ask someone." She gazed outside the window. "He still looked so handsome, like his old self. You'd never suspect anything could possibly be wrong with him. If things were different, I would have run out there."

Mitchell countered her thoughts. "Handsome is as handsome does. Isn't that the old saying? He may still have his looks, but I'm telling you, his mind isn't all that pretty, and definitely not like his old self. At some point, I'm going to have to do something. I just simply haven't thought that far ahead yet."

She focused her eyes back on him again. "Don't you wish this were some kind of bad dream, where we could all wake up and have a good laugh, that the whole thing was simply fake, a figment of our imagination? Or maybe we're really in a movie some skit with a horror theme and we just don't know it."

Mitchell let out a light laugh. "Sorry to burst your bubble, my dear, but we don't have fancy script writers telling us what to say, or ambitious directors telling us what to do or how to act." He put his hand on her shoulder. "And this most certainly isn't a dream or a figment of over-active imaginations on our part. This is real, it's ugly, and it could get dangerous if we aren't careful."

"Well, I bathed last night, I have clothes. What's next on the agenda?"

He stood up and headed to the door. "I'll fix breakfast. You get ready. After we eat, I'll make a quick call to Adrian and give some excuse—tell him I'm going out of town to check on clients. Then we get the hell out of here. I'd rather hang around in Memphis for a while than wait here pacing like nervous cats."

"Sounds like a good idea." Claire scooped up the travel bag and placed it on the bed. She pulled out a comfortable pair of white wide-legged trousers, a pale-yellow cotton top, and a white dress with orange-print butterflies and matching belt. Great choices! Gazing at the cheerful styles and colors brought a smile to her face. Finally, some clothes she'd be proud to wear. She selected an outfit and joined Mitchell in the kitchen.

The drive to Memphis ignited a new sense of adventure, and every mile between her and Ash Grove increased the sense of bittersweet victory, with its promise of an optimistic future coupled with a sorrowful past.

Once she set up house in Knoxville, she'd start over, find new friends and hobbies. How she'd handle new romantic relationships remained a mystery. After all, she still had a husband. On second thought, she could emulate Mitchell, remain single without all the trappings or hassles of a mate.

However, she knew spending the rest of her life alone didn't sit well in her mind. Starting a family may have eluded her by this time, but she enjoyed having someone in her life, someone outside herself, someone to touch, someone to love. With any luck, Hatchie River hadn't killed everything inside her, but it had come close.

Soon the rural countryside of small towns gave way to the bigger buildings and hustle of Memphis. The traffic had increased, more people milled about, and the plethora of shops and diners made Ash Grove pale in comparison. As they arrived at the train station, Mitchell found the appropriate parking lot, and after collecting their bags from the trunk, they headed to the ticket counter.

"I'll purchase the tickets. You just stay back and mind the bags." Mitchell scouted the area before leaving.

Claire shaded her eyes from the evening sun, scouring Memphis Union Station. There she saw it, the beauty Mitchell had talked about like a moony-eyed lover. The Tennessean. In the late evening sun, the Number 46 passenger train glistened, its stout frame dressed in magnificent green and white as it waited patiently. Behind it streamed a line of rail cars where passengers could eat, sleep, and watch the scenery passing by.

Deliverance sat before her, a massive steel queen resting quietly on the rails. Reality set in. Once the whistle sounded and those doors closed, her former life would be sealed chapters, quietly tucked away forever in shadows of the past. She thought again of the lonely grave holding her baby, a grave forgotten and desolate, with no flowers illuminating the memory of a tiny life that graced this earth if only for a moment.

Claire turned her eyes away from the train, struggling with tears as they stung her eyes. As ugly as the ending of her life in Ash Grove had been, would Knoxville herald an equally happy beginning? Thinking back on all she'd endured, the truth became clear. She'd handle anything in her path, no matter how great or small. Take it all one day at a time, just as she'd done at Hatchie River.

"Here's our tickets." Mitchell tapped her on the shoulder. "We can go ahead and board."

"When does the train leave?" Claire took the ticket and picked up her bag.

"At seven-fifteen. We'll reach Knoxville about six-forty-five tomorrow morning, so this will be a rather long trip. For now, we can settle in, find some seats, and enjoy the ride." He took her bag away after picking up his own, and motioned for her to follow him. They stepped up to the entrance of the train, where they handed their tickets to a black gentleman dressed in a sleek uniform.

"Have a wonderful trip." He nodded graciously and extended an arm, showing them the way in.

Mitchell paused a second. "This is it Claire, are you ready?"

"Ready." She smiled and they both entered the car.

CHAPTER TEN

Claire and Mitchell selected two seats together on the opposite side of the car. Decorated in muted blues and greens, the interior reflected a soothing appearance, easy on the eyes, yet bright for the soul. She took a deep breath and inhaled the lingering scent of diesel fuel and a spicy cologne fragrance from another female passenger who'd taken the seat directly in front of hers. Mitchell offered Claire the window seat before settling down.

Five minutes before departure time, all seats held occupants, gaily dressed as she and Mitchell. From snatches of conversation, some were going on to Washington, DC, and had reserved spots in the sleeper cars. At least her trip would end early the next day. Claire decided she'd had enough of adventures, and longed for a space of her own, to settle down again and put out new roots. Knoxville, at this moment, held as much excitement for her as if it had been DC.

"Once we get moving, I'll get us some drinks." Mitchell winked at her. "Bet you didn't have a nice cocktail where you were."

She waved him off. "No, we weren't that lucky. We surely could have used them, though."

"Sorry, Claire, bad humor on my part. I just want better things for you from here on out." He smiled over at Claire, patting her on the hand.

"No, you're right. I missed the nice things, like a good drink every now and then. It's odd how we take our luxuries in life for granted." She smiled back at her brother-in-law, who briefly acknowledged another passenger with a light nod of the head. Gazing out the window, she spied others scrambling fast toward other trains, loved ones gathering up bags from those who'd just arrived in Memphis. What lives did their stories tell? What brought them here, and for those leaving, were they running away too?

The whistle blasted at seven-fifteen sharp, and the doors slid shut. With a loud hiss, the train bucked for a second before moving into a lumbersome roll. Several passengers inside waved to their friends and family on the platform. Soon the train rambled onward at a comfortable thirty-five miles-per-hour down the tracks. Claire watched as Memphis Union Station faded out of site. It was done. Life in Ash Grove and her marriage to Adrian would soon fade too. The horrors of Hatchie River might take longer. Mental insults didn't go scurrying into the dark, but held onto one's psyche with more tenacious fingers.

Mitchell stood up. "I'm going to the cocktail car. Still want to go for that drink?"

"Absolutely. Besides, I probably won't see a cocktail lounge on a train again."

The two headed out and passed through a couple of cars before reaching the designated car. At the back stood a pristine bar, outfitted with a handy assortment of liquors and glasses. Several others had found their way here and had already sat down, engrossed in intimate conversation and a heady drink or two. Mitchell led the way to the bartender who greeted them with a broad smile.

"What'll it be for you lovely people? Ladies first."

"Two Side Cars, please." Mitchell placed his money on the counter.

A few pours and shakes later, the pair carried their drinks to a vacant table and sat down. Claire took a sip of the soft golden liquid, and closed her eyes as the hit of alcohol slipped down her throat. She threw her head back, savoring the flavor.

"Best drink I've had in a long time. I was way overdue."

He grinned. "Thought you'd like this one. It's a favorite of mine." He lifted his glass to his lips.

"Tell me more about your buddy George and this house I'll be using."

"Don't know a lot about the house, actually, but I think I remember him saying he didn't live too far away from it. He lives out a bit from downtown Knoxville. His business is, of course, on Gay Street where all the action is, shops, restaurants, you name it. Knoxville's definitely not as big as Memphis, but it's a hell of a lot bigger than Ash Grove." He glanced over his glass at her. "I think you'll like it much better there, Claire. There's more people, more to do."

"I always liked the city. At least in Ash Grove we lived close to town, but the smallness of it all offset the hectic pace of a big city."

Mitchell nodded. "I think you'll get a taste of both in Knoxville, all kinds of choices when you're in town, but you have the privacy of the country when you return home. A nice combination, if you ask me."

"Does George have any children?" Claire tapped her fingers against her glass and glanced out the window. That question somehow magnified her solitary state, no friends, no spouse—no children.

"He has one small daughter. I believe her name's Anna."

Claire turned and viewed her brother-in-law. "Just the one daughter?"

"Mmm, yes, just the one." He eyed her while nursing his drink for a moment. "I've never met her, so I can't tell you much more."

"I bet little Anna misses her mother."

"I'm sure she does." Mitchell shook his head. "I don't know how a man raises a child alone, and a girl at that. For me, that's the least of my worries."

"And what's so bad about girls? Why is that every man wants a boy?" Claire frowned in his direction.

Mitchell grinned. "Sorry, Claire. I think men see their sons as spitting images of themselves. At least we understand maleness. You gals . . . not so sure about you. Ladies are a mystery, warm and soft, loving on the one hand, yet so damn moody and hard to figure out on the other." He sipped from his glass and stared out the window.

She delivered a soft swat on his wrist. "For Pete's sake, Mitchell! You make it sound like we're from another planet. If you want to know the truth, men and women aren't all that different, except you men use brawn and sex for power." Shuddering, she remembered that horrid afternoon when she'd seen Ruth entering the shed, struggling in vain against the male forcing her inside. How much more did she fight once the doors closed?

Her brother-in-law studied his drink. "We do use sex for power, don't we?"

"You think?" Claire fixed her eyes on his face.

"How did you avoid it at Hatchie River?"

"I prayed like the Catholic I'm not. I swear, if I'd had a rosary, I'd have prayed that thing round and round. If there had been candles and matches in the chapel, I'd have lit one for every saint you could think of and then some." The effects of the alcohol had settled over her, and she sensed her muscles relaxing for the first time in a long time. "I kept my mouth shut, tried to keep a low profile, and it seems like no matter what you did or didn't do, you could become a target." She let out a rueful chuckle. "The odd thing, it was another woman who tried to get me, not the men. So I'll say it again, there's not a whole lot of difference between us. Don't ever forget that."

He acknowledged her with a polite smile, but Claire knew he nor anyone would ever understand circumstances and human nature the way she did now. Experience had raped her outlook on life, snatching away her view of the world as mostly a decent place and people basically good. At times, she shamefully longed for the old cloak of ignorance, where she could hide under simple blind trust and modest social intercourse, the sweet glue holding people together in families and community, where a blind eye shut out truth. No one dared hurt another or slight someone else out of spite, at least not in the open.

Evil lurked behind closed doors. Modesty and prudence were cast aside, and the ugly words and deeds flowed without propriety. The meek held themselves together in stoical silence, fearful of flaming the fires of fury if anyone uttered a protest. In Hatchie River, she'd seen what happens once the doors closed, and instigators ruled freely and without prejudice, picking random victims for the sheer thrill of it, while the community turned away. She'd done it beforehand, just like the others, paying light lip service to the plight of the poor, the infirm, and the insane. Her heart, however, had remained steeped in darkness and ignorance. Her time in the asylum shined a light on her social folly, and now she cringed with shame. She turned her face toward Mitchell, who'd lightly rested his hand on hers.

"I hope all the nightmares and boogey men go away soon, Claire. And once again, I hate that all this happened. I really thought you were safe in that place." He stared at her with an imploring look in his eyes. "I mean, how could you not be safe and sound, with doctors and nurses around?"

Claire's face held a wan smile. "I thought just like you did, once upon a time. It doesn't dawn on people that those in positions to protect and heal actually don't. How could one believe otherwise?"

"Still, you asked me for help the first time, and I heard you, desperate and scared, yet somehow I couldn't believe it was that bad." He shuddered. "Never would have believed it." He swallowed the last of his drink.

"Sometimes, Mitchell, situations can be that bad. I don't go around looking at my surroundings and people, friends or strangers the same way I used to. I know now there's the ugly side to each bright one, and we don't fully know the motives of others."

"I'm hoping Knoxville will give you a chance for another lease on life, an opportunity for living the way you want, to have the things you want, without someone coming along and stripping the rug out from under you."

"Me too." She grew silent, gazing out the window a few seconds before trailing her eyes back over the room, studying the occupants with mild interest.

"How about we head on back to our seats and get some sleep. We still have several hours to go."

The two vacated the lounge car and slipped back to the passenger car, where they sank down in their seats. As the train rumbled over the tracks, the vibration and hum of the car lulled Claire into gentle sleep, while the world, bathed in night black, passed by in silence.

In the early hours, the train slowed to a stop, bringing an end to a dreamless sleep. A warm, light touch from Mitchell, and Claire awakened, squinting at her surroundings as the momentary confusion dissipated.

"We're here." Mitchell leaned over and gazed out the window.

The rays of morning light stole through the windows, illuminating the passenger car with fresh light. Other occupants stirred, some arising and making their way toward the bathrooms.

Mitchell's asked, "Did you want to freshen up or anything?"

Claire eyed an attractive woman passing by her seat. "That might not be a bad idea. I'll be back in a minute."

Inside the lady's room, she sat on a clean toilet, thankful for a real stall with a door that locked. At the sink, she washed her hands with a thick bar of soap. The reflection she saw in the mirror no longer filled her with disdain. Despite all she'd been through, cosmetics and a good brushing of her hair had done wonders in restoring her old glow.

Ladies in fashionable attire, perfectly arranged hair, and trendy jewelry stood in stark contrast to the women of Hatchie River. For a moment, Claire stopped and focused on a moment of remembrance for those wretched women who would never go home. Only one similarity remained. She was still alone in the world. No spouse stood at the platform, ready for a welcome home kiss. Worse, no children to embrace or smother with sweet words of endearment.

For a moment, Claire battled with sadness as she thought again of the grave she'd left behind. She pulled a fresh paper towel from the rack and dabbed her eyes. A younger woman standing nearby acknowledged her with a brief smile before leaving. Claire was glad for the moment of privacy. This morning, polite conversation didn't interest her. She inspected herself in the mirror once more and returned to Mitchell, who'd gathered up their bags.

"Let's head on out and find George." Her brother-in-law nodded toward the door.

Fresh, cool air hit her face, and she inhaled a deep breath, enjoying the first hints of fall as it filled her with a new vibrant energy. This day held the promise of brilliant skies, and an occasional light breeze.

"Claire, I think I see George over there. You okay?" Mitchell took a few steps toward her, concerned.

"I'm fine, Mitchell, just getting used to it all."

Several yards away, she spied a gentleman waving at them.

Within seconds, Claire found herself in the presence of a man near the same age as Adrian, with a warm smile, and sparkling eyes. A quick breeze ruffled a few locks of his hair, giving him a lightly tousled look and a certain boyish charm. For a moment, her pulse quickened. She hadn't expected such an attractive man. Of course, she'd not given much thought about George, other than he bought hats for his store from Adrian's company and owned a vacant house.

"Well, well, so you're Claire?" George stretched out his hand, clasping hers securely, holding a little longer than customary in such a simple greeting. The energy he exuded suggested strength, determination, and from behind those chocolate brown eyes, a flash of kindness and compassion. His stare held a fleeting connection with her own. She noted how well his grey suit fit, and how the quality of the material and burgundy silk handkerchief peeking out of his breast pocket suggested an eye for men's fashion.

If he carried Adrian's hats as part of his merchandise, George definitely had taste. He eyed her with intense interest, a smile brightening his face as he spoke. "I just have to tell you, I love Mitchell's hats. I sell every one of them faster than I can get them in. Men and women, they're all sell-outs."

The sound of his voice fell against her ear, strong yet silky, putting her immediately at ease. His delicacy in word choice, using her brother-in-law's name in association with Wright Hats, filled her with a sense of relief. Had he avoided Adrian's name for her benefit?

"Glad you like them. I'm rather partial to them myself." Claire smiled, giving Mitchell an obligatory pat on the shoulder.

Mitchell reciprocated Claire's gesture with a good-natured glance. "Bet you didn't know Claire comes up with many of our designs. We at Wright Hats believe in the value of a woman's touch."

Claire's eyes widened, and she turned back to George and offered her broadest smile.

"Doesn't surprise me one bit. As good as she is, no wonder she's your best kept secret." George chuckled.

So far George had shown himself as gracious and sensitive, but Claire knew time revealed everyone's true character. The notion of the present moment hit her full force. Hearing him, touching him, seeing him, sealed reality for good. After all, he'd be her landlord.

"Mitch, I've got my car in the lot over there. Let's get this pretty lady settled in." He turned and offered Claire his arm. "I'm so glad you're using the house. It's a great place, right on the bank of the Holston River. When Mitchell and I talked, I knew it would be the perfect place for someone like you."

"It sounds lovely. Thank you so much for helping."

Their eyes met, and a wave of self-consciousness rolled over her, as she and George, for the first time, acknowledged the real impetus behind why she was here.

George leaned over a little and whispered in her ear. "You'll be okay, Claire. I'll see to that."

Downtown Knoxville pulsed with a rhythm altogether different than the sleepy little town of Ash Grove, with cars continually cruising up and down the streets, while shoppers walked the sidewalks flanking taller buildings filled with more shops and businesses than she cared to count. Street cars carried passengers to and from town. Anywhere she could possibly want to go, a street car or bus could take her there.

"I'll bring you here tomorrow, and I'll show you around town, let you see the sights. And of course, I'll show you my store." George beamed at Claire.

"I'd love nothing better. This all looks much more exciting than where I came from."

"It's a faster pace, but you want to see fast, go to New York. Been there, and there's nothing like it. We'll never see that here. The South's a different world, but one I like just fine." He smiled that easy smile, the one Claire found almost addictive, more so when it came on the heels of his eyes lighting up when he talked about a subject of interest. "What about you? Are you originally from Ash Grove?"

"My family is from little unheard of South Dakota. I left home when I graduated high school. Thought I go out and see the world, seek my fortune. Memphis was the place I finally called home."

"Now here you are, still seeing the world. And who knows, you might just get that fortune yet. Good things happen, even here in a modest town like Knoxville." Another intoxicating smile, coupled with those hypnotic eyes.

George took the luggage and placed them in the trunk. Mitchell climbed into the back seat, while Claire took her place in the passenger's seat. Soon the car sped along the streets leading to the new mystery house both Mitchell and George had spoken so highly of. The Holston River. She liked the idea of living on the bank of a river. The image filled her mind with adventures, boats traveling up and down, sailing to far-off towns, children splashing and playing in the calmer inlets and around the shorelines, floating in black soft inner tubes and splashing their buddies.

The city disappeared behind her, leaving her with a new vision of countryside, old homes, and open fields. She'd heard East Tennessee beat West Tennessee hands down when it came to beauty, filled with rolling hills, smoky mountains, and wild forests. In the distance, the Holston River sparkled in the sun, moving onward with blind determination, oblivious to carrier, cargo, or crew. A few more miles, and George turned down a road that delved deeper into the country.

About two miles later, he turned into a gravel driveway leading to a two-story stone-block house fronted with four stout columns shrouding a porch. The back lawn stretched toward the river. Large bushes shielded the home and away from prying eyes. George turned off the ignition, and Claire opened the door, eyes scanning in all directions.

In an instant, she learned that the land of "milk and honey" consisted of rolling pasture land covered with the greenest grass, where birds quarreled in nearby trees, and the sweetest perfume scented the air with an earthy blend of grass, soil, and wildflowers. A quick breeze wafted up from the river, bringing with it the characteristic smell of mud and the faintest hint of fish. At once, she decided she liked this place, didn't know why, didn't care; but this would be home for a long time. Something inside her suggested forever.

"Think you'll like it here?" George had come around to her side and placed a hand on her arm.

She smiled and nodded. "This is perfect."

"I'll get your bags." He turned around and walked to the trunk.

Mitchell came up beside Claire, giving her a light hug. "This is exactly what you need. I couldn't have picked a better place myself."

A long wooden porch held two wicker rockers on either side of a black-painted wooden door. George pulled out a key, inserted it into the lock, and opened the door. Claire stepped across the threshold into an open living room, which opened into the dining room on the far left. On the right, two steps led to a small landing, offering a quick cross-over into the kitchen and the upstairs bedrooms.

"As you can guess, the dining room over there leads back to the kitchen. It's one continuous area." George turned and grinned at Claire. "I've aired out the place and had everything dusted and cleaned. It's all ready for you."

"Just beautiful." She gazed around at the simple, but functional furniture. The right side of the room held a sofa, coffee table, and some wingback chairs sat by a small fireplace. The area on the left side of the living room had been sectioned off into a study area, complete with a larger fireplace, bookcases filled with books, a love seat, and writing desk with chair.

"Let's get your things upstairs, so you'll know where to lay your head at night." Mitchell and Claire followed George up the solid wooden steps. The upstairs housed four ample bedrooms, with the master bedroom at the end of the hall on the left. "You can go outside and sit when you want to." He pointed in the direction of a door in the middle of the wall. "It's kind of nice at night when you want a breath of fresh air."

Claire surveyed the room, with its large four-poster bed, with a nightstand and lamp next to it. A divan sat in one corner. She spied the door leading into the bathroom. An antique dresser and armoire completed the furnishings. "I like having the bathroom so close by."

"It's handy and private. There's another bathroom to the right of the stairs as we came up. You'll have three other rooms, in case Mitchell ever comes to visit. Or if you have other guests."

Heat flared through her cheeks, and all she managed was a quick nod.

"Your phones work, all the electricity and appliances work, and the water runs. I made sure of that before you came."

"George, you've done an awful lot. This home is wonderful."

"You'll like the river too. There's a back door in the kitchen that leads right down to it, but the bank is steep. You won't have such an easy time getting down to the water."

Laughing, she said, "I highly doubt I'll be jumping in for a swim, but I'm glad you warned me."

Mitchell had left the room.

"Tomorrow I'll take you back downtown, and we'll get you some more clothes, some food, and anything else you need. You do have a change of clothes for one more day?"

"Absolutely. I'll be fine. And I want to see your store. Mitchell has spoken highly of it."

He beamed. "My store's the best department store around. There's some nice things in there, and I have a women's section too. Of course, there are other dress shops, so you'll have plenty to choose from. And we have drug stores for anything else you'll need."

"We'll have it covered, so don't worry. I'm easy to please." Her gaze trailed up to his. The way he stared at her, face filled with intense interest, set off a quick burst of excitement. For a moment, her mind shot back to the early days when she and Adrian had first fallen in love. Blushing, she averted her gaze and focused on the divan in the corner, anything to break the spell. Whether or not she liked it, Adrian was still her husband, even if only for worse instead of better.

She considered her new home far away from home, with no support, no vehicle, and no money. The realization of needing an income hit her with startling surprise. Adrian's money wouldn't be accessible any longer. "I'll need a job. I don't have any money right now for rent." Earlier excitement gave way to cold fear. How would she support herself? Adrian had cared for her and made all the money. She hadn't much in the way of skills.

George stood closer, brushing against her shoulder. "Not to worry,

Claire. Won't charge you a penny of rent. I'm just glad you're here." His hand lingered in the middle of her back. "You're helping me more than anything by using this house. I really hated to see it empty."

The sincerity in his eyes and the softness of his voice nearly sent her reeling. His cologne held the gentle fragrance of a fine brand she knew must have been ordered straight from some fancy Parisian men's shop overseas. She held a hand on her cheek, hoping the coolness of it might calm her.

"Maybe we can discuss a job for me once I've settled in a bit?"

His only answer, a tender look, caring eyes, and a light nod.

Claire glanced up toward the door. Mitchell rested easily against the frame, watching them.

CHAPTER ELEVEN

Mitchell slipped Claire some bills. George had already opened the car door on the driver's side. "Keep this safe and sound until you get to a bank and open up an account."

She took the money, knowing this amount was a more than a generous gift for the current times. "I don't know how to thank you enough. I'll definitely pay this back."

"Don't worry about paying me back. This should hold you over a bit until you get on your feet. We'll find a job somewhere for you." Smiling, he opened the passenger door. "Take care of yourself, and let me know when you need something. I'll be in touch."

"Can't you at least stay one night and leave tomorrow? That's a lot of train-riding." She grinned down at her brother-in-law, who'd finally settled himself in the seat.

"I'm going to check on a few accounts while I'm here, and then it's back to the factory. And don't forget, someone has to look after you-know-who."

She winced and nodded. "True. What'll you tell him if he keeps asking about me?"

"I may just tell him you've escaped for good because nobody could find you. With any luck, he'll simply forget about the whole thing. As sad as it sounds, I wish he would."

"Me too. Let's just hope for the best, because it's all we can do." Claire glanced down a moment, kicking at the gravel.

George leaned over. "Claire, I'm just dropping Mitchell off at the trolley stop. I'll come right back." His reassuring smile lifted any trepidation inside her. At least his presence eased her mind, lightened anxiety, and instilled a sense of security. This time in her life more than ever, she needed security and the comfort of someone strong. In her quick estimation, George seemed strong in many facets of his life, as a businessman, friend, and perhaps a father.

"Bye, Claire." Mitchell waved one last time and pulled the door closed.

She stepped back as the car moved out of the driveway, tires crunching against the gravel as it glided out onto the main road. In the distance, the drone of the engine soon faded, leaving nothing but the twitter of birds, buzzing insects, and teasing whispers from the breeze.

She was finally alone. For the first time, she didn't know what to do with herself. There was no food in the house yet, so drumming up a quick meal remained impossible. A quick walk to one of the streetcars, and she'd be on her way to a local store for groceries, but he said he'd be back. No reason to scare poor George by running off somewhere strange. He'd seen her through this far. Surely, he wouldn't let her starve.

Claire turned around and headed toward the porch. Inside a pocket, she held the house keys. Hers. Not Adrian's, not Mitchell's, but hers—and George's. As a property owner, she knew he had a spare key secreted away, but he'd promised more than once that this house was for her use and enjoyment.

Closing the door behind her, she studied the open living room in more detail, taking in the decor with a keener eye. His wife had fine, simple taste. Just enough furnishings for comfort and utility. Dark wooden floors and paneling along the room cast the area in gloomy darkness, and she walked around the room, opening the curtains in each window. The dining room and kitchen held more ample lighting, giving off a cheerier ambiance.

Prowling through the drawers and cabinets, she found elegant china stored in the china cabinet, with sterling silver inside special lined drawers.

Crystal glinted behind the glass panes, water goblets, wine glasses, relish bowls, fruit bowls, vases. In the kitchen, the everyday ware held as much a beauty and elegance as the formal ones. The cabinets held a host of drinking glasses, coffee cups, and teacups with saucers, and below the counter, a blender, and mixer had been stored. The drawers held another set of flatware for daily use, napkins, and dish cloths and towels. A small table for two sat next to the window.

She wondered if George and his late wife had shared secrets while sipping coffee or tea at that table. Did they rent this house out after they married and lived where George did now? Mitchell hadn't told her much information. But a house this comfortable surely couldn't have been without occupants. The river. Claire viewed the back door. The lawn outside led to one place, and she wanted to see it. With a quick twist of the lock, she stepped out into the back yard, flanked by green pastures on either side, with more trees scattered in the distance. The back lawn remained empty, wide and grassy green, stretching to the river.

How she longed for girlhood, to be young again, when youth caught you up in its hands and you danced, carefree and happy. Today the old feeling stirred inside her, and along with it an urge to go barefoot, to touch the ground with bare soles and wiggle her toes into the soil. She quickly slipped off her shoes and waded through the yard, giggling as blades of grass crushed against her feet. Pure earth hit her skin with magnificent coolness, infusing energy and vitality she'd lacked for such a long time. She'd been too rushed, too urgent, too anxious, and the timing too cruel, to appreciate the woods the day she slipped out the back door of the asylum. At last she'd enjoy nature the way one should enjoy it, raw, wild, untamed, yet tender and loving.

Several paces later, she reached the river, gazing down a steep embankment at muddy water careening by, it's lazy whisper barely audible. Yards away a barge moved onward, with slow but sure determination. Where would it go, and what did it carry? Much to her disappointment, George was right. There were no steps or dock leading down to the water's edge, and picking one's way down the bank seemed harrowing at best. So much for wading in the water, but she envisioned future picnics here, a blanket spread across the ground and an eyeful of scenic beauty and peace. With a smile, she turned away and walked back to the house.

Upstairs, silence hit her ears as loudly as the strongest boom from an explosion. The paradox of it might have almost suffocated her, driven her mad had it not been for a recent life of never-ending clamor. Now she welcomed silence as a gift, a luxury allowing the mind a chance to think, plan, and dream. Heavy wooden doors to the rooms held their original hardware, brass locks outfitted with their corresponding skeleton key. She shuddered, remembering tales from her grandparents as they recounted times when they'd been locked in a room for what she personally determined as mild transgressions at best. No access to the outside world or dinner if behavior had been "bad" enough. Yes, in the hands of a wicked master, one could be locked inside a room as easily as using the key for shutting oneself in for safety.

Claire explored each room, admiring the ample space and furnishings. All drawers in the dressers were empty, except for one holding bed linens. Closets held nothing but a few hangers. The rooms seemed sunnier than downstairs, and the ambiance in this space wrapped her in a blanket of tranquility. She ended up back in the master bedroom where George had left her bag. Everything she owned in the world filled that simple travel bag. Sitting on the bed, Claire thought back to her old room in Ash Grove, where she had a closet filled with nice outfits, drawers filled with jewelry, cosmetics, and glinting hair clips—a room where she'd once shared a bed with Adrian. What would it be like sleeping alone? Would her body ever feel a man again, with strong arms around her, whispering loving words?

How long would it take to make friends, become self-sufficient, settle into a new life of living in a new town with strangers? In Hatchie River her friendships, no matter how small, had meant the world to her; they were important not only for companionship, but for survival. The clock on the nightstand showed eleven o'clock. In another hour, Ruth would be eating soon, along with Millie and the others. Part of her felt a twinge of guilt about the women she left behind. While they languished, she'd have sunshine, a beautiful house—and George. She shook her head and got up from the bed, making her way to the dresser.

Why did this new man suddenly intrigue her so much? She'd never been one for believing in love at first sight. She didn't know him, a widower with a young daughter, who still remained an enigma. Claire walked to the dresser, reached out, and pulled one of the knobs of a smaller drawer, cringing when the bottom gave off a shrill squeak as it scraped across wooden runners. Inside she spied an ornate metal jewelry box with a motif of rosebuds and vines in relief over the top. Furrowing her brow, she pulled out the box and opened it. Resting on light blue silk lay a pearl necklace, complete with matching earrings, bracelet, and ring. Pushing aside the pieces, she discovered a matching brooch.

She held up the necklace, noting the cold touch of pearl against her fingers. Studded with small emeralds and tiny seed pearls, the ornate clasp gleamed in the sun. Claire's eyes widened. Either this was a family heirloom or George lavished expensive gifts on his wife. Why on earth would he have left such a box like this? She replaced the necklace into the box. Her jewelry boxes in Ash Grove held pretty paste imitation pieces, but she had loved the small ruby pendant Adrian gave her as an anniversary gift one year, and a set of gold-drop earrings for Christmas. What she'd give for her old jewelry right now. She wished Mitchell had taken a few extra minutes and found those pieces. Focusing her attention back on the box, she admired even more this breathtaking set. How irresistible.

Gripped with temptation, she fingered through the pieces and slipped on the pearl ring, holding out her hand and marveling how it slipped effortlessly onto her middle finger. A ray of morning sun from the window lit up the small row of brilliant green emeralds cushioned within a pearl cluster. She picked up the brooch and fastened it on her blouse. How elegant it looked, though too ornate for casual wear. Some of the dresses and scarves she owned back home would have gone quite nicely with this piece. Losing all sense of discretion, she lifted up the earrings and slipped them on, shaking her hair away so they showed off elegantly against the side of her face. Engrossed, she gazed down and took up the necklace, scrutinizing the pearls and fingering the stunning gold and gem-studded clasp before wrapping the piece around her neck and fastening it. When she lifted her head to admire herself in the mirror, she froze in horror at the reflection.

George had entered the room and stood studying her with intense interest. In his eyes, she couldn't determine if they reflected quiet irritation or some other emotion. He moved quietly behind her, placing his hands lightly on the sides of her shoulders. Claire didn't know what initiated the weakness in her knees more, the fact that she'd been caught snooping or him touching her with an ease as if they'd always belonged together, in this house, in this room, and these jewels were nothing more than a token of his love and undying devotion. She decided it was most likely embarrassment.

In the mirror, Claire noted her crimson cheeks in glowing contrast to George's white ones. The longer they stood together, appraising each other, the brighter his eyes lit up. Stranger still, his hands on her didn't create the slightest unease, and for a moment, she forgot the past and Adrian. Standing tall and proud behind her, she shamelessly enjoyed the sense of protection he provided. After her ordeal in the asylum, protection rated high on her list of wants, like breathing, eating, and sleeping.

"You look beautiful wearing those." His voice rolled over her as easily as the water traveled down the Holston River.

"I-I'm so sorry. I was just looking at everything, and I opened this drawer and found this." She turned around and faced him. "When I saw what it was, I should have just told you so you could take everything home for safe-keeping."

"No need for apologies." He rubbed his finger over the pearl necklace, and the heat from his hands radiated through the rest of her. As if aware of his behavior for the first time, George stepped back. "I'm the one who needs to apologize. You must think I have no regard for boundaries or respect for a lady. Normally, I'm not this forward."

"Now it's you who doesn't need to say I'm sorry." Claire smiled up at him. "I took the liberty of handling something that didn't belong to me. That was forward of me." She removed the jewelry and placed each piece gently back into the box. "Here you go. Are there other boxes in here I don't know about?"

"Keep the jewelry where it is. It's already home." He sat on the bed and stared off into space, lost in thought.

"Are you okay?" Concerned, she sat down beside him.

He smiled, eyes warm yet reminiscent. "You see, Anita and I lived here after we married and stayed until her dying day. This was her parent's old place, along with thirty acres of surrounding property. When she died, I just couldn't bear living here alone. So, I bought a small farmhouse on down the road. Before you came, I removed her clothes, cosmetics, perfumes, but not the jewelry. Part of me just couldn't do it. I really didn't see any harm in leaving them. This house and everything in it was Anita's, and getting rid of things meant getting rid of her." His eyes filled with tears, and he pulled a handkerchief from his pocket. "Seeing her personal items made me sad all over again."

"You two did live here, then. I wondered about that." Claire rested her hand lightly on his shoulder. "Then you caught me trying on her jewelry. Thoughtless on my part."

"I don't blame you. They were in the drawer. But seeing them on you . . ." He turned away, dabbing his eyes.

"I'll put them away and never touch them again. But those pieces were the most beautiful things I've ever seen. It's been such a long time since I've enjoyed something feminine and pretty." She lost her train of thought and stared down at her hands.

He gazed at her with wet eyes. The silence between them spoke volumes, of pain, loss, futures that didn't turn out as planned. When he spoke again, his words came out in a hoarse whisper.

"You've seen the ugliest of humanity, haven't you? Mitchell came clean and told me just a little bit about what happened to you."

She nodded. "There's an ugly side, all right. Nastiness I wouldn't wish on my worst enemy. But your wife, you loved her, didn't you?"

"I did. Anita was the best thing that ever happened to me, other than my little girl Anna. She's the living memory of her mother. She's the most important person in my life right now." George blinked a few times and wiped his eyes again. "You don't have children of your own, do you? I vaguely remember Mitchell telling me you didn't."

Claire sighed. "Tried several times. Almost had two, and the last one didn't make it very long after he was born. I don't have much luck in the motherhood department, I'm afraid." Rubbing her finger over the bedspread, she smoothed out imaginary wrinkles as her mind drifted back to Ash Grove. "Everything I ever loved is back home, and now I find myself in a new place, alone, confused, not knowing what will happen."

"You're scared, aren't you?" His hand found hers, and the touch settled her nerves. "I was scared, too, after Anita left me. How would I get on without her? How would a man like me raise a little girl by myself? How could I be a good father and successful businessman without her?" His eyes fixed on Claire's. "Those questions weren't much different from the ones you have now. It seems at some point we find ourselves in a new place, thrown there, kicking and screaming, demanding an explanation for such injustice. I hadn't done anything to deserve that loss." He lightly squeezed her hand. "Nor did you deserve what happened to you. Let me tell you something. We have an asylum here, Eastern Psychiatric Hospital, and I've heard the horror stories. Everybody here avoids that place."

Her eyes widened, and the pressure in her chest increased. The thought of another mental institution here hadn't crossed her mind. "How close is it?"

"It's a little distance from here." George leaned over, his face inches from hers. "As long as there's breath in my body, you'll never go to a place like that ever again."

She looked away, aware of the heat in her cheeks. Why did he care so much? Was he always this nice with everybody? "Thanks, George. I'd really like to not ever go back to a place like that. I think I'll be plagued with nightmares forever."

"Time does heal wounds. May not seem like it now, but the pain will slowly ease, and you'll be ready to live again." His lips turned into a soft smile.

"Are you living again, George, after being without her?" Claire's eyes had found their way back to his face, one that captivated her.

"I'm a little more ready now for the other part, for feeling, for letting others in. It's time for more than just going through daily routines, pretending nothing's wrong and everything's okay."

The feeling part, letting others in. She understood well what he meant. Though her ordeal didn't last anywhere near the length of time since Anita's death, the toll it took on her spirit equaled the time, and in her opinion, surpassed it. It didn't take long to learn that shutting others out became a survival mechanism at Hatchie River. Shutting down and not thinking kept you from going mad, because actual living acknowledged a hellish existence and death staring you in the face. Each day survived only reinforced your choices.

George stood up and offered his hand. "Mighty heavy talk, but it felt good to get it all out. Tell you what, let's get back to town and grab a bite. While we're out, maybe you can run some errands."

Claire patted the pocket where the money Mitchell had given her lay tucked away. "Good idea." As she followed him out of the room, she briefly acknowledged the jewelry box out of the corner of her eye. That box would go back where she found it, and there it would stay, untouched.

CHAPTER TWELVE

Activity in downtown Knoxville had picked up a vibrant pace compared to the earlier part of the morning when she and Mitchell had stepped off The Tennessean. More cars moved up and down the streets, and people slipped inside the department and furniture stores. Claire's stomach rumbled, and she wished George would take her to a diner.

Much to her relief, he led the way on down the sidewalk until they reached S&W Cafeteria. Claire stepped inside first, and with his hand resting in the small of her back, George led her to the food line. Workers busied themselves loading food onto plates as patrons pointed out what they wanted. She picked up her tray and silverware and move down the line. From the dining room, she marveled at the sound of an organ, its vibrant notes blending with the hum of voices.

"Get whatever you want, Claire. I'm picking up the tab for this." George smiled as he slid his tray along the railing. How unusual the notion of having a choice on what to eat. The passage of time had almost buried the notion of ever having choices again. Her mouth watered at the smell of cooked meat and vegetables. The taste of succulent roast beef with some tasty broccoli and mashed potatoes hit her fancy as she voiced her selections to the ladies behind the glass. George picked out his food and both maneuvered their trays to the cashier.

George's eyes held a warm glow. "Miss, we're together, so ring up hers and mine." Claire's heart quickened as he paid the tab and guided her toward the dining room, his hand resting against her back again, as if they dined here together on a regular basis. The waiter, a sophisticated black man in uniform, had taken their trays and requested they follow him. An empty table not far from the organ sat clean and ready. George tipped the waiter, who offered a polite nod and a statement of thanks.

Claire sat comfortably in the chair George pulled out for her. When he seated himself, they both ate in silence a few minutes. She glanced around the dining room, watching people as they conversed, women's eyes lighting up as their friend filled them in on family secrets or the latest gossip.

Eager young men courting pretty women, chatted away, becoming more animated the more their date expressed agreement. Focusing her eyes back on George, she noted with surprise that his face showed the same interested expression Adrian's had when they first started seeing each other, the look of new interest, new excitement. A flutter of nervousness gathered in the pit of her stomach, and a giddy school-girl feeling rushed over her. She hadn't experienced that feeling in years, obviously, but she hadn't forgotten it, either. This is what being alive meant, a future worth living for, good food, secure home, and the company of good friends.

"Mitchell told me the amount he gave you and begged me to get that money in the bank as soon as possible. When we finish eating, we'll take care of it. Hamilton National Bank isn't far from here, just up the street."

"Is there a drug store and a place for groceries nearby? Though I could eat here and listen to that beautiful organ every day, I know I'll be in the kitchen cooking." Claire grinned.

"You bet. There's Lanes Drug Store, and after that, we'll head on out to Magnolia to Cas Walker's for groceries." As George leaned forward, he rested his leg lightly against hers. He didn't seem inclined to move it, and Claire sat nodding, taking in every word, trying not to focus on the heat building up inside her. She took a sip of water from her glass, fixing her gaze on George.

He continued, "You'll need some more clothes. I know you only brought a few things, so maybe we can finish up the rest of the shopping this weekend." His eyes burned with intense interest, planning out her needs as if they were his own.

"I really appreciate this, George. But I have one big concern, and that's finding a job. I'll need more money, and Mitchell isn't a bank."

"Would you like to help me with my store?" He jogged his eyes to hers and back to the fork-load of fish he held before popping the food into his mouth.

Claire stopped eating and stared at him. "Help you with your store? Like how, a clerk, stock person?"

"I mean help me run the business the way Anita did. How does that sound?" His eyes blazed with new excitement. "Oh, come on! Don't look so surprised. You've helped in a manufacturing business, so surely you can help with a humble department store like mine." He winked at her and dug his fork into the fish for another bite.

Her face flushed. "The manufacturing business, I left to the men. I sometimes helped with new hat designs and wore some of the models to see how they'd hold up. But I didn't get too deep into the accounting or the more detailed aspects."

"Nonsense." He secured his fingers around her wrist for emphasis. "You probably know more than you think. It won't be hard to show you the ropes, the merchandising, ordering, pricing, that sort of thing. If numbers bother you, I can teach you that later. I really could use the help, Claire, and I can't think of a better person than you."

"Don't see why not. I'm a quick study, and I love retail."

"You seem to have an eye for pretty things, and I agree with Mitchell, a woman's touch makes all the difference."

His expression had turned into one riddled with pleading, and she found his suggestion endearing. Mostly, she felt relief. At least she'd landed a job. This had been pure luck.

She beamed back at him. Prospects of having a job, something productive, filled her with excitement. Working kept her mind sharp and gave a sense of purpose. Even in the asylum, hard work in the garden or kitchen had served as some consolation, allowing a semblance of safety while away from the unit. Work turned the focus on getting a job done and off getting belted by someone who didn't have better things to do.

"When do I start?" Claire kept her eyes on him as she reached for her tea.

"Since today's Friday, I say Monday. It'll give you the weekend to rest up and get ready."

"Good. Gives me something to look forward to." She took in a deep breath. He'd not moved his leg from hers since they'd sat down. Though the diner's air conditioner hummed full force from across the room, the heat from his body had warmed her all over. When he stood up, the absence of him shot a chill through her system, filling her with a strange sense of aloneness.

"All right, my dear, let's get you to a bank." George's lips turned up into a kind smile as he guided out of the diner and down the street.

***

Claire waved as George pulled out of the driveway. Setting up a bank account and shopping for the necessities had been tiresome, but he'd been patient through all of it.

"That's why I have employees," he had told her. "It lets me help lovely people like you." The tone fell on her ears, sincere and pleasant, and she detected hesitancy when he left.

The Friday afternoon sun had turned into the hot glow of early evening, when rays burned their brightest. Fall would come soon in the next few weeks, bringing with it a certain characteristic crisp freshness, an air of vitality before the setting in of death, the winter season that wound its way into all living things.

She walked back inside and finished putting away groceries. Eyeing the stove, she laughed. The prospect of using appliances again seemed foreign to her right now. She'd get used to it quickly, though. What should she cook for dinner? And for one person? That's all she was now, one person. This situation would be the most difficult to deal with. She'd only been totally by herself when she first struck out on her own. When she ended up in Memphis, Adrian had come into her life several weeks later.

After neatly folding and putting away the grocery sacks for future use, she turned her attention upstairs. When she entered her bedroom, she saw Anita's beloved jewelry box on the dresser. Claire shuddered. With a grimace, she strode forward and glared at it. She still felt guilty about George catching her red-handed.

She should never have tried on those pieces. What surprised her most was that he clearly didn't want the box with him. While women oftentimes embraced sentimental tokens, weaving them into their memories, men took a different stance, perhaps. She'd learned this through living with Adrian.

George had found his own way for dealing with his grief, just like she'd find a way to deal with hers. They shared this common thread, her and this new man, one who's heart and words expressed understanding. He knew how existence changed like the breeze outside, and how the leaves must feel as they are caught up and carelessly tossed around, floating helplessly to the ground once again. Through all her trials, Claire learned one thing. She had not totally shut herself off from desire and longing. They may have been buried deep in her psyche, put away for a bit, but she always believed hope sprang eternal.

With a sigh, she picked up the jewelry box and returned it to its rightful drawer. She checked each drawer for additional stray boxes and found none. One by one, Claire arranged her purchases in the dresser and closet, and placed new cosmetics and hair care products in the bathroom. On the counter, she placed a small bottle of fragrance. She already had sprayed a little on her skin and enjoyed the smell. A pair of new rhinestone hair clips sparkled under the light over the sink. In the mirror, she gazed at her hair, longing for the moment when she'd dress up and wear these beauties.

One bag remained on the bed. It held a small jewelry box for housing a few pieces of costume jewelry, which she'd also purchased. At least she'd start Monday morning in George Parker's store looking fresh and presentable. She'd wanted to see the store, but George wanted to keep things private until Monday. Customers apparently liked his merchandise. She'd spotted them filing out the doors, bags in tow. She arranged her new box and jewelry on top of the dresser and stood back surveying the room. Finally, everything was put away. Rays of light stole through the window, shrouding the room in a soft glow.

Her eyes roved over the bed, the empty one, one that would hold one lone person tonight, and for a moment, she envisioned George and Anita, snuggled together, Anita's fingers playing through George's hair, while his hands slid over her satiny flesh. In her mind, she viewed the passion in his eyes, and the glow of love on her face. Claire shut off the vision, feeling like an intruder. She hadn't forgotten the way she and Adrian gave each other longing looks, tender touches.

Would she ever resolve her anger toward Adrian? Should she view him as dead, one who'd graced her life for a short while? After all, he might as well be dead. He didn't exist in her life anymore. Though she resolved to live life again, she knew there would be parts of her wishing for the past, wishing everything had turned out differently.

Old ghosts didn't die easily, but she could try and fight them off one day at a time. Right now, she possessed everything she needed, home, food, clothes, Mitchell, and George. For this abundance, she mouthed a quick prayer of gratitude.

A twitter of a bird sounded from the window; the outside called. If she didn't get out of this house right now, her own thoughts stood a great chance of suffocating her. Claire made her way carefully down the stairs. When she opened the front door, her eyes widened in surprise.

Next to one of the wicker rockers sat an unexpected guest, a small young girl with blonde hair falling in loose ringlets around her face. A set of ten metal jacks lay scattered, and in her hand, she held a tiny red rubber ball. After tossing the ball up in the air, she grabbed a jack and caught the ball after it bounced on the porch. Ignoring Claire, the little girl continued this game until all jacks lay in a neat pile by the rocker.

"There, I got 'em all." She gazed up at Claire with shining eyes. "And I did it without touching any of them." Her lips turned up into a wide smile. "You can't touch any when you're playing. It's against the rules." She lowered her voice. "Sometimes I make up my own rules, but don't tell anybody." Her eyes remained steadfast on Claire's face, while her small hand stifled a giggle.

What an angel. Claire marveled at the child's sweet little nose and cherubic lips. The set of eyes she bore sparkled glacier blue, and her smile lit up like the brightest lights. Seating herself in a rocker, Claire smiled back. "That's okay. Sometimes you have to make up your own rules." She paused a moment, and the girl continued staring as she tossed the ball lightly from one hand to the other.

Leaning forward toward the girl, Claire asked, "I don't think we've met. What's your name?"

"Anna." Former excitement trickled down to sudden shyness, and her gaze turned into one of caution.

"Hello, Anna. I'm Claire." She smiled at the girl. "You're awfully pretty."

Anna responded by turning her face down and staring at her pile of jacks.

"Aren't you far from home?" Though George told her he'd purchased a house nearby, she had no idea where nearby really was.

"Hunh uh." Anna shook her head, scattering blonde curls across her face.

"Is your house close by?"

Pointing past Claire's right shoulder, Anna answered, "It's over there."

Claire turned and, saw nothing but fields, but determined one could reach George's house if they kept driving past this one. "You walked here, then." She turned back to the little girl, who'd gathered up her ball and jacks.

"It's not far." Anna turned her eyes homeward for a moment before facing Claire. "I don't have to go to school tomorrow or the next day." She grinned. "I can play for two whole days, can't I?"

"You sure can, precious. And you can play right here anytime you want." For an instant, Claire wanted to take the child in her arms and hold her tight. If she could smother her cheeks and forehead with kisses, she'd do that too.

"Anna, how old are you?"

"Five." Another big smile crawled across her face.

"Five? Why you're almost grown up." Claire reached out and patted her on the shoulder.

"I gotta go home." Anna, turned and stepped gingerly down the porch steps.

Worried, Claire got up from the rocker. "Let me walk with you. That way I'll know you got home safely."

Anna waited by the steps, and the two picked their way down through the yard and onto the main road. Embraced by the light cool of evening the two walked together, breathing in the scent of clover and thistles, while fields rolled lazily around them. The sky had faded into a comfortable baby blue, streaked with orange-pink tints as if an artist had carelessly tossed color on a canvas. The September air exhaled cooler draughts, and any humidity lingering from the day had passed.

A cow stopped its feast of grass, eyed the visitors, and let out a soulful moo. Anna paused by the barbed wire fence, mooing back in between giggles. When the cow bellowed in response, Anna mooed louder and with more determination. Claire fought the urge to laugh. Bored with human company, the cow turned an eager mouth toward the grass for another juicy bite of dinner, ignoring the interlude altogether.

At times, Anna skipped down the road, kicking at stray gravels along the way. One time she picked up a stick and threw it as hard as she could, but not before asking Claire to kindly hold her ball and jacks.

"I can't lose these. They're my most favorite." She gently placed them in Claire's hands, making sure the ball and all the jacks had been accounted for, counting each piece. "Do mother squirrels sing their babies to sleep?" Anna pointed in the direction of a tree, where a bushy tail flicked wildly back and forth, followed by noisy, excited screeches.

Claire grinned. "I don't know. But I'm sure they take care of their babies in their own special way."

The little girl turned a sideways glance at Claire. "I sing Lulabelle to sleep every night. She says it helps her sleep better."

"Lulabelle?" Claire nodded, pretending she knew exactly who or what "Lulabelle" was. "She really said that?"

Anna snickered. "No, she's my most favorite doll, but I pretend she talks."

"Do you sing a lot, or do you just sing to Lulabelle?"

"I don't know. I sing when I feel like it, or when I know a song. But I don't feel like singing right now." She picked up her pace. "I'll race you to that fence post."

Laughing, Claire raced forward, deliberately holding back her speed. Anna's shrill laughter cut the stillness of the country road, and her curls flew out about her head. Her little feet crunched against the gravel as she charged as fast as she could toward the post.

"Yay, I won!" She jumped up and down, clapping her hands. "I knew I'd beat you." Her eyes flashed, and her lips turned up into a wide smile.

"My goodness, you are fast. I think you're a natural-born runner." Claire laughed, wiping back a lock of hair from her forehead.

"I'm very fast. I win all the races at school." Anna skipped ahead a few paces and stopped for Claire.

Several minutes later, rounding a small curve, George's house came into view. Surrounded by flowers and neatly trimmed bushes, the white-washed house sat tucked away from the road. In the gray of evening, it looked like a cottage out of a story book, entrenched in its own world, nearly hidden away from the casual eye. So, this quaint place had been George's sanctuary from death, his hideaway from a broken heart. She followed Anna to the front door. Before she'd begun her good-byes, the door opened.

George stepped outside, taking Anna in his arms and smothering her with a kiss on the cheek.

"Thanks for walking my little girl home." He patted Anna's shoulder as she edged her way inside the house. "I'll have to talk to her later about not wandering off. She's quick."

"Didn't mind a bit." Claire viewed her surroundings. The back of the house inched up to a cozy forest, and several yards down the road she spied a serene pond with a few ducks gliding across the surface. Across the road an old barn sat on a rolling open field.

He rested against the door frame, relaxed and unhurried. "I'd told Anna a nice lady had moved into the house. Her running off down there shouldn't have surprised me. When she got home from school, she said she was going out to play. I thought she meant out back."

The evening air had grown cool. Claire shivered. "I enjoyed meeting her. She told me some of her 'most favorite' toys on the way here."

"I think she wanted to meet you." George smiled. In the cool of evening, his eyes and kind expression warmed her.

"Anna is a darling little girl. No wonder she's the most important thing in your life." Claire's eyes drank in the features of his face, the texture of his hair, his eyes and the way he looked at her. She found conversation challenging.

"I was putting dinner on the table. Now that you're here, why don't you join us?" He moved closer, resting his hand lightly on her shoulder. "You shouldn't have your first dinner alone."

"Oh, I couldn't intrude like that. You treated me to a wonderful lunch. I should cook for you."

His eyes lit up as he chuckled. "I'll take you up on that offer. For now, come on in here. I'll set another plate." He propelled her inside before she could protest further, and shut the door.

George's farmhouse exuded an air of simple comfort, much smaller than the open rooms and hard wooden beams and flooring of his first home. In the quaint living room, crocheted covers and throw pillows covered the sofa. Lamps on the tables emitted a cozy glow, and for a moment, she considered her new home rather austere and cold. The furnishings in this room displayed modest designs, more for utility than artistic beauty. She followed him down the hallway to a small kitchen, where she sat at a wooden plank table outfitted with four straight-back chairs.

The smell of food hit her full force as she watched George remove another plate, glass, and a set of utensils from cupboards and drawers. Before placing everything in front of her, he'd filled her plate with an aromatic thick stew, a baked sweet potato, and a slice of cornbread. From the refrigerator, he pulled out a bottle of milk.

"I hope this is okay." I can't cook like you women, but Anna and I have survived mine." He chuckled and placed the food on the table.

"This smells so good, George. My father was a great cook, better than my mother."

He disappeared briefly, and returned with Anna, whose feet pattered against the floor as she ran to an empty chair. Facing Claire, she smiled. "Are you staying with us? Forever?" She blinked her eyes, and somewhere in them Claire swore she saw sincere hope.

"Anna! Miss Claire's our guest for dinner tonight. We'll take her home later." George frowned, seating himself across from Claire.

"Oh." The little girl hung her head down and picked at one of the carrots peeking out of the stew.

"Here, use your fork, or spoon. We don't eat with our hands." Her father pointed to the silver fork resting on a napkin.

Anna lifted her head, lips puckered in a soft pout. "We eat some things with our hands, like fried chicken or pickles or french fries, don't we, Miss Claire?"

Claire's eyes trailed from Anna to a stunned George, whose frown had turned to a look of embarrassment. She smiled at Anna, patting her hand. "Well, sweetheart, we do eat some foods with our fingers, but tonight we don't have any of those. Would you like a fork or spoon?"

The little girl's lips puckered into a nice round "O." "A spo-o-o-o-n, Miss Claire, a sp-o-o-o-n."

"Good choice, darling. Here." Claire retrieved the spoon and placed it in Anna's open hand. "Now you can eat like a proper lady."

"Will I be as pretty as you, when I grow up?" Anna propped up on her elbow, wagging the spoon back and forth with her hand, a dreamy glow in her eyes.

"Oh, sweetheart, I'm sure you'll be much prettier."

"I-I-I don't know-w-w-w." Anna finally dipped her spoon in the stew, and after swallowing her bite, gazed up at her father. "Can Miss Claire have dinner with us every night, from now on until forever?"

George's eyes popped wide open, and his cheeks flushed red. Claire said nothing, but took an obligatory bite of food, wishing this conversation focused on another topic.

"Anna, you just need to eat your dinner right now and be quiet, please."

As he tapped lightly on the table close to his daughter's plate, George's face bore an image of one embroiled in emotional pain more than anger, while his voice rang out with cool but gentle commands. Claire watched the scene before her noting the interaction between father and daughter, a child who behaved no differently than any other, and a father who struggled with a balance of parental authority and display of affection.

"Did you get everything put away?" He turned and focused on Claire, his face more relaxed.

"I did. And once again, thank you. I'm liking Knoxville already."

He took a quick sip from his glass. "Good, I'm glad to hear it. I'm especially looking forward to Monday. I'll show you more of downtown, and especially the store, where everything is."

They finished dinner with small-talk, and Anna kept quiet, but eyed the two of them in silence. When she ate all her dinner, she asked to be excused and quickly disappeared to her room, but not before bestowing a soft kiss on Claire's cheek.

"She really has taken a liking to you," George said, carrying some dishes to the sink where Claire had already filled up one side with hot, soapy water.

"She's adorable, and a really sweet little girl. So curious." Claire took the dishes and began washing them.

"Got an opinion, that one. She keeps me on my toes because I never know what she'll come out with next." George chuckled and wiped off the table. He came up and stood next Claire, rinsing the dishes she'd placed in the empty sink. "I'll admit, I've never had a woman in this house since we moved here." His eyes searched Claire's. She nodded in silence. "She doesn't remember her mother, only two at the time she died."

Claire tried to remember events at two years of age, but couldn't do it. She barely remembered a few occasions when she was four. Of course, Anna wouldn't remember her mother.

"Does she ever talk about your wife or tell you she wants a mother?" Claire glanced over at George, who'd sidled up so close he brushed against her shoulder as he rinsed the dishes and dried them.

"On occasion, we talk about her. We talk about things she might have liked or what would happen if she were still here. That sort of thing." He shook his head. "As she got a little older, the hard part was trying to explain why other girls had women in their lives while she only had me."

"That must be so hard, trying to explain that to a little girl. Adults have a hard enough time understanding some things."

"It hasn't been easy, I'll say that." He smiled and put away the last of the dishes as Claire drained the sink. "But enough of that, let's get you home."

"Miss Claire?" A tiny voice sounded from the entrance to the kitchen.

She and George turned around. Anna stood across the room, dressed in a nightgown and holding out an old composition doll with a bundle of frizzed hair clinging to its head. The smile on the doll's face gave Claire the creeps with its lifeless stare and row of white teeth.

"Yes, sweetheart. Are you ready for bed, already?"

George held out his wrist, glancing at his watch. "It's getting a little late. Maybe all the excitement today has worn her out."

Anna ran toward Claire, clutching the doll next to her chest. "Will you give Lulabelle a kiss goodnight before you go?"

"Of course, I'll give her a bedtime kiss." Out of the corner of her eye, she caught George stifling a grin. Anna handed her the doll, at which point Claire dropped a tiny kiss on its cheek. Taking back her doll, Anna stood, twisting lightly from one side to the other, turning her eyes toward the floor and then back up to Claire. "Is there something else you need, dear?"

Anna didn't answer, but turned shy again like she'd done earlier at the house. Claire glanced up at George, who stood with his hand propped up against his mouth, lost in thought.

"Do you know what she wants?" Claire whispered to him.

"If I didn't know better, I think she wants you to kiss her goodnight too." He pursed his lips and bounced his gaze from Claire to Anna. "Honey, are you wanting a kiss from Miss Claire?"

The little girl's eyes lit up, followed by a vigorous nod.

"Well, if Lulabelle can have a kiss, you most certainly can." Claire's heart nearly burst with emotion. She'd dreamed of moments like this, family dinners with Adrian and tucking children into bed, soothing boo-boos, and comforting them when they had bad dreams. She stooped down, and delivered a light kiss on the girl's cheek. Thrilled, Anna grabbed Claire around the neck and returned the gesture.

"Night, night, Miss Claire." Anna turned and ran out of the kitchen.

"She seems to be smitten with you." George smiled at Claire, who'd still not recovered from what just transpired. A little prompting, and she'd have sailed out of the kitchen and into Anna's room so she could see her safely in bed, snuggling with her doll. Or she might have read stories until those sleepy eyes shut for the night. "You okay? Not used to kids, are you?"

"I'm quite fine. And you're right. I don't have little girls who ask me to kiss their dolls or throw their arms around me." She grinned up at George. "It's fine. I don't mind a bit."

He studied her for a few seconds before hanging the dishtowel over the oven handle. "I need to get you home. You must be worn out after today."

"We've done a lot, and you're right. Bed would feel really good right now." Peering into his face, she smiled. "Thank you for inviting me for dinner. It was nice having company."

"Wouldn't have had it any other way. Don't know why I didn't think of it myself."

As George drove her home, Claire thought about how his smile showed a familiar warmth she'd come to expect, even for such a short time of having known him. She liked it, the way his face lit up, the way his eyes sparkled, and the way his voice spilled out, ruffling against her ears like the smoothest silk. He could have been a radio personality or a star on the big screen. Most of all, she liked the way he gazed at her with interest, taking in her words as if they were gold, as if she mattered.

George seemed to pick up where Adrian had left off. Where Adrian had left her in the realm of what-might-have-been, the man before her quietly held her hand and seemed to lead her into a realm of good-things-to-come. She slipped into the passenger's seat of the car, and found herself within minutes at her own front doorstep.

She watched George drive off, her mood dimming along with the headlights as they faded out of sight. When Claire entered the house, an old chime clock sounded out the nighttime hour, a harsh clang that nearly sent her heart pounding right out of her chest. She climbed the stairs, legs like dead weights as she lifted each one. A lot of activity for a first day in a new town, but she was grateful for it. Keeping busy had helped her settle in just a little, and the prospects of working at G. P. and Sons alleviated immediate fears about how she'd care for herself. Other than George showing her around, she planned on resting and preparing for Monday. Perhaps she'd spend time listening to the radio in the evening. During the day she could take advantage of what little warmth was left in the season and laze by the river, her nose buried in a good novel. What better time to sip some iced tea from one of those gorgeous goblets winking at her in the china cabinet and let the day pass. Who would care if she used the fine crystal? She rather liked the idea already.

Fatigue hit her now with all its force, and she fought the heaviness in her eyes. Every step took more effort than the last one, but she welcomed silence and solitude at last. Inside the bedroom, she shed her clothing and slipped on a new nightgown she'd purchased, an attractive soft pink silk. The airiness of it hit her skin. For the first time in a long time, she doubted that princesses in far off lands felt any more privileged or special than she did right now.

She slid between the sheets, sinking into a fluffy pillow and a firm mattress. No bedsprings gouging into her back, no gown with a godawful stench, and most of all nothing but the sound of night and the occasional creek of the house. Tonight she lay down and closed her eyes, her mind still clinging to fresh tender memories of the evening, of happy faces, a warm home, and Anna's sweet kiss.

CHAPTER THIRTEEN

By eleven-thirty Monday morning, Gay Street pulsed with new life, sidewalks filled with people. Several customers browsed the shelves of G. P. and Sons, wandering from one side of the store to the other. Others still filed in. Housewives had come to town, some intent on buying, while others seemed more interested in killing time before hurrying off somewhere else. Claire noted with pride how women eyed the hats, those made by Adrian and Mitchell. The ladies picked up different styles, trying them on and twirling around in front of the mirror for a better view. One lady had come in when the store opened and purchased one, while a handsome young gentleman came along behind her and selected a man's hat, a grey fur felt fedora.

George had shown her every department before he opened the store, and walked her through all the aisles filled with everything from men's shirts to women's dresses, to kitchenware, fine china, sewing machines and shoes. In the middle of the store, glass counters glistened with cosmetics, fancy face creams, and make-up, guaranteeing a woman would look twenty-years-old forever. Jewelry winked under showcase lights, and rich, cut-glass bottles of perfume bore exotic European labels.

G. P. and Sons had it all it seemed, brimming over with the finest brands of merchandise Claire had ever seen. He'd properly introduced her to his eight clerks, who'd greeted her with a warm welcome.

Oma Brooks, his head clerk, had gladly taken Claire under her wing. Claire had decided she liked the older woman, most likely in her late fifties, with her upswept greying hair and crisp suit with a shiny rhinestone pin on the lapel of her jacket. Around her neck, she wore a string of round bright red beads, and when she drew close, Claire caught the light scent of lilac perfume. In her opinion, a scowl would have just as easily suited Oma, who reminded her of stern secretaries and snooty business staff she'd encountered before. Instead, the woman's face gleamed with a warm smile as she peered over her spectacles, and her voice wafted out soft and kind.

Oma had ushered Claire to the back side of the store, showing her where everyone clocked in. They passed George's office and ended up in another room where the ladies placed their purses on a wooden shelf against the back wall. A small table with four chairs sat in the middle of the room. Oma informed her that this area was the break room. At Oma's invitation, Claire placed the brown paper bag holding her lunch inside the refrigerator next to the shelf. She gazed at the coat rack in one corner of the room, with its one, lonely white sweater. It wouldn't be long before her sweater would take its place on one of the hooks. October would soon be in full swing, bringing with it golden days, and nights of breezy, chilly air and clear black skies littered with a million glinting stars.

"Did Mr. Parker tell you anything about your position or what you'd be doing?" Oma turned to Claire.

"He didn't go into detail, really. Just said that maybe I'd help him with the business like Anita did."

The smile froze on Oma's face as she nodded several times. "I see. Um, well, I'll ask Mr. Parker later if he wants you to clock in and out like the rest of us, or if he wants you helping customers or helping him."

Claire returned the smile, sensing the woman's reaction. "You know what, I'll follow your lead, and you tell me what I need to do. I can do anything, wait on people, ring up sales on the register, clean the shelves. I'm not too good to do any of it."

"I'm sure you'll be wonderful. None of this is hard, except maybe standing on your feet all day. Let's go back to the floor, and we'll get started.

Having chatted with a few of the customers, satisfied they were taken care of, Claire stood back and watched everything and everyone around her. Two of the clerks, Ruby and Joy, had taken up post in the sewing and housewares department, helping some ladies with kitchen appliances and a woman interested in a sewing machine. Roy had positioned himself between the shoe department and men's wear, presently helping a gentleman with shoes while keeping a watchful eye in the direction of the rack of men's suits.

Dahlia and Minnie stood proudly behind the center counters, oohing and cooing over ladies when they tried on perfume or applied a new shade of eye shadow or lipstick. Oma and Claire shared three departments, children's wear, lingerie, and women's wear. Jack and Leona served as runners, shifting between all the departments as needed. Of course, Oma had informed Claire that she'd soon be expected to know all the departments as well as everyone else, and had instructed her already on how to ring sales on the cash register.

George had holed himself up in the office since the store opened, not once coming out to check on anyone. As more customers came in, managing all the people presented a challenge at times. But no matter, the work would help pass the hours. How good it felt to be back with real people again, normal people who weren't hollow shells housing shattered spirits. How wonderful to wear fresh clean clothes, bathe, eat savory food, and sleep in warm beds. Luck had been on her side, and she knew it. Had George shared any of her past with the others? And why had Oma given her such a puzzled look when they were in the breakroom?

She turned when a hand touched her lightly on the back. "At twelve-thirty, did you want to go on your break?" Oma had slipped up behind her. Claire looked at her watch.

"Oh, yes, that's fine with me. I guess we do need those, don't we?" Claire grinned.

"I've worked for many a slave-driver in the past, but Mr. Parker has made it clear he wants us refreshed and in good working order. Says we make more sales when we're spry and perky." Oma winked.

"I guess he has a point." Claire nodded, glancing around the store one last time before she headed to the break room. How she disliked the dullness of it. She would have rather skipped lunch and stay on the floor.

"Claire." The sound of a man's voice sounded off right behind the two women.

Oma's face sobered as she squared up her shoulders, ready to speak. George cut her off. "Good, I'm glad I caught you. Have you had lunch yet?"

"I was just telling her to take her break, Mr. Parker." Oma grinned. "She's done a nice job so far. A real natural, I think."

George waved her off, nodding in agreement. "I knew that from the start. I can pick a winner when I see them." He smiled at Claire, tilting his head toward the back of the store. "Why don't you get your lunch and we can eat in my office." Oma lifted her brows, staring at Claire in silence.

"Okay. I'll bring yours too."

"Yes, please." He turned to Oma. "Claire and I rode in together. She doesn't have a car yet."

"That was nice of you to offer. Sure beats riding a noisy trolley to work." Oma wore her ingratiating expression. "I'm sure she'll settle in better as time goes on."

"I think so. We're breaking her in good here." He grinned one last time at Oma before turning in Claire's direction. Together they walked to the back of the store. "I thought we could go over some things. I'll only keep you about an hour."

"Sounds good to me. Whatever you need."

Inside the break room, she gathered up her modest lunch sack from the refrigerator. In the back, she spied his lunch box crafted of aluminum, sturdy, roomy. Her mind shifted to thoughts of him, standing in the kitchen, making his lunch after sending Anna off to school. What a lonely figure, she thought. No one should be alone, raising a small child.

A swift pang of sympathy shot through her. In her mind men were nothing but overgrown boys, really. No matter how tough they presented themselves, a mere boy resided underneath. Oma had driven her point home about using the trolley. How long would George plan on bringing her to work every day? But then again, why not? They worked in the same place. So what if he happened to be the owner?

She carried the lunches to George's office. He sat behind his desk, and she sat in a vacant chair across from him on the other side. Claire watched, vision fixed on the box as he pulled out a sandwich, two small yellow apples, and something wrapped in waxed paper. A matching thermos held some juice, which he poured out into the top that doubled as a cup.

"So tell me, Claire. You say the only thing you had to do with the factory back in Memphis was wearing the hats after they were created?"

"Yes, just the prototype, to see how it looked, how it wore. Sometimes I helped with the designs too. I can do some simple sketch work. Nothing too fancy."

George swallowed a bite of his sandwich, studying Claire with such intensity that she sensed her cheeks growing warm. "Anna really took a fancy to you the other night. I've never seen her warm up to someone that fast."

"She's a darling little girl. I liked her too."

"She's asked me last night when we were having 'Miss Claire' over again."

Claire stared briefly at her sandwich. A dull ache roiled inside her stomach. She could have a child like Anna one day. She hadn't given up on this notion at all. "Maybe I'll invite you and Anna over, and she can bring Lulabelle."

His gaze remained fixed on her face. "Do you have any special things you enjoy doing? Any talent or skills?" He shifted in his chair and reached for one of the apples.

As Claire thought of an answer, someone knocked on the door.

"Come in." George's voice rang out.

"Excuse me, Mr. Parker." Ruby stepped inside the office.

Claire caught the brief annoyed expression slipping over George's face. "Yes, Ruby, can I help you?"

"Thought you might want some fresh coffee for lunch. I made another pot." Ruby politely acknowledged Claire with a light nod. "I'll let you get back to your business. Sorry for the interruption." She turned briefly to Claire, mumbling, "I know how he enjoys his coffee."

The door closed, and George spoke up. "Sorry about that. We were talking about things you like to do."

She thought a moment. "If I were given the chance, I could do a lot of things. I catch on fast. But there is one thing I've missed, and that's looming."

George raised an eyebrow. "Really?"

"Uh-huh. I had a nice loom at home. Created several pieces. Even made up my own designs and patterns. I always wondered if I could sell them, if people like them well enough."

"Did you ever try? Maybe suggest that your work be included as a different product line when they were selling the hats?" George tapped his fingers lightly on the desk. "They could have sold your work, you know. I'm sure your husband had lots of accounts that were more than just hat shops."

"I sometimes made pieces for gifts. Simple towels. They were quicker to make and still had my special look, but everything else was just for family use."

"I see." He popped the last bite of sandwich in his mouth and washed it down with some juice. "I guess you didn't happen to bring some of your work, did you?"

"Are you kidding? If things had been a little different, I definitely would have, even just for sentimental reasons." Claire grimaced. "Mitchell and I were in a hurry. Didn't know when Adrian might show up." She shuddered at the memory of her husband and Mitchell's flash of anger. How the look on his face terrified her in that moment. Any less sympathy, and he could have started her nightmare all over again. She turned an eye up at George.

"It's funny how important some things seem one minute, and how in other circumstances not so much."

"True." George acknowledged agreement. A few seconds of silence, and he spoke again, "Claire, what's happening with Adrian is a crying shame. I only thank my lucky stars Mitchell is around to see things are taken care of. Call me selfish, but when I have quality product lines that sell, I want them. I don't want anything interfering. At the same time, I feel personal admiration for both of those men. To me, Adrian and Mitchell are the epitome of quality and class, and anything they touch, create, or make part of their lives echoes those traits.

"In his good mind, several years ago, Adrian caught himself a star person. You. That alone is good enough for me. The truth is, I trust you. I'm sure whatever craft you do, you do it with vigor and perfection. I just sense that about you, the way you dress, speak, the way you carry yourself."

Claire gazed at him, attentive. "I'd say that about sums me up. I like nice things, I can pick them, have a good eye for it. And yes, I take pride in everything I do."

"Good. Just as I'd thought." George smiled, thumping the small stack of invoices in front of him. "Here's what I'm hoping you can help me with. I need a woman's touch and intuition back in this store again. I've been making do with Oma, but it's not enough."

"How's that?" Claire's eyebrows raised. "She seems like a nice lady to me, and very patient when training people."

George chuckled as he ruffled through a few sheets of paper. "Oma's a great gal. I think she'd like to move up higher in position, though. She's poured it on a little thicker since my wife died, offering to take on more responsibility. Being extra nice when she doesn't need to. Honestly, I think she's gone as far as she can in my store. Hate to say it, but I need someone more youthful and vibrant. Someone to liven things up." He sat back in his seat and gazed at Claire.

Now she knew the reason for the strained expressions. Claire's heart went out to the woman. Here poor Oma thought she'd nearly had it in the bag career-wise, only to have a stranger waltz in and take away any chance at climbing that payroll ladder one more time.

"At any rate," George continued, "I'll always be grateful to her for helping out with Anna when I needed it. Sure took a load off me. Anna likes her okay, but she adores you. I'm a dad; I know these things." He winked at Claire, voice dropping to a whisper when he uttered the last words.

"I'm sure you do." Claire laughed as she plucked a grape from the cluster in her sack. "Any ideas, then? What do you need from someone 'more youthful and vibrant?'" She grinned back.

"You could start out by being a buyer for this store. That would help me out a lot. I feel like I'm growing a little stale. I need some new ideas, change some things out. That sort of thing."

Popping another grape in her mouth, she considered his words, thinking about how she'd go about doing this. Making hats from furs and materials and glues was one thing, but how would she ever determine which blender was the best or which fancy perfume bottles and fragrances other women would like? But that wasn't her biggest question.

"There is something that bothers me, George, and I want your honest opinion." Claire closed the sack with the remaining grapes. "I'm concerned about the war in Europe. Being away from a radio so long, I didn't realize how out of touch I was with the world. Everything has been rush-rush until now."

George pursed his lips, nodding, his eyes locked on hers with a steady gaze.

"This past weekend, I spent time relaxing, enjoying myself, but I also listened to the news. It's not pretty over there, and I don't know how this is going to affect us. Haven't you felt some of the anxiety in your business? I know before I went to . . ." She stopped, glancing away. Any talk of the asylum bothered her now. Somehow, she felt it made her seem sub-par in the eyes of others. "I know Adrian and I were talking about it not too long ago, and we were seeing a little drop in sales even then. Not enough to scare us too bad, but just enough that we perked up and paid attention. You know?" Her eyes searched his face. He seemed like a man in control, but she knew quite well some things in life couldn't be controlled, no matter how badly the desire to turn away and pretend the ugliness didn't exist.

George got up from his chair, overtaken by what seemed to Claire a quick fit of anxiety. His jaw tightened, and his brow furrowed while he struggled with finding the right words. At last he said, "I don't know, Claire." He ran his hand over his hair, pacing back and forth behind his desk. "By the grace of God, I don't know what to do, really. Business as usual like there's nothing going on?" He shot a quick glance in her direction. "I'd love nothing better than to bury my head in the sand, pretend it's all silly hearsay, but that would be foolish. We all hoped the last war years ago would be the final one, but I'll be damned if the ugly old Devil didn't rear his horns again."

Claire turned her gaze on the sack in her lap, regretting she'd brought up the subject. "I'm sorry, but a responsible buyer for a successful department store needs to look at things going on around them. Beyond our world here at home too. Like it or not, it all affects us, or will at some point if things change. And sometimes life doesn't change the way you want it to." She hung her head, fighting with herself to keep her thoughts from wondering off in the recent past again.

He came around from behind the desk, up to her chair, and covered her hand with his. She marveled at how warm and soft it was, yet strong.

"That's what I need right now, someone to talk to who has some good common sense and isn't afraid to say what she thinks. Do I like dealing with it? No. But I need someone to keep me grounded and practical in these matters, especially in business."

"So, you have been thinking about this." Claire loosened her grip on the sack.

"Yes. I had really hoped to carry some European lines in here, maybe some fine china, some exotic colognes for men and women. I'm just not sure I'll be able to get it shipped, for one thing. On the other hand, I could be sitting on all this merchandise until the cows come home. The uncertainty of times scares people. They don't part with their money as easily."

"Then let's keep it practical, neat, affordable. Let's not overthink it so much." Claire leaned forward in her chair. "I'm sure you have catalogs, don't you? Ones you've ordered, or that salesmen have left? Let's keep everything home-based, meaning here at home."

"I've got several different catalogs you can look through. Take another look around the store, really study it. Think about what you think you'd like to see or what you would buy or recommend for a customer." George smiled that disarming smile of his again, the one Claire found her pulse quickening whenever she saw it.

"The catalogues will be a great start. If it's not too forward to ask, can I meet with the salesmen who stop in? I know they come by, peddling their wares."

George snapped his fingers. "Good idea. They'll be surprised dealing with a woman, but don't let that throw you. If they give you any lip, I'll tell them they'll have to talk to you if they want to sell anything to me." His facial expression emphasized his sincerity, which relaxed Claire. She knew from experience with Adrian's hats that salesmen could be a persnickety lot, sometimes taking their business elsewhere if they didn't want to deal with a store owner—or a woman. "Besides," he continued, "I'm a good buyer, and they know it. I have a solid reputation in this town."

"I don't know how you buy, but I tend to go with my gut. I look at what calls out to me. Sounds odd, but that's how I go about it."

"And that's how I want you to do it. Let's face it. Men and women think differently, but I always try and please the woman first because she's a heavy influencer. Don't let anyone fool you. A man who doesn't pay attention to his wife's judgement, especially a sound one, is a fool himself."

Claire's eyes focused on George Parker's face. "Do you believe everything you say?"

His eyes snapped open wider. "I do believe it. I feel it in my bones, from the top of my head to the tips of my toes."

Claire laughed. "Good to know."

The worn leather chair squeaked as George got up and headed for a sturdy wooden file cabinet in the left corner behind his desk. He spent several minutes opening drawers, pulling out various catalogues, until he had twenty in his hands. "These should get you started."

"Get me started? You mean there's more in there?" Claire studied the file cabinet.

"There's several more in there, but I thought I'd go easy on you for starters." His eyes twinkled as he placed stack on one corner of his desk. "Take them home, look through them, see what you think. In the meantime, I want you to spend the next two days getting a feel for the store, the customers, the merchandise. Keep an eye on what goes on. We'll talk about what you think would be better as far as departments, how they should be set-up, that sort of thing." He nodded with enthusiasm, grinning. "Sound good? Too overwhelming?"

"No, not at all. I'm excited. I could only get involved so much in the hat making. Nothing like this." Her eyes shined with enthusiasm. "Are you sure you don't want someone more experienced, like Oma? She's been at this a while. I haven't."

"Nonsense." He waved her off. "When we married, Anita didn't have experience, either. But she had an eye for everything from the practical and utilitarian to the sublime. Experience colors our world up to a point, but it's that inner knowing that transcends all. It drives the choices you make and puts the final touches where you need it. You can't teach someone that. You're either wired with it or not."

She sat listening, captivated. His words. His expressions of truth as he viewed them. They tumbled from his mouth without effort, each enunciated word igniting from the energy with which they were delivered. These personal revelations hit at her core. They gave her a brief glimpse into his soul and the passion energizing it. The afternoon sun filled the office. The more she scrutinized him from across the desk, the more she found herself liking him.

He cut a striking figure whether he sat easily behind his desk, or paced the floor, mulling over a problem. Even when he ate, the way he held his utensils or a coffee cup, contained a certain sophistication, an old-school charm—basic good manners. His voice struck her ear like the actors on the big screen, crisp, clear, vibrant. The way he walked, the way he held his shoulders erect, all stemmed from one who comported themselves with confidence, like they owned the world. That was George, and his ways drew her to him, stronger, closer as each day passed.

In unison, each glanced at their watches. "I think our hour is up?" Claire smiled, her angling toward the stack of catalogs on the desk. "I won't forget those at the end of the day."

"Here, take this pen." He handed her a pen, along with a couple of sheets of paper. "Jot some notes down if you need to."

"Will do, sir." She saluted him with a smile and got up from the chair.

Oma greeted her from one of the racks of dresses. "Did you have a nice meeting with Mr. Parker? He was as good as his word. An hour on the nose." The usual polite smile crossed her lips.

"Oh, I hardly noticed." Claire glanced at her watch, feigning surprise. "Yes, he surely did. Right on time."

"I'll take my break now. Will you be comfortable by yourself with these departments?" Oma moved toward the aisle.

Claire motioned for her to go on. "I'll be fine. Leona can pitch in if I get too busy." She watched until Oma disappeared. Just how the older lady would react when she discovered Claire doing certain jobs filled her with a certain discomfort. First day on the job, and already the stage set for beating out a co-worker. At least she'd focus her mind on what George had instructed. She'd worry about Oma and the others later.

The day passed with Claire assisting several customers, including ringing them out at the register. That evening when the store closed, George dropped Claire off at her place, her arms carrying the prized stack of catalogues.

"Are you sure you won't have dinner with Anna and me? She'd love to see you."

Calling on every ounce of will to say no, Claire politely declined. "I'd love to see her too, but I hear these pages calling out to me." She patted the stack.

"I'll let you off the hook tonight, but you have to come one day this week."

"I promise. And give that sweet darling a hug for me." Opening the car door and stepping out, she smiled one last time.

George drove off, leaving Claire alone for the evening. After a light meal for dinner, she showered and settled in bed to review the stack of literature. Taking up each booklet, she familiarized herself with the companies, their products, descriptions, and prices. Way too much to memorize in one night, but she at least had an idea of what products were available. A good ending for her first day at work.

CHAPTER FOURTEEN

"You've been awfully busy back here. Haven't seen you on the floor all morning." Oma had slipped into the break room, Claire had not even glanced up when the door swooshed open.

"Huh?" She reluctantly turned her eyes away from her scattered papers, catching full force the look peering from a pair of silver-rimmed glasses focused on the table. "Surely you don't miss me out there. At least you get to wait on customers in peace, make some extra commission for yourself." Claire smiled at Oma, cringing inside when the lady returned a steely gaze in return.

Thursday had rolled around, and Claire remembered the expression of dismay clouding Oma's face Monday evening when she watched the catalogs leave the store. Tuesday and Wednesday had passed without any questions as to why those books left the store. Her absence from the sales floor, tucked back in a room where she labored over paperwork, had been too much for the poor lady.

"Mind me being nosy and asking what you're working on?" Oma, in a forced casual tone, pulled her sack lunch out of the refrigerator and sat down at the table.

Ugh, the dreaded question. "Oh, just some things that George . . . I mean, Mr. Parker asked me to do."

"I see." Oma kept her eyes steady on Claire as she inched out a parcel wrapped in aluminum foil. "Like what kinds of things? Will this mean some new changes for the store?"

Claire capped the fountain pen she'd been using, laying it easily on the table. She stood up and walked to the refrigerator, pulling out her own lunch before joining Oma.

"If you'd rather not say, or if Mr. Parker wants to keep it secret, I understand." The older lady took a dainty bite out of the corner of her sandwich. "Looks like it's pretty important if he's letting you use his best fountain pen."

"What do you do, watch him all the time? How do you know it's his best fountain pen?"

Oma's face pinked.

Claire's voice trailed down a few octaves. "Sorry, I didn't mean that to sound rude, but it just surprised me."

"I remember the day he received that pen. Anita ordered it for him for his birthday."

No use fighting this anymore, ducking and running whenever Oma looked like she might engage Claire in any long, meaningful conversation. Claire took a few breaths, steadying the whirl of thoughts in her head. She'd never quite put out of her mind the discussion with George the first afternoon in his office.

"Oma, the reason I'm not helping on the floor today is because I'm looking through these sales books. Tomorrow, I can help out a little, but I'll also be talking with everyone throughout the day about product lines they think would be good in this store. Basically, what should stay and what should go."

"He's letting you do that?" Oma's expression displayed sadness. She stared at the table, chewing longer on her food before swallowing.

"Look, I sense that something's bothering you. Let's talk about it for a minute, clear the air."

"I'm fine. I was just wondering, that's all." Oma managed a faint smile, eyes averted toward her lunch.

"Oma, look at me for a second. Please." Claire took a deep breath, hoping this would all go well.

The lady glanced up, lips pursed.

Claire continued. "You struck me from the first day as a responsible person. Of course, I think all of you seem like that. But you're not head clerk for nothing. You've got something on your mind, and I've been feeling it for the past few days."

Still Oma remained silent.

Claire rummaged up her coolest, negotiating voice, one she tried to use with Adrian at times before he abandoned her at Hatchie River. "What are your thoughts? What are you afraid might or might not happen?" Claire searched her co-worker's eyes. "I'm all ears. Let's figure out what we can do to make this store better and how we can work as a team."

"He's put you in charge, hasn't he?" The lady sat back in her chair.

Taken aback, Claire replied, "Well, no, he hasn't. Why do you think that? And is that what's been bothering you?"

Oma sat her lunch on the table, took off her glasses, and rubbed her eyes. Startled, Claire viewed the tears pooling there.

"Are you okay?"

"I've never said anything to anybody." Oma sniffed and dabbed her eyes with a napkin. "When Mrs. Parker died, I hoped that I could move up a little more in the store, help out Mr. Parker with this place like his wife." Oma displayed a half-hearted grin. "Don't worry. An old woman like me has no designs on him whatsoever. Here's the real reason I've been worried lately. I thought if I could help him with the business, it would stall him needing someone else on board to take his wife's place."

Claire stared at Oma. "Why on earth would you say that? What was wrong with Anita?" She sank back in her chair, intrigued. "And just for the record, I don't have designs on Mr. Parker, if that's what you and everybody are thinking."

"Of course not. I wasn't implying that you were, not that it's any of our business what you do or don't do." Oma frowned, waving off Claire's comment. Lowering her voice, eyes darting around the room, she continued, "She was—if you'll permit me—a little hellion. I didn't like her."

With an incredulous look on her face, Claire sat rooted to her seat, mouth opened in amazement. She didn't quite know what to say. Her co-worker was determined to have her say. Shamefully, Claire wanted to hear all the details. Not so much to engage in gossip, but to learn about her boss, neighbor, and more about his character.

"Mr. Parker adored her. Thought she could do no wrong. She'd come in here like she owned the place, which unfortunately she did in a way, and criticized everything we did, made snide comments about what we wore, ordered us around to do the most menial things at the worst times. She irritated customers. I know we lost business at times because of her." Oma hung her head. "I can't deal with another one like her. I'll quit and find something else to do with my life if I have to go through all that again."

Shaking her head, Claire gazed off a moment across the room. "To listen to George, he has her on quite a pedestal, like you said. Myself, I had always envisioned her as kind and gentle. Able to show good judgement and lead with a certain truth and strength about her."

"No. You are kind, and from what I've seen so far, you have good judgement and possible leadership qualities. Anita—never!" Oma enunciated her words, poking the top of Claire's hand gently for added emphasis.

"Oh, dear." Claire blinked a few times before eating a small bite of her food. She looked back at Oma. "You'll never have to worry about me bulldozing my way in. And I'm not his wife, so there's really no danger of anything."

Oma had returned her glasses to their proper place. Her face lightened up considerably. "Men are just fickle. That's all I can say."

Did she dare ask the question? Claire straightened up in her chair.

"Oma, did Mr. Parker marry Anita for any reason other than love? I mean, he's not one to have ulterior motives, is he?"

Wrinkling her brow, Oma sat back, swallowing another bite before speaking. "I don't think he has ulterior motives, like you say, but I do think he chooses people he thinks will be beneficial to him." She gazed at Claire. "I don't mean any of that in a bad way. I think we all make choices. And he's really a nice, honest man. He's been very kind to me."

"Are you married, Oma?"

"I'm a widow. Have been for ten years."

"Do you ever want to find someone else?" Claire maintained eye contact with her co-worker.

"Are you kidding?" Oma grimaced. "Heavens, no. I took care of my husband, loved him dearly, but I don't care about another one. There's a certain freedom in being alone. You can make your own decisions, you can have things your way most of the time, and nobody bothers you. Any company I need I get from work and church. That's plenty good enough for me."

The corners of Claire's mouth turned down as she raised her eyebrows, with more surprise than understanding. Though her experience with Adrian should have soured her desire for any man at this point, the major part of her longed for that old family unit again. She might gain the man one day, but gaining the child seemed elusive at best.

Oma spoke up after a long silence. "Claire, whatever happens, I'll stand behind you. Other than keeping my sanity, I still thought it would be kind of fun to get more involved in the store. I enjoy learning about different parts of the business. The truth is, I adore retail. I love coming in every day, waiting on people, learning their likes, dislikes, getting to know them. There's a personal satisfaction I get from making the sale, making someone happy."

"And you know what, Oma, you'll still get to do those things. We'll do them together, and the others on the floor will help. This will be an even better department store than before."

The mood had lifted, and Claire breathed an inward sigh of relief. Thank goodness this had all been settled. No more walking on tiptoes. The two women finished their lunches and Oma excused herself. Claire tossed her lunch sack away and returned to working on her sheets, her eyes roaming over the titled pages filled with page numbers, names of items, and catalog item codes. Glancing at the stack of remaining catalogs, she grinned and shook her head, relieved at the conversation between her and Oma.

She'd only reviewed three of them, studying each page, taking notes, check-marking items she thought would be good, starring others requiring more thought. Oma's advice might be good for those. As she considered certain products, her mind often strayed back to looming. As she rifled through the stack of books, she spied the catalogue containing the looms. She opened the pages and read through the descriptions beneath certain models that struck her fancy.

Had George ever considered carrying these in the store? And why? Was there a solid customer base for this type of item? She knew one thing. Owning her own loom again would definitely make her happy. Saving up the money to purchase one would prove a daunting challenge. There was probably no way Mitchell could sneak hers out of the house, and getting it here to Knoxville would be expensive. Even in Adrian's wild state, he'd surely miss a huge item like that. Then there were the colorful threads to choose from. For a few minutes, she daydreamed about seeing her towels, runners, and maybe even a tablecloth lining a shelf in the linens section of the store. Maybe she could add some small wraps for covering up when in bed or sitting outside on a porch when the weather got cool.

For another few hours, she spent lording over the books, making notations on new sheets of paper. Leona and Ruby came in for their breaks, and she answered their questions like she had with Oma.

"I think what you're doing is a great idea." Ruby smiled, glancing over at the catalogs with interest. When Leona left, she remained at the table with Claire. "We'll be glad to help too. You'll find we're not shy about giving our opinion." Ruby sat, eying Claire with some consideration.

"What? Why are you just staring at me like that?" Claire looked up, hand poised over her sheets.

"Since you've come to work here, Mr. Parker looks like he's fairly floating on air."

"Oh?"

"I hear you live down the street from him. Do you see much of each other?" Ruby asked the question with no consideration for propriety.

Claire's cheeks warmed. "He owns the house I'm renting from him. Very good landlord. He doesn't pry or get snoopy in my business, if that's what you're asking." Her lips spread into an obligatory grin as she blinked a few times, staring hard into Ruby's face.

Ruby's eyes narrowed as she nodded her head lightly, taking in every word. "That little girl of his needs a good mother."

It was Claire's turn to nod. "Yes. Won't debate you there." She turned back to her papers, scrawling a few numbers across the line.

"Have you met her? His daughter?" Ruby poured some tea from her thermos. "I don't think Anita was all that great of a mother."

"Mmm." Claire kept her eyes on the page.

Ruby ran her fingers threw her hair and stretched a little in her chair, eyes now focused on the sheets of paper. "She'd bring that little girl here to the store sometimes, on the days she came in to work, if you want to call it that. I swear, she was just short-tempered with her. That woman had no business having kids."

Dropping George's "best fountain pen" onto the table, Claire lifted her head and gazed at Ruby. "Was she as bad as all that?"

"Did Oma give you her bit?" Ruby eyes held a determined glint.

The way her lips parted as she gazed at Claire with curiosity gave her an almost sultry look. Too pretty to be in a department store peddling sewing machines. And why on earth had George not tried his luck with her? Claire shook her head, tapping the table with the tips of her fingers. "I'm not sure why, but I've heard more about Mr. Parker's wife today. It's almost like I'm hearing that a witch has gone."

"I think that little song in The Wizard of Oz sums it up pretty good." Ruby's lips turned into a smile, lighting up her face even more.

Grimacing, Claire picked up the pen again. "Far be it for me to judge, but isn't that a bit harsh? Mr. Parker thought an awful lot of her. She couldn't have been that bad."

"I suspect Oma gave you her two cents worth on that too."

"Oma didn't go into detail, but said she thought very highly of him."

"'What a pretty thing man is when he goes in his doublet and hose and leaves off his wit.'" Ruby fluttered her lashes.

"Excuse me?" Claire's eyes grew wide.

Ruby fell back in her chair, her face glowing with satisfaction. "Shakespeare, Much Ado About Nothing. Act five, scene one."

"And that's supposed to mean . . . ?"

"Look, Anita was an attractive woman. She didn't come from much, but she educated herself in the art of wooing a good man. I think she knew if she wanted anything in life, she had to act the part to get what she wanted. He fell for her like a silly schoolboy."

"George seems like . . . Mr. Parker seems like a very nice man from what I've experienced so far. If he wants to think he was happy with her, what harm is it? Anita's gone, so it really doesn't matter anymore, does it?" Claire forced a light smile, hoping the curt tone in her voice didn't seem too emotional.

Ruby yawned. "I suppose you're right. Besides, Mr. Parker is harmless. I just hate to see nice people taken advantage of. That's all."

"Ruby, I'll just get right to the point. Not meaning to sound rude, but I'm pretty sure all of you have chatted when I'm not around. It's obvious to me. From what I've heard, who could blame you? Strange gal in town, owner seems more cheerful than usual, lost one undesirable person only to think you may have another right behind her—"

"Oh, no, Claire. Not at all." Ruby's face clouded as she gently held Claire's wrist. "I didn't mean any of what I said to be taken—"

"I know exactly what you mean. And you, Oma, and all the rest out there are saying the same thing. I'm not stupid. I know human nature and how it goes. Trust me on that one, sister." Claire mentally chided herself for getting riled. She inhaled a deep breath before continuing. "I didn't come here to create trouble, fight with people, or try to get into a man's . . ."

"So why did you come here, Claire? You've really said very little about yourself since you've started. I'm not gonna lie. The mystery is killing us." Ruby did that head tilt again.

"You're pretty bold, aren't you Ruby?" Claire mimicked her coworker's expression.

"I think you are too." Ruby's voice remained calm and even, her expression almost blank. "Again, don't take that to mean a bad thing. I watch and listen to the way you talk, the way you carry yourself, the way you handle customers. You're a woman who's sure of herself." Ruby's eyes glittered. "Tell me, then. What brought you to town?"

Under the table, Claire clenched a fist in one last attempt to keep herself grounded without going off. "Let's just say sometimes a woman needs a change of pace, and I'll leave it at that."

"Point taken." Ruby gave a sign of resignation and scooted back the chair, wincing at the loud screeches from the legs grating against the floor. "Again, I'm not here to fight you, either, Claire. But I'm with Oma and the others on this one. I'm hoping to god the atmosphere in this store stays calm and happy. There will either be mutiny or we're all simply walking out."

"Honestly, Ruby, none of you scare me. I've known true fear." Claire relaxed the muscles in her face, staring hard at her co-worker. Her tone rang out just as even and steely as Ruby's.

"Oh, I'm not trying to scare you. I just thought it might be helpful for all of us if you understood a little history and what it was like before you came. And I'll add this." Ruby patted Claire on the shoulder. "If you can land Mr. Parker, more power to you."

"Have you tried?" Claire didn't flinch. Deep inside, she couldn't resist.

Ruby, merely laughed. "Touché. Let's just say Mr. Parker wants a certain type of woman, and as you say, 'we'll leave it at that.'"

"Let's just say, too, that I have no intention of having history repeat itself. I think you'll find we all have the same goal on this subject."

"Not to worry, Claire. I think we've cleared the air. That's a good thing, don't you think?"

Ruby didn't wait for an answer, but left Claire watching while she placed her lunch box on the shelf and sailed out of the break room. Claire let out a long sigh. At least she gave Ruby some credit for calling out the hand. The ice was finally broken, for better or for worse. No more secrets, but then still the secrets. She and Ruby had either squared off or squared things away for now. With any luck, she might make it through the rest of the day with no confrontation. The men kept to themselves, so hopefully there was no danger with them. Now she understood the frustrations of working with other people every day. The gossip, the opinions, the nosing and prying into personal affairs. When it came to George, she knew Oma was no problem for her at all. Ruby was another story. Ruby possessed the looks, but it seemed he'd dismissed her with any such notions.

What startled her was the fact that her mind had lately turned to comparing herself with the other women in the store, and how they might garner George's attention. Had she fallen into the same trap of using looks and charm to attract a good man, as Ruby had alluded to Anita earlier? She remembered turning up the best side of herself when she and Adrian had first met, but never considered needing to up her station in life. And she knew coming into George's life hung on the thread of mere circumstances and nothing more.

She and Adrian had been more equally yoked in beliefs and social standing. Whether or not she wanted to admit it, she and George fell into the same category. George was merely another version of Adrian, but with his wits about him. And Anna. What a precious little girl. She did need a good mother, whomever that might be, if George felt inclined to see to it that Anna ever had another mother. Too much to think about now. She'd just arrived in town, alone, scared, few supports in place. She couldn't think about all this right now. It all overwhelmed her. Take it one day at a time. Don't rush for anything, and do keep your wits about you. Claire scribbled a few more items onto the page before placing everything into a paper sack and heading back to the floor. Maybe waiting on customers would bring her outside herself and off such intense matters of the head and heart.

✲✲✲

The bonfire rattled and shifted, sending fiery embers floating up to a greying sky tinged with the lightest pink-orange at the edges. Claire watched with mild interest as the burning bits drifted, dying and scattering into oblivion on a light, cool breeze. She stretched her bare toes closer to the heat, enjoying the warmth as the sound of the Holston River lapped, lapped, lapped at the bank below. Anna sat next to her playing with Lulabelle, hosting the most formal tea party, complete with a small child's porcelain tea set resting between them. Claire had poured real tea into the teapot and created some tiny cucumber finger sandwiches to add a flair of realism. Anna helped Lulabelle with an imaginary sip from a dainty teacup, placing it back on the saucer when she thought her imaginary guest had enough.

George sat on the other side of the fire, making himself handy with a skewer, loading on three marshmallows. Beside him on a flat rock were six graham crackers, with three holding a square of chocolate. He grinned at Claire.

"I'll roast these and that'll finish up everything." He held the skewer over the fire, turning slowly and methodically over a flame. When the fire lapped at the sweets bundles, catching them on fire, he withdrew them, blowing hard before they turned into nothing more than black, burnt inedible mush. "There's a system to getting these right." He removed the marshmallows with great care, landing each one on top of a chocolate square and topping off with a cracker. "Here we go." Claire reached out for one, handing it off to Anna who, as if on cue, took it carefully in her small hands.

"Careful, sweetheart, it's still hot." Claire helped Anna steady the confection, holding her hand lightly underneath, lest the little girl drop it. When Anna gained control, clutching the treat and nibbling on a corner, Claire turned back to George.

"And for you, my good lady. Never will such a delicate morsel be touched by fairer lips than yours." His voice took on an actor's brogue. He could have been a lover right out of a movie, and this scene depicting his care and devotion.

"I love these things, but three's enough for one person, don't you think?" She laughed, drowning in the sight of him, while her ears filled with the ambient sounds of the river, a crackling fire, and Anna's soft girlish chatter. It all lulled her into a feeling of oneness with the present moment. She loved the crispness of the early October air. It waved goodbye to the sultry heat of summer, leaving behind lush green for the fanfare of brilliant oranges, yellows, and reds of autumn. What would the days bring? Hayrides? Where would Anna go trick-or-treating? She had to dress up and go out. All kids her age did.

"Daddy, are you going to tell me and Lulabelle some stories?" Anna grasped her doll and made her way onto Claire's lap.

"I don't think Miss Claire wants to hold you. Why don't you come sit by me, right here on this rock?"

"No, I want to be with Miss Claire." Anna's little voice wailed, and she turned her head up, giving the most pitiable expression she could muster. "Can I, Miss Claire?"

"There's one marshmallow left, honey. Don't you want to sit by me, and I'll roast it for you?" George's coaxing may have convinced Claire, but it didn't budge Anna.

The little girl leaned back, tugging at Claire's skirt. "Please, Miss Claire."

"Of course you can, darling." Claire wrapped her arms around Anna, holding her close. When the little girl rested her head against Claire's shoulder, a flashing memory of her baby boy nearly sent her reeling. She blinked her eyes a few times and breathed in. No thinking about that right now and spoiling the mood. It was Friday night after another long week of work. She had all weekend to mourn if she wanted, but not now with George and Anna, who both acted like a balm to her injured spirit.

"Tell me the story about Brer Rabbit." Anna giggled.

For the next hour, George recited a couple of tales from Uncle Remus and some others that Claire had never heard of before, especially a story from the Philippines, about a monkey who turned back into a prince when he heard the declarations of love from a beautiful girl with whom he'd become enamored. Claire enjoyed the stories, but she loved holding Anna most of all. This sweet, innocent girl who definitely missed something or someone in her life.

She glimpsed the expression of wonder in Anna's eyes as they stared up at her or watched intently as she baked or peeled vegetables. Only last week George had come over, Anna in tow, and Claire had prepared a simple meal. It was the least she could do after George insisted she dine with them at their house. Since her arrival, Claire determined that she'd eaten more in their company than alone.

"She's either tired, or I bored her." George chuckled. He'd finished the last story as Anna lay sleeping, her hands still clutching her doll. "I think it's bedtime for her." He got up and lifted his daughter into his arms. Claire doused the flames with a stick, stirring dirt into the last smoldering remnants of the fire.

"We'll have to do this again a few more times before it gets really cold." Claire slipped on her shoes and wrapped a sweater around her shoulders.

"That sounds like fun to me. I love being near the water. It's so peaceful."

All three headed in silence toward the house. George placed Anna gently inside his car and closed the passenger's door. He turned to Claire. "You're really good with her, you know that?"

"She doesn't bother me in the least." Claire smiled up at George, admiring how the light of the full moon illuminated his features, how the breezed rustled his hair. He stood so close she felt the heat from his body warming hers. The touch of his hand on her shoulder quickened her pulse.

"Thank you for all your hard work. I know that was a lot to dump on a new person who's just come to town, and who's been through so much."

Claire didn't flinch, not wanting him to remove his hand. "You haven't dumped anything on me. I'm more than excited about learning the store and what works to bring customers back. You've got a great business. I want to see you keep it around for generations longer."

George stared off at the moon, his hand falling away back down to his side. "I want that too, Claire. I want that too." He opened the car door, sliding easily behind the wheel. The engine started with the turn of the key, and Claire stepped away, waving her hand as they moved out of the driveway and on down the road to their house. She turned and walked back inside. How odd it seemed to her, so close, yet so far away. Two people sleeping alone, and both not more than a mile from each other. What would it be like sharing a bed with George? She forced her mind away from such thoughts. As much as she hated to admit it, she found herself thinking them more as each day passed.

She went to the kitchen and poured herself a cup of tea, carrying it back to the living room where she sipped it alone on the sofa. Claire spent the time now thinking about her baby boy, so far away, with no one near to love him. Would he have loved a bonfire and roasting marshmallows, or would he be trying desperately to scramble down the bank and into the river, drumming up mischief like most boys do? Did Adrian still wonder what happened to her after her escape? Wonder if she were even still alive? Claire didn't like believing that at this point, him not thinking of her may be a good thing. Mitchell hadn't called since he left. Maybe that was a good thing, too. Life marched on; her life marched on, never tarrying despite changes, passage of days, and the seasons that slipped one into the other without a care.

After the last drops of tea, Claire ended the night reviewing some more of the catalogs before she turned out the lights. If only she could get up enough money to buy a loom. Maybe she could teach Anna, and perhaps make a blanket for Lulabelle. Chuckling, Claire entertained herself another two hours reading before falling into a deep sleep.

CHAPTER FIFTEEN

Claire wiped her hands on a towel, tossing it on the counter beside a bowl of fresh cut vegetables. Another series of loud knocks sounded before she grasped the knob and flung the front door wide open. There stood George, all smiles, cuddling a tiny kitten in his hands. Beside him stood Anna who held another in her little grasp. Her eyes sparkled as she held out the furry bundle to Claire, whose mouth dropped open in surprise.

"We got you some kittens, Miss Claire!" Anna squealed with delight, bouncing up and down on her feet while Claire took the animal in her own hands.

"You too?" She looked over at George, one eyebrow raised.

"Of course. I can't let Anna out-do me. Besides, two's company. Um, can we come in?"

"Absolutely. Gosh, what was I thinking?" Laughing, Claire stepped aside while father and daughter passed through into the living room.

"Did we really disturb you? I usually don't just show up un-announced." George turned his attention to the other kitten, delivering a few cooing words of comfort and some finger strokes over its head.

"I was just in the kitchen making some salad for lunch. Would you two like to join me?" Anna, meantime, reached up, petting Claire's kitty on the head.

"This one's Buzzie, and the other is Moo," said Anna. "I named them. Moo looks like a cow."

"Hmm." Claire took note of the kitten in George's hands, admitting that its black and white fur resembled the markings of the cows they'd seen in the fields. "And why did you name this one Buzzie, sweetheart?"

"Because." Anna jumped up and down a few times with excitement. "He looks like a Buzzie." She ran around the room, arms outstretched, making some buzzing noises. Claire admired the markings of Moo's friend, a white kitten covered with what looked like recessive tortie markings.

George chuckled. "She's got an imagination, doesn't she?"

"Where did you find these?" Claire inched closer to George, shaking her head lightly and mumbling some baby-talk words while the little kitten's purrs floated to her ear. "They are darling."

"It's Saturday. Anna and I went to the farmer's market, and some kid and his mom were sitting on a corner. Didn't look like they had two nickels to rub together. They had some sad looking tomatoes to sell and a few spindly carrots. I guess they were selling the kittens for some extra cash. My heart always go out to people trying to survive."

"Oh, dear, George. Can I give you some money just to pay you back?" Claire stared up at George, stunned.

"I wouldn't dream of it. Besides, life treats me pretty good. I believe in giving back and helping your fellow man." George glanced around. "Let's just put them down here and let you get back to your lunch. Or would you want them out in the back yard?"

"And let them wander off or fall and drown in the river?" Claire shook her head, horrified. "They'll be fine right here. We'll have to be careful and not step on them." She motioned for Anna and George to follow her into the kitchen. "I'll finish the salad, make us some sandwiches, and we'll have lunch."

"Can't I stay and play with Buzzie and Moo? I think they need a babysitter." Anna entwined her hands in Claire's.

"Of course you can, darling. You'll have to eat when we're ready, though." Claire stooped down, stroking the little girl's curls.

"I'll come. I'll be real good if you let me stay with the kitties."

Claire smiled, lightly catching George by the sleeve and guiding him into the kitchen, where he sat easily on one of the chairs at the tiny table in front of the window.

"Farmers market, eh? You got an early start this morning." She picked up her knife and finished cutting up a celery stalk.

"I like to get my produce when it's fresh. Get up late and all you'll get are scraps." George stood up, stretched his arms, and walked over to the counter. "Can I make some coffee? I ran out this morning without having my usual cup or two." He rustled through the cabinets as if he did it here in this house every day. Claire pointed to a cabinet holding the coffee. From a lower cabinet, she removed the glass Chemex coffeemaker.

Both worked in easy silence. While George boiled water, Claire finished the salad and started on the sandwiches. She liked the feel of this moment, him making himself at home and Anna playing quietly in the living room. Coming over on weekends as of late had become a habit of his, one she wouldn't break. After the first week of using the car for work, they did what many people did and rode in together on the trolley every morning and came home together each night. Sometimes, she made a quick dinner so he could rest a little before walking on home. A neighbor down the road from his house helped with taking care of Anna until he got home. The days were getting shorter, and he'd already discussed taking the car again so they wouldn't have to walk to and from the trolley stop in the dark.

He'd spoken of these arrangements with such a casual air, basically stating each plan, assuming she'd have no problem with any of it. On the weekends, Anna stole away and played jacks on the porch while Claire sat in one of the rocking chairs and read or engrossed herself in some embroidery. The days passed with bright blue skies or somber grey clouds, slipping into chilly nights that left a breath of frost on the ground. The leaves had truly lived up to their role as announcers of fall, trading in rich greens for golds and reds. Every day that passed left memories of Hatchie River and Ash Grove a little more blurry and dimmer than before.

Mitchell had finally called a couple of times to check on her. Adrian was holding on somewhat to his wits, having days that were somewhat normal, while other days found him a little disheveled and with duller mind. "You just don't know. Every day is a surprise," Mitchell had told her during their last talk.

The staff at the asylum apparently gave up on ever finding out how hateful Grace died. At first, Claire had nightmares about Grace, those devil eyes glowing as she sensed ice cold water splashing up all around her, trapped with no chance of escape. Sometimes she dreamt that it was her being led to the shed by powerful, smelly men with leers pasted on their lips. Just when they'd locked the door and force her legs apart, she awoke drenched in sweat. But those horrid dreams were fading too, though she still thought often of the others, especially Ruth and Millie.

"You look like you're miles away from here."

Claire lifted her head, seeing George standing close. Had he been watching her all this time while the water boiled and after he'd poured himself a cup of coffee? "I guess cooking sends me into a tranquil state. I always did enjoy it for that reason."

George poured her a cup of coffee and handed it to her. "Old man Hyde is having a hayride in two weeks. He lives out farther from here."

"Oh? A hayride sounds like fun." Claire added some vinegar, oil, salt and pepper, and tossed the salad with a large spoon.

"He has some acreage, and every year for the past three years, he holds a big party and invites different people. His farm is perfect for these events. People bring food, we eat, talk, the kids play. We all have a big time of it."

"And Anna enjoys it, too, I imagine."

"Yeah." George chuckled. "She loves playing with the other kids, especially since she doesn't have any brothers and sisters."

"Does she get along well with them? I know sometimes children without siblings have a harder time playing with others, if you know what I mean." From the refrigerator, Claire pulled out more items and started making some sandwiches.

"She does better than you'd think. A pretty generous soul, she is. I'll give her that much."

Before she could stop herself, Claire blurted out, "Where does she get her good nature, you think?"

George leaned against the counter, eyes turned up in thought. He shook his head and took a quick sip of coffee. "I don't know," he said softly.

Unable to resist, she continued, "Oh, come on, I bet she takes after Anita. As nice as you are and with your success, I bet she was charming and had a sparkling personality. I can almost see her in my mind's eye." Claire smiled over at him and finished loading the sandwiches on plates.

The expression on George's face had clouded. In the depths of his eyes, she detected deep sorrow, perhaps some hidden regrets he'd kept to himself.

"George, I didn't mean to get anything started. Really, I didn't." Claire placed her hand on the top of his arm. "I was just wondering, that's all."

"No, you're okay. You see, nobody really understood Anita like I did. She was kind of hard to read sometimes. Came from a humble background, but what I admired about her was the fact she rose above it all, conducted herself like a queen. It was like she knew having more in life was her birthright and somehow she'd been cheated at first." George shook his head, chuckling. "She wasn't having anything but the best."

Claire stood transfixed, ears taking in every word.

"I was only too glad to see that she got all she wanted. I enjoyed spoiling her, making her feel special. The only downside is that she sometimes let it go to her head, and people didn't like it, of course." He turned to Claire, peering into her eyes. "I know the staff at the store didn't like her. People think I don't hear things, but I do."

"Did she love Anna?" Deep inside Claire cringed, but at this point, she really wanted to know. From the moment Oma shined a glaring light on the subject of Anita, she wanted to hear George's side of the story. No better a time to find out than now.

He tapped a finger against his cup, lips pursed together. "Hate like the devil to admit it, but I think having children cramped her style. It took the attention away from her, hindered her from the freedom she enjoyed." George warmed his cup with a little more coffee from the Chemex and stared out the window a few minutes.

In silence Claire placed the sandwiches on the plate.

"But I liked Anita's boldness, her overall sense of judgement, and her impeccable taste in things. She was a perfectionist too. Just because someone's not cut out all that great for kids doesn't mean they have no merit in my life."

"And you? Did you want more kids?"

"Sure. That's what we do. We grow up, start making it on our own, and have our own families. It's human tradition, I think." He placed his cup in the sink. "Besides, having Anna around has pulled me outside myself, keeps me on the straight and narrow and makes me think about things before I do them. She always keeps me questioning, keeps me creative."

"I've always wanted children." Claire carried the plates to the table. "I do think they keep you on your toes."

"You think you'll ever try again if you get the chance, Claire? It's a personal question, I know, but I was just wondering." George seated himself at the table again while Claire gathered silverware and napkins.

"If I ever get the chance again, I don't see why not. I don't give up easily, as you can probably guess."

"Good for you. Never give up. No matter what."

Claire filled some glasses with lemonade and called Anna into the kitchen. The little table barely held the three of them, and Anna had to make do sitting on a tiny kitchen stool. That didn't matter today to Claire. She wanted cozy, intimate, a chance to almost feel the heat from her companions. She wanted to enjoy Anna's curls and admire the sheen up close. She wanted to gaze deeper into George's face without being too obtrusive.

"The kitties are asleep," Anna announced. "I petted them until they were sleepy. Their eyes went like this . . ." She narrowed her eyes into slits, tilting her head a little to the side. "And then they went like this . . ." Anna produced her best rendition of a cat purring.

"You're a good little mommy, darling. That's just what those little sweeties needed, a good nap." Claire rubbed Anna's shoulder while the little girl beamed up at her with pride.

"Can I come see them anytime I want, Miss Claire?" The blue in Anna's eyes shimmered. Claire wanted to dive into those two deep pools of blue and lose herself for a while in the realm of make-believe where all children dwelled before maturity snatched them away unwittingly in its gnarly, sneaky clutches.

"Of course you can, dear. If daddy says it's okay, then you can come."

George's gaze burned into her as she uttered her last words. Claire glanced down at her food, trying to squelch the wave of embarrassment washing over her. If daddy says it's okay. Couldn't she just as easily have said, 'If your father says it's okay?'" It all just slipped out. Truly it did. The subject of Anita, she'd egged on. She'd own that one. The rest, not so much. She definitely needed to put more thought into what she said, especially when asking and answering questions. Life had taught her that there were two sides to every story, and sometimes stating what was on your mind wasn't always bad, especially if it didn't get you killed. If she pinpointed any weaknesses in herself, dying of curiosity and testing the waters rated high on the list. Maybe she, Ruby, and the others at the store shared more commonalities than not.

The remainder of lunch continued with normal chit chat. At times,

Anna chimed in with questions not relating to anything in particular. At the very end, George asked a peculiar question.

"Claire, do you need three bedrooms here?"

***

Finally, it was all finished. She'd set everything up to her specifications, attaching parts and pieces in all the right places. Anna sat next to her, sorting through all colors of thread, running her fingers and crying out, "Look at this one, Miss Claire." She held up a bundle of scarlet threads, gently pulling them apart just to watch them fall back into place again.

"It's beautiful, isn't it, Anna?" Claire stepped back, admiring the loom that had taken up residence in the bedroom beside the staircase. Hardly believing she possessed one, she kept touching it here and there just to make sure it was real and wouldn't vanish before her eyes. Another Saturday had rolled around, and George had surprised her early this morning with this treasure.

"You like it?" George stood in the doorway grinning.

"You really shouldn't have. It's too much. You can take the cost of it out of my wages. That's only fair." Claire fingered one of the heddles.

"I'll do nothing of the kind. Besides, you're supposed to make some pieces for the store. I'm holding you to that, you know."

"Let's make something, Miss Claire." Anna held out four bundles of threads, waving them in front of her. "These colors are pretty."

"They are pretty." Claire took the bundles. "Do you want me to show you how they go?"

"Yes, yes, yes." The little girl clapped and walked up close to the loom, inspecting everything. "This looks awfully hard."

"Oh, sweetheart, can you please get the little kitties out of the boxes?" Claire had meant the request for Anna, but George stepped into the room and headed toward the boxes. "Come here, you little buggers. We don't need your two cents worth in here." He scooped up the two cats. "I'll take them downstairs. Have fun up here. I'm going on home." Turning to Claire, he added, "When you two are done, why don't you come over for dinner? My new housekeeper has a nice spread fixed for tonight."

"Edna? She seems like she's working out nicely for you. And for Anna." Claire wrapped her arm around the little body that had surrounded her waist with loving arms.

"She's not a nice as you, Miss Claire." Anna mumbled the words as she buried her face in Claire's apron.

"Anna, surely don't mean that. I'm sure poor Edna loves you dearly." Claire scolded gently, tousling the mound of blonde curls shaking back and forth.

"Does she love me more than you?" Anna looked up with imploring eyes. Claire swore she saw those pink lips tremble.

"Anna, Miss Claire and Miss Edna both love you. How's that for lots of love? And daddy loves you even more." George's eyes darted from Claire to Anna.

"I agree with daddy, little sweet one." Ugh, she'd done it again. Claire took in a deep breath, refusing to look George in the eye. "You've got lots of love. Such a lucky girl."

"Can Miss Claire spend the night? She and I can have a party with Lulabelle."

"Darling, I can't spend the night, but you know what, after church tomorrow, you can bring Lulabelle over and we'll have a bonfire by the river."

"Can we, Daddy?" Anna peeked up, face brightening.

"Of course we can, honey." George, still holding two cats that were struggling to get away, moved toward the stairs. "See you later, Claire."

His steps faded as he made his way down. A few minutes later, the front door closed. Claire spent the next four hours showing Anna how to set up the threads in the loom and how she worked the peddle and threads. Using the colors Anna had picked out, she began looming a small hand towel. Anna watched with fascination as the body of the towel grew longer.

"That's pretty, Miss Claire." Anna gently touched the piece.

"And you know what, precious? Mommy . . . I mean, I'll make a nice blanket for Lulabelle. How would you like that?"

Anna stepped back, surprised. "Yes."

Claire caught a view of Anna's face, her gaze wide with wonder. What was going on inside that little head of hers? Oh, if Anna could only stay with her, they'd have so much fun. They'd work the loom, bake cookies. Anna could play jacks on the porch, and they'd walk on the bank of the river and watch the barges glide slowly over the glassy currents. And she could play with Buzzie and Moo. If only.

✷✷✷

"Good afternoon, Mrs. Wright." Edna, a portly woman with silvery hair slipped back into a tight bun and dressed in a grey cotton housekeepers uniform, held the door wide open, allowing Claire and Anna to pass in side. During their walk, Anna had held tightly onto her hand the entire time, chattering away about the loom, the cats, asking questions about why the cows weren't out today, and the most important questions, how many more days before the hayride and what would she wear for Halloween. Claire answered absently, thinking more about what a beautiful day it was, how grateful she was to have a loom again, and how she'd get to spend more time with George as well as Anna tonight.

The smells from the kitchen wafted out, filling the house with the scent of pan-fried chicken, green beans, mashed potatoes, cornbread, and fried okra.

"And I've made apple dumplings for dessert." Edna smiled proudly.

"Apple dumplings? How fancy." Claire winked an eye of approval. "And why those?"

Edna stifled a laugh and glanced around to see if anyone else was around. "Anna loves Uncle Wiggily, the children's story. She also has the game, which we play all the time. Uncle Wiggily, a long-eared rabbit gentleman, has a muskrat lady housekeeper who makes him apple dumplings as a treat. She likes to think I'm Nurse Jane Fuzzy Wuzzy, and begs me to make her apple dumplings."

Claire snickered. "How cute. And how sweet of you to make them. I've heard of them, but I've never eaten any."

"Mine are really good. I use lots of cinnamon, and I boil the syrup down where it's thicker and goes over the dumpling much nicer without making them soggy." Edna laughed. "I'm pretty sure my apple dumplings would beat out Nurse Jane Fuzzy Wuzzy's any day."

The ladies' laughter drew George from the hallway.

"I'm missing out on something good. Do tell." He came up to Claire, wrapping an arm around her in a snug embrace. Edna looked on with no hint of emotion.

"Mr. Parker, I'm going back to the kitchen and finish dinner. The table is already set in the dining room." The older lady nodded politely at Claire and soon disappeared inside the kitchen.

"She insisted that we eat in a more formal location." George shook his head. "You didn't mind the kitchen, did you?"

Laughing, Claire leaned her head against his shoulder for a moment. "I'm happy anywhere you and Anna are." Within seconds, she stood up straight and pulled lightly away. His eyes stayed on her. The expression on his face showed one in a brief but far-off reverie. George's arm slid away, resting once again down at his side.

"Let's sit for a while until Edna says we're ready." He gestured toward the couch.

"Sounds good to me. And Anna?"

"She's already playing in her room. I told her to wash up and be ready for dinner when she's called."

Claire selected a spot on the couch, George settling down beside her. She saw his hand waver at little, as if he might land it on top of hers. She desperately needed to talk to Mitchell about what to do concerning her marriage to Adrian. A new life awaited her, along with people she'd grown to care about, even in such a short time.

George's hand inched closer to hers. "I'm so glad you're eating with us tonight. It's always so much nicer when we do this together." His eyes lit up.

"Me to. And having Edna around adds more warmth. I like her. She seems so nice, George."

"Did you and Anna have a go at the loom? I really wanted it to be a surprise."

"You surprised me all right. And yes, I've showed Anna how to work it."

"George?" Claire's hand trailed over to his knee. "Do you have a sewing machine?"

"I have the one Anita used. I'd always thought I could at least hire someone to come in and use it, or maybe sell it. Why?"

"No, don't get rid of it. I was thinking about making Anna a Halloween outfit."

His lips spread into a wide smile. "You don't say. That would be a great idea. Have anything in mind?"

"I'm not sure yet. I'll have to see what she wants." Claire look up at him. "I wouldn't be in your way, would I? And I'm pretty fast."

"You are welcome here anytime you want. Anna will be thrilled."

"Good, then it's settled. I'll make her something fun."

Edna gave the notice that dinner was served, and then went off to tell Anna to come to the table. The plates had been filled and the candles burning. No amount of coaxing changed Edna's mind about staying in the kitchen while everyone else dined together. "I know my place, sir, but thank you for asking." She smiled and left the dining room.

CHAPTER SIXTEEN

"Does anyone have any questions? Do we think we've covered everything?" Claire stacked the catalogs neatly on the table.

It was six-thirty in the evening. Everyone had gathered in the break room, agreeing to stay over this night. Claire made sure each one had a say on what they thought should stay on the shelves or go.

Leona spoke up. "I think we've gone through everything with a fine-toothed comb. I like our decisions, but it's all a big gamble like retail always is."

"What do we do next? Run a big sale before we get the new goods in?" Jack raised his hand for attention. "I'm just wondering, how many customers we'll get with all the news on the radio and in the papers."

"Until we're in this war, we keep on like we've been doing. We won't know until we try." It was Oma who interjected. "Keeping stale merchandise doesn't mean anything, either. I say do what you can now, and we'll regroup again later if we have to."

"Smart idea, Oma." Claire nodded in approval. "Who wants to pick a sale day?"

Minnie raised her hand. "I say let's do it the last week of the month. It'll clear out things so we can make way for Christmas."

"Anybody opposed?" Claire scanned the group. "Fine, we'll tell Mr. Parker so he can let the newspaper know. We've got another week left and then that's it for October."

Everyone shook their heads.

"Sounds like we've picked a week for running a sale." Ruby's voice rang out. "And while we're all here, how many are going to Mr. Hyde's party?" A murmur from the group indicated that each person had been invited and they were intent on coming.

"You going with Mr. Parker, Claire?" Ruby's lips twisted up into a half smile. Her eyes had narrowed just a little as she waited for an answer. Oma's quick kick of admonition against Ruby's foot didn't escape Claire's quick eye.

Claire lightly cleared her throat. "Well, Ruby, since you'll be there, too, why don't I just let you find out for yourself?" She took a moment, making brief eye contact with each co-worker. "And I think that goes for the rest of you who are dying to know."

Roy and Jack turned their faces to the floor. Oma sat wide-eyed in her seat, staring straight ahead. The women turned their heads just enough to cast quick glances at each other. Dahlia's nerves escalated to such a point, she chewed on a hangnail, eyelashes fluttering more rapidly than usual. Joy twiddled her thumbs.

Finally, Roy broke the silence. "Aw, look, Claire, I may be a man, but we'd all like to get to know you a little bit better, where you came from and what made you pick Knoxville. It's sort of a getting-to-know-you thing. We don't mean any harm."

Ruby piped up, "Claire and I broached this subject the other day. We'd have talked more, but we had to get back to work." Ruby faced her co-worker head-on. "Claire, isn't there anything you can share with us? I mean, the way you've been so tight-lipped, it makes us wonder if you didn't kill somebody and run away." She shrugged, chuckling. The others perked their heads up.

Claire clenched her teeth, scrambling hard for a story. "Rest assured, I didn't kill anyone. I left West Tennessee in search of a new beginning. I've had some personal changes in my life that were unexpected, and I thought a bigger city in another location would do the trick, get me on a different path in life."

"Weren't you ever married? Did you just up and leave all your family behind?" Dahlia finally had lost interest in her nails.

"My family is not from Tennessee. And my spouse is . . . dead." It was Claire's turn to gaze straight ahead. The words had slipped off the tongue without too much effort.

"We're awfully sorry to hear that, Claire," said Minnie. "You're just so business-like all the time. All about work and very little chit chat."

"Look, guys, I know the other reason you're so worried. I want to take the time now to say we're all a team here. We work together, and I don't run this store. It's not mine. But just know I want an enjoyable place to come every day just like you."

"I think you've done a nice job, Claire." Oma didn't smile, but her faced held an expression of sincerity. "Whatever it is you've been through, just know that we're here if you need us."

Joy managed a small chuckle. "I'm sure us not pestering her anymore will do wonders for her sanity. Sorry, Claire, I hate to admit that we cackle like hens sometimes, but as Roy said, we like to know the people we work with and if we can trust them or not. That's just the way it goes, you know."

"Joy, I couldn't agree more. Thank you for that. And I'm sorry this whole deal with my looking through a few catalogs scared you silly." Claire managed a smile of gratitude.

Everyone stirred at the sound of the door of the break room opening. Mr. Parker poked his head through. "Are we spending the night here or what?" He grinned. "Claire, do you need any more time?"

"No Geo . . . Mr. Parker. We're finished." She turned back to her cohorts. "If we ever need another meeting again, we can have one. It might not be bad to do these quarterly and see where we are with everything."

Everyone murmured in agreement as they reached for their coats and left the room. Claire took extra time slipping on a jacket before following behind. When the last worker disappeared into the darkness, she paused at the main door. George slipped up beside her. He'd already wrapped a light trench coat around him. On his head perched one of Adrian's hats. It looked broken in, worn well. How long had George worn that particular hat, and was it a favorite? The whole outfit gave him an almost mysterious quality, a man with a past who chose to shroud it underneath a coat and hat.

"That was uncomfortable."

"You think?" Claire looked him up and down.

"I always catch bits and snatches of conversation, when they think I don't hear. I'll admit this time I listened outside the door." He rested his arm against the door rail.

"Really?"

"Couldn't help myself. Honestly, I didn't share anything at all with them about you. The day you started was the first day they knew."

Claire frowned. "Don't you think you could have dropped a hint, made up some kind of story? We could have collaborated on it. Or you could have let Mitchell know and he would have told me."

George let out a soft breath, staring absently at the ceiling. "People are nosy, Claire, and I just don't cater to it." He rested his hand lightly on her shoulder. "That's the beauty of owning your own place. You don't have to answer to anybody."

"Don't you think giving them a heads-up would have gotten some buy-in, maybe have settled their fears a little? That's how they all see me, as someone who's just waltzed in here without a care in the world." Claire didn't flinch from his hand.

"Look, I don't disagree with what you're saying, but I keep a distance from my workers. You get in too thick and soon they don't respect you. I try to be fair, but I'm a businessman first."

"I guess Anita dittoed that sentiment, too, didn't she?"

George pulled away, stunned.

She clapped her hand over her mouth. "I'm sorry, George. That was uncalled for."

He turned away in silence, heading to the back of the store where he cut off all but the security lights. Claire faced the door, gazing through the glass into the dark night. She was just itching to learn more about Anita, get to the bottom of why a woman the others didn't fancy was once admired and loved by the man several feet away. She'd milked the opportunity that day during lunch, when Buzzi and Moo made their entrance into her life. Now she'd lunged for another round.

George held the front door open for Claire. In silence, they walked to his car while the brisk October night air whipped around them. Nearly two months in Knoxville, and now this. All she wanted was to seal the past, avoid discussing it, and avoid walking in the shadow of old ghosts.

Gay Street passed by in a blur. The hum of the car lulled her emotions only a little. She still regretted mentioning his late wife.

"Claire, I'm not mad at you at all. Now, I'll admit I was taken off guard by what you said." He reached over and placed his hand on top of Claire's. "It was a critical remark, and you don't know me or Anita enough. That's what got me." He squeezed her hand. "But I forgive you."

"I shouldn't have said it, but the thoughts of anyone knowing about how and why I came here unnerves me to no end, and as far as Anita goes . . . I don't know. I like knowing about people, what I'm up against, that sort of thing."

"Up against?" George let out a light breath and grimaced. "You're not up against anything, Claire. I don't know where or why you'd even compare yourself, as a worker or anything, for that matter. First of all, I like the folks at the store, but they're a gossipy bunch like most everyone in groups are. And Anita and I were a lot alike in many ways, especially when it came to business. That doesn't mean everything she did was right on the mark. As a matter of fact, there's things I admire about you that she could never be."

She got up enough nerve to finally glance his direction. "Really?" Her voice sounded weak in her ears.

"You have a way about you that affects me in different ways than Anita. And that's okay. You're two different women. How could you not have your own style and personality? I personally wouldn't have it any other way." He took his eyes briefly off the road and grinned at her.

"You don't think I'm a total cad?"

"Not at all. What's eating at you, though?"

Claire rested her eyes on the night, shops and houses and trees zipping by. She thought long and hard. Finally, she answered. "I don't want anybody knowing about my past or getting too personal. I want to forget as much of it as I can myself. I don't want people questioning what happened and why I couldn't keep my man happy enough to keep from thinking I was crazy. It's embarrassing."

"And they've been grilling you, haven't they?" George hadn't let up on her hand.

"Not as bad as they could, but slipping in asking questions just the same." Claire turned her head in his direction, taking in the silhouette of his face. "George, I'm going to be honest with you. Remember how you mentioned that people sometimes didn't understand Anita?"

George shot a quick sideways glance at her. "Y-e-e-s."

"They're scared to death that I'll be just like her. For heaven's sake, was she that bad?"

He exhaled a little at a time. "I think what you're going to find here is that each one of us speaks our own truth. And really, it's all a matter of perspective. She liked being the boss, she had her own ideas about how things should be."

"And you just let her run it the way she saw fit." Claire's eyes wandered to the right passenger window, wishing she were at home right this minute. Starting a disagreement had never been her intention.

"Yes, I did, in some ways. Let me tell you something, I make no apologies for it."

Her heart paused a few beats before the heat flared in her cheeks. George's voice wasn't unkind, but she saw more of the man behind the business, one who could be pleasant most times, but when it came to business, he was the one who dug in his heels. Claire said nothing, but this time, she gently pulled her hand back to her lap. Out of the corner of her eyes, she caught sight of him looking at her at intervals. One more turn and they'd be winding down Holston River Road.

When they reached the driveway, George drove to the front porch and let the car idle. "Claire, we had a pretty bold discussion tonight. Some might say an argument, though I'm not sure it quite went that far."

"Well, then, this conversation was as bold as the one I had with Ruby."

His smile reassured her. "Ruby, now that woman's bold."

"Yes, she's a feisty one. I think we had a meeting of the minds, but I'm not sure I trust her. It all put me on edge, and I'll admit I'm snippy too."

"Personally, Claire, I don't think you trust anyone right now." He grew silent at this observation, focusing his eyes on the house. "Do you?"

Her emotions calmed at the softer tone in his voice. "I think I can trust Mitchell. A little, anyway. I mean, what else can I do? I don't have anyone else, and my family isn't around."

George reached over and took her hand in his. "Look, I want to make one thing clear. You can trust me. And Edna. She doesn't know anything, other than you're renting the house." He turned toward Claire, his whole body facing hers. "You can trust me. I'm not perfect, but whatever comes up, we can talk things out." He loosened his grip and rubbed her shoulder. "I'm sorry you've been bearing this alone. I probably should have paved the way a little, instead of focusing only on myself and work."

"I'll agree with you on that. But again, thank you for an opportunity to work." Claire reached for the handle of the passenger door.

"Don't forget you owe me some loomed towels and runners."

"I haven't forgotten." She slipped out of the seat, shutting the door behind her. With a wave, she turned and picked her way through the dark to the front porch, with only the car lights shining. At least she'd have the evening to herself, and this time, she was glad of it.

✳✳✳

Settled into her work room upstairs, Claire gazed at the loom. She'd spent the previous evening winding the warp, threading the heddles, just a few of the steps taken to dress the loom. All this after making the calculations for 12 towels in the color scheme and designs she'd chosen. Everything was in place and ready to go. She sat for the next four hours, concentrating on nothing but the loom and the movement of her hands and feet. The rhythm of working it soothed her. As always, watching her work come to life filled her with pride and purpose. It also soothed her nerves. Buzzie slept by her feet while Moo eyed the loom, swatting at a stray dangling thread.

She thought about the people at work. Nobody had been unkind, really. Curiosity ingrained itself in human nature. That much she knew. And who could blame them? Her mind wandered back to Ruth, Ella, and the other ladies at Hatchie River. How many dresses had they made now? Wouldn't it have been fun to teach them how to loom? Perhaps they could have make some towels and washcloths, instead of using the nearly shredded ones the asylum had. Halloween was coming up, and she desperately needed to make Anna's outfit for the party at Mr. Hyde's.

It finally dawned on her that the outing would be the first one where she and George would be seen together outside the store, where they'd fallen into the routine of turning on their boss/employee relationship. What startled her was the fluttering excitement at the thought of spending an evening with him outside of work. It was kind of like a date, but not. This was for Anna, she reasoned. Why had he asked her to go? He could have easily taken Anna by himself. What fun it would be, the chilly night air, people laughing, the smell of wood and leaves burning.

All around children would laugh and scream, chasing and scaring each other in fun. The little boys would tease the young girls and make them cry. Someone would fight over who got the last marshmallow, while there would be squabbles over who got the best seat on wagon for the hayride. This weekend she'd get with Anna and help her pick out a costume. Then it would be nights of sewing just to finish in time. Again the flutter of excitement. This would mean more time with George nearby. Each passing day she fantasized more about what it would be if there weren't two different houses in their lives, but one where they would have not only dinners together, but breakfast. And lunch on weekends. What would it be like to tuck Anna into bed every night with Lulabelle resting beside her? What if G. P. & Sons was really her business, too, and not just George's, only because they were . . .? She interrupted herself. No need to go that far with all this thinking. Not right now. The clock let out shrill chime. Her eyes heavy, she stopped at last, smiling at her progress. She had several pieces to put on George's shelves at the store. She'd have just as much fun selling them.

✴✴✴

"I like this one, Miss Claire." Anna pointed her stubby finger to the witch's costume on the pattern envelope.

It was Sunday afternoon. On Friday, Claire had brought home an envelope showing children's costumes on the outside. Inside it, the paper templates used to create one of the outfits.

"You like the witch better than the princess? Are you sure?" Claire turned her eyes toward the little girl, grinning at her determined little face. "Why do you like that one better?"

"Because witches can fly and cast spells. Princesses don't do anything."

They're boring." Anna crossed her arms together, brows rumpled together. "Then a witch it is."

Anna rested her head against Claire's arm as they sat together on the sofa in the quaint living room at George's house. "Will you make me a hat to go with it? And a long black flowy thing coming out the top? And can you make the cape a little longer so it makes me look like I'm flying when I run?"

"Anna, don't you think you're being a bit selfish, asking Miss Claire to do all that work for just one night? You'll never wear that costume again." George had wandered into the room, sitting down to read the paper in the easy chair in the corner.

"But Daddy, witches have to fly." She turned back to Claire. "You understand, don't you, Miss Claire?"

"Anna!" George scowled at his daughter.

"George, it's not a problem. This costume is very simple to make." Claire smiled at George, relieved that his face had softened at her reassurance. "Anna, darling, you'll be the best witch of all."

"Really, Miss Claire? And can we take Moo with us so I'll have a cat like witches do? I need a cat to make me a real witch." Her eyes flashed in earnest, lips pursed in firm determination.

Claire shook her head, beating George with a response as she heard the paper rattle where he sat. "No, darling. We can't take Moo with us. Buzzie would be so lonesome. And not taking her would hurt her feelings. You wouldn't want that, would you? To know that poor sweet kittie was home all by herself, crying her little heart out?"

Anna's lower lip quivered, and her big blue eyes filled with tears. Her voice trembled. "No, Miss Claire. I didn't think about that. I just thought it would be fun to have a cat like witches do." She buried her face against Claire's arm. "Please don't tell Buzzie I was only going to take Moo to the party. I love Buzzie."

"Of course you do. And I won't say a word." Claire caught sight of George struggling to keep from laughing. The paper move up more and more until it shielded his face from view.

"We'll get you a broom. That's what people see with witches. A broom." Anna's eyes lit up. "Really?"

"Why don't you go make up some spells to go with your new costume. Maybe you can pretend to turn some of the boys into toads or something." George had peeked out from the side of the newspaper he still held up.

It was Claire's turn to stifle a giggle. "I agree. Maybe Lulabelle can help."

"Yeaaa! Yes, Lulabell can help." Anna threw up her arms in triumph and scrambled off the sofa, leaving George and Claire in peace.

"You handled that well, my dear." George dropped the newspaper and laughed.

"You weren't bad yourself. Tomorrow after everyone leaves, I'll cut some black material from one of the bolts in the sewing section. There's plenty."

"And how do you plan on making a hat? That'll take a little more planning."

"Simple. Take the same material, make the cutouts and soak them in starch so the shape stays when the hat dries. When I push the cone part of the hat through the brim, I'll leave enough material at the bottom to attach everything. It won't be hard at all."

George rested his head back, gazing at Claire. "You're something else. You know that, don't you?"

"What do you mean? Things like this come easy for me. Nothing to get worked up about. And Anna will love it. Does Mr. Hyde have a costume-judging contest?"

"He hasn't before. But maybe I can suggest it to him. That would be something different this year."

"And what would the winner win?"

"Not sure. I'll have to think about that. It might be a quick trip to the Five and Dime for a small toy of some kind."

"Good idea." Claire grinned. She'd spend the next week making the costume. Maybe she'd start with the hat and get that part out of the way.

CHAPTER SEVENTEEN

On a small table, the black hat sat, drying on an old towel George had found in his basement. Anna sat fingering the material Claire had cut the night before, once she was sure everyone had made their way out the door and off to catch the trolley or bus. When the door shut, she'd headed straight to the sewing section. With George's permission, she made her selection, picking up the shears and quickly snipping off some black material in accordance with Anna's size. Another bolt board held the remnants of black chiffon.

Normally that would have been pricey for a child's costume, but only a yard remained, hardly enough for a dress of any kind. The chiffon would become a tassel trailing from the hat. Work on the dress and cape, finishing the project in plenty of time.

"Can I help you cut, Miss Claire?" Anna reached for the scissors.

"No, darling. Those scissors are too sharp for little girls." She grinned. "But you know what else you can help me do?"

"What?" Anna peered up. The eyes which had filled with a sad expression twinkled into excitement.

"You can help me lay all this out and pin the pattern down. You'll have to be careful with the pins and not stick yourself." Claire cast Anna a solemn glance. "Can you promise me you'll be easy and not hurt your fingers?"

"I'll be real careful, Miss Claire. "I won't stick myself." She got up and whispered in Claire's ear. "And if I do, I promise I won't cry or say anything."

"You'll do a good job." Claire reached over and hugged the little girl.

She loved moments like this, when Anna responded with a firm hug right back. These moments were not only growing more frequent, they were becoming a habit, a gentle routine filled with a certain understanding. Though she had to almost pinch herself to make sure she wasn't dreaming, she sensed a certain love growing between her and the little girl.

"Let's get to work, then. Here, grab this corner and let's lay this out on the bed." For the next several minutes, Claire and Anna worked on spreading out the cloth. She taught Anna how to use a thimble and showed her a technique for pinning the pattern to the fabric. Luckily for Claire, she'd taken some time after arriving home from work to cut out the pattern pieces she'd be using. This saved considerable time. Anna watched, wide-eyed as Claire cut out each section of the costume.

"We're lucky this is a simple dress, Anna. I thought it might take me longer, but it seems like we'll get it done today."

"Yeaaa! I'll have all week to wear it. I have to practice being the best witch in the whole wide world." The little girl bounced up and down, clapping. "How long will it take for my hat to dry?"

"It'll take a few hours, and then we'll add this pretty piece for an accent." Claire fingered the black chiffon. Anna picked it up, fluffing the edges, cooing with satisfaction.

"I'll be queen of the witches." Anna whirled around the room, flinging out her arms, and spreading her fingers. From her lips tumbled out an odd assortment of mumbo jumbo words. Claire laughed to herself, focusing her concentration on cutting out the dress parts. She moved the scissors carefully over the fabric, taking great care not to cut the bedspread.

"Looks like you're making pretty good progress. You might be finished with this dress today, if you keep at it like you are." George lounged easily against the doorframe, smiling. "Anna, are you behaving so you don't bother Miss Claire?"

"I'm helping her!" Anna twirled her way to George, nestling against him with affection. "I'm casting spells so she makes the prettiest dress in the world."

George's face took on an expression of solemnity like his daughter's. "They must be very powerful spells, because she's making good time with your outfit." He grinned at Claire.

"Look at this." The little girl ran over to a chair and pulled off the black chiffon, trailing it around her head. "This is going in my hat. That makes me the queen. I don't ever see witches with these."

"Then you must be a very special witch to wear that." George hugged his daughter, placing a light kiss on the top of her head.

"Claire, can you and Anna can take a break for lunch? Edna made some sandwiches and some of the best butternut squash soup."

Claire glanced at her watch. "Goodness. Where did the time go? Give us about twenty more minutes, and we'll be ready."

"And good appetites too, I hope." George tapped the door frame and walked away.

Anna settled on a small stool by the sewing machine. "Hurry up, Miss Claire. Will we have all this cut and ready to sew before we eat?"

"Maybe not all of it, but we'll get this one sleeve cut out."

Twenty minutes later, Claire and Anna seated themselves at the kitchen table. Edna stood by the stove, ladling soup into bowls. She'd already placed the plates of chicken sandwiches on the table.

"Edna, can I help you pour tea, or make myself useful?"

"No, dear. I've got it. You just sit right down and relax." Edna turned around and grinned at Claire.

"You two girls have been going at it?" George smiled over at Claire. "Again, this is so nice of you to come over and spend your weekend doing this for her. It takes a load off me, that's for sure."

"I've enjoyed every minute of it. She's so happy."

Edna came by and set bowls of soup next to each person. A few seconds later, she added the glasses of tea. "Sorry, I didn't have all this ready earlier, but the soup took a little longer than I'd planned."

"We understand, Edna. You can go rest in your room for an hour, if you like. We'll be done by then."

"Yes, sir." Edna nodded at George.

Anna ignored the adults, blowing on her spoon and swallowing a few bites of soup. She savored the flavor, closing her eyes and running her tongue over her lips. Satisfied with the nutty taste, she dipped her spoon into her bowl for another bite.

"You'll stay for dinner, too, won't you?' George placed his hand lightly on Claire's.

"Dinner too? Aren't you tired of me?"

"I'd never grow tired of you. You're not an imposition in the least."

Narrowing her eyes, Claire said, "I can't stay much longer. I really need to get some more looming done."

"True. But you've been working hard every night, and there's tomorrow. Surely missing one night won't hurt."

"I don't know, George. I'd really like to get some other work done this weekend. How about another time?"

"No, Miss Claire." Anna had put down her spoon. Her face exhibited one huge frown. "Stay here. After we finish my dress, we can play a game." She tugged on Claire's sleeve. "Or you could stay 'til bedtime and read me a story. I'd like that."

Claire's eyes remained fixed on Anna. How could she get out of this without hurting the little girl? Maybe one day of not looming wouldn't throw off her plan too badly.

George cleared his throat. "Um, Anna, don't you think that's a lot to ask Miss Claire, when she has other things she needs to do?"

"No." Anna glared. "She always leaves too early. Why can't she stay until bedtime at least once?"

"Anna!" George's voice dropped a couple of octaves.

The sharp tone startled Claire. She looked over at the disapproving father and placed a hand on his arm. "Oh, George, she doesn't mean any harm. Anna, darling, I can't stay until bedtime, but I know we can at least get that witch costume made. Maybe another time we can read a story before bed." She glanced up at George, and lightly shrugged her shoulders.

"Honey, just be quiet and eat your lunch. Like Miss Claire says, we'll deal with this another time." His face had returned to calmer state, along with his tone.

Anna's lip puckered out. "Promise?"

"We promise, darling." Claire squeezed George's arm, indicating he remain silent.

The remainder of lunch passed with the conversation a little strained between the adults. Anna's sulked, barely eating her meal.

When everyone finished lunch, Claire and Anna retreated to the sewing room and went at the costume with gusto. Anna helped unpin the patterns from the fabric, contenting herself with folding each one neatly and placing it back in the pattern envelope.

"We may use these again next year, Miss Claire. Maybe we can make something else with them."

"Good idea, dear. You're so smart."

Anna watched with intense interest as Claire pinned the dress parts so she could sew the edges together. Claire worked with the machine and expertly sewed the sleeves in. Around five o'clock, the dress was made. All the costume needed now was the bottom and sleeves hemmed. The hat continued drying and held its shape without any drooping or sagging in places. Claire felt the fabric. It was solid and would hold up nicely. This would be a good time to stop and go on home. Edna could hem the dress and finish the hat.

The incident at lunch still bothered her. The storm brewing in the little girl's eyes showed an anger she'd not seen before, and the energy and passion unnerved her a bit. She almost felt guilty leaving this time. What did Anna think about alone in her room, just her and her dolls, no one to talk to? What did she really wish for as she played her games on the porch? Did she wake up every morning and feel like something was missing from her life? When Claire left with George to go home, Anna hugged her hard, face buried in Claire's skirt as she poured out a series of tiny heart-wrenching sobs.

✷✷✷

Halloween night was in full swing. Mr. Hyde had set up everything in perfect order. Several tables had been set up, and all of them laden with food brought by guests. A huge bonfire blazed several yards away, orange flames licking the air as if it wanted a taste of the night. Children squealed and chased each other, the girls sometimes chasing the little boys, who yelled and tried to run to their buddies for safety.

George and Claire took their time, slowly picking their way through the grass toward the tables. Anna spied the group of children and ran with all her might, yelling as loud as her lungs allowed. Claire inhaled a long, deep breath, taking in the scent of hot dogs cooking, smoke, and the woodsy scent of leaves. The breeze had kicked up tonight, the chill nipping with no remorse.

"She's so cute, George." Claire laughed as she watched Anna with the others. One of the classmates, a charming little girl in a princess outfit, engrossed herself in Anna's hat, pulling the tassel in the top so she could see it float back into place.

"Miss Claire made it for me." Anna fairly crowed with delight.

"Is she your mom? I didn't think you had a mom." The little princess stared at Anna.

Anna hung her head, the brief moment of happiness snatched away. "No."

"Oh," said the girl, who now seemed at a loss for words. "She still did a nice job with your hat and dress. I wish I had it."

"Miss Claire's the best." Anna perked up a bit.

"Come on, let's go see the fire." The little girl grabbed Anna's hand and pulled her along.

George shifted a large bowl of potato salad to his other arm, and took hold of Claire's. Claire held tightly to her bag of marshmallows, chocolate bars, and graham crackers.

"I'm so sorry about Anna. I don't know what's gotten into her lately. She asks about you all the time now."

"Oh. Really?"

"Yes. I don't know what to do with her."

His body heat radiated out to hers despite the chill. If she had no propriety, she would have thrown down the bag, flung her arms around him and shed a few tears, right there on the spot. As much as she wanted a perfect night, seeing Anna's face saddened her.

"George, I've been thinking. Would it be best if I stopped coming around so much, or maybe we stop—?"

"Absolutely not." His tone of voice took on the same admonition he used with Anna when he tried to maintain discipline.

Claire swallowed hard, blinking back some tears. Was it the chill in the air stinging her eyes, or did she really need a little cry? "I just thought if my not coming around gave you some peace, maybe it would be better for all of us. Especially her. I seem to just rile her up, that's all."

"You'll do nothing of the kind." George slowed his pace. "She needs to learn how to get on in life when things don't go her way."

"Oh, George. She's a little girl and she wants what every child wants. Parents. Both of them."

"Sometimes you just can't have what you want, plain and simple."

She glanced over at George. His face turned down in thought. The gruffness surprised her. His words chilled her almost as much as the night air. What did he mean by his comment, exactly? Did this mean he preferred staying single, rearing Anna alone?

Voices grew louder as they neared the tables. A few of the employees from the store milled about, chatting. Women and men, many she didn't know, stood in small groups, laughing at the occasional story. Claire pushed the conversation with George out of her mind. She'd have to revisit this when she was alone, tucked away in her house, perhaps while she loomed. Too much to take in now.

"Claire, you're here." Ruby walked over with an outstretched arm, landing it easily on Claire's back. "So glad you got out tonight. Mr. Parker, nice to see you." She grinned from George to Claire. "Here, honey, let me help you find a spot for your bag."

"I thought the children would like s'mores, so I brought everything for making them."

"Children, my foot. Adults like 'em too." Ruby laughed, taking the bag from Claire and landing it in a small empty spot on the table. George had found a cozy vacant area for the potato salad. The smell of food hit full force, and Claire's stomach growled.

"Looks like you got that dress made." Oma came up to Claire, smiling and glancing in Anna's direction.

"I worked all last Saturday on that dress. George's housekeeper finished the last touches."

"George's housekeeper? George has one of those?" Ruby had joined them.

Out of the corner of her eyes, Claire caught Oma frowning at Ruby to be quiet.

"Mr. Parker has a lady named Edna who helps. She's so nice." Claire turned to Ruby. "So what did you bring for tonight?"

"I brought a salad, and Oma brought some of her famous peanut butter fudge."

"Let's eat. I'm starved." Oma tugged on Claire's sweater, and all three ladies fell in line, picking up plates, silverware, and cups for drinks. Several chairs surrounded the bonfire, and the ladies moved three close together so they could chat. Jack and Roy had engaged in a lively conversation with Mr. Hyde, while George straightened up Anna's cape that had twisted with all her running.

Casting a sideways glance at Ruby, Claire said, "So Ruby, did you bring a friend, by any chance?"

"Not this time. Just me. I thought why not just get out of the house for a bit and have a fun evening? I don't know about you, but there's still a little girl in me. I love the holidays." She smiled.

"I don't think we ever get rid of the youth in ourselves, no matter how old we are." Oma took a bite of the potato salad. "Gosh, this is so good. Did you make this?"

Claire nodded.

"Claire, you look like something's on your mind. Are you all right?" Ruby leaned forward in her seat.

"Oh, I'm fine. I'm just enjoying the night. It's so clear and starry."

Ruby continued, "So did you and George—or Mr. Parker, I should say—come together? I thought I saw you two get out of his car."

Oma chimed in. "I think it's kind of nice, you two living so close together. It's kind of handy at times, don't you think?"

"Handy?" Claire wrinkled her brow in Oma's direction.

"I mean, if either one of you needs anything, or just . . . I don't know. I think it's nice to have neighbors who can help or just be there. You know what I mean."

"Nothing wrong with that." Ruby took a sip of tea from her paper cup.

"Yes, he and I came together. And if you must know, I spent all Saturday at his house making Anna's dress. We had lunch and everything. I would have read Anna a story at bedtime, but I left after dinner." Claire looked at Oma and Ruby. "I didn't want to wear out my welcome too much, so he took me on back to my house. He left, and I spent my time working on some crafts. I spent Sunday alone. Then it was work, work, work for the week, until today."

The two ladies stared at Claire, Ruby nodding slowly as she chewed her food. Oma dropped her fork on her plate.

Ruby broke the silence. "I'm glad you made Anna's dress. She's just adorable. And asking you to read to her at bedtime. Claire, that's really sweet when a kid asks you to do that, you know."

"Yeah, so I hear." Claire focused on consuming a few bites of food.

Just as the women finished up their conversation, the men joined them. George sat a few chairs away from Claire, striking up a chat with Minnie, who'd just arrived. Mr. Hyde now took the time to load his plate up with food and soon joined the group. Ruby quickly got up from her chair and went back to the table, where she loaded some food on a paper plate.

She joined the group and handed the plate to George. "Here, Mr. Parker. You haven't had a bite all night." George smiled and nodded his appreciation as he took the plate from Ruby. Claire and Oma exchanged quick glances as their co-worker sat down in her chair. Ruby turned her head away, speaking amiably to another lady.

The children had moved closer to the adults, their cries and squeals of laughter being shushed by parents.

"Can you tell us some ghost stories?" Anna slid on George's lap.

"Go on, George, tell us a couple of stories." Jack spoke up, patting his boss on the arm. "Nothing like a couple of good ones to spook us."

"I'd love a good ghost story, Mr. Parker. Do you know any good ones?" Oma re-arranged her chair for a better view of the fire.

Ruby piped up. "I think we should at least let Mr. Parker finish his food. A master story-teller needs his strength."

Ignoring his employee, George placed the plate of half-eaten food beside his chair. "Well, I guess I could tell a couple of short ones," he said. "Let me see, which ones would be good? How about The Black Cat and The Old Mansion?"

Ruby clapped her hands. "Do those, Mr. Parker. I love Edgar Allen Poe's cat story. And you're so perfect at telling anything. I look forward to it every year."

Claire winced in the darkness.

"Sure, I can do those two. I'm sure there are some here who haven't heard them yet." George sat straight up in his chair, Anna balanced on one leg, while the children gathered around his feet. The adults pulled their chairs closer. For the next hour, George told the stories, using his best story-telling voice, along with some added sound effects. The children sat listening, wide-eyed.

Even the adults paid full attention. To Claire's chagrin, Ruby seemed extra attentive, grinning, smiling wider at times, lightly shaking her head or nodding as George came to different points in the story. The fire had died down just a little, giving off the occasional snap while sending a few sparks flying in protest. The moon floated high in the sky. From the woods, an owl sent out a low and lonesome hoot. Claire settled back in her chair, staring into the fire as the sound of George's voice filled her ears. He really wasn't bad with children at all, and Anna loved him telling his repertoire of fantastic fantasies and horrific tales. When the stories were finished, Ruby grabbed the bag of ingredients for the s'mores, and everyone busied themselves making up a couple of treats to satisfy their sweet tooth.

"How about a hayride?" Mr. Hyde stood up. "Anybody up for one, or do we just not do it this year?" At that suggestion, the kids yelled in protest, jumping up and running to him. "All right then, I'll head to the barn and come back. We'll load everybody on and go for a ride."

The children squealed and jumped up and down. Claire smiled, adoring Anna's enthusiasm. She wondered if a sleep-over was in order at her house, where Anna's sweet classmate could be invited. Within moments, the rumbling sound of the tractor sounded from the barn, growing louder as Mr. Hyde drove it near the fire site. The motor belted out its grinding, scratchy tune, sending the children running full force toward the bed attached at the back. Jack and Roy had followed Mr. Hyde and had ridden back to help the children up. A few men and women, including Ruby and Oma, clambered on. Soon the tractor headed off, becoming nothing more than a specter in the dark.

George dragged his chair close to Claire's. "Finally, I can get a moment with you."

"You did a wonderful job telling those stories." She smiled over at him, rubbing his arm.

"I love doing it. There's nothing like the smell of the outdoors, a chilly night, a crackling fire to get the old imagination going."

"Anna should be over any of her fright after the hayride. I'll still be spooked. Going to bed tonight may be more of a challenge than usual." Claire laughed.

The smile faded from George's face, waning into an expression of thoughtfulness.

"What's wrong? You'll have Anna and Edna around. You won't be spooked."

They grew silent. There was one question still nagging at Claire, and she wanted to get it out of her system. If she didn't, it wouldn't be scary ghost stories that kept her up. George's words still rang in her ear.

"I have a question for you, sort of finishing up our conversation we had on our way here."

He glanced over at her. "Oh? What's that?"

Claire lightly popped his hand, pretending to scold. "You said something about not always being able to get what you want. What did you mean by that?"

Shaking his head, George rested his hand over hers. "I just mean there are times in your life when you want something really bad, but simply can't have it."

"Like what?" Claire said, hoping she'd get to the bottom of his thoughts.

"I don't know. There are lots of things I'd like to have right now, things for Anna, as much as anything else."

"What do you want for her?"

George shifted in his seat, his demeanor showing definite discomfort. He turned his head slowly from side to side, checking to see if anyone was nearby. Most had gone on the hayride or had gathered in new intimate groups, leaving the two of them mostly alone. "Of course, I'd like for her to be happy, have things other kids have, if you know what I mean. When Anita died, a part of me closed down for a while. Like I told you before, I'm ready to move on, get on with my life, but . . ."

"But what?" Claire turned, facing him straight on. "Something getting in your way?"

He shook his head. "I don't know. Oddly enough, just when I think I'm ready, there's still that part of me that's a little unsure. Don't get me wrong, being married was wonderful, but maybe with her I got lucky."

This comment left Claire thoughtful. She sat back in her chair, gazing into the fire. She didn't have any words of wisdom. Her situation was no better. What does one do with a spouse who is drifting away, held captive by tricks of his trade, a trade he loved and had lived with a good part of his life? Claire didn't see a need for pushing the issue with George any further. Not tonight. Each one had their own demons to fight. "All in good time," her grandmother had always told her. Granny was never wrong.

She thought about her family now, still not knowing about her situation. Maybe when she got up enough nerve, she'd pen a note. Nothing else regarding this matter was discussed the rest of the night. When the kids had been handed down from the tractor bed after the hayride, George and Claire took Anna, and all headed home.

CHAPTER EIGHTEEN

Claire studied the shelves in the home accents department, re-arranging a towel here and there. She stepped back and tipped her head from side to side, eyes narrowed with indecision.

"Those are so pretty, Claire. When did we get those in?" Joy slipped up next to the shelf, gently fingering the material. "I don't remember us ordering any of this, but they are just beautiful."

Ruby also strode up next to Claire, eyeing the merchandise. "I don't remember us asking for these either, but we were getting low on some towels after our sale." She looked straight at Claire. "Can you satisfy our curiosity, even just a little bit? Or is this a secret vendor we're not supposed to know anything about?"

"Meaning?" Claire sensed her irritation growing. She forced a weak smile and stared back at Ruby.

"Meaning, since we know they weren't on any order list, where did you get them? I'm with Joy. I think they're awfully nice."

There was no way out of this, nor could she keep this a secret no matter how hard she tried. "If you must know, I loomed all these myself. Mr. Parker said I could put them in here and sell them. Thought maybe the customers would like something new, something different."

"Mr. Parker let you make these and put them on our shelves? To sell and no doubt make some extra money." Ruby nodded slowly, her vision fixed on the cheerful red, yellow, and blue towels. She took the liberty of picking up one of the yellow ones, unfolding it, and examining the royal blue pattern woven into the body of the yellow. "You make up your own designs too?"

"Yes, as a matter of fact I do." Claire's voice rang out more hollow and cold.

Facing Claire, Ruby's eyes held a certain anger, as if she'd heard an unjust pronouncement. "He's never considered letting the rest of us do this sort of thing. I make nice soap. Joy knits beautiful scarves and hats. He's never once suggested we put our work out."

"Did you ask him, by any chance?" Claire fidgeted with a lock of her hair.

"Did you?" Ruby countered.

Joy backed away. "Ladies, I'm running over to see if Dhalia needs any help."

Claire sucked in her breath, remembering the day in George's office, when they'd discussed her hobbies and what she'd like to be doing again. "Look, Ruby, if you'd like to place some of your soap in the cosmetics department, something pretty with a nice floral scent, I'm sure it wouldn't be a problem."

"You could make that happen, I presume?"

"Or you could just ask. Why not?"

"Oh, come on, Claire. Let's face it. You've got an in with him." Ruby's face held a look of indignation. She'd done a nice job of keeping her voice low, like they both had, painfully aware of others nearby.

This was the last straw. Time to put this ordeal to rest. "Tell me something, Ruby, when are you going to ever let this obsession with Mr. Parker and me go? Personally, I'm done with it." Claire leaned in closer. "With all this questioning and hinting you do about him and me, and throwing in Anna too, I'm only guessing you still have the hots for him, even after he's made it clear he wants somebody else. And let me just tell you that I don't mean me, either."

Ruby's eyes displayed an expression of shock. For once she had no words, but the pink cheeks on her face spoke volumes.

"I have your number, Ruby. Get over him. He doesn't want you. As a matter of fact, I'm not sure what or whom he wants. As for me, I just want to settle down here in this town and move on with my life. If I were you, with your attractive looks, I'd go find a man who appreciates you and your independent nature. They're out there. You just have to look harder, that's all."

"I hear you loud and clear, Claire." Ruby looked around, swallowing hard.

Claire didn't let the tears brimming in her co-worker's eyes throw her in the least. "I was hoping I had answered everybody's questions during our last meeting, but obviously I was wrong. I don't want any more questions about my personal life, other than how are you, did you have a nice weekend? Yeah, that sort of thing."

Regaining her usual composure, Ruby squared up her shoulders. "That's fine, Claire, not a problem. And I hope you do really well with your towels and runners." She neatly folded the towel, placed it back on the shelf, and walked away. Inside, Claire's whole body trembled. She needed to get away before she screamed at the top of her lungs. Not many people in the store today. The ones who'd made it in were waited on by the other staff. Satisfied that she could steal a moment to herself, she sped to the break room.

Luckily, no one was there, and she sat down in one of the empty chairs. Then she started having second thoughts. Maybe she shouldn't have come down so hard on Ruby. Maybe she should have been getting to know Ruby and asking her questions so she'd understand her better. That would have been a therapeutic thing to do. Anne had mentioned that word several times to Greta, when she overheard them talking behind the desk at the nurse's station. When she and the inmates of Hatchie River gathered together on their sewing days, Anne always knew how to ask questions and quell arguments and sharp tongues among the women.

"Claire, are you okay?" Oma had slipped in. She strode over to another vacant chair and sat down, taking one of Claire's hands in her own. "I have to know you're okay. Can you at least talk to me, just a little?"

Saying nothing, Claire looked up at Oma. Still she couldn't find any words to say. She glanced down again at her lap.

"Look, I saw you and Ruby talking, and Joy mentioned things were getting a little heated—"

"Did we make that much of a scene? We tried to keep it down."

"Nobody noticed. I wanted to see if I could do anything for you."

"Did Ruby say anything?" Claire managed to look over at Oma.

"Not really. We asked, but she played it cool and casual. But you could tell by the look on her face, something was bothering her."

"Hmm, that's a surprise. I thought she'd be all over the place blabbing." Claire turned to Oma. "What is it with you people? Why is everyone so interested in me and what I do or don't do outside this store, with or without Mr. Parker?"

Oma, loosened her grip on Claire's hand and sat back in her chair. "That was what you two were going on about?"

"And she went on at the party this past Saturday. That's why I just rambled on the way I did about Anna's dress the day I made it."

"Look, I'm going to come right out and say it." Oma straightened up her glasses on her nose and looked intently at Claire. "Ruby had her sights on Mr. Parker. He wouldn't give her the time of day. He was nice, of course, always the perfect gentleman. Long story short, he wasn't interested in her at all."

"She kind of hinted that to me, too, without actually saying so." Claire nodded, ready for Oma to continue. "What else happened?"

"Ruby gave up a little and focused more on her work, stopped trying to do those little extra things around the store and basically playing up to him. I think she's trying to make her way in life, too, and she's falling into the trap that most women fall into when they want a man. You know how that goes, Claire."

"Unfortunately, I do. I think we're all guilty, but I think I really came down on her pretty hard. I hope she at least got the message."

"I think she did. And here's the crazy part, she still tries to turn on some of that old charm, like you saw at the Halloween party."

Claire grimaced. "Why does that not surprise me?"

Nodding, Oma continued. "It just bothers me. I like people with some discretion."

"He's never said anything to me about her. But men are secretive about things like that."

Oma grinned. "I don't think I'd worry about Ruby. It's like her to take things to heart, especially when she feels like she's not a favored one or isn't getting the fair shake she think she deserves. She'll get over it and move on."

"Let's hope so." Claire said. "Thank you for talking to me. I do feel a lot better."

"I'm going back out on the floor. See you out there." The older lady got up from her chair and left the break room.

For the first time in weeks, a wave of calm washed over her. Maybe her encounter with Ruby had finally done its trick. Like lancing a boil when it came to a head. The cut, the words, released all her tension, and let the bad flow out. Why had she even doubted for a minute that she'd spoken out of turn to Ruby? Sometimes people needed to be told the truth, whether it hurt their feelings or not.

The conversation with Oma helped her recognize this. She'd keep this incident quiet. If George remained closed-lip about things that happened, then she could too. Still, she needed to sort out her feelings about George, how she felt, what she wanted. Their last conversation still bothered her, leaving her with no more insight into his feelings.

✷✷✷

November had come, running its chilling fingers over everything it touched. Frost covered the grass in the mornings, caked the windows of cars, and sent blasts of cold blowing hard when the wind threw a tantrum. Claire had managed to keep a distance from George for a couple of weeks, feigning fatigue or stating the shelves at the store needed more towels and runners. He'd dropped her off, and she didn't linger too long before heading inside her house.

"I'm really impressed, Claire," he said one night. "Customers just love them and have asked if we'd take some personal orders."

"I'm up for doing anything that will sell."

She hung on to that sentiment with gusto, staying home most nights. Looming let her mind wander, plan, and rest, and then all over again.

This evening after work, he'd held up two tickets in his hand as they sat in the car in front of her porch.

"Oma gave me these. Says she has a cousin who works at the Bijou." He looked proud. "They're tickets to "Life With Father. Dorothy Gish is a lead player in this one."

"Lillian Gish's sister?"

George nodded, smiling.

"I hear everything at the Bijou is just wonderful. How thoughtful of Oma. I'm surprised she wouldn't want those tickets for herself."

"Don't know, but she came into my office and asked if I wanted them. How about you coming with me this weekend? Edna can cook up a nice dinner, and we'll eat before we go."

"I'd love to go, especially if I get to see Dorothy Gish." Claire beamed at George. Backing off from him needed a break, and Claire had no intention of passing up a fine night at a fine theater that had locals raving. Especially if her escort was George Parker.

"Really? You mean it? No excuse that you have to catch up on some craft or book or looming?"

Claire grinned. "I can take one night off."

George's face turned thoughtful. "You know I've missed you? Anna has really missed you. I've been dealing with her bad mood lately because of it."

"Bad mood?" Claire's face changed into an incredulous look. "How strange."

"Not strange at all, if you ask me. Why have you been so scarce lately?"

"Sorry about all that, but my projects don't get done by themselves. Maybe I can have Anna down for a weekend, just her and me."

"She'd love that, Claire. I'm holding you to it."

"Maybe I can let her help me with some of my projects. I'm trying out my hand at soap-making. When I get the perfect recipe and scent, you still up for me putting some in the cosmetics department?" She couldn't help but feel a quick pang of guilt about wanting to "one-up" Ruby. Like it or not, she wanted that last jab.

"I'd love nothing better." His lips pulled into a wide grin.

Claire's heart sped up when he slipped his fingers between hers. Mustering up her willpower she said, "I need to get on inside and let you get back to Anna."

"You sure you won't ride on down with me to the house and eat with us tonight? Anna would love to see you."

"Tell you what, we'll get together this weekend. I'll be looking forward to it."

George squeezed her hand one last time, and she left the car. Claire hated the look of sorrow on his face as he backed out of the driveway. She stood at the window and watched the car lights fade in the distance. She had robbed herself of his company for the past several days, missing the moments he'd slyly place his hand in the small of her back when they walked into his kitchen or he'd follow her to the door.

He'd now made it a regular habit of touching her hand or knee whenever they sat together casually conversing. Every night when they left the store and everyone was out of sight, he'd place his hand in the small of her back, leading her to his car. But playing cool was her decision, with no regrets, either.

She opened the door and slipped into the house. The wind had picked up with a blowing cold that seeped into her marrow. Shivering, she slipped off her coat and hung it on a nearby coatrack. Tonight would be a good night for a fire in the fireplace. At least Adrian had shown her how to build a good fire long ago when they first married. Claire headed for the fireplace. In her mind, flames contained a life of their own, almost animating a room with a certain spiritual force.

It was that force she needed right now, one to extinguish the loneliness swirling around her like an old ghost with no resolution. Why this overwhelming sense of aloneness tonight? Because she found herself missing Adrian yet again? These moments confounded her. She definitely missed George, and sweet little Anna. Even a cup of coffee with Edna the housekeeper would have been nice company. Shrugging, she pulled a few small logs out of the bin beside the fireplace and tossed them easily onto the grate. Some kindling and a strike of a match, and she soon had a small fire blazing.

Tonight, she ate dinner in front of the dancing flames. She treated herself to a generous serving of wine in one of the fancy cut glass wine goblets in the china cabinet. Claire was not big into alcohol, but this time, she welcomed the buzz after the first glass. She poured another and drank some more. Her plate sat next to the sofa on which she'd reclined after eating. Buzzy and Moo settled at her feet, engrossed in grooming their paws. The more she thought about Adrian again, the more she wished they had their old life back.

Did he even think about her at all anymore? Was he sitting alone in front of a fire tonight too? Claire's mind slipped back to the past, remembering special things they'd done. She thought about the trip they made to Gatlinburg and how they spent the weekend there one time, just for a quick getaway and a change of scenery. There were picnics and parties with friends. They'd spent nights laughing, dreaming big dreams, with Adrian of becoming the most famous hatter in the nation, if not the world.

What astounded her most was why part of her still loved a man who didn't love her anymore? Claire pondered this simple question, and after about an hour engrossed in it, finally concluded that love didn't simply shut itself off like flicking a light switch up and down whenever you needed or wanted to.

One didn't readily dismiss another, especially if they'd made a commitment to you one time in their life. Especially if you'd birthed their children and helped them, even in some small way, with their livelihood. One didn't dismiss shared secrets and big dreams. One didn't dismiss the person they once were. The true Adrian was not the man he was now. None of this was his fault, really. They'd both been victims, he caught in one web, she in another. Their webs had tangled, and he'd nearly gotten the better of her.

Her thoughts turned to George. What would it be like to have him with her, cuddling on the sofa, the cats nearby, and Anna playing with Lulabelle? Claire had been giving that more thought lately. She hadn't dismissed him totally because of his words at Mr. Hyde's party, but in truth, George wasn't hers to dismiss. His words didn't match the look he often gave her, nor the way he touched her. She'd need to give all this more time. Men needed it more than women. But three years as a widower? That was enough. She had no problem giving him more time since she was new in his life, but then it would be time to move on at some point.

Claire swung her legs off the sofa, picked up her plate and empty wine glass, and headed to the kitchen. She could work on the loom until bedtime. Tomorrow, she would play with the soap ingredients. Lucky for her, she found a perfumer's catalog with all kinds of oils and colors. All she needed was some labels and nice packaging. Not bad for a single woman who had two product lines to her name.

CHAPTER NINETEEN

"You can't be serious." Claire nearly dropped the phone.

"Of course, I'm serious. Why would I ask you to if I didn't mean it?" George's voice bounded loud and clear through the line. There was a brief silence. "Look, I know it may sound odd to you, but I'm fine with it. I want to see them on you."

Claire shook her head, staring in the direction of her bedroom. "I don't know what to say."

"Say nothing. Just do it." He paused. "You will do it for me? Promise?"

"Okay, I promise."

"Pick you up at six-thirty and we come back here for dinner. After that, it's to the Bijou we go."

"Fine. That sounds good." Claire fidgeted with the tie on her silk robe.

"I've been waiting for this all week. You know that, don't you?"

She laughed. "George, you do know we see each other eight hours a day, right?"

"Not really. We don't."

Now it was Claire's turn for silence.

"Face it Claire, once we walk through those doors, I go my way, and you go yours. And we try to pretend every day that we don't know each other."

"I know. Personally, they know. And Ruby, I hear . . ." Claire winced, sucking in her lips. She almost let the cat out of the bag.

"Ruby what?" George asked, a cautious tone infusing his voice.

"Um, I hear that Ruby would love to put some of her crafted items into the store. Since we're trying to add unique merchandise, would you be up for it?"

"No, not really." His words slid out quickly and with conviction.

She nearly dropped the phone again. "Oh?"

"All I need are your magnificent products. I admire your style and quality. So do the customers. The rest can be chosen from catalogs and vendors who stop by."

"I see. I just wanted to check with you, that's all." Claire turned on the most casual voice possible and turned her gaze to the ceiling, chiding herself for the slip-up. Hadn't she already suggested Ruby approach him directly? Any guilt regarding her co-worker ended here.

"Very well then. I'll see you soon, and I expect you to be wearing what we talked about."

"I promise, George. Not to worry. Goodbye."

When they hung up, Claire walked to the bedroom and gazed at the dresser drawer containing the jewelry box with Anita's prized pieces. She'd purposely avoided that drawer after the first day George caught her thoughtlessly trying them on. Now he insisted, demanded that she wear them. But that wasn't all. There was one more item they'd discussed, one which she'd never realized was in the house.

It was hanging up in the closet in the bedroom across the hall. Other than her bedroom and the one with the loom, she never went inside the other two rooms. No need to, as she didn't have guests over. It always amazed her how foreign she felt in some parts of this house, while feeling so much more at home in others. After being caught prowling the first day, she'd not done it much after that.

Inside the bedroom, she wandered over to the closet and twisted an oval ornate brass knob, flinging aside the heavy dark wooden door. The stale smell of years filled her nose. Through the dim light, she spied a pale pink stiff plastic bag hugged up against the wall. Claire plucked the hanger off the rod, carelessly pushed the door closed with her foot, and carried the small mass back to her room.

Claire thought for a moment how she would feel if Adrian had let another woman wear her jewelry or best clothes. She grimaced. At this point, of course he wouldn't care. But what if things were different? With a gentle grip on the zipper and a steady tug, a soft brown fur came into view. Her pulse sped up. This fur stole reminded her of the one she'd left behind in Ash Grove. She'd all but forgotten about it until now. For a few seconds, her fingers glossed over the fur, running up and down, side to side.

The more she thought about her situation right now, the more it seemed that some semblance of her old life had somehow started tumbling discreetly into place. As each day passed she'd settled more into a normalcy that was hers, as if none of it had really ever quite left her, but had gone temporarily into hiding while she was forced to finish up hateful dreams. The fur would be perfect for a chilly night like tonight, and definitely fine for a date at the Bijou.

A date. How odd to consider it as such, but that's exactly what it was. Kind of. Other than Mr. Hyde's Halloween gathering, she and George had never gone out for any reason. Meals at each other's homes didn't count as dates. What startled her was a near lack of guilt. Still being connected to Adrian, though she missed him at times, was turning into inconvenience, one she intended to discuss with Mitchell during their next phone call.

Claire moved toward the dresser and opened the drawer containing Anita's jewelry box. After opening it, she ran her fingers over the stones. All of it was so beautiful. In her closet, she had a sleek, elegant black dress she'd picked up several weeks after she'd moved in. Articles in fashion magazines had always suggested keeping something black for formal occasions. She'd do her hair in a chignon, like one of the pictures she'd recently seen.

A cut crystal bottle of fragrance sat in front of the dresser mirror. Claire eyed it, shaking her head. Dhalia and Minnie had searched frantically for that sample bottle the next day after they'd received a new shipment of perfume. George had picked it up on a whim and given it to her that night, swearing her to secrecy. "I saw you sniffing that bottle all day long," he said, laughing. "I couldn't resist."

"What'll the girls say?"

"They can sell the other bottles. They'll just tell customers they don't have a sample, that's all. Happens all the time."

"Really? And customer will buy it?"

"Oh come on, Claire, you can still get a small whiff from the box. Besides, most of the customers trust Dhalia and Minnie's judgement." He'd leaned over close to her. "I like a nice scent on a woman every now and then. I know you're not up for springing for a bottle yourself right now."

George was right on both counts. No, she was in no position for splurging on expensive bottles of perfume, and yes, it seemed like customers of G. P. and Sons did trust the judgement of everyone who worked in that store. She grinned. Those same customers were quickly learning to trust her judgment too. The looming had paid off greatly. The soap would too; she knew it. And Ruby would simply have to bear another sting to that poor heart of hers.

Claire meandered into the bathroom, filled the tub full of hot water and bath fragrance, and settled in for a relaxing soak. She still had some time before George would pick her up. He wasn't the only sweet one for giving gifts at times. So was she. She'd ordered a darling rabbit fur purse with a golden chain for Anna. She'd look darling carrying that to church with her. George wouldn't know until tonight when she planned on presenting it to the little girl.

Served him right for leaving the ordering to her. She grinned at the memory of its arrival. When Ruby went on break, Oma quietly rang up the sale on the cash register and placed her money in the drawer. How they'd admired the little purse. When it came to store orders, Claire made sure she included others for their input. They were a team; she'd make sure it stayed that way. Even Ruby had her say. Like it or not, Ruby had ritzy taste. Anyone who quoted the classics like she did had to have some class. Laughing, Claire slid deeper into the bath water.

An hour and a half later, she stood before the mirror admiring her reflection, even though she felt a little shameful doing so. The chignon rested in smart woven coils at the base of her head. The black dress fit her slender form at the top, flaring out in soft waves at the bottom. Claire especially liked the smart white bow she'd tied at the waist.

But it was the jewelry that added the final touch. With some lingering trepidation, she'd put on each piece. Why did a small part of her feel like a thief all of a sudden, or an intruder? George's insistence kept her going, and now she turned her head lightly from side to side, admiring how the earrings bobbled and glistened in the light of the room.

Struck with a clever idea, she'd pinned the brooch to the knot of the bow just to be different. The bracelet and rings found their appropriate places on her wrist and finger. The necklace closed the whole look, with two rows of large white luminous pearls draped around her neck. They settled against her chest, the weight of them almost reproachful.

"Don't worry, Anita," Claire said, gazing into the mirror, "I'll never forget you're the true owner of these. I'm just borrowing them for the evening."

Outside, she heard tires grinding against the gravel. Claire ran to the window and pulled back the curtain. Lights from a car sliced through the dark. George had arrived. She grabbed the rabbit fur purse out of a drawer, slipped on the stole, and sped down the stairs. Buzzie and Moo had settled together in one of the window sills, ears standing at attention. "I'll see you dears later," Claire called out to the two curious cats.

When she opened the door, she yelped in surprise.

"You look just absolutely gorgeous." George stood outside. His gaze perused Claire. "I never thought I'd see anyone wear that fur and jewelry ever again."

"I really hope you're okay with this, George." Claire grinned, closing the door behind her. The night air smelled cold and fresh. A silver moon peeked through the branches of the trees. "Are you sure you don't want these with you after tonight?"

He shook his head, lacing his arm through hers as they headed to the car. "Those need to be worn and often. You think we can make that happen?"

She glanced at him, not answering, but studying the serious expression in his face. Had he done some thinking over the weeks? All this seemed like a bold move for him. Claire seated herself in the passenger side.

George shut the door and moved to the other side of the car. He viewed Claire a few more seconds before starting the engine. He said, "Again, I'm thinking it would be nice to get out every once in a while, go to the Bijou, or somewhere nice where we can dress up, do something special."

"That would be nice. I'd like that." Claire fingered the small fur purse.

"What's that?" George quickly leaned his head in the direction of the purse.

"I thought Anna would enjoy carrying this. The holidays are coming, you know."

"When did you get it?"

"I got it when I placed an order several weeks ago. I paid for it. So we're good." She stroked George's hand, which rested easily between them.

"You know you could have asked me. I would have gladly taken care of it."

"Nonsense. I wouldn't have it any other way."

Claire rested her head back, enjoying the hum and vibration of the car as it moved down the road to George's house. She reveled in the tingle of excitement. Dinner prepared by Edna, a night out with George, and a chance to see Anna's eyes light up when she held the purse in her sweet, excited little hands. It had been a while since she felt like some semblance of a princess. The ride on the magnificent Tennessean should have provided a similar opportunity, but all she could concentrate on at the time was getting out of town fast and never looking back. More than that, she hoped nothing would track her here.

The tires ground into the tiny stones as George pulled into his driveway. From the sky, moonbeams kissed the fields below, lighting them up in a soft glow. She wished for a walk tonight down this road, hand-in-hand with George. She'd love sniffing in the cold and taking in the scent, that chilly scent only the hint of a winter night could give. Thanksgiving was coming soon, and she had no idea how she'd spend the holiday. She could assume George would invite her over, but she didn't want to be that sure of herself.

"Did you want to give the purse to Anna before or after dinner?" George reached over, rubbing his finger lightly over the fur. He smiled. "Cute little thing. I think she'll like it."

"I'll give it to her before dinner. I'm more excited giving it to her."

"Very well, then." He opened the car door.

Inside the house, the smell of food sent her stomach into a rumble. Claire had gone all day without eating, except for a bite of fruit and a small bowl of soup.

Edna came out, wiping her hands on a stained apron, her lips upturned in a warm smile. "Mrs. Wright, how wonderful to see you again." She stopped and surveyed Claire. "And my, don't you look pretty. I think you look good all the time, but tonight you're extra pretty."

"Thank you." Claire returned the smile, while George removed the stole and placed it on the arm of the sofa.

In the distance the small pounding of feet sounded in the house, and Anna burst into the living room, sailing into Claire's open arms. "Miss Claire,

Miss Claire!" She squealed with excitement, jumping up and down. The fluffy curls on her head bounced in all directions, sending her scarlet bow into a lop-sided slant in her hair. The little girl hugged Claire around the waist.

"Anna, be careful. You'll rumple Mrs. Wright's dress." Edna scolded the child, trying a gentle attempt at pulling her away.

"She's just fine, Edna. I've missed her too." Claire ran her hand over Anna's head. "I've got something for you darling. Do you like presents?"

Anna's face lit up, her eyes gazing up at Claire. "For me?"

"Yes, sweetheart. Something for you. You can carry it to church with you, or maybe to a nice party." Claire handed Anna the tiny fur purse.

With wide eyes and open mouth, Anna gently took the purse, rubbing it lightly against her cheek. "It's so soft."

"It's rabbit fur. You can put some money in it or maybe a handkerchief.

"What do you say, Anna, when someone has given you something so nice?" George ruffled his little girl's hair.

"Thank you, Miss Claire." Anna hugged Claire all over again. "Can I go with you to the play tonight and carry my new purse?"

George said, "We'll all go together another night and you can carry it then. For now, why don't you put that in your room, in a special drawer so you don't get it dirty?"

"But I want to go with you and Miss Claire." Anna's lips puckered as the rest of her face showed a scowl."

Anna's father stepped toward her, taking her in his arms. "I will make sure that the next time something good comes to the Bijou, I'll take you and Miss Claire. That's a promise. But right now, I need you to go on to your room and get ready for bed. Edna can read to you."

"Okay," Anna replied in a resigned tone. She hugged Claire one last time before following Edna's lead down the hall.

The housekeeper came back in a few minutes. "I think I got her settled in for a bit. At least until you two get through dinner."

"Do you think she liked the purse?" Claire looked from George to Edna. Everyone broke out laughing.

"I think you got a winner, there, Mrs. Wright," Edna said, looking down the hall. "I need to do some last-minute things in the kitchen, and then you two will be ready."

"Are you sure Anna can't at least eat with us?" Claire sat on the sofa next to George.

"I had Edna give her an early dinner. Tonight, I want it to be just the two of us."

As much as Claire enjoyed times with Anna, she had to admit that dining alone with George would be romantic.

"Are you as excited about tonight as I am?" George cupped Claire's hand in his.

"I've been dreaming of it. I'm sure you've been there lots of times, haven't you?"

"Anita and I would go whenever we got a chance. She loved the theater." George stared off ahead, thoughtful.

"Adrian and I did our fair share of parties and theaters too. He always adored fine dining and a chance to go out for an evening."

"And you wearing one of his fine hats." George grinned at her.

"Yes, I always got compliments on them." Claire chuckled. "Do you know one night when he and I were at dinner, a woman made such a fuss over one style I was wearing, that she bought it from me, right off my head. Didn't matter that I'd already worn it. She just had to have it, she told me."

George laughed. "I don't doubt that for one minute." He glanced in earnest at Claire. "Would you like one of his hats from the store?"

"Oh, heavens, no! I can purchase some shiny hair clips or a nice tortoise shell comb, if I want it."

"Or you can take one of the hats from England. Just got in some of those the other day."

Claire didn't want to look too closely at him. Out of the corner of her eye, she caught him gazing at her, almost like he was memorizing every inch of her face. His thumb grazed over the top of her hand.

Edna slipped into the living room. "Dinner is ready." Her smile spread across her face. She took great pride in her cooking. "I've made roasted quail, some fluffy potatoes with cream mixed in, and some steamed butter carrots. And for dessert, I have my trademark cake, a seven-layer apple spice cake."

"Goodness, that sounds delicious." Claire smiled at the older lady. "You must have been busy all day."

"That's what I live for, Mrs. Wright."

"Maybe I can talk Edna into preparing more of her trademark meals and desserts, and you can join me in enjoying them." George rubbed his hand down Claire's back, pausing just a little to adjust the pearls at the back of her neck. Claire sensed the heat infusing her face.

"I'd love nothing better. It's nice to let someone prepare the meals for a change."

The kind housekeeper ushered George and Claire into the dining room, where candles glowed between two plates. A small crystal bowl held several brilliant dark red roses.

"How pretty. And I love the tablecloth."

"Just one of several I had in a collection. It's pretty, isn't it?" He spoke the words as if he'd picked out the collection himself instead of Anita. Glistening china held fresh food hot from the stove. Beside each plate a linen napkin displayed shiny sterling silver. A crystal goblet had been filled with a brilliant burgundy wine.

"Mrs. Wright, you do take some drink, don't you?" Edna looked at her. "I just assumed, but I know some ladies are adamant against alcohol."

"I take wine, Edna. I'm not one for all these religious rules all of the time." She suddenly regretted what she'd just said. What would George think? "I mean, I believe in moderation." She sat down embarrassed.

"No need for making apologies, Claire. We know exactly what you mean. We'll just keep it between us three." George smiled, while Edna nodded in agreement.

"I'll let you in on a secret, Mrs. Wright. My grandmother kept a small flask hidden in her pantry. Whenever I stayed with her, I'd see her take a small sip from it every morning. One day she caught me looking at her, and she said, 'Honey, we never talk about this. We don't want the church ladies knowing. It's just a little pick-me-upper I take every day.'" At that story, all three broke out laughing.

"I definitely understand your grandmother," said Claire laughing.

"I'll leave you two alone. I'm going to check on Anna." Edna turned and left.

"Mrs. Wright, please feel free to start eating." George held out a hand toward her plate.

Claire couldn't help but detect a certain pained expression in George's tone when he stated her married name, as if the sound of it now struck a certain chord of irritation. Come to think of it, she'd experienced some relief when he didn't talk more about the tablecloths. In some small way, she was getting a little tired of Anita too. The fact that Anita wasn't totally enamored with her daughter still bothered her. George may have his fond memories of her, but like the others, she found the woman rather cold.

"Something on your mind?" George had put his fork down, his eyes intent on hers.

"No. Why?"

"You seem like you're thinking of something."

"I was just thinking about Anna and how she reacted to the fur purse. She was so cute." Claire aimed a forkful of carrots into her mouth.

"That was a nice gift. Really, you didn't need to do that, but thank you."

"I wish she could come with us tonight."

George sipped some of his wine. "I'm glad it's just us."

CHAPTER TWENTY

The Bijou teemed with people strolling leisurely over the flowered carpet, ladies wearing their furs and best jewelry. Off to the sides, groups of gentlemen chatted, their laughter chiming in with the ladies, who also congregated. As women passed, a new scent of the latest cologne filled Claire's nostrils. She'd doused herself with the fancy French scent George had given her. As she and George slipped deeper into the lobby of the theater, she caught bits and pieces of conversation regarding the war in Europe. She wished for one night people would leave politics and the war at home, and not sully such a spectacular place with negative talk.

At least the women still showed interest in fashion and homemaking advice. She wished she knew these people or had acquired a more intimate group of friends. Since her arrival in Knoxville, her focus had turned down a narrow path, pretty much shutting out everyone and everything else that didn't involve the store or George Parker and his daughter. *Maybe I need to start going to church.* She made a mental note to ask George about his church the next time she thought of it.

"George, over here," called out an older gentleman with a neatly groomed mustache. Claire at once recognized the hat style he wore. One of Adrian's styles.

"Mr. Pemberton, how are you?" With an out-stretched hand, George smiled and made his way to the man. At once they shook hands.

"And who's this lovely lady with you?" Pemberton's eyes twinkled as he offered his hand also to Claire.

"This is Miriam Woodsworth, my newest store employee. She just moved here not long ago." George smiled, landing a pointed look at Claire. He rested his hand lightly on her shoulder.

"Just moved here?" The man's face turned a more focused gaze at Claire. "Where did you live before you came here?"

"Ash Grove, not far from Memphis." Claire smiled, following George's lead and hoping Pemberton wouldn't ask too many questions.

"A little ways away from here, but Tennessee still. Did you happen to ride that beauty of a train, The Tennessean?"

"I did," said Claire, smiling. "And it was a beauty. Had everything a body could want."

"I've ridden it once during my travels."

George added, "Mr. Pemberton represents the upper end line of men's suits we carry in the store. Keeps us supplied. Has a good eye for style, don't you, Warren?"

"I try my darnedest. Old George is picky, but I guess you've figured that out by now, haven't you, Miss. Woodsworth? Or is it Mrs.?" He looked at George.

"I'm married." Claire forced an uncomfortable smile. She saw the rise of Pemberton's eyebrow. The heat rose in her face.

"Claire has added a new line to the store. She does looming. Got beautiful towels and runners now." George shifted to the other foot. Claire noted he seemed as uncomfortable with the question.

"You don't say," said Pemberton. "That's wonderful. I'll have to send Emily over to see them."

"Warren, if you'll excuse us, we're going to mosey on. Hope you enjoy the show." George bowed his head and pulled Claire along with him.

"Good," George mumbled in Claire's ear, "we needed to get away. And thanks for playing along."

"Thank you."

"The more we keep things to ourselves, the better off we'll be. That's what I say." George tipped his head, politely acknowledging a young lady as she passed.

"All things aside, he seems like a nice man."

"He's one of the best acquaintances I have. A fine, upright human being. You don't get much better than Warren Pemberton."

"I agree with him. You have high standards."

"A mark of a good man is how high his standards are. Once you stop striving for perfection, you can just crawl in a corner and let life pass you by. Because it just won't matter anymore."

Claire relaxed as she and George mingled into the crowd. His hand had found hers, and she basked in warmth that flowed over her. She'd nearly forgotten the excitement of going out, dressing up, and being with someone she cared about. And George had turned into someone she more than cared about. He was turning into someone she might actually love. She turned her face for a brief glimpse at the man beside her.

His suit was impeccable. Probably one of Warren Pemberton's collection. Like Warren, he also wore one of Adrian's fine hats. Only now did full appreciation for Adrian's talent hit her, the realization cementing itself so strongly into her soul that it would never leave no matter what happened. And what would happen once Adrian couldn't make the hats anymore? What would happen to Mitchell if the business shut down? This was something else she wanted to discuss with her brother-in-law.

George ushered Claire in the direction of the theater. "Let's find our seats. Show's about to start."

When they entered, she gazed all around. The massive room held three levels of box seating on each side. When she turned around for a quick view, two balcony levels loomed behind her. A maroon curtain covered the stage. Hushed tones filled the room with a soft buzzing sound. Conversations continued between new groups of people or just among couples. She and George made their way slowly down the aisle to the main floor, where they ended up on the tenth row from the stage. They squeezed their way into their seats, next to an older man and woman. The woman wore a set of huge white pearls. In her hand, she clutched a shiny pair of mother of pearl opera glasses. She shifted closer to the male beside her as Claire sat down. Off on the far left hand side, Pemberton threw up his hand with an amiable wave, which George returned, accompanied with a smile.

"Oma got us great tickets, didn't she?" Claire smiled at George.

"I'll say. This is just as good as front row seats, if you ask me." He settled himself easily into the chair, letting out a sigh when he'd positioned himself in a comfortable position.

The house lights flickered. All talking came to a quick end. Over the loudspeaker, a voice announced the following:

Ladies and gentlemen, from Lindsay and Crouse's adaptation of stories by Clarence Day, Jr, the Bijou Theater proudly presents "Life With Father," starring Dorothy Gish and Louis Calhern."

As the room darkened, the orchestra struck the first chords of music. The curtains drew apart, revealing a large stage slowly illuminating to full light. The play started. Claire sat, eyes riveted on the stage as she absorbed every move, word, and scene. For all her attempts to remain totally focused, she and George chuckling at the humor demonstrated by a brilliant cast of characters, her mind still wandered at times. She wondered if she'd had a family and Adrian had kept a sane mind, would they be a lot like the Day family on stage? Would Claire have pampered Adrian while trying to make him feel like man of the house? That she would never know.

Somehow, she didn't quite see George like the character Mr. Day. George had a certain strictness about him, which still permeated through kindness and his moments of humor. He also held women in higher regard, especially her. Most likely he did the same with Anita. The more she thought about it, she wasn't like Vinnie, the seemingly frivolous happy-go-lucky stage wife, the one who really held the family together.

In many ways, she was glad. Constant use of cunning and wit exhausted her. She was a straight-shooter, wanting a husband who saw marriage as a partnership of equals. She knew in 1941 this ideal was not the norm. With Adrian, she'd gotten lucky, just like George felt about Anita.

Her reminiscing came to an end when George interlaced his fingers through hers. She always liked it when he rubbed his thumb over her hand. There was something about the gesture that held a more intimate, heartfelt emotion to it. Together they sat, arms and fingers entwined, until the play ended.

They followed the crowd back to the lobby, where Pemberton stood waiting near the door leading outside the Bijou. His wife stood next to him, watching as he flagged down George and Claire.

"That was a terrific show, wasn't it?" He grinned.

"We had a wonderful time, didn't we?" George motioned to Claire.

"Loved Dorothy Gish," said Claire. "I thought she made the whole show."

"Men don't know it, but it's really we women who run the show." Emily winked at Claire and extended her hand. "I'm Emily, by the way. And Warren told me that you have some towels you've loomed in George's store?"

"Yes. They haven't been out too long, so it's a new product line."

"How talented you are," Emily remarked. "I've never tried looming before, but I admire people who do that kind of work." She frowned. "I'm not sure what my talent is."

"Your talent it taking care of me." Warren chuckled, wrapping his wife in a warm, brief hug.

"That does take talent!" Emily chuckled along with everyone else in the small group, and then glanced around. "Claire, Warren says you just moved here. Do you and your husband live near George or in town somewhere?"

Warren's eyes remained steadfast on the ground. Claire sensed George tensing up next to her, and the heat found its way to her cheeks again.

"I'm staying in one of George's houses," Claire answered, forcing an obligatory smile on her face.

"Oh, is it the one that he and Anita used to live in?" Emily's eyes lit up. "I just love that house. Holston River Road is just so beautiful out there with all that green countryside."

Warren spoke up, "Emily, sweetheart, I think we need to head on back home. I think Claire and George are pretty tired." He offered his hand to George for a quick handshake. "Sir, I'll see you at the store. I have some fine collections to show you the next time I come in."

"Looking forward to it, Warren. Emily, so nice to see you again."

Managing a polite wave to Emily, Claire smiled back as the couple turned and headed out the door.

"You okay?" George wrapped his arm around Claire's shoulder.

"Humans are just so inquisitive, aren't they?"

"They are. I hear bears are the same way. At least, that's what I've heard my hunter customers tell me when they come into the store for regular clothes."

Claire couldn't help but giggle at that analogy. "So we're not much better than bears, huh?"

"Not much. Just as curious, and just as ornery at times." He laughed and hugged her tighter. "Let's get on out of here before someone else sees us."

As Claire and George stepped outside the theater doors, someone quickly moved into the shadows undetected. Ruby watched as the couple made their way to George's car.

★★★

George pulled into the driveway of the house, and stepped out of the car. He headed over to Claire's door, offering his hand for assistance as she stepped out.

"Did you want to come in for a quick cup of coffee and a piece of cake? I made it yesterday. Maybe just as a quick treat?"

His face lit up. "I'd love nothing better. You get the cake ready, and I'll make the coffee. Sound like a deal?"

"Let's do it."

Claire opened the door to the greeting of Buzzie and Moo, with Buzzie slinking up next to her leg, while Moo sniffed out George.

"Well, hello there, kitties. Claire takes such good care of you, doesn't she?" His voice changed into cooing adoration at the two cats, both deciding they wanted littles scratches behind the ears and on the top of their heads.

In the kitchen, Claire pulled out the Chemex coffee maker and placed it on the counter.

"They keep you company, don't they?" George sauntered into the kitchen, taking up the kettle resting on the stove and filling it with water.

"Yes, they do. Never a dull moment with those two around."

Several minutes later, both of them had found their seats at the tiny table, complete with cups of hot coffee and fresh chocolate cake.

"This is delicious." George closed his eyes and smiled after swallowing down a bite of the cake.

"You get to enjoy everything Edna makes. I adore her cooking."

"Don't kid yourself, my dear. She's no better than you are."

He took a sip of coffee, savoring the flavor. As he did, his eyes fixed on Claire.

She didn't say anything, but didn't fail to catch the expression in his eyes as he gazed at her. She knew that look, the look of more than platonic admiration. Adrian had looked at her that way, too, before they married.

"Thank you for coming with me tonight. I had a wonderful time."

"I wouldn't have dreamed of missing it, George. I like dressing up and going out. I'll have to thank Oma when I see her Monday."

Claire studied him, allowing their eyes to deadlock for a moment. Tonight she wished he didn't have to go back to his house. She wished for either going with him or having him stay with her. What would it be like sharing a bed with George, his warm body next to hers? Would it be as wonderful waking up next to him? What if things were different and not only he slept beside her, but Anna slept tucked away in her room across the hall? How nice it would be for such a routine, waking up in the mornings, seeing Anna off to school. She and George would go to the store for a full day's work, only to come home together and all of them be together. And the nights could be hers and George's.

"Would you like another piece of cake?" She broke herself away from her thoughts and saw his empty plate.

"I'd love another piece, but I think one will do. I'll take another cup of coffee."

"I'll get that for you." Claire got up from her chair.

"So what are you doing tomorrow?"

"Don't know yet. It's getting colder, so I'll likely do some more looming. The soap-making is coming along. I'll soon have some of it out. I found some really pretty paper and twine I can use to wrap up the bars."

"I love your creativity. You're so smart, Claire. I love the way you and Anna get along so well together. I love . . ."

Claire's heart fluttered in her chest. She brought him a new steaming cup of coffee. "And there's a lot of things I love about you too." She hoped her voice sounded cool and casual, though she swore it came out a bit shaky. "I think you're also smart. You're kind and caring toward Anna. You respect Edna. You're kind to the folks at the store. You're nice, but you set the limits between boss and employee. That's important, you know."

He grinned back at her, his eyes with that far-off dreamy look again. She let the momentary silence play between them. Silence usually made her uncomfortable, but she'd learned through the women's magazines that sometimes a woman needed to be quiet and let the man dream a little, give him time to think about her and the situation. That's what she forced herself to do now.

Let George think about why he might want her, what life would be like without her, or what Anna might think if they might never see each other again. Would Anna's heart break? Would George's? How would she feel if darkness shut out the light, sending the small world they'd made for themselves, perhaps if only by accident, spinning into oblivion? What if she'd found herself once again in that realm of the unknown, where uncertainty would be her shroud in a slow, silent death of virtual non-existence?

With George and Anna, life made sense again, gave her a taste of what a true family life could be. What she and Adrian could have had if everything hadn't gone so horribly wrong. Anna exuded joy and life, reveled in it the way happy children seemed to do when they had everything they needed and more. George had managed to keep himself from being the deserted ship tossed on an open stormy sea. Maybe men had an advantage over women, only because they identified with life in different ways. Fatherhood may have been a part of their personal backdrop, but it didn't wrap them up in a tight cocoon like motherhood did women.

She a certain joy in freedom now that it was hers. Making her own living brought out a more self-sufficient side she'd never known before, especially indulging her creative side. All had been squelched because of her ties to a man and potential family. This would change if she and George became more than what they were now. In one moment of clarity, she enjoyed an epiphany, of fully knowing that her existence right now revealed much of what she was, and how much more she could be when left alone with her own devices. But it also revealed a desire to have it all, or as much as she could in this life while she was living and breathing.

She couldn't control George or anyone else, that much she knew, but she could make her way and hope that someone like him saw great value in having her around and would love her until his last breath. Anna needed a mother, and Claire knew she'd love that little girl as if she had given birth to her. Would she and George have more children if they somehow stayed together? There were so many possibilities at this moment that she felt a rush of emotion, happy to be alive, glad that the tables had turned in her favor.

At the touch of a warm hand on hers, Claire snapped out of her dream world. George still had maintained that sense of wonderment toward her, his face glowing with emotion. His fingers wrapped around hers, infusing his energy straight into her.

"I wish I didn't have to go," he whispered.

"I wish you didn't have to, either."

In a remarkable display of feelings from the heart, George got up and moved in front of Claire, taking her head between his hands. She didn't know why but she stood up, a reflexive action that took her by surprise. Or was it instinct?

He turned her face up toward his, pulling her close until their lips met. George kissed her with a passion that nearly took her breath away, if not frightened her just a little. His touch warmed her with an intense heat, and the hint of the remaining cologne on his skin stirred up a deep attraction. She wrapped her arms around him, allowing herself the intoxicating joy of being in a man's arms again. She'd sensed a connection the day they met. Now she knew it for sure.

The kiss ended, and George stood gazing down at her. "I need to go."

Claire just nodded, still reeling from what just happened.

They walked to the door. He grabbed up his coat and hat, and turned around once more, gracing her with another quick kiss. In a flash, George stepped into the darkness and into his car, driving off toward his home. She had never felt her solitude more acutely than now. The kiss, however, still burned with a heat she hadn't felt in a while.

CHAPTER TWENTY-ONE

Claire stood in front of a shelf in the cosmetics department. In another week, her hand-crafted soap line would go right here, and then would be the start of a new additional product line for her. She needed a catchy name for the labels, instead of simple merchandise descriptions on the hand-cut paper she'd created, cleverly edged with a set of pinking shears.

In the back of the same closet holding Anita's fur, she'd prowled in more detail and found several sheets of flowered paper lying on top of a shelf. It looked similar to the designs lining the dresser drawers in her bedroom. In the basement, she'd managed to dig out some fine twine in an old wooden box. This wrapping style and her special tags would be good until her new wrappings arrived.

"Did you and George have fun seeing the play this past Saturday?"

Startled, Claire whirled around at the sound of the voice beside her. "Excuse me?"

Ruby stood by, eyeing Claire with a light grin on her face. "I saw you two outside The Bijou." She touched Claire lightly on the arm. "You looked really pretty in Anita's fur and jewelry. I guess that's a big deal when a man lets you wear his dead wife's trinkets, don't you think?"

This announcement by her co-worker stunned Claire so badly, all words failed her. Worse, the blood nearly seemed to boil inside of her. If she lacked propriety, she would have slugged the woman who stood close to her, ripping out every bleached-blonde lock of her hair. In all probability, she might have beaten her to a bloody pulp. All this talk and the way Ruby angled her head, the way her lips curled back when she made her jabs reminded Claire so much of Grace at Hatchie River.

"Oh, and Claire, I was talking to my aunt about you. She's here on vacation for several days and she's coming to the store to see me."

Claire said nothing, but kept her eyes fixed on Ruby, fists clenched at her sides.

"I've told her all about you and all the fine work you've done here. She's very interested in meeting you."

With a racing pulse, Claire fought for the right thing to say or do. Why would some aunt have any interest in meeting her? Should she just walk away and say nothing? Or tell Ruby to mind her own business, and that she had zero interest in meeting anyone in her family?

The front door of the store opened, letting in a cold gust of wind. Both ladies turned in the direction of a woman dressed in a long black wool coat. Her hair, which was probably curled and pinned neatly in place earlier, had been lightly tossed by the wind. She had briefly turned away, sweeping back a lock of hair behind her ear and quickly grabbing a handkerchief out of her pocket. Before the lady finished with a few quick pats on her forehead and face, Ruby rushed over, calling out an animated, warm greeting, which ended with a hug. In a matter of seconds, the woman turned fully around, and Ruby propelled her straight to Claire. Beaming, Ruby proudly announced, "Claire, this is my aunt I was just telling you about."

Claire grabbed the shelf for support. The room spun for a moment, and she breathed deeply to keep from fainting.

The woman in front of her, Ruby's so-called aunt, was none other than Greta Shultz.

Both pairs of eyes locked onto each other, and without missing a beat, Greta held out her arms.

"Claire, how wonderful to see you again! I just knew from Ruby's description, it had to be you." The nurse from Hatchie River stepped forward, with a wide smile on her face, taking Claire in her arms for a warm hug like a long-lost friend. She even gently patted Claire's back for added effect. "You didn't tell me you were leaving Ash Grove. We could have had coffee one last time, at least."

Wide-eyed with the biggest smile she could muster, Claire fought for control of her voice. "Wonderful to see you too, Greta. Yes, coffee would have been nice, but I simply had things come up, and time … well …" Claire managed a light chuckle. "Time just got away from me. You know how that is." She rubbed Greta's arm in mock affection, the smile plastered on her face so hard she swore it may never truly leave again.

"Are you liking Knoxville? I always love it here when I visit my favorite niece." Greta wrapped her arm around Ruby.

"Enjoying it a lot. Don't miss West Tennessee that much at all." Claire's eyes darted toward Ruby, who stood transfixed, watching everything going on between her and the aunt. "So how is everything back home?" Claire managed another nod of feigned interest.

"No changes, really." Greta presented herself in the most convincing casual manner that would have rivaled the characters in the play Claire and George saw the other night. "All the girls are still around, chatting, still getting together and sewing a couple of times a week. It helps them pass time and makes them feel productive." Now Greta managed a light chuckle.

Ruby piped up. "There's nothing Claire can't do, Aunt Greta. You should have seen the Halloween costume she made for Mr. Parker's daughter. And look at these gorgeous towels she made for the store. She loomed them, each and every one." Ruby picked up a hand towel and handed it to Greta.

"How beautiful." Greta cooed, turning the towel in her hands. "Too bad you weren't able to teach our sewing circle this skill. The girls would have loved it."

"I'm sure they would have. But you know that time thing I mentioned."

Claire fluttered her lashes a little, hoping she sounded as convincing as Greta. This showdown had to end before she vomited from a huge anxiety attack. "Greta, if you'll excuse me a moment, there's something I need to do in the back."

Overcome with a new strong wave of nausea, Claire turned and sped toward the back of the store, where she headed for the break room. If she hadn't cut out then, she surely would have fainted dead on the spot. She considered losing herself in the storage room and quietly skedaddling out the back door.

With any luck, she'd hop the next trolley and be back home before anyone could think twice. Maybe it was time to take The Tennessean and ride it all the way straight to Washington, DC. No one knew her there. It would be time to cut all ties with anyone she ever knew before and truly start from the beginning all over again. The thought wearied her, but this episode that just happened was simply too much.

In the end, she found herself staring out the window of the break room several minutes, praying hard Ruby would distract Greta with something else. She wasn't sure what her excuse would be. Maybe she'd say a stomach illness had gotten the better of her.

"Claire." Ruby's voice filled the room. "Are you okay? You've been gone a while." She strode over to Claire, placing her hand lightly on her shoulder. Her face clouded with concern. "Can I get you a cold cloth or something to drink? You look pale—and you're shaking a little."

"No," Claire answered in a weak voice. "I'm sorry. I'm just not feeling well at all today." She managed an even weaker smile. "I nearly stayed home. Must have picked up some bug over the weekend."

Ruby walked over to the water cooler and pulled off one of the paper cone cups, filling it and bringing it back to Claire. "Aunt Greta is so happy she's finally seen you again. I would have never imagined you two would have been such good friends."

Claire downed the cup of water, nearly choking.

"When she and I talked before, she said you sounded like someone she may have known back home. I just think this is wonderful that two old friends have met up again."

"Mmm," Claire said, choking back another sick feeling in the pit of her stomach.

"I'm sorry you're sick. Is there anything I can do for you?"

"Ruby, I have to ask you something." Claire pushed herself off against the wall and squared up her shoulders, sensing some of her old exasperation coming back. "Just why was it so important for you to bring up me and what I do here to Greta? And another thing, why was mentioning the play such a priority for you?"

"Would you have rather I not have mentioned it? I didn't see any harm with two co-workers sharing their love for a play." Ruby stepped back, dismayed.

"Really, Ruby? We're not necessarily the best of pals, in case you haven't figured that out by now. Personally, I think you couldn't wait to mention the play. It's like you wanted to rub my nose in it, like you wanted to make sure I knew you saw me with George." Claire's energy regained more momentum, and the old anger flared again. "You saw what you needed to last Saturday. Don't you think that's enough? And on top of that, you have to gossip about me to your aunt. What is it with this obsession you seem to have about me, for heaven's sake?"

Ruby shook her head, grasping at Claire's hand. Claire stiffened. "I'm not trying to fight. Honest, I'm not."

"You don't give up, do you?" Her voice held a charged, frantic tone.

Not loosening her hand on Claire's, Ruby continued, "Look, you've really hurt my feelings lately. I've tried to sort everything out in my head that's been said between us. I've decided to try and be a bigger person and not hold a grudge. You said what you wanted to say, and I read you loud and clear. I just don't want to walk on pins and needles when I'm around you. When it comes to Mr. Parker, I can see it, you've won fair and square." She dropped her gaze to the floor.

"I've won fair and square?" Claire arched an eyebrow.

"Look, I'm not going to lie. There was some jealousy on my part at first, because I really tried to get his attention before. But what you said to me last time we talked and then last Saturday … I see that he's made his choice. That's fine. Really, who could blame him?"

Claire stared hard at the younger woman in front of her.

"Can you blame me if I want to better myself, Claire? Anita did, and you are, but it seems that you were already the better one." Ruby turned her face up to Claire's. "I admire you. I really do. You're so pretty, smart, talented. I wish I was like that. I just want someone in my life so I can be that woman people admire. Have someone who's handsome and successful that adores me. That's all."

For once, Claire's heart softened a little. "Look, Ruby. I can say the same about you. You definitely seem very well-read, quoting Shakespeare and knowing all the classic stories you do. You seem to like the arts. You'll find what you're looking for if you just keep at it. Know when to pursue and most of all, please know when to keep moving on. That's the best advice I can give you."

"Thank you, that means a lot." Ruby grinned. "Now that we have that all cleared away, what about Aunt Greta? She mentioned wanting to have lunch with you."

Claire's stomach lurched again. At this point she and Greta had acted their parts to perfection. Why not finish with a grand ending and do lunch? "I guess we could grab something at the S & W across the street?"

Ruby winked. "I'm sure Mr. Parker wouldn't mind you taking a little time on your lunch hour to visit with an old friend."

Claire's lip turned up in one corner as she nodded in agreement. "Sure. Always nice to see old friends, yes?"

"I think it's pretty nice." Ruby grabbed Claire's coat off the rack and handed it to her. The two women filed out of the break room and out on to the sales floor. Greta had engaged in what seemed a chatty, friendly conversation with Dahlia and Minnie at the cosmetics counter, where the sales ladies had apparently been offering perfume samples.

"Aunt Greta, Claire wants to go for lunch."

Greta's eyes lit up. "Wonderful. All the excitement has given me an appetite."

"I thought we'd go to the cafeteria across the street. Maybe we can catch up a little."

"I guess they still have the organ player there?" Greta's lips pulled back in a wide smile.

"They do."

"Then let's go, and I'll let my niece get back to work." Greta hugged Ruby. "I'll see you later, dear." Turning to Dahlia and Minnie she added, "I'll come back and purchase one of those bottles of perfume you showed me. I love the scent."

Keeping up their act, Claire slipped an arm under Greta's, and led her to the S&W Cafeteria.

✳✳✳

The ladies moved down the line in silence, only speaking with selecting their food to the staff behind the glass divider. The black assistant found a vacant spot and led them to a table for two in a less crowded corner of the dining room. Each woman slipped of a coat and sat down. The next few minutes consisted of each one opening a napkin and pulling out the silverware, which ended up neatly placed beside the plates.

Greta spoke first, surveying Claire from across the table. "Found you at last." A light smile flickered across her face. "I've been wondering what happened to you." Her voice had lost the higher pitched animated tone she'd displayed earlier in the store. She sounded more like the nurse back in the asylum.

Claire fidgeted with her napkin that she'd placed in her lap. She stirred her bowl of chowder aimlessly with her soup spoon. "Now you know. So, I'm busted, right?"

"Absolutely not." Greta sat straight up, leaning on her elbows, hands folded primly under her chin. "I'd never dream of saying anything. We'll simply call this our dirty little secret and move on with life. If you tell me exactly what happened, the truth, then I'm agreeable if you are."

"Oh, I'm more than agreeable. And there's really no dirty secret about anything." She stared hard at Greta. "Can I really trust you, or does it really not matter, since I'll have you and a hundred others against me if authorities had to choose?" Claire's face turned cold in earnestness.

"Mrs. Wright, I would hope that you still remember how we were back in Hatchie River. Anne and I were supportive of you a hundred percent." She shrugged lightly. "As best we could be in a place like that. As you well know, there are not many choices, and good can only go so far. Eyes and ears can only see and hear so much."

The older lady cut a piece from her pot roast and placed a bite in her mouth. Claire managed a bite of her corn chowder.

When Greta had taken a few bites of her food, she sat back, resting her hands in her lap. "Tell me everything in great detail. I really want to hear your story."

For the next several minutes, Claire shared the event once again with someone who demanded an explanation of how she'd escaped hell and left the devil dead, though not by her own hand.

"And that's how it all happened." Claire sank back in her chair, surprised at how much retelling the story left her drained and exhausted. "All I ask is that you believe me. Grace truly died by accident. I'll add this. If she hadn't slipped, I'm not sure I would have made it out alive. I had Providence on my side, I guess."

Greta sat straight up, lightly wrapping her hand against the table.

"Providence works wonders. We need miracles every now and then in our lives, lest we be swept away by an evil hand. Grace Neil was exactly that, the embodiment of all that is black and cruel in the world, the embodiment of evil. She lived it, breathed it, worked for it. It finally got her." Greta leaned forward, lowering her voice. "Mrs. Wright, I say good riddance. And it's really your word against the dead. The problem is that no one would believe you. When you passed our doors, any respectability you once had was gone."

Claire stared down at her bowl. "Did they ever try to find me?"

Placing her hand on Claire's, Greta said, "Mrs. Wright, they did their brief search. But rest assured, they didn't spend lots of time on it. Once they decided you were not an immediate danger, they let it go." She leaned forward, lowering her voice. "Besides, we keep lots of secrets at Hatchie River. We don't want the public frightened or thinking we can't do our jobs properly."

"But do you believe me?" Claire insisted on an answer.

"Of course, I believe you. And Anne will believe you. I have to tell her. She's been so worried about you."

"Really? Why would she be worried about me?"

"Mrs. Wright, we both were worried. We would have been saddened if something bad had happened to you." Greta's thick German accent kicked in harder, the more intense she became. "You want to know the real truth? We would have been more devastated had you returned. Your fate would have been much worse, and Anne and I would have been nearly powerless to stop it. Honestly, I don't think we could."

"Am I really safe here?" Claire searched Greta's face.

"You're safe as long as Anne and I have breath in our bodies. Sounds like you have a very caring brother-in-law." Greta smiled. "Sounds like you have a new admirer too, from what Ruby tells me."

Irritation shot through Claire. Her face clouded in a reflexive movement that had grown difficult to try and cover. "Yes. Dear Ruby. She's persistent. Sometimes I look at her and see Gra …" Claire stopped, wide-eyed, pursing her lips together. She may have had her reservations about Ruby, but Greta seemed fond of her niece. No need to loosen her tongue and say hateful things to a doting aunt.

Greta clucked her tongue. "Come now, Mrs. Wright. You surely don't mean that. To compare Ruby to someone so awful."

"I'm sorry. It just slipped out. Just so you know, Greta, I've had to ward her off on several occasions. She's a little too inquisitive for my taste."

"I'll allow you your sentiments, Mrs. Wright, but you have my word. I assure you that Ruby is a good girl. She means no harm."

Claire narrowed her eyes and tipped her head to one side, gazing at the nurse. "A little biased, maybe?"

"Of course." The old light grin slipped in on Greta's face. "The truth is, I would have nothing to do with Ruby if she were anything but a good girl. She's persistent. Has an odd way of showing how she really feels." Greta swallowed a quick sip of tea from her glass. "Ruby's not polished, I agree. A young lady who still has far to go. And Mrs. Wright, whether or not you believe it, she admires you so much." Greta beamed at Claire with fondness. "She couldn't have picked a better role model. I'll be happier knowing you're nearby. She needs that in her life, someone to whom she can aspire."

"You'll never say anything to her about what I've told you? It's her … and anyone else finding out about my past that concerns me a great deal. I don't want to be hauled off back to the crazy house because somebody has it in for me."

"Of course not. I wouldn't dream of it." Greta lifted her gaze briefly to the ceiling. "Again, your secret's safe with me. Now, let's talk about other things. Tell me what you've been doing here. I'd love to know."

The two ladies spent the rest of the lunch hour in as much pleasant conversation as they could, under the circumstances. Claire, though she would always be grateful to Greta, still held on to a bit of caution. It may not be Greta, or even Ruby now, who would concern her as much, but the older lady's presence had rudely stirred up a fear deep within her gut, and she couldn't quite put her finger on why it wouldn't let go. The longer she conversed with the nurse, the more dismal things seemed. If confession was good for the soul, why did she harbor such ominous feelings?

CHAPTER TWENTY-TWO

"Simply amazing." George shook his head, taking Claire's free hand in his. Both sat at the kitchen table sipping coffee that Edna had made after pulling a reluctant and tearful Anna away from Claire, promptly sending the little girl off to bed for the evening. "That's why I had you over for dinner tonight. I just knew something wasn't right after you came back from lunch with that woman . . . Ruby's aunt."

"You're the third person I've told in detail what's happened. And this is the last time I ever want to mention any of this again."

"I don't blame you. People are nosy and look for any way to knock you down. My lips are sealed." George squeezed her hand in reassurance.

"Did Mitchell ever say anything more about me once he got back to Ash Grove? I thought he would have. That's why I never made a point to bring it up to you." Claire managed a quick swallow of her cooling coffee.

"No, he's not one to gossip like a chatty woman." George smiled. "You know how we men are. No details. Just the quick down and dirty, and then carry on."

"You do believe me, don't you, George?" Claire's eyes searched his face. "I despised Grace Neil worse than the devil, but I'd never deliberately kill her."

"Of course, you wouldn't. Listen, she slipped. Simple. Handy stroke of luck."

Claire placed her cup back in the saucer. "But I know the others at Hatchie River think I did."

"Who cares what they think. If they felt the same way as you, they probably didn't care. Their only concern would be you harming someone else. You're here. They're done."

"Since we're talking candidly, I want to ask you something."

"Go on."

"Did Ruby ever try to get in good with you? Even lately? Because I swear I still have trust issues with her, though Greta adores her."

George grinned. "I won't lie. She flirted like everything before you came to town. And yes, she still tried a little after you started at the store. She'd knock on my office door and bring me a small bite of some cake she'd made. Or she'd bring me some coffee. She's not done anything for the past few weeks, and she had cooled down a bit before that."

"You loved the attention, didn't you?"

"Claire! That's a bold comment." George wrinkled his brow, unable to totally stifle a light chuckle. "It's always nice to get attention from someone, but she's also young and somewhat impressionable. I'm not the kind of man to take advantage of that."

"She saw us at The Bijou." Claire drummed her nails lightly against the tablecloth.

"So what? She can see anything she wants. Maybe that'll finish off whatever thoughts she had in her head." George locked his gaze on Claire. "Over all, I'm in Greta's camp where Ruby's concerned. She stands toe-to-toe, but her bark is worse than her bite." With a quick grin, he leaned over and kissed Claire lightly on the lips. "Don't worry about a thing. I think you've cleared the air for the last time."

"I'm hoping it's the last time. I don't know how much more my nerves can take."

"You'll be fine. You're not alone, Claire." He stared at his cup. His lips twitched as if he wanted to say something else, but couldn't quite get the words out. He picked up the cup, swirled the remaining coffee, and downed it in one gulp. Claire reached for the coffee pot and poured him another cup, freshening her own cup too.

"Do you have something on your mind, George? You suddenly seem preoccupied."

"I'll just come right out and ask it, since we're talking candidly, as you say."

Beneath the table, Claire landed a light kick on George's leg. "Quit stalling. Out with it."

"What are you going to do about that husband of yours? Have you even spoken to Mitchell lately?"

"I keep thinking I'll get a letter in the mail, or I start to pick up the phone, and then I get busy with something else."

"So the answer is no."

"Right. No." Claire grimaced and sipped from her cup.

George shifted lightly in his seat. His face showed signs of one struggling with strong emotion. "Do you plan on being with him forever? I mean, after what he's done to you? You're here, miles away. You've started a new life …" He sank back in his chair.

Claire's heart pounded in her chest. For George to bring this up surely was a sign that he'd been thinking in more detail about his future too. Why hadn't she spoken to her brother-in-law? She couldn't even pin down the reason for it. Perhaps the thoughts of having to deal with Adrian in any way exhausted her before she could even think of getting started.

"I'll call him tomorrow. I promise." Claire angled her head to the side, studying George. "Why the sudden concern for him?"

"Sudden?" His face hardened. "There's nothing all that sudden about any of this. I'm thinking at some point you want that behind you too, don't you?"

"Of course. You're right about that." She frowned a little. Not totally the answer she was expecting, but still a move forward. She would definitely make it a point to call Mitchell. At some point she needed the freedom to make any choice she wanted unencumbered.

George glanced at his watch. "I need to get you home. It's late."

"I'll help you clean up first."

Claire picked up the dishes and the coffee pot, carrying them to the counter. She quickly washed everything and placed them on the drainboard. From the living room sofa, she plucked up her coat and slipped it on. Outside the night was colder, the moon and stars brighter and shinier than she'd noticed before. Somehow it hit her senses that way as she gazed briefly at the black sky.

She breathed in a healthy dose of cold air, noting the burst of internal energy as opposed to the warm, sleepy lull creeping over her in George's kitchen. If she had lacked propriety, she would have asked if she could at least sleep on the sofa for the night. But the cold had awakened her, and now that she'd be away from George and his cozy abode, it riled up the old fear she experienced earlier in the day while conversing with Greta. She didn't want to go to her place. She wanted to stay with him where she was warm and at least felt safe.

The car rumbled down the street toward the stone house. As it came into view, an unexplained chill of uneasiness shot down Claire's spine. She shivered. In the moonlight, the house seemed lonely, filled with something darker than the darkness. The pale shadows from the moon gripped the stone blocks like desperate ghosts. More than ever a sense of dread filled her, starting in the pit of her stomach and moving throughout her. Not understanding from where it came only intensified a certain beginning of madness if it continued for any length of time. That much she knew.

What if she simply came clean with George and said she wanted to go back to his place? No one else would know but him. Of course he wouldn't say no, if she told him her nerves were getting the better of her. Claire turned in her seat toward him, but no words came out. He smiled at her quickly and turned his face back toward the road.

"Did you want to say something?" He asked.

"I . . . um . . ." Claire sat back in her seat, viewing the frosty night through the windshield.

"I'm glad I got to spend some time with you tonight." He reached over and grasped Claire's hand.

"Yeah, me too. I needed that. I really did." She smiled lightly, hoping she'd get up the nerve to talk more about what was bothering her.

At last he pulled into the gravel driveway and stopped the car in front of the porch. Claire drew up her shoulders and reached for the door handle.

"Uh, uh, uh," George said, waving a finger in mock admonishment. "You're forgetting something." He leaned toward Claire, wrapping a hand around her neck. Their lips met in a fiery kiss. Drowning in his kiss, she savored a moment of brief perfection. She tossed aside her uneasiness about entering the place she called home.

George finished the kiss and lightly pulled away. "Take care, dear."

"I'll do just that." She forced a weak grin on her face and got out of the car.

He didn't pull away until she'd entered the front door and shut it behind her, locking it. Glancing around her, she strained her ears in the silence. From the kitchen, the sound of the refrigerator whirred in monotone sounds. Strange. Where were Buzzie and Moo? They usually greeted her at the door, rubbing against her ankles and voicing their hellos with emphatic meows. Maybe they were napping somewhere else tonight. She jumped at the cracking sound of the house settling. The colder temperatures had set in. The stone comprising the house seemed to have trapped all the cold air, sending it straight inside.

The chilly air held a certain thickness to it she'd not felt before. Or maybe it was simply her imagination. Part of her wanted to check out all of the rooms downstairs to make sure everything was okay. But she couldn't deny that the desire to spring up the stairs and into her bedroom compelled her to do just that. Where were the cats? When she reached the top of the stairs, she called out to them. "Buzzie? Moo? Where are you two hiding? Come out, come out wherever you are." She listened hard again. Nothing.

Walking down the hall, she passed by the phone sitting in its designated small recess in the wall. Mitchell was only an hour behind her in time. It wouldn't be that late to call him. She could check in now, see how everything was going. Instead Claire quickly entered her room, shook off her clothes, and threw on a flannel nightgown. The rushed movements warmed her a little. Throwing back the covers, she crawled into bed, wishing the sheets didn't feel so cold. The clock on the nightstand showed nine o'clock. Maybe if she closed her eyes and cleared her head, she might fall asleep.

Closing her eyes, Claire tried focusing on nothing. Instead of drowsiness, images of lunch with Greta popped up. As seconds passed, Hatchie River welled up, looming large and awful inside her mind's eye. She flinched, struggling to see white like she always did for blotting out unpleasantness. To her horror, she saw Grace again, lips twisted up in a smirk, the flashing mockery in her eyes, which slowly morphed into glassy eyes of death. Claire tossed a little between the sheets.

After fifteen minutes, she finally settled into a comfortable position, sleep creeping over her. Heaviness in her body set in, and she felt herself sinking into the realms of sleep. Just as she drifted off and began dreaming, the lamp on the nightstand switched on. A rude light beamed down on her face. Her eyes fluttered open. Through the blinding light, she viewed the image of a man standing over her, staring down with a wild look in his eye. Claire let out a scream and scrambled to the other side of the bed.

"Adrian!" She threw the covers off and tumbled out of bed, wrenching her foot free from the sheets before she nearly hit the ground. Her breath came hard and loud in her throat, deafening in her ears. She grabbed the edge of the dresser for support. The surprise and fear had set of a wave of dizziness.

Adrian moved with jerky steps in Claire's direction. "So this is where you are. I've been wondering about you. Obsessed. Can't sleep, can't eat."

"What are you doing here. How did you know—"

"Maybe my brother shouldn't be so careless leaving your name and information on his desk."

Claire glanced around the room for an item she could use as a weapon. Just in case. "Careless with his papers?" She tried desperately to keep her voice from reflecting the shaking of her body. "What are you talking about?"

"Are you that dumb?" His gaze drilled into her own. "You can't keep things from me. I'm smarter than that." He swiped a loose lock of hair away from his face. "Might take me a little time, but I figure things out. You know that."

"No one said you weren't smart, Adrian. You've always been a bright, creative person." Claire forced a light smile on her face. If she didn't get control of her breathing, she'd faint for sure. The last thing she wanted was him more riled. Just as her husband move in on her, she scrambled back on the bed. If she could reach the door, she'd make a run for it. Too late. Somehow In a clumsy but quick move, Adrian grabbed her leg, pulling her back to him. His hair hung limp around his face. From so close, she viewed the large dark rings under his eyes. He looked haggard and worn, nothing like the strapping, handsome man he used to me. The fine tremors in his body reverberated against her. Was it truly the mercury toxins that had kicked in over time, or was it his temper flaring?

"Why did you run away from me? I had you where I wanted you. Home with me." He gripped her arm so hard she cried out.

"You put me in hell. I'd be damned if I was staying there. When I had a chance, I ran for it." She pushed her face close to his. "Maybe staff shouldn't be so careless with their keys."

He grabbed her arm. "Don't get sassy with me. You remember your place, woman."

Claire pulled hard, finally wrenching herself free. She took several small steps back. Maybe if she moved slowly he wouldn't get more upset. "How could you do this to me? To us? I tried calling you. You shut me out."

His steps kept pace with hers. Adrian's eyes narrowed. "You were always such a whiney thing." his voice floated out in a soft whisper.

"Are you kidding me? Have you forgotten the life we had?" Claire quickly caught sight of the lamp on the nightstand—and the clock. She could use those if things got really ugly.

"Life we had?" He glanced around, squinting, as if trying to remember.

"And how did you get all the way from Ash Grove to here? You don't look fit to travel anywhere, let alone have a mind enough—"

"There's nothing wrong with my mind. I'm perfectly fine." As he shouted, his eyes burned with hot fires of indignation. "I can drive and I can read, can't I? I can figure out a schedule and ride a fancy train along with the best of them." Adrian strode toward her. Claire had backed away some more, but was still several feet from the door. She didn't want to risk doing anything too quickly or startle him. She stepped back a few more steps, holding out her arms to ward him off.

"How did you get in this house?" Claire's tone had risen in her throat.

"Maybe you shouldn't be careless when it comes to locking the door. Like the Bible says, when you can't come through the front door, check the back."

Claire stared at her husband stunned. "The Bible doesn't—"

"Don't argue with me, woman. I know what the Good Book says." A crooked smile crept across Adrian's face. "I guess here in the boondocks, folks don't lock up. Gets you in trouble, doesn't it? The Bible says you'll never know the hour or the place, but when it comes, it comes." He attempted another grab at Claire.

She backed away, horrified at her husband's statements. Adrian had always been well-versed in scripture. He'd been so well-versed when they first married that he treated her with kindness and respect.

Adrian, continued, "I still have enough wits about me to outsmart you."

A chill ricocheted through Claire. "Adrian, honey, listen to me. Since we've been apart this long, and you're not happy, why don't you just go on back home? I promise I won't bother you at all. Won't say another word about anything."

He shook his head. "No, you'll be coming home with me. A wife lives with her husband."

"I won't be living with you Adrian, no matter where I go. And I'm not about to go back to that nasty place you sent me. And for what reason, I'm still trying to figure out."

"Nasty place?" He looked at her again, a confused look on his face. Clenching his fists, he shouted, "You'll go where I say you'll go. A woman abides by what her husband tells her to do. It's written in the law."

"Would you just listen to yourself? I still can't figure out how you got here." She challenged him. "You sound like a crazy person. Are you even listening to yourself?"

He stomped his foot hard against the wooden floor. "You listen to me. You'll do everything I tell you to do, no matter what. No wife of mine is going to stay away from me, acting like a common trollop." Drops of spittle sprayed from his mouth. Without warning, he lunged forward. Claire screamed and attempted a run for the door. Adrian had just enough speed, grabbing Claire and pulling her into his arms. He shook her hard. "Don't you run away from me."

"Stop it, Adrian! You're hurting me." She jerked and pulled in all directions, beating at him with a hand she'd loosened from his grip. Resorting to action movies again, she slammed her foot on top of his, before kneeing him in the groin. His grip loosened as he buckled in pain. Claire took advantage, breaking loose at last. The ringing of the telephone both startled and relieved her. Whomever it was on the other line, she only had one chance at a cry for help.

She managed a head start to the hall and grabbed the phone, screaming into the receiver, "Adrian's here. Help me."

Mitchell's distant voice cracked through the line. "Claire... Claire, can you hear me?"

A strong arm reached around her and yanked the telephone from the shelf. Adrian slammed it against the wall, cracking the plaster and sending phone parts scattering in all directions.

Claire didn't look back, but made a rush for the stairs. Everything in her field of vision passed in a blur. The only plan in her head was to get out of the house as fast as she could and make a run for George's. Thoughts of running through the bitter cold night, with sharp rocks digging into her nearly frozen feet, scared her. Would she be able to do it, bear the pain?

Adrian's steps pounded loud, much too close for comfort, but Claire knew she surely had to be steadier and more sure-footed. It must have been sheer will that kept her husband charging forward, shouting her name. Her breath came hard, and her chest ached. Just as she landed mid-way down the staircase and thought she could make a run for the front door, she screamed in pain. He'd grabbed a handful of her hair, yanking her back. She heard strands ripping from her head. If he didn't let her go, she'd be bald. Forced to stop, she tried clawing at him, slapping her hands back and around his face.

Relentless, he caught one of her arms, wrenching it down and wrapping his own around her. Claire winced as the joint in her shoulder made a popping sound. "You think you'll get away from me?" He lowered his face down so that his voice filled her ear. He grabbed the other arm, yanking it down and behind her back. Adrian held her fast. Try as she might, she couldn't move.

He'd twisted her arms around tightly so that each pull or tug ended with pain. The only thing free was her head, which she could move. She thought of one last idea. This was it, one last plan before sure death. She leaned her head forward as far as she could, and brought it back up, not stopping until she smashed into Adrian's face. He cried out in pain.

She scrambled down the remaining stairs to the landing. Only two more small steps down into the living room, and the door was straight ahead. The lock would delay her a little, but she'd dealt with it so much, she knew just how to twist and lift the little knob to its smoothest spot and open the door. No matter how cold or how hard the run would be, she'd grit her teeth and wouldn't stop until she was safe inside George's house. She knew careening her head into her husband's face only made him madder and stronger. Claire didn't know quite what happened, or even how he'd thought clearly enough, but the last thing she remembered was a sharp pain to the back of the head and spiraling down to the hard wooden floor. All went dark.

CHAPTER TWENTY-THREE

Light from the window ignited a searing pain through Claire's head as she opened her eyes. She closed them again, shutting out the world a few seconds longer before attempting another peek through narrowed lids. Her mind reeled and slowed as it slogged through a jumble of information that had somehow become muddled and broken. Where was she? Why was she here? Was this a dream? When coherence managed a toehold somewhere in her scrambled memory, a part that still remained somewhat intact, she cried out in panic. Her body tensed. She finally remembered remnants of what happened before now.

"It's okay, Miss Claire, I'm here." The tiny voice tinkled in her ear, a sound so soft and sweet, it must have been a cherub. That's how cherubs sounded, didn't they? Claire winced, stirring and turning toward a small form sitting beside the bed. "I'll take care of you, Miss Claire. You'll get better. I promise." The last words came out in a soft whisper, falling on her ear like a soft breeze. Yes, that was an angel's voice.

The form must have moved because Claire felt a sense of emptiness beside her. In the distance, she heard the patter of feet moving quickly along something hard. Within moments, she detected the warmth of a body. The energy from this being seemed big, strong, a force that should have frightened her, but somehow didn't. A heavy, warm hand rested lightly on her forehead.

"Claire, are you awake?"

She knew this voice from somewhere. It sounded kind. The touch, firm but gentle, soothed her as she acclimated to the world of the living. Where did her world go? Nothing had prepared her for disappearance, a brief touch with darkness that could have easily been oblivion.

"Claire, it's me, George. And Anna's here too."

"Is she finally awake?" Another strong voice filled the room, and Claire sensed another energy not too different from the one who had touched her the first time. This voice had a hand, too, that rested lightly on her own, gently rubbing her cool flesh. "Are you sure we don't need to get her to a hospital?"

A hospital? No. The word rang in her mind as a somber tone of recognition, a fleeting remembrance of a place she didn't like. She did not want to go there or any place like it. She'd rather slip away into darkness forever than go to anything resembling a hospital. She tried clasping the hand on hers.

"Claire, we're all here. Me, Anna, and Mitchell."

Finally, she knew names. They all connected now. With one last struggle, she opened her eyes, viewing all three people through a hazy blur. She didn't say anything but just stared at them, blinking, focusing.

"She's not going to die, is she, Daddy?"

"Anna, that's not a proper question to ask right now."

"Why not? We need to know so we can keep her here." A small sob sounded from the little girl.

"Miss Claire is going to be fine. Don't worry, sweetheart." That was Mitchell's voice. Anna sniffed back more tears. George let out a sigh.

Claire forced her eyes open wider. Over the next few minutes, her vision improved. Croaking out her words, she managed to ask, "What happened?" When George lifted a hand, she saw it had been bandaged. "What happened to your hand?"

Mitchell spoke up. "Let me go downstairs and make some coffee and some hot broth. Anna, dear, would you like to help?"

"No, sir. I'll stay with Miss Claire."

"Anna, you'll go downstairs with Mr. Wright this instant." George's voice sounded firm, but not unkind.

Anna whimpered.

"Come on, Anna. Don't you want to make Miss Claire better? You can only do that by helping me." Mitchell, motioned for the girl to follow. Anna left the bedside, and she and Mitchell disappeared from the room.

George leaned over Claire's face, and kissed her lips. "I'm so glad you're coming around. I was worried sick about you."

"My head is so sore."

"I imagine so. You have a nasty bump back there. I had a doctor look at you."

Claire narrowed her eyes, confused.

"I found a doctor who made house calls. He stopped by for a quick look at you. Said to keep watch and take you to the hospital if anything got worse."

"I think I'll survive. I've had enough of hospitals." She managed a small smile. "But you never told me about your hand—and Adrian was here. Did he get away? We have to catch him."

George shook his head. "I got a frantic call from Mitchell last night. Came right over."

"Was Adrian still here?" Claire tried to sit up, but gave up on the notion.

Grimacing, George nodded. "Yeah, he was. He was trying to pick you up, shouting your name. When he saw me, it set him off."

"Oh, dear." Claire frowned, turning her eyes toward George's bandaged hand. "Looks like he put up a fight."

"I hate like everything that I had to punch out my favorite client, and old friend, but I had no other choice. He was determined to take you with him, where ever he thought he was going."

"Adrian was bound and determined to take me back to Ash Grove. You should have heard the nonsense. It was crazy."

"I bet it was."

"So where is he, George?" Claire's panic returned. "He didn't just go on back to Ash Grove, did he?"

"Not exactly." George scratched the back of his head, stalling.

"Then tell me where he is." The loud tone in her voice startled Claire. At least her energy had come back a little.

"Shh, Claire. Don't get upset. You won't believe me when I tell you."

"Try me. I'm all ears." She scowled.

"He's at Eastern Psychiatric Hospital. It was either that or jail."

Claire gasped. George grew silent, eyes locked on hers.

✶✶✶

Mitchell, Claire, and George sat at the dining table. George had let the store employees know that he and Claire weren't coming in this day. He'd give no other explanation. Oma had been assigned to open the store. Anna had insisted she have a day off from school to help. As the three adults conversed together, Claire noted that this was the first time she'd used her own formal dining room. She rather liked it, sitting with the others, conversing. After this ordeal, she'd determined a change was in order—with or without George. Anna, having rounded up Buzzie and Moo from their hiding place, played quietly in the other room.

Mitchell poured each one at the table a cup of coffee from the Chemex. Claire brought the chintz ware cup to her nose, inhaling the aroma. She definitely needed something with a bit of kick to it. In front of her sat a matching chintz bowl full of seasoned chicken broth and a few vegetables Mitchell had thrown in for good measure. She enjoyed the simplicity and comfort of it. Her head still felt a bit heavy and sore, and her appetite had kicked in a bit.

"I still can't believe I let him get away. He hopped the train all the way here, broke in, and stayed around until he could get you." Mitchell shook his head and took a quick sip from his cup. "I'm still speechless. When I couldn't find him anywhere, something told me to call you, Claire."

"Why did you have my address out on your desk? Adrian mentioned something like that."

"I was going to call you. I needed your number. I walked away to answer a question out on the factory floor. He must have slipped in just as I left."

"Then he's not totally gone, but listening to him carry on last night, I'm curious as to how long he'll last." George reached over, taking Claire's hand in his. "The question is, what do we do with him now?" He looked over at Mitchell.

Claire spoke up first. "I want him as far away as possible. Otherwise, I'm leaving here and going somewhere else." Though she had no idea where "somewhere" would be.

George stared hard at her, silent.

Mitchell's face had turned down toward his coffee. He seemed lost in thought, his lips twisted in what seemed an expression of sadness and regret. "Honestly, I'm not really worried about Adrian as much as I am the business. Adrian can be dealt with. But he ran the production side of our business. I'm not sure whether to shut the whole thing down or try and find another partner."

"Ah, you don't want to do that, shut your business down. I want those hats." George grimaced, shaking his head.

"You got any ideas on who can run the place, then?" Mitchell shot his friend a pointed look. "I'm in a quandary."

"You'll figure it all out, Mitchell. You've got workers who know the job, and I'd start chatting with some people in the industry, make a few calls or visits." Claire cast a reassuring look at her brother-in-law.

Mitchell shrugged and rested an elbow on the table, a forlorn look covering his face.

"Can you get Adrian back to Ash Grove?" George asked.

"There's one thing I want to do first, and that's see a lawyer while I'm here. I think it would be easier while we're all together." Mitchell aimed his gaze at Claire. "My dear, we're getting you a divorce."

"How do you intend to pull that off, Mitchell? Doesn't Adrian have to be present? And how do you get a madman to sign anything?"

"I've got an acquaintance who's a lawyer. I don't see why he couldn't help, or at least think of something." George peered at Claire. "This is now or never."

"I know. I just never thought I'd see myself in this situation. Life was supposed to be simple and good. That's all I ever asked for."

All three sat in silence while a war raged in Claire's head. Just the sound of the word "divorce" grated on her. Never would she have ever guessed her life would come to this. Being a widow would be better. At least that was respectable. People understood it, treated you with sympathy and respect. You could even marry again without someone batting an eye. But divorce? Society looked down on that. She'd be "used goods," a sullied woman.

Maybe George didn't care. Still, he'd never clearly discussed a future with him. In an instant, a keen sense of lost youth and her current lot in life engulfed her, shrouding her with a sense of time slipping away so fast it seemed life was passing her by before she could grab the reigns and stop it. She didn't feel like a fresh young woman anymore.

Now an underlying sadness lingered most days than not. The future wore a hazy veil. Life carried far too much mystery and uncertainty for her liking, and all she wanted was the comfort of house and family again, someone she could trust, and children she could love and nurture. This wish still seemed elusive at best, all but lost at the worst.

"Miss Claire," said a small voice beside her. "Do you want to stay with us until you feel better? I can take care of you." Anna had slipped into the room and snuggled up to Claire.

"Darling, thank you. I think I should be all right here. That bad old man is gone." Claire took Anna in her arm and pulled her close, kissing her on top of the head.

"But what if he comes back? I won't be here to scare him off." Anna peered up, tears welling in her eyes. Her small pink lips trembled.

Claire suppressed a smile. "Maybe you can spend the night over here." She glanced at George.

"Honey," George said to his daughter, "I'll have to think about what we need to do for Miss Claire. We haven't thought that far ahead yet."

"You don't need to think far ahead. She can stay with us." Anna backed away, her face contorted with a certain irritation that Claire hadn't seen before. The little girl's clenched fists alarmed her most. Something about this exchange didn't feel right.

"Sweetheart, it's okay." Claire tried one more attempt at supporting George's statement while soothing Anna. "We'll figure out something. Don't worry." This time, she reached toward the girl, wanting to pull her close again.

Anna stepped back a few more steps. Her breath came in rapid successions, and her eyes had changed from concern to almost wild with pent up rage. "No!" she screamed, stomping her foot. "I want you to stay with me!"

"Anna." George's voice rang out with disapproval. "Don't ever talk back. What's gotten into you?" He stood up, face clouded with anger.

"I want Miss Claire to stay with me forever!" Anna stomped one foot, then the other. "I want my mother!"

Claire winced as the little girl's shrill voice pierced her ear.

George moved in his daughter's direction, fists clenched. Tears had fallen over Anna's cheeks. Without another word, she let out a wail and bolted for the front door.

The adults remained rooted in place, stunned. When the front door opened and the sound of Anna's footsteps echoed on the porch, Mitchell spoke, "Go after her." He sped toward the living room window. "George, she's headed toward the road."

Claire jumped up from her chair, nearly fainting. She took a deep breath, steadied herself, and moved as fast as she could, calling out Anna's name. George brushed by her, tearing through the room and on toward the yard. His voice sounded loud and urgent in the distance. Claire made it to the front porch, Mitchell behind her. She saw George at the road's edge.

Out of nowhere, it seemed, came the grinding sound of a car. At the same time, a honking horn, a shrill scream, and the screech of brakes. It was the slamming of car doors and the frantic talking of multiple voices that nearly did it for Claire. Mitchell grabbed hold of her arm, pausing a moment.

"Claire, are you okay?" His face had grown ashen.

Before she knew it, she could hardly breath. Tears streamed out, but she managed enough energy to keep walking. "I-I think something bad has happened, Mitchell," she said between sobs."

CHAPTER TWENTY-FOUR

To her horror, Claire saw a man and woman, along with George, kneeling by a small, limp body. The woman, who was much older, spoke in a tearful voice as she stroked Anna's ashen face. Claire pushed George and the woman gently away, dropping by Anna's side. Placing her ear on the little girl's chest, she detected the faintest sounds of a heartbeat. In Anna's hair, spots of blood had matted some of the blonde locks together. Claire fingered through the strands until she discovered the small gash that had been the source of the blood. The wound was turning into a thickened ooze. She inspected as much as she could, satisfied there was no further damage. The top left side of Anna's temple bore another nasty scrape, with bruising around a larger part of that area. Anna didn't move. The chilly November air whipped around them.

As Claire cradled the girl, her own head throbbed full force now. A fullness settled in her chest. Supporting Anna's head and upper body, she drew her close for warmth and security.

"Anna, darling, can you hear me?" Claire gave up on stifling tears and putting on a brave front. She rocked gently back and forth rubbing the little girl's back.

Mitchell said, "I'll call an ambulance." He ran full speed back to the house.

"She came out of nowhere," the driver said. "I tried to stop, but it was too late."

The woman had now started crying. "I'm so sorry. I'm so sorry. Is she yours?"

"No," Claire answered, glancing up at the woman.

Claire turned her lips toward Anna's cheek and kissed her. She kissed her forehead, her lips, her neck. "Please tell me you're all right, sweetheart." Unable to contain her emotions, Claire broke into another round of sobbing. She could hear the woman sniffling above her, and the man exchanging words with George.

"No," the man said, "we're actually visiting. You know the Palmers?"

"I do," said George.

"We just left there. Heading home. I keep to my business when it comes to driving, but she just shot out from the bushes. I couldn't stop in time." His face showed hard lines of age, and he also showed extreme distress. He leaned against his car and pulled out a handkerchief, wiping his forehead and his eyes. His lower lip trembled.

"They're on their way." Mitchell had returned, and he placed a large blanket around Claire and Anna. "Is she all right?"

"I think so." She looked up at her brother-in-law through tears. "I really don't know."

"Here, let me check." Mitchell knelt next to Claire. He placed an ear on Anna's chest and nodded. A light reassuring smile covered his face. "I hear her heart. The car simply may have knocked her out. Does anything seem broken?"

George moved into place and tenderly examined his little girl's legs. "I'm not seeing anything but some skinned areas. Maybe a little bruising around the ankles. She could have twisted them when she fell." Claire unzipped the back of Anna's dress, and noted large bruised areas. The sight of it sent her into another round of tears.

"She okay?" George asked, alarmed.

"I don't know. Looks like there's some more injury on her back. Can't check her out much more." Claire pulled Anna closer, rubbing her back, and trying to keep her warm. She whispered in the little girl's ear, "I love you, little munchkin. Please don't leave me. I can't lose you too."

This incident was too much for her soul to bear. Even the worst moments at Hatchie River didn't compare to this. The loss of her own children, yes. But to witness possibly losing another one—she couldn't take anymore. It didn't matter that Anna wasn't her flesh and blood. They had bonded the moment they first met when Anna played jacks on the front porch. She buried her face in Anna's neck and cried until the ambulance crew arrived and pulled her away.

Claire watched as two men placed Anna on a stretcher. She seems so tiny, like the orange blanket they brought might swallow her up forever. If she was aware of anything at all, was she scared and unable to say so? Claire clapped a hand over her mouth to steady her nerves and keep from crying.

"Where do you want us to take her?" asked the driver.

"St. Mary's," George said.

"Did you need us to come with you to the hospital?" The driver of the car stood by George. The older woman had come up to Claire and had wrapped an arm around her for comfort.

"Tell you what. You two go on home. If I need you, I'll contact Mr. Palmer. Honestly, there's really nothing else to do."

The man nodded, his face still twisted with emotion. He motioned for his wife and the two drove off.

"I mean, what else could they do?" George looked from Mitchell to Claire.

"It was a horrible accident. There is nothing to do." Claire shivered, placing the palm on her forehead, hoping to lessen the pain. "The important thing is that Anna is alive."

"Let's go. I want to be there with Anna."

***

The antiseptic hospital smell overwhelmed her the moment she stepped inside St. Mary's. A plump lady at the front desk pointed the direction to the children's wing, and the three adults headed off. Mitchell had remained silent during the drive. George had not let go of Claire's hand, and now he'd wrapped his arm around her. When they landed on the designated floor, nurses in neat, snow-white uniforms and starched caps moved about, doing their duties, hardly acknowledging the arrival of George Parker and his two friends.

Following the signs, George led the way to the nurse's station. A young nurse smiled as they walked up.

"Excuse me," said George, "but I think my daughter is supposed to be on this floor."

"What's your child's name?" The nurse leafed through a register book.

"Anna Parker. She came by ambulance. Hit by a car."

"Oh, goodness." The nurse winced and stopped moving her pen over the list of names. "Came by ambulance?" She reached for another book and turned the pages until she came to the last one with a list of names. "She's still in the emergency room. When they clear her, they'll bring her here." The nurse stepped out from behind the desk. "You can wait in her room. Right this way, please."

"You already have a room for her?" George had slipped his arm around Claire again.

"A bed just came open, so we saved it. We keep our lists updated for potential new patients." The nurse briefly smiled at Claire and George.

Midway down a long hall, the nurse finally stopped at an open room. "This is where your daughter will be. We'll keep you informed of any information we receive, but I'm hoping she'll be released to come up here soon. I know you and your wife are so worried." The nurse turned in George and Claire's direction.

Claire startled at the words "your wife," and she didn't fail to catch the quick, wide-eyed look Mitchell cast in her direction. George didn't correct the lady, but merely nodded and ushered Claire into a vacant chair.

Mitchell glanced around the room. "If you don't mind, I think I'll head back to the lobby and wait there. I'll check back up here in about an hour or so."

George, expressionless, merely nodded and waved as Mitchell left. He sat on the bed, staring at the opposite wall. Claire's heart sank even more as she watched the man she saw as so strong and brave lift his hands to his eyes. When he heaved with the first tears, she nearly thought she'd lose her mind.

"She's everything to me, all I have left," he said, the muffled words coming out in a jumble. "If something happens to her, I don't know what I'll do." He shook his head, trying hard to stifle the sobs.

"Maybe everything will be okay after all, George. What if it just looked worse than what it really is?"

"She looked so small, fragile. Just looking at her reminded me of a broken doll."

"I'd like to think she's much stronger than that. She's a tough, determined little thing."

"I can't lose her, too, Claire," he said, peering through tearful eyes. "I just can't." He buried his face in his hands once more.

Unable to remain in the chair, Claire got up and sat on the bed next to George. She didn't say anything, but let a frightened man have his cry. After all, he had good reason to be scared. Heartbreak, tears, and fear weren't emotions only felt by women. Men felt it all too. They felt it deeply, their heart and soul equally wounded by life's transgressions. Each brush with loss or the possible near miss with it only made joy and triumph sweeter, no matter how small or large.

Claire wrapped her arms around George. This time she became the wall of security he'd always been for her. It was that way between people who loved and cared for each other. She knew love and caring surrounded her and George, each one reciprocating these actions with ease. No thinking. Just doing. Their relationship had been born out of necessity, but so far, it endured with constancy, a dance of give and take. If it endured further, there would be wins and losses. She could only hope that this instance with Anna would end with a win. It had to. She'd heard it in the heartbeat of the little girl she'd come to love as if she were her own.

Two hours later, the sound of rolling wheels filtered down the hallway. A young man filled the doorway, pushing a stretcher holding Anna. George and Claire got up, and Claire turned the covers down. George offered support, assisting the orderly in placing Anna in the bed. The little girl's face still retained a pallid shade even after the transport from home to this room.

"Can you tell us anything about what they found? Is she going to be all right?" George asked the orderly.

"The doctor will be in soon. He'll be able to tell you everything. She's up here now, so that's a good sign." The young man smiled. "If you need anything, here is the call button." He showed Claire and George a small box with a button on it. "Do you need any extra pillows or blankets?"

Claire had already fluffed Anna's pillow and pulled up the covers. "No, I think we should be fine right now. Thank you, though."

The orderly smiled again, and with a light nod, turned and left the room. Claire busied herself again, examining the bandages around Anna, lightly lifting some of the edges for a better look.

"She should be better and able to leave in a few days," said a voice in the doorway.

George and Claire both turned and viewed an older male wearing a lab coat and holding a chart.

"You must be the doctor," George stepped forward, holding out his hand. "I'm George Parker."

"I'm Dr. Grayson. I'll be the one directing your daughter's care. I'm sure you're wanting to know what we found."

"Yes, we are," Claire stated.

"As you can guess, she's bruised up, especially on the upper part of her body. On her back were several scratches. Her ankles were strained, with the right one being worse. We found a small hairline fracture there. Any more stress to the area, and it would have broken. Her head has a nasty little gash. We shaved the area so we could clean everything and put some antibiotic ointment on it. Also had to add a few stitches. She also suffered a broken rib. We've got her in a splint. Not much else we can do for that. When she complains of pain, just tell the nurse. We've ordered some medication for her." The doctor shook his head. "You're lucky it wasn't worse. She could have been killed. She'll be sore for a while."

"Has she said anything or moved at all?" George asked.

"They said during the ambulance ride, she moved a little and responded." Dr. Grayson replied. "She cried when we had to clean her up in the ER, but we managed to calm her down enough. I think the whole ordeal has shocked her as much as anything. We didn't see any other obvious head injury, and everything else checked out. But time will tell. Just watch for any nausea, vomiting, any other behavioral changes. Hopefully she'll talk more in a little while. We'll be keeping an eye on her."

Both George and Claire nodded.

"Very good. You two have a nice day, and I'll check on her tomorrow." Dr. Grayson left the room.

A small rustling sound came from the bed. Claire turned around. Anna had both eyes slightly open as she fidgeted with the covers. Her face wore a frown. George sped to her side, gently kissing her forehead.

"Sweetheart, you're awake. You feeling better?" His voice came out in soft tones, soothing.

Anna blinked a few times as tears welled up in her eyes.

"What's wrong, honey? Do you need something to help you feel better?"

She shook her head. Claire went over and placed her hand over Anna's. "You're okay, darling. Do you know where you are?"

The only answer, a few more blinks and a whimper.

Claire answered for her. "You're in the hospital. You're safe, and you're going to be okay."

"You won't leave?" Anna's voice wavered. The boldness she usually possessed had disappeared, and under the covers she seemed more small and fragile. A hint of color had seeped its way into her skin, making her look a little more alive than before. Claire had decided she'd never forget the lifeless look of Anna's body, just like she'd never forget her baby boy's. She'd surely have nightmares long after this incident.

George spoke up softly, "You're really worried about that, aren't you? Do you love Miss Claire that much?"

The little girl's lips curled up into a sweet smile. "I love her this much." She lifted her hands from under the covers in an attempt to stretch them wide apart. Her mouth opened in pain.

"That's okay, Anna. We know exactly what you mean." George placed his hands on his daughter's arms and helped situate them in a more comfortable position.

"My arms can't go wide enough to show you how much I love you, too Anna." Claire leaned down and kissed the girl's cheek. "I'll be staying right beside you."

Anna's only answer was another smile and a few blinks of her eyes before she snuggled back down in her pillow and fell asleep holding Claire's hand.

"I don't even want to move," said Claire, glancing over at George.

"I'll move the chair for you so you can sit next to her for a while. You don't mind, do you?"

"Absolutely not. I'll stay here as long as it takes." She smiled as George kissed her.

Claire settled in the chair, making sure her hand never slipped away from Anna's.

About an hour later, Mitchell came back up to the room. "I can let you two get some fresh air while I sit with her, if you like. They should be serving the patients dinner soon. I heard a couple of the nurses talking to each other."

"That would be nice," said George. "We'll take a walk, maybe."

"They've got some nice grounds outside. Kind of chilly, though. But there is a cafeteria, if you want some coffee."

George patted Mitchell on the back. "Don't worry about us. Be back in a little while."

Mitchell took Claire's place on the chair.

"We won't be gone too long." Claire turned back toward the bed. "I don't want her crying or scared when she wakes up."

"She'll be fine. I'll tell her that you're coming back." Mitchell smiled and waved them off.

Claire and George walked down the hall and took the elevator to the bottom floor. Struck with an idea, they decided to go to the chapel, hoping they would be alone. The lobby had filled up more since their arrival. Inside the chapel, the sun blazed outside, lighting up the stain glass windows, casting a kaleidoscope of colors on the floor. George ushered Claire into a pew, where he slid in beside her. As they sat in silence for a while, Claire said a prayer for Anna, for her, for George, Mitchell, and people she cared about.

For the first time she welcomed the communion with spirit, the chance to simply be silent and pray. She'd learned the power of prayer at an early age. The only time it wavered was at Hatchie River, but even then, she knew it saw her through the worst of times. Her internal solitude dissipated at the touch of George's warm hand on hers. His face showed a certain preoccupation, very similar to the one at dinner the last time they ate together.

"You okay?" she asked him.

Though they were alone, he glanced around before focusing his attention on her. "I need to ask you something."

Claire indicated for him to continue.

"I'm serious about Mitchell, you, and me going to see the lawyer. That needs to be done. But there's another person I want to see, but I can't decide if it's a Justice of The Peace or a minister."

She arched an eyebrow. "What exactly are you saying? Are you asking me to marry you?"

"What do you think?" He smiled at her.

"You sure about this, George?"

"I couldn't be more sure. First of all, Anna loves you more than I've ever seen her care about anybody, and it's not like she hasn't been around other women. But there's one more thing."

"Go on." Claire fought to keep her heart from pounding right out of her chest. This was the moment she'd been wanting, pretty much since she'd arrived in Knoxville and laid eyes on George Parker.

"I love you too. I think something hit me the moment I saw you. There was this connection. Don't know how to describe it, really."

She smiled. "I know a man who told me the story of when he was a little boy and saw another little girl on the playground. He looked at her and told her he was going to marry her. And years later they did."

"Men know these things, Claire. They carry the feelings and that inner knowing deep in their hearts. Even if they're too young to understand, they know. I knew it, too, when you stepped off that train. As time went on, I'll admit it scared me a little, and I started doubting."

Claire nodded in agreement.

"But this has brought me back around full circle." The tears welled up in his eyes. "Seeing my little girl nearly dead scared me more than I've ever been scared in my life. I didn't know true fear until I saw that little body lying there on the cold hard gravel. Even Anita's death didn't affect me like that. And why was Anna on the road, her little heart about to beat its last? Because she wanted a mother. She had an inner knowing too. She wanted you to be that special person."

George's eyes fixed on Claire, a look so intent it drew her in like a magnet. He continued. "To deny her that wish would be cruel and thoughtless. To deny myself wouldn't be good, either. And this all hinges on the hope that you even agree with what I'm saying."

When Claire found her voice, she said, "Of course I agree with you. I think I knew all of this much earlier, or I admitted it to myself. But women have to be careful. You men spook too easily. Then all is lost."

"If a man spooks that easily, he's not worthy." He wrapped his arm around hers. "I want to be worthy, and love you every day until our dying day. I want Anna to never cry and run away again because she doesn't have a mother who'll love her and care for her the way she deserves."

"You'll never have to worry that I don't feel the same toward both of you. Somehow I almost feel like Anna's mine." Claire managed a small chuckle. "Not sure why I would feel that way, but I do believe there is that connection as you say."

"It was meant for you to be her mother. I see that now."

"I think things happen for a reason. There's a big picture that we may not see at a certain time, but when all is said and done, even the bad fits in for the greater whole of the good."

"So it's settled? We have a plan once Anna gets out of here?" George pulled Claire closer to him.

"We have a plan." Claire closed her eyes as George kissed her again.

"Let's go back upstairs. Mitchell will think we ran off and left him."

CHAPTER TWENTY-FIVE

Harland Chadwell sat behind a gargantuan maple desk, leaning back in his red leather chair. He appraised the three people sitting in front of him. His law office was a couple of blocks down from George's store, and he'd come to work that morning with a notice from his secretary that he had an urgent appointment first thing.

"That's the craziest story I've heard in a while." He let out a light whistle and shook his head. "So your old man just dumped you like that? And then he shows up again, and nearly kills you?"

"I thought I'd seen my last," said Claire, gazing hard at the pudgy man behind the desk. He looked like one who enjoyed his food and drink to a fault. George gave her his oath that the man was honorable, or she'd have walked out the moment she saw him.

The lawyer squinted at George, Mitchell, and Claire, silent with his own thoughts. The tops of his fingers drummed a little rhythmic beat on top of the desk pad. He finally let out a sigh. With a little tilt back for leverage, he threw himself forward out of the chair and headed straight for a group of wooden filing cabinets. "Well, I think there are some options we have. My question is how are we getting Mr. Wright to sign any of them? He sounds like he's turned pretty cantankerous." He glanced over at George. "Mr. Parker, have you and Mr. Wright thought about that?" He angled his head further in Mitchell's direction.

"A little," said George, "but I'm like you. I'm not sure how to go about it. You'd have to try and trick him, make him think he was signing something else. I think he'd catch on. Something tells me he isn't totally off his rocker." Mitchell grimaced. "No, but he's sliding off pretty fast, in my opinion."

Claire spoke up. "Mr. Chadwell, I'm going to propose something. It's very unorthodox, but if nobody ever challenged it, I don't see how it could hurt."

"And what's that, ma'am?" Chadwell pulled out some papers from a couple of different drawers and settled back down in his chair, the springs blaring off a grating sound against his weight.

"What if Mitchell signed the papers and simply put Adrian's name?" She eyed each man quickly and stared down at her lap.

"It's not unorthodox, ma'am. It's really illegal." Chadwell tapped the papers lightly against his chin.

"Couldn't we do a signature by proxy, some sort of emergency thing like that? I'm sure people have done it in some dire situations." Claire was determined to have this divorce if it was the last thing she ever did in life.

The lawyer let out a loud laugh. "They have." He gazed at the group.

"Oh, come on, Harland," George said, shrugging. "Claire's right. How could it hurt? Nobody is ever going to make a huge deal about this, let alone ask to see papers. They don't have children. I've never heard her talk about being close with family. Mitchell will take all this to the grave with him. And of course, I'd die before I ever said anything. You definitely aren't."

"Can't we just keep this our dirty little secret, an ugly necessity, and just get on with our lives?" It was Mitchell who chimed in.

Harland sucked in his breath. "There is what's called an ex parte divorce. It a divorce where the other party is not present." He shrugged. "Okay, I'm game if you are. Let's do it." He flipped through some papers and spent a few minutes filling out some of the blanks on the pages. When he finished, he pushed them toward Mitchell. "There you go. I need your signature as a witness."

Mitchell looked quickly at Claire. "You sure you want me to do this?"

"You're the one who brought all this up first. So why are you asking me?" She frowned.

"Just checking."

"Sign the papers, Mitchell." George lightly pushed his client toward the desk. With a few flourishes of the pen, Mitchell signed his name on the blank.

"Mrs. Wright, you sign here."

Claire grasped the pen and dutifully placed her name on the line above Mitchell's. She pushed the papers back to Harland and handed him his pen.

"There, we're done." Harland grinned for a second. "That wasn't too bad, was it?"

"How much do we owe you, Harland?" George got up from his chair, extending his hand to his friend.

"Aw, George. I won't charge you for this."

"I'll give you a free hat. Your choice," said Mitchell.

"That's an offer I can't refuse, Mr. Wright." Harland shook Mitchell's hand with enthusiasm.

"You come to the store, and I'll also let you pick out something for the wife," George said. "That's my contribution."

"I'll take you up on that, Parker. You'll see me soon." Chadwell laughed. "Mrs. Wright, glad you're here in Knoxville. It was a pleasure meeting you. I'm here if you ever need me."

"Thank you," Claire stated, shaking the attorney's hand.

All three left Chadwell's office and returned to Claire's house. Anna had insisted on taking up residence in the room across from Claire's, and Edna had followed, determined she needed to perform her work no matter where she was. When they arrived, Anna was resting on the sofa, Buzzie and Moo curled up around her. Edna had retired to the kitchen, where the most wonderful smell floated out.

"Did you get everything done?" she asked, wiping her hands on her apron and greeting them at the door.

"We did, Edna," said George. "That's a big load off us."

"I'm sure it is." She turned to Claire. "I bet you're so happy now that this is all over. You can move on."

"That is so true." Claire smiled.

"Miss Claire, can I stay here forever? I'll be really good." Anna peered up.

"Darling, how could you ever think you were bad? You're always good." Claire walked over and stroked Anna's curls.

George rubbed his lower lip, thinking. "Anna, how would you like to stay here for a really long time?" He walked over to his daughter and sat on the edge of the sofa next to her. "How would you like for Miss Claire to be your mother?"

The room grew silent. Mitchell stared straight at Claire. George gazed at his daughter and she back at him. Edna stared at the floor, too emotional to move.

Anna's eyes had grown wide. "My mother?" She looked at Claire and back to her father. "It's not a dream?"

"Of course not, Anna. This is real. I love Miss Claire too."

"And we can all stay here with Buzzie and Moo? And Edna can stay too?"

"Of course." George smiled and nodded to Edna, who's mouth had spread into a wide smile. She lifted her hand, wiping away a tear that had trickled down her cheek.

I'm sorry," she said in a quivering voice. "I just love beautiful moments like this." She sniffed and smiled again. "I'll just go on back in the kitchen and get lunch ready."

"When will Miss Claire be mother?" Anna whispered the words.

"Probably by the end of the week. We'll do it all really quick. Does that sound good?"

"It's perfect." Anna sang out, her eyes sparkling. She didn't try to move too much, still sore from the accident. "Miss Claire, are we going to have a wedding with flowers and pretty dresses?"

"I don't know about that, but we'll have a quick ceremony." Claire wrapped her hands around Anna's face, kissing her lightly on the top of the head. The wound was healing well and the hair would be grown back out soon. The bruising was taking it's time going away, but all in good time for that too.

"The quicker we do the ceremony, the faster she becomes your mother. A wedding takes months to plan."

"We can't wait months, daddy. That's too long." Anna looked intently at her father.

"I know, honey." George laughed. He stood up and looked at everyone. "Now we all know what's going on. Don't know about you, but it's lunchtime, and I'm starved. Mitchell, you lead the way, and I'll get Anna situated."

★★★

"I'm so happy for you. I think you and Mr. Parker will be so good for each other," Oma had said earlier in the week to Claire. "I'd be honored to stand with you." Mitchell also expressed his pleasure in being asked to join George and Claire on their special day, and agreed to stay until he saw Claire safely married to George. Anna was beside herself with excitement, moving carefully back and forth all over the house as the adults dressed before heading to the church. Edna said she would stay behind and have a special meal prepared when they returned.

"You've never looked more beautiful than you do now, Mrs. Wright . . . um . . . I mean Mrs. Parker." She giggled, face flushed with pleasure, and returned to the kitchen.

Inside the church, George and Claire now stood before the minister, no one else present except for Mitchell, Oma, and Anna. The minister smiled at the small group before him. "I love small ceremonies like this one. It only shows that true love, bound by God, needs no fanfare, no pomp and circumstance to make the pledge between man and woman any stronger. Shall we begin?"

The group smiled in approval. Within minutes, Claire's life changed all over again. The relationship with George, and the marriage especially, had been fast. But it had seemed so right. True love didn't get caught up in the trappings and expectations of time as humans dictated. One's path in life held twists and turns, heartache and happiness, and oftentimes it didn't hold to man-made traditions, either. Maybe that was what "be still and know that I am God" really meant. That you learn from the silence and follow what feels right in the gut. She and George had both felt it simultaneously, and so did Anna.

Claire smiled down at the sweet little girl grasping her hand as if her life depended on it. Edna had fixed Anna's hair and added a darling bow that fell nicely in place, covering the wounded part of her head. Beneath the cream-colored dress, no one really noticed the bandages still covering the scrapes that healed. Now Anna was her little girl. Harland Chadwell had suggested a couple of days earlier that she and George stop by, and he would draw up some papers that made Claire the legal, adoptive mother to Anna.

When Anna heard this, she insisted she wanted her own certificate to hang on her wall. Harland had been delighted to create a special adoption certificate for the little girl.

After eating lunch at the house, Mitchell went upstairs and packed his bags. When he finished, he carried them downstairs and placed them by the front door.

"Do you have to leave today? Can't you stay a little longer?" Claire hated to see those bags packed. Having Mitchell around added life to the family. And he'd been so kind, though it all had gotten off to a rather slow start.

"Gotta run, Claire. My employees are good, but they still need a leader. You know how that goes." He smiled.

"What are you going to do with Adrian? I don't want him here at all. Nothing to even remind me of him anymore."

"Yes, just what are you going to do, Mitchell?" George had entered the living room.

"He'll be coming with me on the train tonight." Mitchell eyed both Claire and George.

George's face went solemn. "And just how do you intend on doing that? Do you need some help? Want me to come with you? My wife can run the store if I need to leave." George kissed Claire quickly on the cheek. "You don't know how happy it makes me feel to say that."

Claire laughed. "I love hearing it. And Mitchell, George is right. You surely can't handle Adrian all by yourself."

"Well, I've been doing it this whole time. I just let him get away. That was my fault. Let's just say alcohol can be your best friend when you need it. The Tennessean has a wonderful bar, and I intend to let Adrian make full use of it. I'll whisper for the bartender to make everything a double." Mitchell chuckled.

"Hey, Mitch," said George, "have you ever thought of moving your business to Knoxville?"

Mitchell's mouth curved into an expression of consideration. "That is an idea. There are buildings here that would make a good place for a hat factory."

"You can rent or even buy my house up the road. Anna and I are moving back in this one. No need to have another house sit empty. Think about it, and let's see if we can't work something out. Workers can either follow you or not. I guarantee you'll get excellent people here."

"Oh, Mitchell," Claire said, beaming, "why don't you do that? And I can still help the way I used to. It would be wonderful to have you here. This area is a beautiful part of Tennessee. Not the flat land you see on the western side."

"The more I think about it, I must admit that the idea hits me pretty well." He nodded. "Let me get Adrian settled, and George, you and I will talk more about this."

"You bet," said George.

Later that evening, George drove Mitchell to the train station.

✽✽✽

A rich woody scent from large, old oak trees hung thick and heavy in the West Tennessee afternoon air, penetrated by the occasional breeze carrying floral top notes from nearby bushes and wildflowers. A mixture so intoxicating at times, one good whiff lulled a person into a state of gentle relaxation, if not momentary sweet oblivion. Songbirds still found enough energy to muster up a healthy competition of trills and soprano chirps against the drone of insects. Summer had come around again, and Hatchie River Asylum For The Insane sat on its expansive green lawn, a powerful ruler, fit with gothic pointed windows and arches, lording over the whole world, it seemed. Faces of gargoyles on top of the structure leered down, some with lolling tongues, others with brutish grins, not unlike the faces of many an occupant who lived inside. An interesting paradox, this peaceful world outside, and the cruel, shocking world inside.

Adrian Wright sat alone in a chair on the lawn, resting his head against one of the trees, grateful for a quick moment of peace. Out of kindness, he'd been granted permission to sit here each day for a while, most likely a small reward for his former position in town. Yes, his former place in society, where his work had not only been sought after here in the sleepy little town of Ash Grove, but in various shops in the Southeast. His fine work as a hatter had given him license to practice his art with gusto, and in the end had made him a rather enviable living. Now he found himself here in this place, forgotten, struggling to make sense of the chaos in his mind.

A few moments ago, he'd watched in forlorn silence as his brother, and business partner walked away, deserting him. Again. He thought when they'd left that other town, he'd finally be going home. Now he lifted his head and stared at the empty chair beside him. Mitchell apparently had no intent on taking him back home, though he'd pleaded with promises to control his temper and to refrain from losing himself in forgetful moments. When he'd inquired about his wife, her whereabouts, demanding to see her, Mitchell's answer proved shocking enough.

"She's never coming back, Adrian," Mitchell said, a mixture of pity and irritation flashing from his eyes. He patted his brother's shoulder in sympathy.

"Never? What do you mean? Of course, she is. I nearly had her back one time, I think." Adrian scratched his head. His lips trembled, and his eyes filled with tears as he stared up at the man sitting next to him, hoping he'd surely been joking. But the solemn expression he viewed gave no indication of such a thing. With shaky hands, he reached in his pocket for a handkerchief.

"I mean never, and that's the end of that. Just let it go, let everything go. Nothing will ever be the way it was before." Mitchell shrugged. "Some of it's the nature of things, and some of it was your own doing."

Mitchell had spent their visit together this time launching into a monologue of events that had now turned Adrian's world upside down for good. His mind, riddled with past memories and the exhausting effort of trying to digest his present situation, sent him into a tailspin, finally plummeting him into an abyss of despair. Had he, in fact, created the mess in which he found himself, wrenched from an old life and thrust into a dark world where no one heard his cries for help, where no one understood him anymore? Is that what all the sympathetic looks he'd seen and the gentle pats on the hand had meant? He always tried to answer back, explain, but he only received silent nods, and those damned, gratuitous pats on the hand. Then they walked away, leaving him alone to wrestle with his own demons.

A small grey and blue-striped lizard scuttled close to his feet, making its way to the trunk of the tree. Startled by the rustle, Adrian jerked his head down and glared at the creature. The tiny reptile, somehow sensing the pair of eyes glaring down at it from above, stalled and waited. In anger, Adrian kicked out, trying to flick the poor, innocent creature away.

"Get out of here, you devil! You're a mean, no-account devil, that's what you are!" He yelled and struck out his foot again. This time the frightened animal made a bee-line for the tree and scurried out of sight. "There, that'll teach you." Adrian repositioned himself back on the chair and drew up his shoulders. Out of the corner of his eye, he caught sight of someone, a young male, staring in his direction. Turning his head around, he faced the unknown gentleman and delivered a fierce scowl.

He threw up a fist, shaking it. "And damn you to hell too. You're another devil if I ever saw one!"

The man answered back with nothing more than a silent shake of his head before hurrying to the front door of the building, where he quickly disappeared inside.

Adrian shook his fist one last time for good measure and turned back around, resting his head against the tree. At least he hadn't received that infernal pat on the hand. And speaking of hands, his own hands trembled now, nothing like the steady tools for crafting the finest hats around. He wiped the drool pooling in the corner of his mouth before it dripped its way onto his shirt.

With a deep breath, he inhaled a hearty dose of air, the sweet aroma carrying him back to another time, a not so distant past where everything had seemed perfect—almost. He closed his eyes and tried again to recount in his mind the story his brother had just told him, especially about the part of her never returning. How long had she been away? How long had he been here without her? Was Mitchell coming back? What a chore, sorting fact from fiction! Determined, he spent the remainder of his time outside by the tree putting the puzzle of his life back together little by little.

Meanwhile, back in Knoxville, miles away on the other side of Tennessee, Anna and Claire sat curled together on a sofa in the wonderful stone block house they all called home. While the breeze floated through the open windows, Claire read Anna's favorite story, Uncle Wiggily, while Lullabelle sat between them. Buzzie and Moo contented themselves with sitting on the floor and grooming their fur. Edna busied herself in the kitchen, preparing fresh-baked cookies. Up the road, George helped Mitchell move into his former home. Not far from Gay Street, movers and new employees readied a new hat factory for production of the finest hats around.

As Claire read to Anna, she couldn't help but feel like a queen, the richest, most content person on earth. She'd come full circle, tasting the bitter with the sweet. Her losses had been many, but her wins embodied triumph at its best. Inside her, a new life grew, a new baby brother or sister for Anna. Her intuition had grown stronger as days passed. She felt happier than ever, more vibrant. Somehow, she knew beyond reason that her new life held even greater gifts than she could ever imagine.

END

ABOUT THE AUTHOR

Scarlet Darkwood wields a mighty pen, or at the very least, delivers mighty punches to the computer keys when she's typing furiously on a story. She likes dark and twisted, and the weirder, the better.

Always preferring avant garde themes, her stories take the reader on unusual adventures, exploring the darker parts of the human psyche as she whips out cunning prose wrapped in provocative themes. Sometimes she veers from her beaten path and takes a happy-go-lucky romp in the brighter sides of life, kicking up her style into sharp, snappy dialogue and clever descriptions.

Writing in several genres unleashes her imagination so she never grows bored. From a young age, she's enjoyed writing and keeping diaries, but didn't start creating novels until 2012. She's a Southern girl who lives in Tennessee and enjoys the beauty of the mountains. She lives in Nashville with her spouse and two rambunctious kitties.

For more information about the latest concerning Scarlet and her work, sign up for her newsletter: http://ow.ly/HUyz303E5Oh

You can visit her BLOG at: www.scarletdarkwood.com

Follow her on Facebook at: https://www.facebook.com/scarletdarkwoodauthor

Follow her on Google+ at:http://ow.ly/VvZ82

Follow her on Twitter at: http://twitter.com/ScarletDarkwood

See the snarkier side at Tin Hats: http://www.tinhatsblog.wordpress.com